THE BONE SEASON

SAMANTHA SHANNON

Praise for THE BONE SEASON Series

Sunday Times Bestseller

New York Times Bestseller

Asian Age Bestseller

USA Today Bestseller

Indie Bestseller List

Daily Mail Book of the Year

Stylist Book of the Year

Huffington Post Book of the Year

Nominated for a FutureBook Innovation Award
Bookseller Ones to Watch

Today Book Club Pick

GoodReads Choice Awards Fantasy Nominee

Amazon Rising Star

"Like treasures unearthed by mudlarks, Samantha Shannon's alternative world is studded with fabulous language: mime queens and mime lords have their mollishers; gutterlings jostle with amaurotics . . . the country groans under the rule of the Scion Republic." —*The Daily Mail*

"Ever since HG Wells' *The War Of The Worlds* there has been a slight aversion to looking at the global consequences of such dystopias and Shannon seems to be taking that wider view . . . Done with an understated elegance." —*Scotland on Sunday*

"Shannon's exploration of a futuristic, perilous Europe remains engaging and evocative, especially with the depiction of the so-called Unnatural Assembly and its tradition of catchy, almost folkloric nicknames. The narrative is fueled by a constant sense of tension." —*Publishers Weekly*

"Constant, fast-paced action . . . Mesmerizing . . . Intricately imagined . . . This seven-part series climbs to its highest point of tension. Shannon's world begins to feel more generically dystopian, but as Paige fights to locate and understand the spiritual energy powering Senshield, it is never less than captivating." —*Kirkus Reviews*

"Fans will be rewarded with more character backstory, and new double agents on both sides of the insurgency. When those within the Mime Order are branded enemies of the state and discover that their spiritual powers are being harnessed for warfare through a device called Senshield, the novel hits its stride, effectively mirroring current debates on immigration, violence, and equality . . . Shannon's writing shines." —*Library Journal*

"Shannon's hybridized world combines sci-fi and fantasy as the perfect backdrop for a human rights thriller." —Shelf Awareness

THE
SONG
RISING

AUTHOR'S PREFERRED TEXT

The Third Book in The Bone Season Series

SAMANTHA SHANNON

BLOOMSBURY PUBLISHING

NEW YORK · LONDON · OXFORD · NEW DELHI · SYDNEY

BLOOMSBURY PUBLISHING
Bloomsbury Publishing Inc.
1385 Broadway, New York, NY 10018, USA

BLOOMSBURY, BLOOMSBURY PUBLISHING, and the Diana logo
are trademarks of Bloomsbury Publishing Plc

First published in 2017 in Great Britain
First published in the United States 2017
This author's preferred text edition published 2024

ISBN: HB: 978-1-63973-460-3; PB: 978-1-63973-347-7; EBOOK: 978-1-63973-541-9

Library of Congress Cataloging-in-Publication Data is available.

2 4 6 8 10 9 7 5 3 1

Typeset by Integra Software Services Pvt. Ltd.
Printed and bound in the U.S.A.

To find out more about our authors and books visit www.bloomsbury.com
and sign up for our newsletters.

Bloomsbury books may be purchased for business or promotional use.
For information on bulk purchases please contact Macmillan Corporate and
Premium Sales Department at specialmarkets@macmillan.com.

For the silenced

Author's Note on this Edition

The Song Rising was originally published in 2017.

The Author's Preferred Text you're about to read has been significantly revised. It follows roughly the same course of events, rewritten with a bit more experience under my belt.

I hope you enjoy this series as much as I've loved working on it for the last decade.

Samantha Shannon, 14 February 2024

Silence is all we dread.
There's Ransom in a Voice
EMILY DICKINSON

Contents

THE REPUBLIC OF
SCION ENGLAND
*also known as the
Republic of Scion Britain*

Inverness

HIGHLANDS

Edinburgh

LOWLANDS

ULSTER

Belfast

CONNAUGHT

NORTH
WEST

NORTH
EAST

Leeds

LEINSTER

Manchester

Dublin

MUNSTER

Feirm na mBeach Meala

MIDLANDS

Birmingham

WESTLANDS

Cardiff

SOUTH EAST

Bristol

THE REPUBLIC OF
**SCION
IRELAND**

SOUTH WEST

London

Capital
Citadel
Paige's Family Home

The Mime Order

The UNDERQUEEN, Paige Mahoney,
also known as the Black Moth *or* the Pale Dreamer

Her MOLLISHERS, Nicklas Nygård,
mollisher supreme, *also known as* the Red Vision,
and Eliza Renton, *also known as* the Martyred Muse

THE HIGH COMMANDERS
of the Unnatural Assembly

I Cohort – Ognena Maria – Strategy
II Cohort – The Glym Lord – Recruitment
III Cohort – Tom the Rhymer – Communication
IV Cohort – Minty Wolfson – Proclamation
V Cohort – Wynn Ní Luain – Medical
VI Cohort – The Pearl Queen – Provisions

THE HIGH COMMANDERS
of the Ranthen

Terebellum, Warden of the Sheratan – Resources
Arcturus, Warden of the Mesarthim – Instruction

NO SAFE PLACE, NO SURRENDER

Prelude

2 November 2059

The lights scalded my borrowed eyes. I was still inside a different body, standing on the same floor, but everything had changed.

There was a smile on his lips. That old gleam in his eye, like I had brought him good news from the auction house. He wore a black waistcoat embroidered with interlinked gold anchors, and a scarlet cravat was tied at his throat. One silk-clad hand grasped an ebony cane.

'I see you have mastered possession at a distance,' he said. 'You *are* full of surprises.'

The cane's handle was porcelain, shaped like the head of a white horse.

'I believe,' Nashira said, her voice soft, 'that you are already acquainted with my new Grand Overseer.'

I let out my first breath since laying eyes on him.

He had tried to stop me. The scheming worm had silenced me for weeks, keeping me from telling the world about the Rephs. Yet here he was, looking as easy with them as he was with his own shadow.

'Oh, dear. Have you swallowed that pilfered tongue?' Jaxon Hall let out a deep laugh. 'Yes, Paige, I am here, with the Rephaim. In the Archon, wearing the anchor! Are you aghast?

Are you oh-so scandalised? Is this all a terrible *shock* to your fragile sensibilities?'

'Why?' I finally managed to speak. 'Why the hell are you here, Jaxon?'

'As if I had a choice. With you as Underqueen, my beloved syndicate is doomed to destruction. Consequently, I have decided to return to my roots.'

'Your roots?'

His smile widened.

'Allow me to shed light upon your situation,' he said. 'To Terebellum Sheraton, you are a convenient pawn in an age-old game. Arcturus Mesarthim is nothing but her lure. Her bait. He took you under his wing in Oxford on her orders, to entice you into their net. And you, darling – you fell for it. Everyone but you can see it.'

A chill warned me that something was wrong. Elsewhere in the citadel, someone had touched my body.

'This is a fight you cannot win. The syndicate was never meant as a weapon of war, and you were never meant to rule,' Jaxon continued. 'If we must pull off your wings to stop you casting yourself into the fire, so be it.' He offered a hand. 'Come to us, Paige.'

The three bodies flashed through my mind. Lotte Gordon, Ella Giddings and Charles Lanvin, swinging from the gallows on the screen behind me.

'You have chosen the wrong side. Join this one,' Jaxon said. 'I can't tell you how it hurts me to see you serving the Ranthen. Unlike the Rag and Bone Man, I have always believed you could be saved from their indoctrination. From Arcturus Mesarthim's . . . seduction. I thought you had more sense than to blindly obey the man who was once your master.'

'You're asking me to do that now,' I said.

Jaxon smiled.

Another shiver in the æther. Little by little, I was losing control of my host.

'This is your last chance, Underqueen,' Jaxon said, his tone hardening. 'Step back from the brink, before you lose any more of your allies. Before the anchor crushes you all into the dust.'

He had shocked me. We both knew it.

If he thought he could scare me, he would have to try a lot harder.

'I'd rather burn,' I said.

———

My brain was molten, slithering out through my nose and down my front. I had to get out, get air into my lungs . . .

A hand took hold of my arm, but I shook it off. I clawed off the oxygen mask, got the door open, and spilled out of the car in a jumble of limbs. The stitches in my side peeled apart, wetting my shirt.

Jaxon Hall was many things, but I couldn't believe he had gone to Scion. He had made his career out of living in their shadow, not their arms.

My wounds from the scrimmage flared, deep and throbbing. I pitched into the night, down the wet steps to the Thames, cursing my own stupidity. I crumpled to my knees by the water, heaving.

I will find other allies. His words from the scrimmage rang in my ears. *You have not seen the last of me.*

I should have killed him in the Rose Ring. The blade had been against his throat, and I had been too weak to cut. My thoughts raced.

Looks like you'll have to make some new friends, I had said to Nashira, full of myself.

Oh, I but I have an old one. One who returned to me in the early hours of this morning, after twenty long years of estrangement . . .

'No,' I whispered. 'Not you.'

I have decided to return to my roots.

Jaxon had been standing so calmly with the Sargas. And there were other things – things I had brushed off, or hadn't seen, that now came surging to the front of my mind. He was so much wealthier than other mime-lords, even though he claimed to come from nothing. Even though there was so little coin in pamphleteering.

How had he leapt from pauper to prince?

There was more. He had spearheaded my rescue from Oxford with no exit plan, no apparent knowledge of what lurked there.

That was foolish. Jaxon was no fool. It wasn't in his nature to go blindly into anything.

But if he had left that prison once before . . . if he had *known* there was a way . . .

We weren't sure how to establish what was happening in Oxford. Another memory rushed back. *Jaxon was the one who found the missing piece, a rumour of a tunnel under Whitehall.*

There was no such rumour.

Of course there wasn't.

Twenty long years. Those were the only words I needed to realise who Jaxon Hall had once been. I had no absolute proof, but I knew in my bones that my instinct was right.

Jaxon wasn't just a traitor.

He was *the* traitor.

The man who had betrayed the Ranthen twenty years ago, buying his freedom from Oxford. The man who was responsible for the scars on their backs; who had left his fellow prisoners to die.

And I had been his mollisher.

His right hand.

A shout in the near distance stopped time, or started it again. The crunch of footsteps broke through the roar in my ears. Out of the corner of my eye, I saw Warden sink into a crouch beside me.

'Paige,' he said. 'What is it?'

I had to tell him.

I couldn't carry this knowledge alone.

'I know who betrayed you twenty years ago,' I said. 'I know who gave you the scars.'

Nick ran to the railings above us. 'Vigiles,' he shouted. 'Warden, bring her up!'

Warden stayed exactly where he was. I was afraid he would lack the ability to read my expression – that I might have to say the name myself – but as each agonising moment ticked past, I watched it dawn on him, just as it had on me. A fire rose in his eyes.

'Jaxon.'

PART ONE

GOD IN
A MACHINE

I

UNDERQUEEN

War has been called a game, with good reason. Both have combatants. Both have sides. Both carry the risk of losing.

There is just one difference.

Every game is a gamble. Certainty is the last thing you want when you begin. If victory is guaranteed, there is no game at all.

In war, however, we crave certainty. No fool ever went to war without the cast-iron belief that they would win – or that the likelihood of losing was so small as to make the bloody price of every move worthwhile. You don't go to war for the thrill, but the gain.

The question is whether any gain, any outcome, can justify the way you play.

SCION CITADEL OF LONDON
27 November 2059

In the heart of its financial district, the Scion Citadel of London was burning. On Cheapside, Didion Waite – poet of the underworld, bitter rival of Jaxon Hall – was howling over the remains of Bow Bells.

Once a fixture of the capital, the derelict church was now a mass of charred and smoking rubble.

In his powdered wig and tailcoat, Didion was conspicuous (even by underworld standards), but everyone was too engrossed to notice one madman – all but those of us who had answered his call. We stood at the mouth of a lane, masked and shrouded, taking in what was left of Bow Bells. A message had been sprayed in red across the street.

ALL HAIL THE WHITE BINDER

TRUE UNDERLORD OF LONDON

A distinctive orange flower had been painted beneath it. Nasturtium. In the language of flowers, it meant *conquest*, or *power*.

'Let's get him out of there,' said Ognena Maria, one of my commanders. 'Before Scion does.'

I didn't volunteer to help. Didion had demanded that I come in person, but I couldn't risk speaking to him when he was this upset. I knew from experience that he would have no qualms about exposing me to the whole street.

'I'll go.' Eliza checked that her hood was fastened. 'We'll take him to Grub Street.'

'Be careful,' I said.

She hurried towards Didion, who was now pounding the cobbles with his fists, screaming. Maria followed with her mollisher, Witcher Cully.

I stayed behind with Nick. We had taken to wearing the winter hoods that had come into fashion in recent weeks, which covered most of the face, but by now I was so recognisable that even that might not protect me.

After the scrimmage – when I had fought my own mime-lord for the right to rule the voyants of London – Nick had quit his job with Scion, only staying long enough to steal a few cases of medical supplies and take as much cash from his bank account as he could. Within days, his face had appeared on the screens alongside mine. Now he nodded to the wreck of the church.

'You think this was Jax?'

'His loyalists,' I said. 'They're clearly more committed than we thought.'

'It's a tiny group of troublemakers. Not worth your time,' Nick said. 'You know everyone hated the auction house. It's probably a good thing it's gone.'

His tone was reassuring, but this was the third assault on a syndicate landmark in as many days. The last time, they had raided Old Spitalfields, scaring the traders and looting stalls. Those responsible considered Jaxon to be the rightful Underlord, despite his conspicuous absence. Even after I had told them the facts, they refused to believe that the White Binder could be involved with Scion.

In the grand scheme of things, this was a minor nuisance – the majority of voyants did seem to support my rule – but these attacks were indisputable proof that I had not yet won all of my subjects' hearts. I supposed it came with the territory. Haymarket Hector, my predecessor, had been widely despised. Those who had obeyed him had done so out of fear, or because he made it worth their while.

Eliza and Cully coaxed Didion away. A fire engine drowned out his sobs of denial, but anyone could see that the church was beyond saving – as was the Juditheon, the auction house beneath it. We retreated, leaving another part of our history to be swept away.

Nick was right, of course. The whole syndicate had resented Didion for poaching spirits from other sections and auctioning them to fill his own pockets. Still, it had been a good place to socialise. I had whiled away many an afternoon at the Juditheon. Once, I might even have mourned its loss – but since Jaxon had revealed his true nature, all of my memories of life as his mollisher were tainted. I wanted to scrape them into a pit, close the earth on top of them, and build again on the new ground.

'Nearest safe house is Cloak Lane,' Nick said.

'Right.'

We slipped into another backstreet, away from the heat and light around the church. I kept us clear of other people, while Nick checked for security cameras. Since the scrimmage, we were no longer just unnaturals, but fugitives, with ever-growing bounties on our heads. Even if we hadn't yet made a bold move against Scion, they knew our objective.

I had to wonder how much longer we could survive in London. It was dangerous for us to be out after dark, but when Didion had sent for me, I had wanted to come, if only to convince him that we were on the same side. After all, he loathed Jaxon, which now made him a potential ally.

The safe house was a cramped apartment, rented by a former Nightingale who was keen to help the Mime Order. About half of the gang had fled after the Abbess died, while the others had pledged their loyalty to me.

Unlike most of our hideouts, this one had central heating, a fridge, and a decent bed. The warmth was a relief after a long night on the streets. Over the last two weeks, snow had fallen every day, leaving London as thickly iced as a birthday cake. I had never experienced a winter so ruthless. My eyes streamed every time I stepped outside.

Nick dropped on to the bed. He, at least, got a few hours' rest. A hint of moonlight shone on his pale face, drawing out the crease that pinched his brow even in sleep. I lay on the couch in the dark, but I was too restless to close my eyes for long. The image of the burning church – a promise of devastation – was scorched on to my mind. A reminder that, while Jaxon Hall was gone, he wasn't yet forgotten.

In the morning, I took a bob cab to the Mill, an industrial ruin in Silvertown – one of several abandoned buildings we had recently occupied across the citadel. It was home to our largest cell of voyants.

Changing the structure of the syndicate, with the aim of turning it into an army capable of fighting Scion, had not been easy. I had ended all disputes over turf and shut down every den Jaxon knew about, though I had tried to keep gang members together wherever possible. Syndicate voyants were now organised into cells, each based in a location known only to its members and the local mime-lord or mime-queen, who received their orders through a high commander. Forcing my subjects to limit contact outside their cells hadn't exactly thrilled them, but it was the only way to evade Jaxon, who had known the old syndicate inside and out.

Now anyone who was captured would only be able to betray a certain number of people to the enemy.

When I arrived at the Mill, I climbed the stairs. Leon Wax – one of the few amaurotics who worked for the syndicate – was at the end of the hall in his wheelchair, handing out clothes to a pair of soothsayers. He was sixty, with skin of a deep, rich brown and grey hair.

Eliza had convinced Leon to pledge his loyalty to me. In exchange, I had obtained a vial of amaranth for his spouse. Bea had since moved to the relative safety of Kent, while Leon had stayed on to forge papers and money for the syndicate.

Just one way Eliza was proving invaluable as a mollisher. I still couldn't quite believe I had my own mollishers, after being one for so long.

'Underqueen,' Leon said.

'Leon.' I nodded to the newcomers, who were staring at me. 'Welcome to the Mime Order.'

Both of them looked awestruck. They must have heard plenty of gossip about me. The mollisher who had stabbed her mime-lord in the back. The dreamwalker with mysterious allies from the æther. I wondered how I matched up to their expectations. All they would be seeing now was a woman with dark circles under her eyes.

My hair was back to pale blonde, with a streak of black at the front. The only evidence that I had been in the scrimmage were my fading bruises and the conspicuous welt on my jaw where a cutlass had caught me. Proof that I could fight and win, written on my face.

One of the soothsayers – a pale redhead – actually curtseyed. 'Thank you, Underqueen. We're honoured to be part of the Mime Order.'

'You don't need to curtsey.' I turned to Leon. 'Let Terebell know if we run low on anything, won't you?'

Leon raised his eyebrows. 'Do I just . . . approach her?'

'She won't bite, Leon.'

'If you say so.' Pause. 'Perhaps you could ask her for a few more pairs of boots?'

I breathed out through my nose. 'All right.'

'Thank you.'

Leaving the soothsayers in his capable hands, I made my way upstairs. My deepest injuries still throbbed, but I had just enough medicine to keep the pain under control.

I couldn't blame Leon for being unsure of the Rephs. There was hardly a voyant in the syndicate who didn't break a sweat around our benefactors. I usually spoke to Terebell on their behalf, but I wanted them all to be able to work together, with or without me as a mediator. I was also starting to feel like her secretary.

The surveillance room was eleven floors up. When I entered, I found Tom the Rhymer and the Glym Lord – two of my high commanders – eating breakfast and poring over a map of the cita-del, which showed the positions of recently installed Senshield scanners. Numa were spread among the paperwork and data pads on the table: shew stones, keys, a knife, a crystal ball.

'Good morning to you, Underqueen,' Glym said.

'We have a problem.'

Tom raised his bushy eyebrows. 'Now, that's no way to greet anyone at this time of the morning. I've not even finished my coffee.' He pulled out a chair for me. 'What's the matter?'

'Jaxon's supporters burned down the Juditheon.'

'Maria told us. They're small fry.'

'Even so.' I poured a coffee. 'We need to replace Jaxon. I've left it for too long.' I said it more to myself than to them. 'How are you both getting on?'

'New recruits are arriving daily,' Glym said. 'We need far more, of course, but I have no concerns at this stage. Many voyants seem to be taking to the idea of the Mime Order, now we've announced that all orders and skills are welcome. Of course, the more that join, the more will feel emboldened to follow them into our ranks.'

'We rescued two mediums from a scanner yesterday. I had a vision,' Tom said. 'Glym sent the Linkboys to get them away.' He glanced at his old friend. 'They had an . . . interesting story. Said the scanner went off, but they couldna *see* it. They just heard the alarm.'

I frowned.

Not long after my surprise victory in the scrimmage, Scion had installed multiple Senshield scanners in the Underground. It was an unwelcome development, but they were big enough to avoid.

'They must have seen it,' I said. 'Where was this?'

'I havena heard all the details yet.'

'Send your mollisher to investigate. I don't like the sound of it.'

'All right, Underqueen.'

I filched a ginger bun before I left, causing Tom to gather the rest protectively into their box.

Downstairs, in the training room, daylight spilled through the broken windows, dappling the concrete and the disused machines. There were rings for voyants to train in physical and spirit combat, as well as a knife range.

As promised, the Ranthen were helping our recruits to hone their abilities. Pleione Sualocin stood in a ring on the left side of the room, teaching spirit combat to a group of beginners. The voyants around her were visibly transfixed by their instructor.

'. . . spool strikes your opponent's dreamscape, it will unleash a sequence of images called *apparitions*, disorienting them. However, a weak spool can be deflected or broken,' she was saying. 'To hold true, spools must be tightly bound.' She cast a gloved hand in front of her, lacing several wisps together. 'Most voyants can spool by instinct. Think of it as weaving with spirits.'

A few voyants nodded. I had learned to spool at sixteen, but many of our recruits were newcomers to the underworld, with no idea where to start.

'There are plenty of spirits here. Try your hands at spooling,' Pleione told the class. 'I will continue your instruction in due course.'

Several of the voyants saluted me as they dispersed. Pleione watched them leave. So far, she was proving to be a decent instructor.

'Underqueen,' she said. 'The sovereign-elect has asked me to inform you that she will carry out an inspection of all cells in I Cohort next week.'

'Fine,' I said. 'Anything else?'

The light in her eyes burned low. I had forbidden all the Ranthen from feeding on the voyants in my care, forcing them to lie in wait for those who lived outside the syndicate. It hadn't done much to improve their temperaments.

'Terebell is disappointed,' Pleione said, 'that you have not erased the influence of the arch-traitor from London.'

9

'Trust me, I'm trying.'

'I advise you to try harder, dreamwalker.'

She gave me a wide berth as she left. I was used to it by now. Mutual hatred of Jaxon was holding our alliance together, but barely.

All of the Ranthen knew now that he was the human who had betrayed the Novembertide Rebellion, when they had first revolted against the Sargas, the ruling family of Rephs. I wasn't wholly sure that I had been spared from guilt by association. After all, I had worked for the arch-traitor, their sworn enemy, for three years – it was hard to believe that I had never noticed anything, never learned his dirty secret.

The intermediate class was in full swing nearby. An augur rolled a spool together and hurled it at the Rephaite instructor. One sweep of a gloved hand shattered the spool, putting the spirits to flight.

Arcturus Mesarthim is nothing but her lure.

Warden spared me a glance. I hung back, nursing my coffee.

Everyone but you can see it.

The augur sighed and retreated. Warden beckoned two more voyants from the line. First was Felix Coombs, one of the other Bone Season survivors. He stepped into the ring and filled a bowl with water for hydromancy. His opponent was Róisín Ní Chonaill Jacob, whose plaited hair was dark with sweat. Since I had released the vile augurs from Jacob's Island, she had given herself, heart and soul, to the cause, training every day.

'Felix,' Warden said, making Felix start (he was still jumpy around Rephs), 'you are slouching. I assure you, a Vigile will still see you.'

Felix squared up to Róisín, who was a head taller than him.

'Róisín, strike true,' Warden said, 'but give Felix a chance to attempt the technique.'

'A quick chance,' Róisín agreed.

Clearing his throat, Felix spooled a few spirits. Warden paced around the ring.

'Turn your backs,' he said. They did. 'Now, take three steps away from one another.'

He always made combat a duel, a dance. A train of observers wound all the way around the ring. As Felix and Róisín waited for their cue, the audience called encouragements.

'Now,' Warden said.

Felix turned and sliced his arm down. The spirits wheeled after it and dived into the water, making its surface tremble and the æther strain. I watched in amazement as the spirits rose again, carrying a chain of sparkling droplets with them. The other voyants stared, riveted.

Róisín put a sudden end to the grace period and sprang towards Felix. She threw him against the ropes before her fingers bit into his shoulder. His body gave a violent jolt, causing the spirits to panic and flee. Water sprayed everywhere as he slid into a heap on the floor.

'Yield, I yield,' he yelled, to gales of laughter. 'That hurt, Róisín! What did you do?'

'Róisín used her gift against you,' Warden said. 'Your bones responded to her touch.'

Felix recoiled. 'My bones?'

'Yes. They may be enveloped in flesh, but they will still answer to an osteomancer.' He gave her a nod. 'Well done, Róisín.'

Róisín nodded back and offered Felix a hand up, earning a smattering of applause. I put my coffee down and joined in. Warden had transformed her osteomancy into an active gift, something she could use to defend herself. Even the brief feat Felix had managed was nothing like the hydromancy I had seen before.

'Told you we should never have released them,' a whisperer muttered. 'Vile augurs don't belong with civilised voyants.'

'Enough,' Warden said. 'The Underqueen has forbidden that sort of talk.'

Several people started. Rephs, as it turned out, had keen hearing. Anyone else would have quailed at his tone, but the whisperer recovered quickly.

'I don't have to do what you say, Reph,' he sneered. Felix swallowed and glanced at Warden. 'I'll take my orders from the Underqueen.'

'Then listen to this, Trenary,' I called. Heads turned in my direction. 'We don't hold with that attitude any longer. If you can't let go of it, take it elsewhere.'

There was a long pause before Trenary stormed out of the hall. Róisín looked tense, but no one else spoke.

'Warden, what can you teach me?' Jos Biwott piped up, breaking the silence. 'All I can do is sing.'

'That is no small gift,' Warden said. 'All of you have the potential to use your clairvoyance against Scion, but my time is short today.' Groans of disappointment rang through the hall. 'I will return soon. Until then, keep practising.'

With clear reluctance, the voyants went their separate ways – some upstairs, more to the canteen, and the rest to the knife range, where Maria was hitting targets with practised ease. Warden reached for his coat.

It had been weeks since we had spoken more than a few stiff words to one another. Trying to shake off my apprehension, I crossed the hall to stand beside him.

'Paige.'

His voice warmed me like a glass of hot mecks. The tension in my body unwound, and I felt steady for the first time in days.

'Warden,' I said. 'It's been a while.'

'Indeed.'

I tried to appear as if I was observing the knife range, but I was too aware of the eyes on us – of those who were regarding the Underqueen and their Rephaite instructor with open curiosity.

'That was very impressive,' I said frankly. 'How did you teach Felix to use hydromancy that way?'

'We call it *fusion*. An advanced form of spirit combat for certain soothsayers and augurs. You saw the Wicked Lady use it during the scrimmage.' He watched as a medium allowed herself to be possessed. 'With the exception of breachers, spirits cannot usually affect the corporeal world. But they can be persuaded to interact with certain numa.'

'So the spirits lifted the water for Felix.'

'Yes.'

This could give us a real advantage. Before the Ranthen had come along, soothsayers and augurs could only really use spooling against an opponent. It was part of why Jaxon thought them so weak.

'That one has been speaking against the vile augurs. And, less openly, in favour of Jaxon as the rightful leader of the Mime Order.' Warden nodded after Trenary. 'Apparently he often quotes the more incendiary passages from *On the Merits of Unnaturalness*.'

'I'll keep an eye on him. We can't have any discord in the ranks.'

'Very well.'

There was a brief, uncomfortable silence. I closed my eyes for a moment.

'Well,' I said, 'I've business elsewhere. Excuse me.'

I had already taken a few steps towards the door when Warden spoke again.

'Did I do something to insult you, Paige?'

I stopped. His voice was as soft as ever, but it cut right the way through me.

'No,' I said. 'I've just been preoccupied.'

My tone was too defensive. We both knew full well that something was wrong.

'Of course,' Warden said. I avoided his gaze. 'The company you keep is yours to decide. But if you ever desire counsel, or someone to listen, I am here.'

All at once, I was even more conscious of him. I was also conscious of the stiffness in my back. The chill of unease that I still couldn't shake.

After the scrimmage, we had decided to keep seeing each other in secret. I had been looking forward to it. From his perspective, my cold shoulder must have come out of nowhere. I was only surprised it had taken him this long to question my sudden withdrawal.

It wasn't anything he had done. Unlike the other Ranthen, he had accepted that I had spent three years working for Jaxon Hall without knowing who he was. He had treated me no differently, excusing and believing in my ignorance without question.

No, it wasn't him. It was the warning Jaxon had given me, lodged in the back of my mind like a splinter. And I couldn't admit that to Warden. I couldn't admit that Jaxon Hall – a serial liar – had got to me.

'Thank you,' I said quietly. 'I know.' Noticing the interest we were attracting, I turned away, schooling my face. 'I'll see you soon, Warden.'

I spent the rest of the day taking stock of our supplies. As I left the Mill at dusk, Nick and Eliza were on their way in, looking for me. They had taken an urgent report from Mary Bourne, who was convinced there were Vigiles watching a phone box in her section.

'One of her voyants made a call and never came back,' Nick told me as we trudged through the snow. 'She wants someone to investigate.'

I pulled my gloves on. 'Didn't we have something like this last week, with the medium who vanished into a pharmacy?'

'Yes.'

'Is it a box they've used for a while?'

'Yes, for syndicate business.'

'Tell Mary to abandon it, then. Scion must have got wind of their calls.'

'I'll send a courier,' Eliza said. 'Back to the den?'

I nodded. We had been out for too long today, and we needed to assess our finances.

Cully gave us a lift. Given that she was one of the few syndies with a car, Maria had entrusted her with driving to the Unnatural Assembly between safe houses and meeting points.

She dropped us off on Limehouse Causeway. From there, we went on foot, keeping our heads down. Eliza stuck to my side like a body-guard, already committed to her new role as mollisher supreme.

All around us, partygoers were out in force, high on Floxy (or fanaticism), jostling past dockworkers from the Isle of Dogs. Oxygen bars were always busy in the run-up to Novembertide. Eliza stopped at a cash machine and took out a pickpocketed bank card.

Stolen cards were useful, even if they only lasted as long as it took for their owners to realise they were missing. Terebell often refused my requests for money, something I was convinced she enjoyed. Nick glanced over his shoulder, checking for observant passers-by, as Eliza fed the card into the machine and tapped her foot.

An alarm shrilled.

Eliza flinched back with a sharp intake of breath. The ear-splitting wail drew the eyes of everyone in the vicinity. For a moment, we just stared at each other.

I knew that sound.

That was the sound a Senshield scanner made when it detected the presence of a voyant; a sound that portended arrest – but it was coming from *inside* the cash machine.

And that wasn't possible. Senshield scanners were massive contraptions. You could see one from the other end of the street. If you stayed alert, you might never go near one. They weren't *hidden*.

Were they?

I thought all of this in the split second it took me to react.

'Run,' I barked at the others.

As one, we fled from the machine. 'Stop them,' someone bellowed. 'Unnaturals!'

A hand snatched at Nick. His fist swung up, punching the man away. I looked back to see night Vigiles in pursuit, flux guns at the ready, bellowing 'halt' and 'get down' at the tops of their voices – a roar that made people scatter in panic around them.

The telltale *click-hiss* of a flux gun made me drop into a roll and veer into the next street, hauling Eliza along with me. Shock had already ramped up my heartbeat; now terror carved my body, cutting my breaths short. I hadn't felt fear like this in a long time, not since the day I was taken to Oxford. The three of us were the highest-ranking members of the Mime Order. We could not be detained.

We sprinted towards the dockworkers' shantytown, where we could vanish into the close-knit labyrinth of shacks. Just as it came into sight, a vehicle screamed into our path. Like cornered animals, we turned to face the Vigiles. There were eight of them.

'Shit,' Eliza whispered.

Slowly, I raised my hands. The others did the same. As the Vigiles formed a circle around us, shock batons glowed to life and flux guns were levelled at our chests, no doubt loaded with the newest version of the drug.

I glanced at Nick. His aura was changing, reaching farther into the æther.

I couldn't dreamwalk. After overusing my spirit in the scrimmage, then having to possess a Vigile to confront Nashira, I was still too fragile to be of much use in a fight.

That didn't mean I couldn't kick some turncoats to the kerb.

Nick's gift exploded out of him. He blinded them with a torrent of visions; Eliza chased them with a string of spools. Complex weaves of spirits twisted around the Vigiles, trapping them in a gyre of apparitions. In the confusion that followed, I snatched a flux gun. The ballistic syringe sprang free, hitting the commandant between the shoulder blades.

We were fluid, working as a team, as we had in the past when we fought rival gangs. Nick made a grab for one of their shock batons and snapped his elbow into an unprotected chin. With a sizzle of electricity, a Vigile dropped to the ground. Eliza rammed her shoulder into another and ran past the vehicle, tossing one of our precious smoke canisters. As it broke open, swathing us all in a dense grey cloud, I fired off one more dart and raced after her, keeping hold of the empty gun. Nick's footfalls soon caught up with mine.

One leap took me over a low wall. We crawled under the graffiti-coated fence that marked the boundary of the shantytown, closed in on the first shack we came across, and flung away the tarpaulin that served as a door. Even as we crashed through occupied dwellings, even as the dockworkers swore at us, we didn't slow down.

It was only when we emerged at the very end of the Isle of Dogs, stumbling on to an oily ribbon of sand beside the Thames, that we stopped. A stitch was biting into my side, but it was nothing in comparison to the abyss of dread that was opening inside me.

We had always been so careful, so sure of our ability to blend in. I had thought nothing could touch us. Yet we, of all people, had been taken by surprise.

'What the fuck was that?' Eliza said, between gasps. 'A *concealed* Senshield scanner?'

I felt too shaken to speak. We had to move, but every bone and muscle protested my return to combat. Nick shook his head, panting. Finally, I gathered enough breath to say, 'Come on. We have to warn the Mime Order. This could – this could end everything.'

2

EMERGENCY

I called an emergency meeting at once, sending Nick to Poplar and a trusted courier to the Mill. By the time we got to Candlewick, Glym, Tom and Maria had already reached it by car. Opposite them was Danica Panić, the other member of the Seven Seals who had stayed with me after the scrimmage. I would usually have wanted all six of my commanders to attend a gathering like this, but it seemed unwise for us all to be under one roof.

When I entered the hideout, they stood. My ribs ached as I lowered myself into a chair. The bitter cold wasn't helping my injuries from the scrimmage.

'There you are.' Maria raised her eyebrows. 'What's going on, Paige?'

Nick walked in a moment later, his cheeks pink from the cold. 'Terebell wasn't there,' he said to me. 'Sorry. I left a message.'

I forced myself to nod. The Ranthen had taken up residence in a derelict library in Poplar, but they were often away, which Terebell rarely saw fit to explain.

Her absence was beyond frustrating. Nothing could be more important than this. We had always expected Scion to increase the number of Senshield scanners, but we had also expected to be able to see them.

'Thank you all for coming at such short notice,' I said. 'I'll get straight to the point. Eliza just tried to use a cash machine, and an alarm went off. It seems like a Senshield scanner was . . . built into it, somehow.' I paused, letting them take it in. 'We barely escaped.'

Deep breaths were drawn. Glym lowered his face into the palm of one hand.

'The implications for the Mime Order could be catastrophic,' I said. 'If we can't see the scanners, we can't avoid them.'

'In a cash machine.' Maria scraped a hand through her hair. 'Such an ordinary thing . . .'

'This might explain the phone box,' Nick said. 'And the voyant who disappeared from the pharmacy.'

I had been too quick to brush off those reports.

'This is the most significant threat we've ever faced,' I said. 'Depending on how many hidden scanners Scion has installed, some members of the Mime Order may have to go into hiding until our numbers are great enough to overcome the Vigiles. It could be too dangerous on the streets.'

'Some members,' Maria repeated.

'The Ranthen have a spy on the inside. From what they've learned, Senshield can only detect certain voyants in its current state,' I said. 'The first three orders, as classified by *On the Merits*.'

The news sank in.

'Paige,' Eliza finally said, 'we can't just hide.'

'As a fellow medium,' Glym said, 'I agree. Despite the danger, it would be impractical to freeze most of our recruits.'

'It would also be impractical to allow Scion to capture them,' I said. 'We have other voyants to do the footwork.'

'Not many.'

'Enough,' I said, but I could tell that they weren't having this. 'You'd rather hide in plain sight, then?'

'As we always have,' Maria said. 'How sure are you?'

'Terebell told me a few days ago. I was hoping for proof before I caused any panic.'

'It sounds like a barrel of shit to me. You're telling me Scion has *miraculously* been able to target us according to Jaxon's inane hierarchy?'

'Whatever Senshield can do, it's time we tackled the threat. Hector buried his head in the sand, but we have to face the facts about how serious this is,' I said. 'This is a god in a machine. An all-seeing eye.'

'And you're going to find it hard to blind it,' Danica remarked.

She sat with her arms folded. Her hair was a thatch of auburn frizzles, her eyes bloodshot from overtime. With her job in the engineering sector of Scion, she was one of our best sources of information on Senshield.

'Dani,' I said, 'did you have any idea this was coming?'

'I knew as much as you did, which is that Scion planned to install the large scanners across London. We all knew that they would eventually target essential services. What I did *not* know,' she said, 'was that they had created a version that could be concealed, or would target certain orders.'

'Jaxon asked you to build a device to block Senshield,' Nick said. 'Did you get anywhere with it?'

'Clearly not.'

'I asked the Ranthen for alysoplasm to help Dani,' I said. 'Buzzer blood conceals auras and dreamscapes – I'm hoping that could be the key – but so far, they've declined my request. I had to grovel just to get that amaranth for Bea.'

Maria sighed. 'Why are they like this?'

'In their defence, it's very difficult to harvest both substances, and I'm not the one risking my neck.'

'Okay,' Nick said. 'Do you have any idea how we can get rid of the scanners, then, Dani?'

'You can't destroy or remove the large ones,' Danica said. 'Each scanner is watched closely, not to mention welded in place.'

'Do you know how they work?' Glym asked her. 'Anything about them at all?'

'Obviously.'

'And?'

She shot him a dark look. If there was one thing Danica Panić hated, it was being rushed.

'The Senshield scanners are powered by a single energy source, which they call its *core*,' she said, with deliberate slowness. 'I don't know what it is, but I do know that every scanner is somehow connected to it.'

'So if we get rid of the core, we disable the whole thing,' I said.

'Hypothetically. It would be like removing the battery.'

Tom stroked his beard. 'And where do we find it?'

'The Archon, surely,' I said.

'Senshield is a ScionIDE project,' Danica said. 'More likely it's in a military facility.'

Scion: International Defence Executive. I had last encountered them thirteen years ago, when they had invaded Ireland.

'ScionIDE,' Maria murmured.

I looked at her. Wearing an odd expression, she took a leather case from her jacket.

'I didn't know Senshield was a military brainchild. That's very interesting.' She removed a cigarette and lit up. 'A link to the army gives its increased presence an even more sinister touch.'

A chill darted up my spine. We had security measures in place to protect us from Vigiles and enemy Rephs, but I hadn't seriously considered the army a prospective threat at this stage. The bulk of it was thought to be overseas, keeping control of Ireland and Scion East.

'I'm all for going after Senshield, but if we bait the beast, we have to be prepared for one hell of a bite,' Maria said, 'and that bite might well include a certain Hildred Vance, Grand Commander of the Republic of Scion.'

Tom muttered some choice words.

'Vance,' Glym said. 'She spearheaded the invasion of Bulgaria.'

'That's the one. The mastermind behind their conquests.' Maria blew out a fine mist of smoke. 'She may have accelerated the expansion of Senshield. For military purposes.'

Eliza swallowed. 'What does it mean if she comes here?'

Maria drew on her cigarette again. 'It means,' she said, 'that we will be fighting one of the most intelligent and ruthless strategists alive. One who is accustomed to dismantling cell-based rebel groups.'

There was a long silence. Our movement wasn't strong enough to deal with the army yet.

'Well,' I said, 'whether or not it *is* linked to Vance—'

I stopped when the door opened again, and Warden appeared, wearing his black overcoat. The commanders regarded him with the usual degree of trepidation, taking in his glowing blue eyes.

'I saw your summons, Underqueen,' he said. 'I came as soon as I could.'

'Thank you,' I said. 'Could Terebell not be here?'

'She is engaged tonight.'

He took the seat beside Glym. His eyes were unnerving, reminding me of exactly what he had to do to survive, but I couldn't resent him for it. For his sake, I briefly explained the hidden scanner.

'You were close to the Sargas,' I said. 'We could use your advice if we're going to have any chance of disabling Senshield. Dani heard it has a single power source, the core. Does that sound possible to you?'

'Danica may be right,' Warden said. 'If so, this core is likely a form of ethereal technology, which harnesses the energy created by spirits.'

Tom knitted his brow. 'I've never heard of such a thing.'

I recalled the ethereal fences in Oxford, and the strange padlock held in place by the spirit of Sebastian Pearce. My jaw tightened a little.

'Even most Rephaim know precious little about it,' Warden said. 'The Sargas are the only family to have spliced the energy of the æther with human machinery. Many of my kind consider it obscene. Unfortunately, I was not trusted with any specific knowledge about Senshield. I do not know the workings of the core.'

I nodded slowly. 'Do you think it might be in the Archon?'

'I will ask our double agent, but I imagine that if it was, he would already have told us.'

Alsafi Sualocin, the spy in the Westminster Archon. I had known him in Oxford as a brutal Sargas loyalist. It had been a shock to discover that he was Ranthen, working in secret to undermine Nashira.

'This may be the time to consider something we *do* know of the scanners.' Warden glanced around the table. 'Senshield can only detect three orders of clairvoyance. So far, Scion has been unable to tune it to detect the higher four.'

'Yes, Paige just told us,' Maria said. 'I still think it sounds a tad convenient, but I'll indulge you. How do they do this . . . tuning, exactly?'

'No one knows, but I have long suspected that exposure to aura is involved. It would be logical for Senshield to recognise what it has already encountered.'

'And the first three orders are the most populous,' Glym said, catching on.

'Yes,' Warden said. 'It is possible that any of you could be used to improve its ability to detect aura.'

This was all we needed. If walking the streets could not only get us arrested, but potentially make Senshield more dangerous, then going into hiding had to remain an option, even if we only used it as a last resort.

'On the subject of the core, do you think it could be easily replaced?' I said. 'If we destroyed it, would they just build another?'

'Not being a Sargas, I am no specialist in ethereal technology,' Warden said, 'but I know that it is complex, volatile, and delicate. If you destroyed the existing core, I imagine it would take Scion many years to return it to its current operational state.'

I could hear in his voice that this was educated guesswork, but it was something to go on, at least.

'Something else to bear in mind,' he said, 'is that an improved Senshield will pose a great danger to the Night Vigilance Division. If it can be adjusted to detect all seven orders, there will be no need for sighted clairvoyant officers. They will be redundant.' He looked at me. 'Some of them may well be willing to help you imperil the core.'

'Absolutely not,' Glym said. 'The syndicate has *never* worked with Vigiles.'

I had always thought Glym was a bit of a prankster, like Tom, but he was quite the disciplinarian. He was taking the revolution seriously, at least, which was more than I could say for some of the Unnatural Assembly.

'If you do not extend the hand of friendship,' Warden said, 'the night Vigiles will be eliminated.'

'Good,' Glym said.

'Warden makes a salient point,' Maria said. 'The night Vigiles have never betrayed the Garden — we all know that some of them must still go there — and they *are* potential recruits. Why waste them?'

'It would only be a temporary alliance,' I said. 'Once Senshield is down, there's no risk to their jobs.'

'By which point, they may have been persuaded of the merits of revolution,' Warden said. 'But a temporary alliance may be all that is needed.'

There was silence while I mulled it over. I could listen to counsel all I liked, but in the end, this was my call. I was beginning to understand why Hector had been able to abuse his power to such an extent – syndicate leaders were handed a lot of it. The voyants in this organisation bowed to strength, and in the scrimmage, I had proven mine. That didn't make me an expert in starting revolutions.

My instinct had always been to steer well clear of Vigiles, but what they could offer might be worth the flak I would get for giving them a chance. It would also drain recruits from Scion.

'If we ever find ourselves in a situation where the Vigiles' help would be vital to our success, we can return to this subject,' I concluded. 'Until then, I don't think we should risk approaching them.' Everyone seemed satisfied. 'Dani, I want you to do your utmost to find out what – and where – the core is. That's our priority.'

'Wait.' Tom gestured to Danica. 'Doesn't the White Binder know that you work for Scion?'

'Yes,' Danica said.

'And you're still happy to do it?'

'Unless the Mime Order can match my existing salary.'

It definitely couldn't.

Nick looked troubled. 'It's strange, but Jaxon doesn't seem to have given her away. I don't trust him, but if he hasn't said anything after three weeks—'

He trailed off.

'Warden has already checked with the double agent,' I said. 'As far as we can tell, Dani isn't being monitored. He'll alert us if the situation changes.'

'Good to know,' Danica said.

'While we investigate Senshield, you should all warn your mime-lords and mime-queens about these hidden scanners I want reports about any their voyants encounter,' I said. 'We need to work out which kinds of places have been targeted and keep the syndicate aware. I'll have Grub Street distribute maps of all the known locations. We also need to deal with the few voyants who still support the White Binder.'

'They will forget any lingering fondness for him once I-4 has a new leader,' Glym said.

'No one has declared themselves to me.'

'They think Jax is coming back,' Eliza said. 'They're all too scared to take his place.'

Of course. Even now Jaxon was gone, his shadow still lay across the citadel, as it had for decades.

Usually, the only way to change the leader of a section was if the current one was killed, and if no mollisher came forward to claim the title. There would be a power struggle before the victor announced themselves to the Unnatural Assembly.

I didn't know if Jaxon had chosen a new mollisher before he left, and in truth, I didn't care. I also didn't want chaos while the syndicate tried to work out who the best replacement was.

'One of you must have a candidate in mind,' I said. 'I'd like you to encourage them to present themselves at the trial tomorrow, so we can put this to bed.' I stood. 'I'll send orders in the morning.'

With nods, my three commanders left the hideout. As Nick and Eliza went to secure the building, I cleared away the papers on the table.

Warden was last to stand. For the first time in weeks, we were alone together. I kept my head down as he stepped towards the doorway.

'Are you leaving?'

'I must,' he said. 'To discuss what you have learned with Terebell.'

I couldn't stomach this atmosphere between us. The golden cord – the fragile link that connected our spirits – was supposed to tell me what he was feeling, but all I could sense was an echo chamber.

'You must remove Jaxon's remaining supporters. Terebell will insist upon it,' Warden said. 'Fail to do this, and you risk her displeasure.'

'You just heard me address that.'

'You know which supporters I mean.'

I paused, my chest tight. 'Does she know I haven't evicted them?'

'No, but she may raise the subject with me.'

'And you'll tell her.'

'You seem exasperated.'

'Do I really, Warden?'

'Yes.'

I rubbed the bridge of my nose. He really could be oblivious sometimes.

A few days after the scrimmage, Chat had come to me with news. Nadine and Zeke were still in Seven Dials, apparently trying to hold the fort. So far, my conscience had stopped me throwing them out. I had sent them an offer of shelter, regardless of their feelings towards me, but received no reply. Chat had since got out of dodge and moved his cookshop to Leadenhall, the same beautiful market where Eliza had been meant to sell her forgeries. So far, her duties as a mollisher supreme had prevented her from doing it.

Other than Nick and Eliza, I had only told Warden about Nadine and Zeke. That was the last time we had spoken in private.

'Terebell is fixated on the minority who support Jaxon,' I said, forcing myself to sound calm and reasonable. 'She needs to let me handle this my way. I know she hates Jax – I know it's personal for her, and for you – but having to think about it is distracting me from things we actually need to focus on, like Senshield.'

'She views your reluctance to replace Jaxon as evidence that you still hold some affection for him,' Warden said. 'Your refusal to expel Zeke and Nadine will only increase her suspicion.'

'For goodness' sake—' I pulled on my jacket. 'Look, I'll deal with it. Give me a few days.'

Warden regarded me. 'You have deferred your decision because of Nick's feelings for Zeke.'

'You might know Terebell's mind, Warden, but don't presume you have any insight into mine.'

He fell silent, but his eyes burned.

Heat fanned across my face. Before I could say anything else, I headed for the door.

'Terebell is my sovereign-elect. I owe her my loyalty and allegiance,' Warden said, 'but do not think me some mindless instrument of her will.' I stopped. 'I remind you that I am my own master. I remind you that I have defied the Ranthen. And still do.'

'I know,' I said.

'You do not believe me.'

A long breath escaped me. 'I don't know what I believe any more.'

His gaze darted across my features. I lingered by the door, watching him.

It had been so easy, before the scrimmage, to believe that things could work out between us. I still didn't know where I had gone wrong, to let Jaxon keep controlling me.

When I didn't leave, Warden came to me and touched the underside of my jaw, lifting my face. My heart thumped as I looked him in the eye.

The contact awakened something that had lain dormant for weeks, since the night before the scrimmage. As we regarded each other, linked by the barest touch of his fingertips, I didn't know what I wanted to do; what I wanted *him* to do. Leave me. Talk to me. Stay with me.

My hands moved as if by instinct – smoothing up to his shoulders, settling at the nape of his neck. He stroked down my back. I searched him the way I might search a map for a path I had known long ago, chasing the familiar, learning what I had forgotten. When our foreheads met, my dreamscape danced with the flames he always set there.

'I missed you,' I said.

'Likewise.'

We stayed like that for a while. I traced the hollow of his throat, where his pulse tolled – and I wondered, as I had before, why a deathless being would have a heartbeat. It only made my own run faster.

His fingers grazed up my nape, into my curls. For once, I didn't care that he was still wearing his gloves. I sensed his aura flit along mine, felt warmth race and rise beneath my skin. When I couldn't stand the separation any more, I wound an arm around his neck and closed what space was left between us.

It was lighting a fire after days in the rain. I pressed my mouth to his, feverishly seeking a connection, and he gave it. I tasted wine first, a hint of oak, then him.

The strain of staying away from him had almost snapped me in half. Now I was cradled to his chest, I had thought that strain would ease, but I only wanted him to hold me tighter, closer. We kissed with a hunger that was almost a hurt, an ache deepened by weeks apart. I reached for the door handle, finding no key or bolt to protect us from discovery, but I couldn't stop. I needed this.

His lips unlocked mine. Our auras intertwined, as they always did. My heart pounded at the thought of the other Ranthen walking in. The alliance unravelling. I said his name; he stopped at once – but now I had him back, I couldn't bring myself to end this. I moved his hand to my waist. As he drew me into his embrace, his thumb brushed the scar on my jaw, turning my skin as delicate as paper. I felt tender all over, like his touch had stripped off armour I hadn't known was there.

He sat down on the table, keeping me with him. I let him fill my thoughts, my senses. Gently, he opened the top of my shirt and kissed my throat, brushing the pendant that rested between my collarbones. A shiver worked its way down my body as his lips came to mine again.

I only sensed the dreamscape when it was far too close. With a jolt, I broke away from Warden and threw myself into the nearest chair. Maria strode in a moment later.

'Forgot my coat,' she said. 'Still here, Warden?'

He inclined his head. 'Paige and I had a private matter to discuss.'

'Ah.' She grabbed her coat from the back of a chair. 'Paige, sweet, you look . . . feverish.'

'I do feel a little warmer than usual,' I said.

'You should see Nick about it.' Maria looked between us. 'Well, don't let me keep you.'

She slung her coat over her shoulder and left.

Warden stayed where he was. My blood was hot and restless in my veins. There was no one else close, no one else coming.

'I forgot about the hazards of being in your company,' I said, trying to sound light.

'Hm.'

Our gazes met again. I wanted, needed, to trust that this was real – but I was frozen by the reminder of the danger, and by the memory of Jaxon, that mocking laughter in his eyes. *Arcturus Mesarthim is nothing but her lure. Her bait. And you, darling – you fell for it.*

'I meant to ask,' I said. 'Has Alsafi heard anything more about my father?'

'He is still imprisoned in Coldbath Fields.'

'Is there any chance that we can get him out?'

'From what Alsafi told me, he is watched around the clock,' Warden said. 'Nashira knows your abilities. That means she can take precautions. If I believed he could be freed, I would be honest, Paige.'

I nodded stiffly. Perhaps it had been too much to hope.

'I should get some sleep.' I stood. 'Ivy goes on trial tomorrow.'

For being part of the grey market. For helping the Rag and Bone Man sell voyants to the Rephs.

'You will come to the right decision,' Warden said.

He knew, somehow, that I wasn't sure what to do with her. 'Is Terebell sending someone to witness it?'

'Errai.'

Great. Errai was about as friendly as a punch in the mouth.

'Do not give me that look,' Warden said softly.

'I'm not giving you a look. I *love* Errai.' I paused. 'Warden—'

He waited. I wrestled with what I wanted to say; what I still couldn't.

'Never mind.' I opened the door. 'I'll . . . see you soon. Goodnight.'

'Goodnight, little dreamer.'

The others didn't ask why I had taken so long to join them. Nick knew about Warden, and I had a feeling Eliza suspected. I sometimes caught her glancing at me and Warden, eyes sharp with curiosity.

As we fought our way through a blizzard, I tried not to think about what had just happened. Maria had almost seen the truth. She would never have gone to Terebell, but I doubted she would have been able to resist telling at least one of the other commanders. Our secret could have been out. I had no idea what my subjects would say – perhaps they wouldn't really care – but Warden was a Reph, and I didn't want to be accused of favouring the Ranthen. No matter how good it had felt to be close to him again, it was too dangerous.

But I missed talking to him. I missed being near him. It had seemed so much simpler before I won the Rose Crown.

When we passed a pharmacy at the end of a line of shops, Eliza hung back. Nick and I turned to look at her.

'It's okay,' Nick said. 'Come on. We'll keep away from—'

'Everything?'

'You'll be fine.'

Eliza hesitated before pressing on. We walked on either side of her, as if our auras could shield hers. A driver picked us up on Hart Street.

We never stayed long in our safe houses, but my favourite was the one that overlooked the Limehouse Basin. The plumbing worked, which meant I could have a hot bath. Once we were locked in, Danica and Eliza retired for the night, while I went straight for the tub. As I soaked away the cold, I let my eyes drift shut.

One side of my head was beginning to throb. I didn't know what we would do if we couldn't get rid of Senshield. The nature and location of its core must be top secret. It was hard not to give way to dread. I was exhausted from doubting everyone and everything.

No matter what I did next, I had to repair my relationship with Warden. I had to find a way to shake my sudden doubt in him.

I know the syndicate must always come first. His words came back to me. *I will be there to meet you in the interludes, Paige Mahoney.*

I wanted to keep meeting him. But for days, a poison of misgiving had been spreading in my mind. I had started to question his motives; to wonder if he was manipulating me on behalf of the Ranthen. They had chosen me to lead their rebellion, but they needed me to be pliable. Perhaps they thought a lovestruck human, overcome by emotion, would be easy to influence. Perhaps they thought that if I wanted Warden badly enough, I would do anything for him.

Now paranoia swelled when I saw him. More than likely, this was just what Jaxon wanted. More than likely, I was playing right into my enemies' hands. I just couldn't seem to stop it.

There was only one thing to be done. I needed to tell Warden, giving him a chance to defend himself. It would take courage, but I wanted to be able to trust him again.

I had so few people left I could trust.

In the parlour, Nick was by the fire, leafing through reports. I could smell the wine on him from the doorway. Until recently, he had always refused to touch alcohol.

'You miss him,' I said quietly.

'Every minute.' His voice was hoarse. 'Have you told Warden what Jax said to you?'

I glanced at him. 'How did you know?'

'Same way you knew I was thinking about Zeke. I always know.'

'If only Rephs were so easy to read,' I said, joining him on the couch. 'No. I haven't told him.'

'Don't leave it too long. You never know when the chance to say things will just . . . disappear.'

He stared into the fire like he was trying to find something. I had always thought I knew his face, down to the dent in his chin and the slight dip at the end of his nose. I had memorised the way his pale eyebrows sloped upward, giving him a look of perpetual concern. But when the light found him at this angle, I sensed the unfamiliar.

'I keep imagining what Jaxon might have planned for him,' he said. 'Look how badly Jax hurt you in the scrimmage.'

'Zeke didn't take his crown.'

'Terebell wants them gone, doesn't she?' Nick said. 'Why haven't you done it?'

'Because I still want to understand why,' I said. 'And I might be a criminal, but I like to think I'm not heartless.'

'They sided with him in public. You can't ignore it.' His voice softened. 'Do what you have to do. Don't take my burdens on to your shoulders.'

'Like you've never done that for me.' I nudged him. 'I'll always have room on my shoulders for you.'

Nick smiled and draped an arm around me. I didn't know what I would have done without him on my side. If he had chosen Jaxon instead of me.

Neither of us wanted to be alone with our thoughts, so we stayed together on the couch, resting in front of the fire. Night had become a perilous time, when I confronted all the paths I could or should have taken. I could have shot Jaxon in the Archon. I could have cut his throat during the scrimmage. I should have had the mettle to tell Warden the truth. I should have done better, done more, done otherwise. Apparently, it wasn't enough to have the whole underworld watching my every move. I had to be my own judge, too.

I needed to plan our next steps in detail, but I was so worn out that I soon lost my train of thought, dozing off. Every time I woke, I thought Warden was with me. Every time I woke, there was less light in the fire.

Arcturus Mesarthim is nothing but her lure. Her bait. I remembered that long night in the chandlery, when our dream-forms had touched for the first time. How easy it had been to laugh when I danced with him in the Old Lyre. *And you, darling – you fell for it.*

It felt real when he held me, but I might have been too trusting. Had he done it all for Terebell?

Was I a fool?

Nick fell asleep at some point, and then it was his words on my mind. *I keep imagining what Jaxon might have planned for him*

I imagined, too. And so imagination became my nemesis; my mind created monsters out of nothing. I imagined how Scion would punish us if they found our nests of sedition. How Nashira would hurt the people I loved if she ever got her hands on them. My father was already in the Steel, at her mercy. All because of me.

Even when the fire went out, I didn't sleep again.

3

JUDGEMENT

'The Unnatural Assembly recognises Divya Jacob, a chiromancer of the order of augurs, also known as the Jacobite. You stand accused of assisting the Rag and Bone Man in the capture and sale of clairvoyants to Scion, resulting in their detainment, enslavement, and – in some cases – death, in the prison city of Oxford. Tell us how you plead, and the æther will determine the truth of your words.'

The Pearl Queen, leading the proceedings, was standing on the stage in a suit of black velvet and pearl embroidery, a pillbox hat perched on her hair. Seated behind her, I was also dressed more elegantly than usual – a shirt of ivory silk with belled sleeves, pressed trousers, and a sleeveless jacket of crimson velvet, embroidered with gold roses and lilies. My face was painted. I felt like a doll on display.

Ivy stood before the stage in a moth-eaten blazer. One of her wrists was bound to a brazier with blue ribbon.

'Guilty,' she said.

Minty Wolfson scratched down the proceedings in a ledger, which looked as if no one had touched it in a century. Apparently, all syndicate trials had to be chronicled for posterity.

'Ms Jacob,' the Pearl Queen said, 'please tell the court about your involvement with the Rag and Bone Man.'

I hadn't seen Ivy since the night of the scrimmage. She had been staying in a cell north of the river with two voyant bodyguards to prevent revenge attacks. She had gained a little weight, and her hair, which had been shorn off in Oxford, was coming through soft and dark.

With composure, she repeated the story she had told after the scrimmage. The story of how she had been taken in by the Rag and Bone Man, become his third (or fourth) mollisher, and been ordered to find talented voyants for him – voyants who she never saw again.

The Rag and Bone Man had vanished after the scrimmage, along with his surviving allies. Ivy was our last clue as to where he might have gone.

We were in an old music hall on Graces Alley, closed down for showing blacklisted films. My high commanders and mollishers were fanned out in seats on either side of mine, listening to Ivy describe the suspicious disappearances. Errai Sarin stood in a corner at the back of the hall. In the gallery was a crowd of observers from across London.

'You noticed that these voyants were disappearing, and you became worried. You informed Chelsea Neves, known as Cutmouth, who was mollisher supreme,' the Pearl Queen said. 'You must have thought her trustworthy. Will you describe your relationship?'

'I made friends with Chelsea when she was brought to Jacob's Island,' Ivy said. 'We . . . only got closer as the years went by.'

'How close?' the Pearl Queen prompted. 'Were you ever lovers?'

'Objection, Pearl Queen,' Minty said. 'The accused has no obligation to—'

'I don't mind,' Ivy said. 'She shacked up with Hector when she joined the Underbodies. Before that, we were together.'

Minty shot the Pearl Queen an exasperated look, but noted down the information.

The Pearl Queen combed through it all in painful detail. How Cutmouth had inspected the Camden Catacombs, found a voyant in chains, and reported it to Hector. How his lust for coin had persuaded him to join the grey market instead of suppressing it.

My gaze strayed to Errai, who wore all black, as the Ranthen usually did. I knew he had little patience for syndicate politics, but I felt his scrutiny. He would report every word of the trial to Terebell.

'Were you ever aware that the missing voyants were being sold to Scion?'

'No,' Ivy said.

Minty continued scribbling as if her hand would drop off.

'Who else was involved in the ring?'

'The Abbess, obviously. Faceless, the Bully-Rook, the Wicked Lady, the Winter Queen, Jenny Greenteeth, and Bloody Knuckles. Other than Jenny and the Wicked Lady, I don't think they involved their mollishers,' Ivy said. 'Too greedy to share the coin.'

A small relief. Halfpenny, the Swan Knight and Jack Hickathrift were all well liked. I hadn't wanted the evidence to force me into banishing them.

'At any point,' the Pearl Queen said, 'did you see the White Binder associate with the Rag and Bone Man?'

'No.'

Murmurs from the gallery. I found it very difficult to believe that Jaxon, who had been entangled with the Sargas for two decades, hadn't known about the grey market.

The Pearl Queen hesitated. 'To your knowledge, did any members of the grey market have dealings with the White Binder, or speak of his involvement?'

'I wish I could say *yes*,' Ivy said darkly, 'but I never heard of any. It's possible he could have been involved without my—'

'No speculation, please,' Glym rumbled. 'This is a court, not one of your palm readings.'

Ivy dropped her head.

'For what it's worth,' she said, 'I'm sorry. I should have done more, and sooner.'

'Yes, you should have, vile augur,' someone bellowed down at her. 'You earned your name!'

'Scum!'

'Enough,' I barked at the gallery.

Some of them shut up, but the abuse soon rose again. The deep-seated hatred towards vile augurs was never going to fade in a few weeks. Another one of Jaxon's glorious contributions to the syndicate.

'Silence.' The Pearl Queen banged her gavel. 'We will have *no* interruptions from the observers!'

Hearing the story for a second time had made it no less disturbing. I wondered how much more there was to it than Ivy knew. From the sound of it, she had been little more than a pawn.

'Now,' the Pearl Queen said, 'the accused will be judged by a member of her order. The æther must determine if any lie has passed her lips.'

Ognena Maria sprang down from the stage. She was a pyromancer, using fire to reach the æther. She struck a match and tossed it into the brazier, which was already piled with wood and kindling. Once a fire was burning, she said, 'All right. Come here, Ivy.'

Ivy shuffled towards the brazier. Maria placed a hand on her shoulder and drew her closer.

The æther quavered. Maria leaned towards the flames, sweat dewing her face.

'I can't see a great deal,' she said, 'but the fire is bright and strong, and it was easy to light. Her words were truthful.'

She patted Ivy on the shoulder before leaving her. Ivy shied away from the flames.

'The high commanders will now cast votes,' the Pearl Queen said. 'Guilty?'

She raised her own hand. A moment passed before Maria, Tom and Glym also held up theirs. Nick, Eliza, Wynn and Minty kept theirs down.

'Underqueen, the deciding vote is yours.'

Ivy kept her head down, waiting. Even from this distance, I could see her scars from Oxford.

I remembered her so clearly from that first night, with her electric-blue hair, hiding the terrible burn on her arm. She had endured more than any of us – yet she had lived to shine a light on the corruption.

I had also spent years grafting for a mime-lord whose true nature I hadn't known. I had carried out his orders without question. If I could work in the service of a traitor and end up as Underqueen,

I had no right to deprive Ivy of a place in the syndicate for committing the same crime.

'I have to find you guilty.'

Ivy didn't flinch, but Wynn did.

'Under my predecessors, a crime like this would have been met with a death sentence,' I continued. Wynn stood with a screech of chair legs. 'However, these are exceptional circumstances. Even if you *had* known about the trade with Scion and sought help, you would have found none from the Unnatural Assembly. I also believe your crimes have been punished enough by the time you spent in Oxford.'

The scrabbling started again. Tom leaned towards me. 'Underqueen,' he whispered, 'the lass was brave to come forward, but to have *no* sentence—'

'We must send a message that sympathy with the grey market will not go unpunished,' Glym said. 'Clemency will show contempt for your voyants' suffering.'

'I wouldna go that far,' Tom said, 'but a soft hand, aye. And you canna afford that.'

'Hector would cut voyants' throats if he was in the wrong mood,' I pointed out. 'In comparison to that, any punishment I give will seem weak. I can't win this.'

'Death would be too extreme,' Glym conceded, 'but she must serve as an example. Too much mercy, and your voyants will assume that mercy will be your answer to all crimes.'

Wynn hadn't taken her eyes off me. Whatever I did next would estrange someone, whether on the stage or in the gallery.

'I'd like you to be a part of the Mime Order, Ivy.' My voice resounded through the hall. 'I'm giving you another chance.'

Ivy looked up. Maria cursed under her breath, while Glym shook his head and angry mutters rolled from above.

'Underqueen,' the Pearl Queen said, 'this is an extraordinary decision. For the sake of the gallery, may I confirm that you intend to give no punishment at all?'

'Her confession was instrumental in exposing the grey market,' I said. The fury on the observers' faces was already making me doubt my decision, but I couldn't backpedal now. 'Without it, the Abbess and the Rag and Bone Man might still have influence over this citadel.'

Shouts rained from the gallery. 'Who cares?' I heard one of them say. 'She sold us out!'

'Hang her!'

'Let her rot!'

These were the people who would spread the news of my first trial as Underqueen. If they went away dissatisfied, the syndicate would soon rally against my verdict.

'Ognena Maria deems Ivy honest,' I said firmly, 'and I see no reason why she would continue to have loyalty to the Rag and Bone Man, but there is a risk. For the time being, she'll remain under house arrest in one of our buildings, or with a chaperone.'

The commanders seemed placated, if disgruntled, but many of the observers still clamoured for a harsher judgement. Ivy, who looked close to passing out, recovered enough to give me a small nod.

'The Underqueen has given her verdict.' The Pearl Queen brought down her gavel. 'Divya Jacob, your trial is over.'

A roar of outrage went up. Glym sliced the ribbon that bound Ivy to the brazier. As it fell, Wynn hurried down from the stage, enveloped Ivy in her arms, and rushed her away from the bellowing in the gallery.

She had the right idea. Best to lie low while things cooled off. I was about to get up when a newcomer strode from the sidelines, ending the commotion.

I recognised that easy gait, the heeled leather boots, the cloak of olive silk. This could only be Jack Hickathrift, the new mime-lord of III-1, who was usually shadowed by a doting admirer or ten. He had taken over from the Bully-Rook after the scrimmage. Maria clicked her fingers to get my attention and pointed to herself.

Jack Hickathrift bowed low. 'My queen.' His voice was soft and honey-smooth. 'With your permission.'

'Please,' I said.

He lowered his hood, revealing a smooth, chiselled face, white as milk. Thick red hair coiled over one eye. The visible one was clear hazel, more amber than green, framed by long lashes. He smiled at the gallery.

'Thank you, Underqueen. I am still grateful to have survived our fleeting encounter during the scrimmage,' he added. 'Even though you stayed your hand, I thought I would be struck down by your beauty.'

My face must have said it all. Nobody had commented on my beauty in my life, least of all in such a public setting.

'You *were* struck down, if I recall correctly,' I said, almost without thinking, 'though I doubt my beauty was to blame.'

Laughter echoed through the music hall. Jack Hickathrift grinned, showing that his perfect teeth had survived the scrimmage intact. He carried an array of bruises from the fray, like all the survivors, and was missing his left thumb.

'Jack, you scoundrel,' Maria said, in mock outrage. 'Are you trying to seduce your way into the Underqueen's good graces?'

'I would *never* do such a thing, Maria.' He placed a hand over his heart. 'I'm far too in love with you.'

'I should think so, too.'

Whistles rang from the gallery. I sat up straighter and threw on a coolly amused expression.

'Tell me, Jack,' I said, 'did you open your meetings with Haymarket Hector in this manner?'

'I might have done,' he said, unperturbed, 'had Hector been as exquisitely lovely as you, my queen.'

He had caught me by surprise at first, but now I relaxed into my chair, trying not to smile at his cheek. This was nothing but a performance, a power play.

'For the sake of your ego, I'll allow you to believe your flattery has worked,' I said in a jaded tone. 'What do you want?'

More laughter. Jack winked.

'I have come here to declare myself before any other can,' he said. 'I wish to rule I-4.'

'You already rule a section.'

'I have greater ambitions.'

'And what makes you think you can control such an important territory?'

'I survived the scrimmage in one piece. That should prove my strength. I ran III-1 for years while the Bully-Rook soaked himself in drink and debauchery.' He dropped to one knee. 'I will be devoted to you, Underqueen, and to your cause. I slew the Knife Grinder in the Rose Ring to stop him killing you, knowing you would make a good leader.'

He had done that. I didn't believe for a moment that it had been to protect me, but he also hadn't attempted to fight me – not even when his mime-lord had been out for my blood.

'Let me prove myself to you,' Jack said. 'Let me bring I-4 to heel.'

I looked to my commanders. Maria nodded. Tom gave me a thumbs up, while the others seemed ambivalent. Doing this would leave III-1 without a leader, but I-4 needed one far more.

'Very well,' I said. 'Jack Hickathrift, I declare you mime-lord of I Cohort, Section 4, there to reign unchallenged for as long as the æther permits.' Applause thundered from the gallery. 'Who is your chosen mollisher?'

'I might have to get back to you on that front, my queen. Not that I haven't considered it,' he added, 'but I have, ah, a few options to contemplate.'

'Yes,' I said. 'No doubt you have.'

Jack went straight to Seven Dials. At my behest, he promised to give Zeke and Nadine an ultimatum. They could join the Mime Order or go their own way, without fear of attack from the syndicate. Either way, they had to leave the den. I had delayed the inevitable for too long.

Several of my commanders had eyed me with displeasure as I stepped down from the stage. Over the last few weeks, I had learned that the Pearl Queen and Glym had the toughest approaches, and the utmost respect for syndicate tradition. Tom had a softer heart than he let on. Maria was unpredictable, while Minty tended to do whatever she thought would cause the least offence. Wynn tried to protect the vulnerable.

Usually, they produced a good mix of views, but only Wynn, out of all of them, had shown real approval of my verdict on Ivy.

After I left the music hall, I had found her standing alone in Graces Alley, having sent Ivy away in a cab. She had taken my hands and promised that my kindness would not go unnoticed.

Elsewhere, kindness was not seen as an admirable quality. News would be spreading through the syndicate now, warning my voyants that their Underqueen was weak.

It couldn't be helped. Ivy had been through too much for one lifetime. I knew what Thuban Sargas had done to her. I hadn't been able to save her from him, but I could protect her in London.

Back at the hideout, Nick set about making supper while I tended to my injuries from the scrimmage. The slash along my side was itching as it healed, driving me spare. It blazed from underarm to hip in a trail of pink and red. Another gift from the White Binder. Warden had far deeper scars, his punishment for betraying the Sargas – punishment he would never have received if not for Jaxon. I hadn't seen them, but I had felt the scar tissue that laddered his back. Jaxon Hall had left his mark on all our lives.

One day soon, he would pay for it.

I faced the mirror and sluiced the greasepaint off. Beneath it, my dark lips looked bruised, and my eyes were steeped in shadow. Weeks of living on broth and coffee had urged my bones against my skin.

Ever since the scrimmage, my appetite had shrivelled. Nick thought it was down to stress, but I couldn't do very much about that. At least he was there to make sure I kept eating, even if my stomach churned. I couldn't afford to lose any strength.

Downstairs, Nick was at the wood-burning stove, stirring whatever was steaming in the pan, while Eliza pored over a map. As soon as I entered, she looked up.

'You,' she said darkly, 'are a very lucky woman.'

'Yes, I often reflect on how *lucky* I am. Lucky enough to be detained by Scion and banged up with the Rephs for half a year,' I said. 'Let's bottle my good luck and sell it. We'll make a killing.'

'Jack Hickathrift flirted with you, and you're not even a tiny bit hot and bothered. Do you know how long I've been in love with that man?'

I sat down. 'You're welcome to offer yourself as *his* mollisher, but I think you'll have to queue.'

'No, thank you. I'd want to be his one and only lover.'

I raised a faint smile at that, but it faded when I saw the map. 'What is that?'

'We've had a few more reports about Senshield. It doesn't look good, Paige.'

The map was marked with every location where a scanner had been seen or heard. Cash machines, phone boxes, oxygen bars, hospitals, schools, supermarkets and homeless shelters had all been reported as potential deathtraps. Even registered taxis had been fitted with the alarms. No voyant could go about the citadel for long without encountering something on that list.

'This has happened so quickly,' I murmured. 'I thought we'd have longer.'

'We all did.'

Nick presented us both with a mug of tea and a bowl of hearty vegetable soup. The wan light from the oil lamp made his face look pinched.

'There's discontent in the syndicate, Paige,' he said. 'They're not pleased with the outcome of the trial.'

'Hector gave them a taste for bloodshed, but they don't have a right to it,' I said. 'Ivy needs protection, not more punishment.'

'I'm glad you weren't hard on her. I'm just warning you that some of your voyants aren't.'

'If they could stomach Hector's decisions, they can learn to stomach mine.' I rubbed my aching eyes. 'When is Dani back from work?'

'About seven, I think.'

I checked my watch. The chances that she had been able to find anything out were minuscule, but other than Alsafi, she was the only one left on the inside – and if anyone had the tenacity to find out where Scion was hiding the power source of Senshield, it was Danica Panić.

'Errai spoke to me after the trial,' Nick said. 'He said that Terebell wants to see you tonight. I'll go with you.'

'Great,' I said. 'I can't wait to be told off for an hour.' (Among other things, I would have to ask Terebell for money.) 'Do you have the accounts?'

Eliza found the ledger and pushed it across the table. I scanned our many streams of income from across the underworld, which included syndicate tax and rent, as well as the lump sums from Terebell – but the financial needs of the Mime Order were growing by the day. Hector had seemed effortlessly rich, but I now realised it was because the grey market had been raking in so much extra income.

Besides, Hector had only ever needed to spend his money on himself. He hadn't been trying to build and fund an army. I closed the ledger.

'Let's make ourselves presentable,' I said. 'Eliza, double-check that the Unnatural Assembly have all handed over their rose tax for November, will you?'

'Sure.'

————

Terebell had summoned us to the derelict library in Poplar. Two of our moto drivers picked me and Nick up. Unfortunately, we didn't get far before the transmission screens came to life. An announcement from our glorious Grand Inquisitor was imminent.

The motos swerved to the side of the road. Across the river, Frank Weaver appeared.

'*Denizens of the citadel, this is your Inquisitor,*' he said. '*For security reasons, a curfew will be imposed in the capital from eight p.m. to five a.m., effective immediately. Scion key workers are exempt, but must be in uniform when they travel. We ask you to trust that this extraordinary measure has been put in place for your protection, and we thank you for your cooperation. There is no safer place than Scion.*'

He vanished, replaced by the anchor on a white background. All I could hear was my breath inside the helmet.

'Take us back to Limehouse,' I said to my driver. 'Let's not draw attention.'

'Right you are, Underqueen.'

As the moto turned, I glimpsed people gesturing at the screens, frustration etched on their faces. Still, they did begin to trickle back to their homes.

Our drivers returned us to the docklands. My mind whirred like an overworked machine, drilling out every potential consequence of this announcement.

Eliza looked up from the taxes as we trudged back in. 'What's happening?'

'Official curfew,' I said. 'Eight to five.'

'Oh, great.' A sigh escaped her. 'Well, we're already used to working by daylight. It's not the end of the world, is it?'

'Not for most of us, but it will make it harder for the Ranthen to get around.'

'And the fugitives,' Nick pointed out. 'We're more likely to be spotted in broad daylight.'

I hadn't even thought of that. It must be the reason Weaver had done this.

'Well.' I shed my jacket. 'Let's just hope he doesn't put night Vigiles on the street in the day, too.'

We had all heard rumours, but so far, they were unconfirmed. I hoped they would stay that way.

Whatever Terebell wanted, it would have to wait. We set about locking down the building, with Nick doing the final check. Once it was done, he joined me and Eliza at the table, where the setback kept us all silent, lost in our own thoughts.

As we sat there, I tried to think of ways we could work around the curfew. It was already a challenge to keep syndicate voyants safe as they moved across the citadel, with Jaxon advising Scion. His knowledge of London, built up over decades, was far greater than mine. He also knew every trick in the book when it came to avoiding detection.

The best way lay beneath the streets. London had many underground passages, but the mudlarks and toshers would stop us from going too deep. They were homeless Londoners, mostly amaurotic, who made their living by scouring lost rivers, storm drains and sewers for trinkets and artefacts to sell. They claimed most of the tunnels under London as their territory, treating the manholes as their front doors. The syndicate respected their claim, and they, in turn, didn't bother the syndicate.

Someone hammered on the front door. We flinched to our feet, spools quavering around us.

'Vigiles.' Nick was already moving. 'We can—'

'Wait,' I said.

Two more crashes. Those weren't human dreamscapes outside. Slowly, I released my clutch of spirits.

'No,' I said. 'It's just the Ranthen.'

I stepped across the hallway and cracked the door open, leaving it on its chain. A pair of inhuman eyes flashed. The chain tore away from the frame, and the door was flung wide open.

The impact caught me in the shoulder. Next, a gloved hand seized the front of my jacket and pinned me against a wall, making Eliza and Nick shout in protest. For the first time since the scrimmage, my spirit snapped out like an elastic band – only to ping off an armoured dreamscape and slam back into my body. Red-hot pain streaked up one side of my face and burrowed deep into my temple.

'I see now,' Terebell Sheratan said, 'that you were a poor investment, dreamwalker.'

Several of the Ranthen followed her into the hallway. Nick pointed his pistol at her hand.

'Let go of her, Terebell.'

The ache was swelling. I tried not to let it show, but my eyes watered.

'If you were a Rephaite, I might excuse your lack of punctuality, but you are mortal. Each moment chips away at your lifeline,' Terebell said. 'Do not try to convince me that you cannot tell the time.'

'There's a curfew,' Nick said. 'We had to turn back.'

'It does not supersede your duty to meet me.'

'You're being unreasonable, Terebell.'

'Rich words for a human,' Pleione said. 'Your species is the very definition of *unreasonable*.'

A storm of black flecks crossed my vision. As the iron grip tightened enough to leave bruises, Warden arrived. He hadn't observed the scene for more than a second before the light in his eyes ignited, and he addressed Terebell in rough Gloss. She threw me, like I was nothing but a sack of flour, towards Nick, who caught me by the arms.

'How dare you?' Eliza said hotly. 'Don't you think she took enough punishment in the Rose Ring?'

'You will not speak to the sovereign-elect in that manner,' Errai said.

Eliza bristled. I pressed my hands to my forehead, willing the pain to disappear.

'Paige,' Nick murmured. 'Are you okay?'

'I'm fine.'

'Do not affect illness,' Errai sneered.

'Please, Errai, just give it a rest,' I forced out.

'What did you say to me, human?'

'Enough,' Warden said curtly. 'This is not the time for petty disagreements. Along with Senshield, the curfew may restrict syndicate activity if we cannot agree upon a plan of action.' He closed the door. 'The Mime Order is a union of both humans and Ranthen. We pose a far greater threat to them together than divided. If you cannot see that, you are all fools.'

Every hair on my arms stood on end. I had never heard Warden speak with so much authority in the presence of the other Ranthen. Nick lowered his gun.

'If everyone's cooled off,' I said, 'perhaps we could have the meeting now.'

Terebell swept into the parlour, shadowed by Errai. 'Bring wine, dreamwalker.'

A flush crept into my face.

'Paige, I'll get it,' Nick said, but I was already heading for the kitchen.

Terebell wanted a reaction. I wasn't going to give her the pleasure. I reached under the sink for one of the bottles she had left with us for safekeeping. I filled the glasses, sloshing red wine all over the counter, and took a few gulps of my own from the bottle. The alcohol scorched down my throat.

In the hallway, Nick lurked outside the parlour door like a security guard. As we made to go in, Lucida Sargas barred our way.

'Alone,' she said.

Nick frowned. 'What?'

'The sovereign-elect wishes to speak to the Underqueen alone.'

Eliza squared up to her. No easy feat, as she was more than a foot shorter. 'We're Paige's mollishers. What she needs to know, we need to know.'

'Not if you want your revolution funded.'

'Don't you mean *our* revolution?'

'It's fine,' I said to Eliza. 'I'll tell you everything later.'

Neither of them looked happy, but they stepped away. I held out a glass to Lucida.

'I do not partake. I have no scars to soothe,' she said. 'But you will find that Terebell becomes ill-tempered without amaranth to numb the pain.'

'And I thought it was just her personality,' I said.

Lucida tilted her head. 'Is that a *joke*, as you say?'

'Not really.'

Balancing the tray of glasses on my hip, I opened the parlour door. My head continued to throb. Usually, I had a chance to warm up before dreamwalking, but the shock had caused an involuntary jump.

Errai stood beside the window. Pleione was lounging on the couch (she never seemed to *sit*, Pleione; she lounged), while Warden was a statue in the corner, his back against the wall. There was also a stranger among them, with sarx of pure silver and a bald head, like Errai.

Terebell, who stood beside the fire with her usual ramrod posture, took a glass of wine. She added a drop of amaranth before drinking.

I put down the tray a little too hard. Terebell emptied half her glass at a draught.

'This is Mira Sarin,' she said. 'She has been in exile for many years.'

I inclined my head to the stranger, a gesture she returned. Her eyes, which were large and wide-spaced, betrayed her recent feed on a sensor.

'I summoned you,' Terebell said, 'to inform you that we are leaving.'

'I see,' I said. 'For how long?'

'As long as necessary.'

'Why?'

She approached the nearest window. The other Ranthen watched her in silence.

'We have found other Rephaim who are willing to confront the Sargas with us,' she said. 'They have asked us to prove our commitment to rekindling war before they will take up our cause. To do that, we must persuade an influential member of each family to join us – preferably a Warden, past or present.'

'Those who went into exile after our civil war may be sympathetic to our cause,' Lucida said. 'First of all, we mean to seek out Adhara, the former Warden of the Sarin.'

I picked up a glass of wine for myself. 'What if you can't persuade her?'

'We must,' Warden said.

Reassuring.

'It would help our cause,' Terebell said, 'if we could demonstrate that you are a loyal and capable associate. Many of our old friends are disturbed by the notion that we must work with humans, given what happened last time.'

'How would you like me to prove that, exactly?'

'Show us that you are willing to do whatever is necessary for this movement to make progress.' She handed back her empty glass. 'I understand that you have finally replaced the arch-traitor. I assume you have also hunted down his loyalists, in accordance with my orders.'

'Jaxon is gone, Terebell. He's not coming back,' I said. 'We need to focus on disabling Senshield, or we're likely to find ourselves unable to leave the house, let alone start a revolution. Warden said it might be powered by ethereal technology, and we have a list of places where we know the scanners have been hidden, but we need more information.' When none of them volunteered any, I pursed my lips. 'Lucida, you're a Sargas. Do you know why they're rolling Senshield out earlier than they originally projected, or what could be powering it?'

Lucida turned away. I doubted she liked to remember which family she belonged to.

'Only the blood-sovereigns know how Senshield works,' she said. 'Perhaps the Grand Commander, too. As to why they are moving so quickly, I can only suppose that they wish to counter the threat of the Mime Order.'

'Senshield may be powered by an ethereal battery,' Mira said. Her voice was soft and cool. 'They store and channel the energy created by a breacher, most often a poltergeist. Something to consider, Underqueen.'

'Say it *is* an ethereal battery,' I said. 'How could it be deactivated?'

'By exorcising the spirit or destroying the physical casing, I should think.'

That had worked in Oxford. I had broken the binding on Sebastian Pearce, unlocking the padlock his spirit had been holding shut.

'Desecration,' Errai muttered. 'The Sargas continue to disgrace us by meddling with human machinery.'

I raised an eyebrow. 'What's wrong with human machinery?'

'It poisons the air and taints the ground. Much of it feeds on fuel made of putrefied matter. It is inelegant and destructive,' he shot back. 'Harnessing the energy of the æther with such contraptions is profane.'

When he put it like that, I had no argument.

'Errai speaks the truth. I approve of your proposal to rid us of Senshield,' Terebell said to me, 'but I expect you to seek my authorisation before you take any specific action.'

'Can I expect to authorise your decisions, too?'

'Not until you fund my decisions, as I fund yours.' She turned her back on me. 'You can seek my approval through Lucida, who will stay behind. The rest of the Ranthen will cross over to the Netherworld.'

When I understood what she meant, my throat knotted.

'Warden is our best instructor,' I said. 'I'd prefer him to stay with the Mime Order. And I'll need him to help me if I'm planning to dreamwalk again.'

'I am putting an end to your training with Arcturus.'

'What?'

'You heard me. If you require assistance with your ability, you may ask Lucida.'

Warden kept his gaze on the fire. My pulse quickened.

'Lucida doesn't train voyants,' I said. 'She wasn't even in Oxford.'

'True,' Lucida said airily, 'but one has to start somewhere.'

'I don't know how my recruits will respond to you. I do know how they'll respond to Warden – that they respect him – and I need that certainty. Things are about to get a lot harder for them, with the curfew and Senshield.' I turned to him. 'Warden, we need you here.'

My tone was even, but it sounded all too much like an entreaty. Terebell looked at him.

'I must do as the sovereign-elect commands,' Warden finally said.

Such a small number of words to drain so much strength from me. One look, and he belonged to her.

To Terebellum Sheratan, you are a convenient pawn in an age-old game. I had stifled that voice for a few hours, but now it filled my ears. *Arcturus Mesarthim is nothing but her lure. Her bait.*

I should never have kissed him in Candlewick. Not only was he content to see me humiliated, but to undermine my orders in front of Terebell, who was supposed to be my equal – *and* to abandon me to handle the Mime Order alone while they left on their own business.

'We leave in five nights' time,' Terebell said. 'Until then, stay the course, dreamwalker.'

She strode away. Errai opened the door for her, and the Ranthen filed into the hallway, leaving a chill in their wake. Mira gave me a fleeting look – one I couldn't read – before she left.

Only Warden stayed. He shut the door, so the two of us were ensconced in shadows.

'Your nose is bleeding.'

'I know,' I said curtly.

I hadn't known, but I could taste the blood now.

'Errai reported to us that you chose a new mime-lord for I-4,' Warden said, 'but that the ceremony was casual, and your attitude throughout was flippant and . . . improper. Would you disagree, Paige?'

Of course. I should have known that Errai would find something to criticise.

'With all due respect, none of you know the first thing about syndicate politics,' I said. 'That's why you needed a human associate.'

'How did you choose the replacement?'

'The usual way. The first candidate to declare themselves to the Unnatural Assembly is considered for the position. I deemed Jack Hickathrift suitable.' I lifted my chin. 'Look, the reason Errai called it *improper* is because Jack made his entrance by flirting with me.'

'I trust your judgement. Errai did not.'

'If Terebell wanted me to cross-examine every candidate, she should have said.' I tried to sound calm, but my insides were boiling. 'I know the syndicate. I know how it works.'

'That is not her only qualm. If she discovers that you have not punished his loyalists—'

'I am getting really sick of pandering to this obsession with Jaxon. I'm sorry if publicly betraying him wasn't enough to show I've rejected him. Or if risking my neck in Oxford didn't prove my loyalty to the cause. Maybe I was the wrong human to choose.' I held out a glass. 'Some more *wine* for you, blood-consort?'

'Stop, Paige.'

'You never manage to tell Terebell to *stop*, do you?' It took effort to keep my voice down. Every word quaked. 'You fucking coward. She belittles me, treats me as her waitron, and you do nothing. Not only that, but you make me look like a fool for all the Ranthen to see. So much for being my advocate.'

Warden lowered his head, so we were at eye level. I folded my arms.

'If I speak for you too loudly,' he said, his voice rumbling from the depths of his chest, 'you will pay a price far higher than wounded pride. If you suppose that I enjoy upholding the façade, you are mistaken.'

His voice was no sharper than before, but there was a simmer in the softness.

'I wouldn't know what you enjoy.' I stared him down. 'I need you here. You know what we're facing.'

'If I press the matter, she may not allow me to see you at all.'

'Don't pretend you care, Arcturus. I know what you are.'

'What am I, Paige?'

An open invitation to explain it all. The accusation was on the tip of my tongue.

Lure. Bait.

'If all you're going to do is tell me how much you *can't* do, then go,' I said coolly. 'Deal with your Ranthen business. Go to the Netherworld and let me run this organisation my own way. And unless you ever plan on sticking up for me when Terebell treats me like dirt, don't bother coming back.'

Warden was silent for some time, never taking those golden eyes off me.

'I cannot tell what you think you know of me,' he eventually said, 'but remember this, Paige. The Sargas want you isolated. They want the Mime Order divided. They mean to sow the seeds of mistrust. Do not prove to them that human and Rephaite cannot join forces.'

'That was an order,' I said.

My shoulders were rigid. There was another silence before Warden answered.

'As you command, Underqueen.'

When he stepped away, our auras pulled apart, leaving me colder than ever. I sank on to a chair and held my head between my hands.

4

THIN ICE

29 November 2059

I was losing him. Little by little, he was slipping out of reach. We were the bridge between the syndicate and the Ranthen, and unless I could somehow preserve our relationship, everything we had built together would crumble. The Mime Order would not survive.

Don't bother coming back.

My stomach tightened. I was fuming with Warden, but I hadn't meant to go that far.

Danica finally came in, wearing her boiler suit, and stamped the snow from her steel-capped boots. I was nursing my headache by the fire.

'Give me some good news,' I said.

'I've found the core.'

I sat up. 'You're serious?'

'I don't really like to joke.' She folded her arms. 'Do you want the bad news, too?'

I was still reeling from the good news. 'Okay.'

'It's underground. And we need to move quickly.'

I went to wake the others. A few minutes later, the four of us were sitting in the parlour. Danica unlaced her boots and kicked them off.

'My supervisor is involved with the installation of the large scanners. Today he learned that the core needs urgent maintenance. Scion is pushing it too hard.'

'That checks out,' I said.

'Yes. I wasn't chosen to work on it,' she said, answering my unspoken question, 'but I did some eavesdropping. I know where it is.'

'Go on.'

'Chelsea Creek in Fulham. There's an abandoned warehouse on top of the facility. While they're carrying out the maintenance, the alarms will be deactivated . . . but there is a catch. The work is being carried out tomorrow night. You will have to flout the curfew.'

'Why not straight away, if it's urgent?'

'They need to fly the team leader from Greece. She took some time off for Novembertide.'

Nick was frowning. 'And you still have no idea what the core *is*, Dani?'

'My guess is that it's volatile, which is why it's kept underground, but now might be your chance to find out. If you can go tomorrow, Paige could possess one of the engineers and see for herself.'

'Dani,' I said, 'you are brilliant.'

'Yes.' She wiped her oily hands on her boiler suit. 'I'm going to bed. I had a long day.'

The stairs creaked as she trudged upstairs, leaving us to contemplate our options.

'We have to make a quick decision here,' I said. 'The core might not need maintenance again for months or years. This could be our only chance.'

'I don't know.' Nick rubbed his chin. 'This seems too convenient.'

'Scion doesn't suspect Dani. The double agent would have told Warden.'

We had a lead. I needed to quash the exhilaration and think clearly. If we did this, it would be our first direct assault on Scion, targeting its infrastructure. It was risky, but it could be decisive for the Mime Order.

'Fulham.' I stood. 'That's the Glass Duchess, isn't it?'

'Yes, but there was fighting along Chelsea Embankment while you were in Oxford,' Eliza said. 'The Bunch of Fives pushed west and claimed Chelsea Creek, so the warehouse *just* belongs to Jimmy.'

'Fine, but ask them both about it. Tell Jimmy to meet us in the Arches.'

She took a burner from her pocket. In the kitchen, I dug out a detailed map of the area.

'Paige,' Nick said, 'should we get permission from the Ranthen?'

I clenched my jaw, considering.

'No,' I said. 'If Terebell is ever going to trust me, I need to prove I can make decisions on my own, and that they can pay off. Otherwise she'll never respect me, let alone treat me as her equal.'

'She could cut off the money if something goes wrong.'

'I'll call her bluff. She needs us, too.' I looked at him. 'Can you get Maria and Glym to meet us in the morning?'

'I can do that.'

———

It was a long night, waiting for the curfew to lift. As soon as it did, we made for the Vauxhall Arches, where Maria and Glym met us with Jimmy O'Goblin, mime-lord of II-1. His hair was a mess and he smelled of moonshine, but at least he was upright.

'Afternoon, Underqueen,' he rasped.

'Jimmy, it's six in the morning.' My breath came white and thick. 'Dani found the core.'

'That was quick,' Maria said.

I imparted to them what Danica had told us. Glym listened with a frown.

'We need to go for it,' Maria said. 'It's worth the risk if we can kill this thing.'

'I agree,' I said. 'Jimmy, have you noticed any Scion activity around that warehouse?'

'No,' Jimmy said, 'but there *were* a few Vigiles sniffing about in that area yesterday.'

He described what we were up against. The derelict warehouse stood right by the Thames, in a complex surrounded by a security fence, with a single guarded entrance on Lots Road. The fence couldn't be cut or scaled, and approaching in the open was likely to get us shot.

'But there is one option, Underqueen.' Jimmy flashed his stained teeth at me. 'One way you could get inside without being seen . . . but you'd have to be mad to try it.'

'Let's assume I'm mad,' I said.

'Well,' he said, 'you know how bleedin' cold it's been?' I nodded. 'There's an old service ladder at the back of the warehouse that leads right down to Chelsea Creek. Normally you wouldn't be able to access it, but with the weather being what it is, the water's frozen in that spot.'

'You're suggesting we walk *across* the ice?'

'That is a truly mad idea,' Maria said, looking impressed.

My hands pressed together, so I felt my pulse in my fingertips. I had fought to be Underqueen so I could make decisions, but now I had to trust myself to make the right ones.

'The local courtiers use the place to stash regal and blank,' Jimmy said. 'I can send you a seer who knows her way around. Mad it may be, but I reckon it's the only way you'll get in without the Vigiles seeing.'

I was swiftly becoming convinced by the idea.

'It's Novembertide,' I said. 'Weaver will probably lift the curfew. The celebrations might give us cover.' Everyone nodded. 'I say we send in a small armed team. We get into the underground facility, locate the core, do as much damage as we can – or at least find out what the hell it is – and then get out of there.'

Eliza hesitated. 'When you say *we*—'

'I'll lead the team.'

'Paige,' Nick said, 'you're Underqueen. You need to stay behind the lines.'

'Dani said I could possess one of the engineers to see inside the facility. I'm better up close.'

'You haven't used your gift that way since the scrimmage. If you insist on going, you should ask Warden to train with you today.'

'He can't.'

'Why not?'

I gave him a look that said we would talk about it later. His mouth thinned, but he didn't push it.

'I need to show that I'm not just using the syndicate as cannon fodder. That I'm happy to put my neck on the line, too,' I said. 'I'm not going to run things like Hector did, from a safe distance.'

Nick exchanged a silent glance with Eliza, but neither of them argued.

Next up was the matter of who should come with me. Maria volunteered first. As well as the local seer, we decided to take a few voyants who had passed Warden's intermediate training, chosen by Glym.

'I'm coming as well,' Nick said.

Eliza nodded. 'And me. We're your mollishers.'

'I can't risk both of you being captured.' I considered them. 'Eliza, I think an oracle would be more useful for this mission. You can coordinate our exit.'

'Right.' She forced a smile. 'I can do getaways.'

I shot her an apologetic look. She had been waiting weeks for a chance to shine, but I couldn't put her in the team for the sake of it.

'I will ask Tom to check for portents, Underqueen,' Glym said. 'The æther may be able to offer us guidance.'

'And I'll try to source a few explosives. If we do find the core, we can blow it to smithereens.' Maria was already leaving. 'I owe Vance a little pain.'

The sun shone like a silver coin behind its gauze of cloud. All over London, people were singing around pianos and exchanging gifts for Novembertide, the day Scion celebrated its official foundation and naming. The Grand Inquisitor of France had been expected, but apparently he was unwell again. I wondered if it was the same illness that had kept him away from the Bicentenary in Oxford.

At noon, Frank Weaver announced that the curfew would be lifted for one night to allow for the usual fireworks and bonfires. So far, everything was going to plan.

As the day wore on, we prepared for our mission. Glym, as the commander in charge of recruitment, assembled and briefed the infiltration team. A backup group would be ready to cause a distraction if anything went wrong. I worked out the route across the ice, based on what Jimmy had told us.

Nick was right about my gift. I If I was going to use it, I would need practice; I was badly out of form. I swallowed my pride and tried the golden cord, but there was no answer.

If that was how Warden wanted to play, so be it. It only stiffened my resolve to break Senshield without him. Even if he *had* come, he would likely have gone straight to Terebell with our plans – so I practised alone, trying to push my spirit into birds. It was late in the afternoon when I successfully possessed a magpie and amused Nick by having it perch on his head. Less amusing was the headache that followed.

We set off as dusk fell. Even the night Vigiles were distracted by the festivities. When we reached our meeting point in Fulham, Eliza handed out boiler suits that resembled engineers' uniforms, sourced from Petticoat Lane. Maria strode in last.

'No decent grenades at the Garden, *again*,' she groused.

I laced my boots. 'Do you often comb the citadel for grenades?'

'You never know when you'll need one.' She accepted a boiler suit. 'ScionIDE has never been stationed in London. That means you rarely find military-grade weaponry.'

'That's how it works, is it?'

'It's the one and only advantage to having krigs around – you can steal their equipment, like we did in Bulgaria. That, in turn, allows rebels to become militarised. You cannibalise one army to create another.'

'Krigs?'

She waved a hand. 'Soldiers. It's from the Swedish word for war, *krig*. As Nick will know, there are a lot of them in Sweden.'

Nick nodded without comment, zipping up his suit.

Glym had found us one more pyromancer, three summoners, and a pair of capnomancers, who might be able to use smoke to mask us if we needed a quick escape. There were also two augurs from the Glass Duchess, who refused to show their faces, and the waifish seer from Jimmy. As agreed, none of them said which cells they were from.

We waited to hear from Tom, who had checked with our scrying squad that there were no ill omens in the æther. After an hour, we decided we couldn't delay any longer. I gathered the infiltration team around me.

'This is the Mime Order's first move against Scion,' I told them. 'We're basing this plan on stolen intelligence, but I can't guarantee that it's watertight. Or that something won't go wrong.' I looked at each face in turn. 'None of you are under any obligation to do this. Just say the word, and you can return to your cells.'

The silence lasted for some time. The seer gnawed her nails, but said nothing.

'We're all with you, Underqueen,' one of the capnomancers said. The rest of the team agreed.

It was utterly dark by the time Nick led us out. 'We'll be back before you know it,' I said to Eliza.

'You'd better be.'

A perishing wind howled around us, shot with snow. There was no moonlight to betray us as we approached the ice, taking care to erase the footprints we left in the snow. Every so often, fireworks crackled.

The old warehouse towered over the Thames. It was exceptionally rare for the river to freeze to this extent – according to the records, it hadn't happened in over a century. Most of the surface was clearly too brittle to stand on, and the middle was as swift-flowing as ever, but a shelf of thick ice led into Chelsea Creek, the last of a stream that had once flowed here from Kensington. It was frozen solid.

Eliza was keeping watch nearby. If anything went wrong, she had drivers on standby.

I tested the ice where the stream joined the Thames. A web of silver threads spread from my boot. Nick hovered nearby as I risked the other foot.

'On a scale of one to lethal,' I said, so only he could hear, 'how dangerous is this?'

'I think we've done more dangerous things. Maybe.' He joined me on the ice and rocked his weight. 'It's a plan, Paige. That's more than any of your predecessors have had.'

I turned to the rest of the team. 'Here we go. Spread out as much as possible.'

We set off. The capnomancers stayed behind to watch the fire they had prepared.

Every step ratcheted up my pulse. If the ice gave way, the cold alone could finish us off, and if it didn't, the current would. The great artery of London had never been known for its mercy.

The crossing took time. Nobody dared walk too quickly. The seer led the way, skirting around the thinnest patches. After what felt like days, I spotted the rusted ladder, almost hanging off the wall and missing several rungs.

As we inched closer, one of the summoners hit a weak spot. His booted foot splashed through it, into the dark stream, before one of the others grabbed him. The impact quivered right the way along the ice shelf, turning us into statues. When it became clear that we weren't about to meet a watery end, the young pyromancer – a redhead – steadied the shaken summoner.

When we were in the shadow of the warehouse, I turned to him. 'Are you all right?'

'Yeah,' he said, keeping his voice low. 'Sorry, Underqueen.'

'What's your name?'

'Driscoll.'

'He's fine, Underqueen,' the redhead told me. 'We'll be more careful.'

Nick gave the seer a boost on to the ladder. I went next. The relief at being off the ice was almost enough to tame my nerves.

The seer led us into the skeletal warehouse. Most of its roof was missing; I could glimpse stars beyond the rusty iron girders that remained. I reached for the æther, goosebumps darting up my arms.

'There's nothing below us,' I said to Nick. 'No dreamscapes. No activity.'

'Maybe there's nothing to sense.' He held a pistol. 'This could be a dud lead.'

'Or the workers could be using alysoplasm to conceal themselves as a precaution. It would stop me from being able to sense them.'

'I thought Buzzer blood was hard to get?'

'Scion could still have some.'

Beneath my boiler suit, my skin was clammy. Driscoll stood guard, while the rest of us split up to search the silent, cavernous space.

Our footfalls echoed. Nick switched on his torch. As we walked the length of the warehouse, Maria tripped on a glass bottle, making us all start. It rolled through threads of aster and unsettled several plastic bags.

We stopped at the end of the hall, and I looked through a grimy window. To the northeast, the building was bordered by a desolate stretch of snow, where a SciORE vehicle was parked, apparently empty.

'They are here, then,' I murmured.

'I don't like this. If you can't sense them, they must suspect you're coming.' Nick looked to our left. 'Wait. What is that?'

I followed his line of sight. The adjoining wall was taken up by a vast transmission screen, clearly new. An unsettling chill went through my body. It was such an odd thing to see in a derelict; I couldn't think of any logical reason it would be there.

'Look,' the seer whispered. 'In front of it. I don't remember that, either.'

Nick pointed his torch, and we saw. There, sunk into the floor, was a trapdoor.

'Paige,' Nick hissed, but I was already crouching beside it. Finding no evidence of a lock or bolt, I grasped the handle and heaved it up.

Beneath it, there was only concrete.

I stared, my mind emptying. It took only moments for panic to engulf me.

Not a trap*door*. Just a trap. I turned to warn the team, to tell them to run – but before I could get a single word out, I found myself wrenched upside down, high above the others' heads, pinioned in a net.

Blood surged through my body as shouts came from below. The mesh around me was so tight that my elbows dug into my waist and my knees were jammed together. Gritting my teeth, I pushed my fingers towards the knife inside my jacket, but moving my limbs was agony.

As I struggled, the transmission screen glowed white. The light stretched our shadows across half the room. When my eyes adjusted to the glare, I found myself looking at the face of a woman.

She had to be at least seventy. Thin lines branched through her sun-beaten skin. A pinched nose, a seam of a mouth, and a head of white hair, combed back from a raw-boned face.

The eyes in that face chilled me to the heart of my being. They were black as pits.

'*Welcome,*' she said. '*Paige Mahoney.*'

Her voice was crisp as pressed linen. The feeling it induced in me was terrible – detachment, numbness, followed by a rush of dread. The way she said my name was oddly thorough, each syllable enunciated, as if she was determined not to let a single part of it escape her tongue.

Maria seemed hypnotised by the screen. I could see the whites of her eyes around the iris.

'*I am Hildred Vance, Grand Commander of the Republic of Scion England. As you are no doubt coming to realise, you have not found the core of Senshield.*' She didn't blink. '*Such information would never be allowed to fall into the wrong hands. There is no . . . underground facility.*' Nick stepped back, knocking a piece of rubble across the floor. '*This building is derelict. Tonight, however, it has been prepared for your arrival.*'

She had lured me here like a lamb to the abattoir. I thrashed against the net.

'*As we speak, your unique radiesthesic signature is being used to recalibrate Senshield. Thank you for assisting us.*'

A light beamed from above, blinding me.

The æther trembled, pushing shudder after shudder through my body as I hung there, sweating and powerless, feeling my pulse twang in my fingers, suddenly certain that something was *looking* at me.

'Shoot it, Nick,' Maria barked. 'Paige, don't move!'

A loud *beep* sounded in the building.

'*You have already made a grave error by coming here. Do not make the mistake of resisting detainment.*' Vance watched soullessly from the screen. '*Your allies may be spared if you allow my soldiers to take you into Inquisitorial custody.*'

My mouth rang with the taste of blood. The air was too thin, weak and spidery in my lungs. I was going to black out.

Danica.

Somehow, Vance must know about her.

Alsafi had been wrong.

A bullet snapped the hook that held the net. I plummeted – only to have my fall broken by Nick. He let out a faint *oof* before we both slammed into the concrete, hard enough to awaken all my old hurts from the scrimmage. Maria was already dragging me up by the back of my jacket.

'*There can be no escape for those who defy the anchor,*' Vance said. '*No mercy for those who pervert the natural order.*'

Chased by her voice, we sprinted back across the warehouse. Floodlights blazed from outside, exposing our position, but there were still no dreamscapes closing in – at least, I thought there weren't. Not until my sixth sense rang, and I looked up.

Eight shadows bloomed above us, blotting out the stars. Maria understood before I did.

'Paratroopers.' Her hands viced my arms. 'Run. Back to the ice!'

Driscoll was already making for the exit. As the seer and the other summoners ran after him, two explosions went off in front of them, destroying our way back to the service ladder. Maria aimed her pistol, her shots nicking a parachute.

'Paige,' Nick roared, 'get down!'

Gunfire rattled from above. One of the summoners fell. When the seer died, too, a gasp of 'no' escaped me. Maria wrenched me behind a crate.

'Through those windows,' she called over the din. 'Make straight for the Thames.'

'But the fence—'

'I'll handle the fence.'

She reloaded her gun. I struck out from our hiding place and ran like I never thought I could, keeping Nick in my sights. He shot the glass from two of the windows, and together, we vaulted into the snow, the others hot on our heels. My thoughts seemed to vanish, crushed by the breathless, overriding need to survive. Now we were outside, we were fully exposed.

A light flared behind me. I glanced back to see a string of burning spirits hit one of the paratroopers, who had just landed in front of Maria. The parachute went up in flames, but the other soldiers were already shooting. Driscoll and the redhead returned fire. Nick grabbed my hand, pulling me towards the security fence, which still loomed between us and the Thames.

Everything about this trap had been perfect. Vance had known I would sense a ruse if her people were waiting nearby to arrest us; that dropping them in would keep them off my radar until it was too late.

'Take cover,' Maria shouted.

Nick and I ducked behind the parked vehicle just as she hurled something at the fence. A heartbeat later, another explosion blew it apart.

I didn't stop to ask questions. Nick ran for the smoking gap, and I followed, my ears ringing. Now only a short drop stood between us and the frozen Thames.

Nick went down there first. The ice took his weight. There was only a narrow vein of it here, following the edge of the industrial estate. Just as I was about to go after him, I heard a gunshot. Maria let out a sharp cry. At once, I threw my spirit towards the nearest paratrooper.

What happened next was a blur. I aware of tearing through a grey dreamscape; of throwing a spirit into the æther; of seeing a rifle fall into the snow. Before I could do anything more, my silver cord whiplashed me back to my own body. Through tears of pain, I saw another soldier approaching from the north, his rifle trained on the redhead. I tried to dreamwalk again, but it was as if two rusted gears were grinding in my skull, locked in place.

A spray of bullets tore through her midriff.

Nick helped Maria down and swung her arm around his neck. Her face was white. My nose bled as I joined them. Driscoll just about got through the gap before the soldiers opened fire again.

'The others are dead,' he told me. 'Go, go—'

There was no time to absorb it. We forged on as quickly as we dared, ice straining underfoot. So far, there was no way off it – the wall to our left was too high, slick and green – but not too far ahead, I glimpsed a jetty, carving out into the Thames. If we could reach it before the soldiers did, we had a fighting chance.

Eliza would have seen and heard the explosions. All we had to do was make it back to solid ground, and she could get us out of here.

A helicopter appeared to our right, shining a searchlight across the river. A voice from inside told me to surrender. I thought of the six dead voyants I had left behind. With a surge of breathless fury, I turned to face the chopper, throwing my arms wide. I motioned for Driscoll to move behind me and made sure I was shielding Nick and Maria. My hair whipped across my face as we gathered together.

'Paige,' Nick said, panting, 'what are you doing?'

'They won't shoot.' I kept my eyes on the helicopter. 'They can't risk breaking the ice.'

'Why would they care?'

'Because they have to take me alive.'

Nashira wanted my spirit. If I was swept away by the river, she would never get it.

We were deadlocked.

The chopper hovered above the water. It might not shoot while we were here, but as soon as we left the ice, it would incapacitate me and kill the others. Sickening fear took hold as I pictured it. We might have eluded Vance for an instant, but she had us cornered, all for nothing.

I caught an acrid smell and risked a look over my shoulder. Smoke was billowing across the ice, carried by a stream of spirits. The capnomancers were giving us cover. I held my breath and took a step back, forcing the others into the darkness. The helicopter banked before it disappeared from view.

The cover wouldn't last. We kept moving, making for the jetty. As we neared it, a deep fracture coursed beneath my boots and forked off in all directions.

There was no time to think. I shoved Driscoll back, away from the splintering, just before my foothold collapsed.

For a blinding instant, I thought I was dead.

Somehow I resisted gulping as I plunged into the Thames. The cold ripped through my body, a blade that skinned me in one slice, but I didn't let the water in. I went down like a diving bell.

As I sank deeper, my lungs bayed for oxygen. I was burning without heat, on fire without flame. I wrestled with the river, screaming inside as it scourged me, but my limbs had turned to stone.

London does not forget a traitor, nor forgive the weak, Jaxon whispered from my memory. *It will suck you down, Paige. Into the tunnels and the plague pits, the sewers and the lost rivers. Into its heart of shadows, where all the traitors' bodies sink.*

Damn him to hell. I would not die like this. Some deep reserve of strength glowed within me, warming my arms enough to get them moving. My hands tore my boiler suit open; I freed myself from it and clawed through the foul-tasting water, but the darkness was disorienting. I kicked and clutched the darkness, not knowing which way was up, until my head shattered the surface. White breath plumed from my mouth. A vicious current roared against my body, carrying me faster than my shocked muscles could fight.

I was too far from the shore, too cold to swim. I wasn't going to make it out of this alive.

My head slipped under again. The river took hold of my body with greed.

That was when I felt an aura against mine, and an arm scooping me back to the surface.

My hands found a pair of shoulders. As I gasped and coughed, I found myself faced with burning eyes.

'Warden—'

'Hold on to me.'

I had no idea how he could have reached me so quickly – what he was even doing here – but in that moment, I didn't care. My arms were losing strength, but I managed to wrap them around his neck. His muscles worked as he cut through the Thames, swimming as if the current was just a whisper against him.

I must have passed out. Suddenly I was aware of being lifted from the river. When the night air hit me, I felt as if frost was encasing my organs, creeping between my ribs, covering every inch of skin.

'Paige, breathe,' Warden said, and I did, retching up water. He pressed me to the heat of his chest and wrapped his coat around me, sheltering me from the snow. I shivered uncontrollably.

We huddled together behind a hedgerow, under an oak by Battersea Bridge, until Pleione got there. Nick kept me awake on the drive to safety, talking to me, asking me questions. I swung between moments of painful clarity, like seeing Driscoll break down in tears, and darker periods, when all I could do was try to keep warm.

The team retreated to our safe house on Cranley Mews, another donation from a former Nightingale. As soon as we were inside, Nick transformed into a medic. On his instructions, I took off my remaining clothes and washed in tepid water. Once he had checked for open wounds and ordered me to tell him straight away if I felt sick or feverish, I was swaddled in thick blankets and left to dry. I burrowed into my snug cocoon and focused on preserving heat.

I drowsed for a while. When I lifted my head, there was a Reph in the armchair nearby, gazing into a fire. For a chilling instant, I thought I was in Magdalen – that we were in Oxford again, in that tower, still uncertain of each other.

'Warden.'

His hair was still damp. 'Paige.'

Prickles raced along my skin. I pushed myself up on my elbows. 'Dani,' I said, my voice thick.

'False information about the warehouse was planted across multiple sectors. Scion has no way of knowing which one sprang the leak.'

Vance must have only suspected that I had someone on the inside, then. As I drew the blankets closer, I noticed that my hands were steady.

I wanted them to shake. I wanted to feel myself responding to my voyants' lives being pointlessly lost, but I had seen death on the screens since I was a child; it was drip-fed to us every week, breathed into our homes. Our lives had been steeped in it, until blood was as commonplace a thing as coffee – and after all I had seen in the last few months, it seemed I had stopped being able to react. I hated Scion for it.

'You got me out of the water.'

'Yes,' Warden said. 'Tom told me about your mission. The scrying squad had sensed a portent, but the Glym Lord encountered a scanner on his way to stop you. Pleione and I went in his stead.'

'Is Glym all right?'

'Yes. He escaped.'

We had all come so close to death. If not for Warden, the river would have swallowed me.

'Thank you,' I said. 'For saving me.'

With a nod, Warden rested his elbows on the arms of the chair and clasped his gloved hands in front of him, a posture he had often adopted in Oxford. I waited for the axe to fall.

'Terebell is angry that I went without permission,' I said, when the silence had gone on for too long. 'Isn't she?'

He reached for the table in front of us and held out a steaming mug.

'Drink this,' he said. 'Dr Nygård says your core temperature is still lower than it should be.'

'I don't care about my temperature.'

'Then you are a fool.'

The mug stayed where it was. I took it and drank a little of the saloop, if only to make him talk.

'Paige,' he said, 'are you deliberately trying to provoke Terebell?'

A question, not an accusation.

'No,' I said. 'Of course not.'

'You entered the warehouse without her authorisation. You ignored a direct order to seek her approval before taking any specific action.'

'I had a lead, and a limited amount of time to follow it.' I kept my tone as calm as I could. 'And I did call you, Warden. I used the cord.'

There was a brief silence.

'While you were sleeping,' Warden finally said, 'your commanders received a report. Two hours after your excursion to the warehouse, a polyglot was detained. According to a witness, her aura triggered a visible Senshield scanner outside an Underground station.'

I hadn't thought it was possible to turn any colder. Polyglots were from the fourth order. An order that Senshield shouldn't yet be able to detect.

'Of course, this could be nothing but hearsay. But if it is true,' Warden said, 'then the technology has been significantly enhanced overnight.'

A dull flutter started, low in my stomach. I tightened my fingers around the mug.

'It's not hearsay.' My voice was hoarse. 'Vance told me herself that she used me to recalibrate Senshield, but . . . I'm from the seventh order. How could exposure to *me* help it detect the fourth?'

'I could not say.' He sought my gaze. 'It may not be true, Paige.'

'If this *is* my fault, Terebell will—' I fought to keep my breathing under control. 'We can't lose your funding. Without it, the Mime Order will fall apart.'

'Terebell is unlikely to withdraw our financial support as a result of one setback. It is as much in our interest for the Mime Order to survive as it is in yours. She will reserve judgement until the consequences of your actions become apparent.'

'They're already apparent. I fell into a trap, helped them improve Senshield, and lost six people. I could have saved at least one if my gift had been stronger.' I couldn't keep the exhaustion from my voice. 'I wanted to train with you. Why didn't you answer me?'

'We were dealing with another Emite.'

I tensed. 'Where?'

'Epping Forest.'

The shiver that went through me had nothing to do with my fall through the ice.

Now there were no Rephs left in Oxford, the Buzzers were starting to appear in London instead. While I was fixated on deactivating Senshield, the Ranthen were trying to stop us falling prey to their ancient enemies. Our problems were closing in from all sides.

'War requires risk,' Warden said. 'This may yet prove to be a strategic error, but from what I heard, you took what precautions you could. No one knew that Hildred Vance had been recalled to the capital, or that she would lay a trap for you. Even Alsafi was unaware.'

'Six voyants are still dead for nothing.'

'They knew there was a chance of failure.' His face was cast into shadow. 'I asked Alsafi about the core. He does not know its location. Since he works in the Archon, we may safely assume that it is not there.'

I looked into the fire. 'I will find it.'

A log crumbled.

'Paige,' Warden said quietly, 'there is something else. Alsafi visited Coldbath Fields, but he could not find any trace of your father.'

'Was he moved?'

'I will endeavour to find out.'

Despite its bleak nickname, the Steel was one of the more comfortable prisons in London, built for amaurotics. If my father *had* been transferred, I doubted his living conditions would have improved.

I refused to consider what else might have happened.

'Thank you for telling me,' I said. 'I appreciate you trying, Warden.'

'I am sorry I could not see you earlier.'

'It's fine. You were busy.' I set the mug aside. 'Did you get rid of the Buzzer?'

'Yes.' He paused. 'You should not have risked leading the team in person. You are Underqueen. If you fall, there will be no Mime Order.'

'You could always find another human.'

'None that the syndicate would accept. There is no time for another scrimmage,' he said. 'And there is no other human I trust as I trust you.'

I looked him in the face. He was offering me a chance to let him back in – exposing a vulnerability, a break in all that Rephaite armour. This was a door I needed to open.

'I need to speak to the others,' I said. 'I'm sure you'd like to get back to Terebell.'

Warden held my gaze for a long moment. And in that moment, I thought I felt the softest flicker of sorrow through the cord. Or perhaps that was just me.

'As you wish.' He stood. 'Goodnight, Paige.'

5

VANCE

The image of Hildred Vance was too fresh for me to get any more sleep. I dressed in dry clothes and left the fire behind, taking a blanket with me. Glym, Tom and Nick were in the next room, sitting around a tired Maria, who was tucked up on the couch, ladling broth into her mouth. Nick got up and crushed me to his chest.

'Paige,' he said. 'I tried to reach you. If Warden hadn't been there—'

'But he was.' I patted his back. 'I'm fine.'

'You saved Driscoll, you know,' Maria said. 'He would have gone under if you hadn't pushed him.'

I looked her over. 'Are you all right?'

'Bullet graze. I've had worse.'

'You saved our necks by blowing up the fence,' I said. 'I thought there weren't any grenades at the Garden?'

'I said there weren't any *decent* grenades. I'm convinced that one was a genuine antique. Fortunately,' she said, 'it still worked.'

'Thank you.' I sat by Nick. 'I don't suppose anyone else made it out?'

'One of the augurs,' Nick said. 'Driscoll didn't realise.'

'We'll make sure the others aren't forgotten,' I said. 'And that their sacrifice isn't wasted.' I looked at the others. 'Warden told me about the report.'

'Let's not worry too soon, Underqueen,' Glym said, with his usual confidence. 'The mime-lord who reported it is not even certain the captured voyant *was* a polyglot.'

'We need to find out quickly. If the fourth order can be detected—'

'There's no evidence of that yet,' Tom soothed. 'It would be . . . bad, I admit—'

'Bad?'

'All right, *very* bad, but it's just like Glym says, it'll be nothing but misinformation. Or scaremongering.'

'I disagree,' Maria said. I looked at her. 'I know Vance, and I don't believe she would lie unless she absolutely had to. She told Paige she was using her aura to change Senshield. That means she was.' She paused to draw a breath. 'If that *is* the case, the syndicate must never know.'

Because if they learned that my error had exposed the fourth order, the Unnatural Assembly would almost certainly move to depose me.

'Tell me more about Vance,' I said.

Maria put the bowl of broth to one side. 'I'll tell you what I know of her,' she said, 'but trust me. She already knows about you.'

From the way Vance had looked at me, even through a screen, I didn't doubt it.

'Let's have a little history lesson,' Maria said. 'Hildred Diane Vance joined ScionIDE at the tender age of sixteen and was posted to Inverness. During that time, as Tom will remember, she helped crush several uprisings in what was then called Scotland.'

Tom, who had been watching her from beneath the brim of his hat, now came into the lamplight.

'Believe it or not, I'm a wee bit younger than Vance,' he said. 'I remember how people whispered her name when I was a lad, even in Glasgow. Like they were scared she might be able to hear them.'

'Sounds like she was very young to have so much power,' I said.

'So are you,' Maria pointed out.

The thought of any similarity was unsettling.

'Young Hildred's superiors noticed her appetite for slaughtering unnaturals, and they rewarded her for it. Her rise through the ranks was meteoric,' Maria said. 'She's now seventy-five, and has served Scion for longer than anyone else in its upper echelons.'

I had to wonder how close she was to the Sargas. She sounded like their sort of person.

'When the anchor launched the Balkan Incursion, Hildred Vance was at the helm. While other Scion commandants stayed comfortably in Cyprus, she was on the ground,' Maria continued. 'Faced with local resistance, Vance gave no quarter. As soon as her boots touched Bulgarian soil, she planted double agents among us. Within days, she knew the names and backgrounds of all of our leaders and key fighters.' A shadow winged over her face. 'She soon learned that my unit commander, Rozaliya Yudina, was one of our best – and that Roza had once had a younger brother, who died when he was ten, before the family moved to Bulgaria.

'The surviving insurgents were thin on the ground when Vance set the trap,' she went on, her face hardening. 'She knew that Roza's death would devastate morale. Don't ask me how, but her soldiers found a boy who looked very like Roza's brother. During our final stand in Sofia, this child was thrown on to the street and told to beg Roza for help. And Roza hesitated.' Her fist clenched. 'The boy had been given a toy bear to hold. Inside was a plastic explosive.'

The small amount of warmth in my body disappeared.

Scion had killed many children in Dublin. I had almost been among them.

'One reason Vance is lethal is because she doesn't underestimate her foes,' Maria said. 'I suspect we escaped today because she truly didn't think we'd be mad enough to take the ice.'

'So we outfoxed her with our stupidity,' I said.

'Exactly. But she'll remember that you took that risk.' She tapped her temple. 'It goes into her mental database. The more she learns about you, the better she becomes at predicting you.'

I had to wonder how much she already knew. My official record would give her a starting point. Jaxon might have told her things, if he had sunk that low. It was clear that she understood how my gift worked.

And she knew I had a father.

'If Vance had a hand in the Balkan Incursion,' I said, 'I assume she was also involved in the conquest of Ireland.'

'Aye,' Tom said quietly. 'Inquisitor Mayfield was the one who made her Grand Commander.'

I nodded slowly.

'Okay,' I said. 'We need to work out whether Vance has more than a few paratroopers with her. Are we taking on an army?'

'No. ScionIDE won't come here,' Maria said firmly. 'This is the heart of the empire. Martial law has never been declared in London. They have to give an impression of peace and safety in the capital, or the whole idea behind Scion will collapse.'

Nick shifted closer to me. 'Then why is Vance here at all?'

'To deal with Paige, most likely,' Glym said. 'The syndicate would slide back to its old ways without her, and would no longer pose a threat.'

It was true. The syndicate could survive if I was captured, but old habits died hard.

'We need another lead.' I rubbed my arms, which were peppered with goosebumps. 'Nick, talk to Dani. Glym, I need you to double-check the report about the fourth order. We also need to prepare for whatever Vance is planning next, which means that all of the Unnatural Assembly have to be properly armed, for starters. Get the Pearl Queen on to every arms dealer in the Garden. What time is it?'

'Eight in the morning,' Glym said.

'Good.'

When I got up, Maria said, 'And where exactly are you going?'

'To make sure Jack Hickathrift has evicted the remaining members of the Seven Seals.' I buckled my jacket. 'It's past time.'

'Hildred Vance is on to you, Paige. You should lie low for a few days.'

'If I hide away, she's already won. We might as well go to the Archon and bow to the Rephs now.' I stepped into my boots and laced them. 'For the time being, we keep what happened at the warehouse between us. We'll regroup with the others at the Mill tonight.'

I hadn't been back to Seven Dials since the scrimmage. The thought had been too painful. That aside, Jaxon knew its every corner, which meant that it was no longer safe. Even the Old Lyre might be compromised.

The commanders wanted me to take bodyguards. I agreed to have Eliza with me. As we waited for our rickshaw, Nick emerged from the safe house.

'I want to come with you.'

'I really need you to liaise with Dani,' I said. 'We have to know if she can find out anything more about Senshield, even if it's just—'

'Paige,' he said, his voice thick, 'please.'

When I took a second look, I understood. There were crescents of shadow under his eyes.

'I know why you want to do this,' I said, 'but Maria is right. Vance is on to us, Nick. I need you focused.'

'You think Zeke will make me lose focus.' He shook his head. 'Does that mean you're not focused, either?'

It took me a moment to recognise what he was implying. What he had just implied in front of Eliza, who frowned. When it sank in, my jaw hardened. Even Nick looked shocked at himself.

I drifted to the corner of the street, my arms folded. Nick came straight after me.

'Paige,' he said, 'I'm sorry.'

'No one else can know.' I spoke quietly. 'Nick, I trusted you when I told you about Warden. I need to be able to trust *you*, of all people.'

'You can.' He took one of my gloved hands. 'I'm sorry. I nearly lost you. I've already lost Zeke. I just feel so . . . powerless. But it's not an excuse.'

Powerless was the right word for it. It was how I had felt in the river, and in the warehouse, knowing that Vance had played me right into her hands. I was a queen at the mercy of pawns.

The rickshaw appeared at the end of the street. Nick looked wretched. I had never argued with him, and I didn't want to start today.

'It's okay.' I squeezed his hand. 'Look, if Zeke's there, I'll be as kind as I can. I'll try my best to persuade him to join us.'

Nick embraced me. 'I know,' he said. 'Take this. You must still have a chill.' He tucked a heat pack into my pocket. 'I'll talk to Dani now.'

'Thank you.'

I wrapped my hand around the heat pack as the rickshaw trundled away from Kensington, but the cold was in my blood. Snow floated around us, catching in my eyelashes and the wispy curls around my temples.

'Paige,' Eliza said, 'what did Nick mean, when he asked if it meant you weren't focused, either?' When I failed to conjure a suitable lie, she nudged me in the ribs. 'You'd better not have slept with Hickathrift behind my back.'

'I wouldn't dare.'

Eliza smiled, but it didn't quite touch her eyes. She knew I was keeping something close to my chest.

A blood-smeared sky greeted us in Covent Garden. Early shoppers were out in force, waiting around the stalls and outside shops for the sales to begin. I smoothed my scarf over my face, watching for any hint of a military presence. I imagined the wind taking my scent right to Vance.

An alarm went off as we crossed a junction. Across the street, Vigiles wrestled a weeping augur away from an oxygen bar, cuffing her hands behind her back. We moved on as quickly as possible, going in the same direction automatically. After all, we both knew where Jack Hickathrift would be. There was only one place the mime-lord of I-4 could reside if he expected to be taken seriously.

Seven Dials had been garlanded with red and white lights for Novembertide. In mutual, wordless understanding, we walked past the entrance to the den, to the sundial pillar. I laid a hand on the pale stone.

This had been the keystone of our chaotic world – the heart of the syndicate as we had once known it. I had stood before this pillar when Jaxon had made me his mollisher. Eliza circled it, as if to remind herself it was real. Behind it, on a nearby building, a line of bleached graffiti was just about visible.

BACKSTABBERS NOT WELCOME

Amaurotic workers and shoppers were giving it nervous looks. Our underworld was invisible to the people around us, but it was dangerous to linger. Eliza blew out a breath, reached into her coat, and took out a key.

We opened the gate to Ching Court and passed the blossom tree, which the bitter cold of winter had stripped bare. Eliza unlocked the back door. As Underqueen, I had the right to enter any syndicate building.

In the hallway, we stamped the snow from our boots. As Eliza started up the stairs, her muses flew in and swirled around her. Pieter was overjoyed, bouncing about like a firecracker.

'Oh, there you all are,' Eliza said, laughing. 'I thought Jaxon had taken you!'

I left them to get reacquainted. 'Hello, Phil,' I said, when Philippe did a celebratory twirl around me. Pieter gave me a sullen nudge before he returned to his beloved medium.

They couldn't leave this place. Jaxon had long since bound them to the den, and unless we could find and scour away the blood he had used to tie them here, they were trapped until he died. Probably for the best. Eliza could do without the possessions.

On the second floor, I paused outside my old room, feeling as if I had wandered into a museum. When I entered, I found it empty. Nick had rescued most of my belongings – including my precious, lovingly curated chest of antiques and curiosities from the Garden – but Jaxon, for whatever reason, had taken my record player. The painted stars on the ceiling were the only evidence that I had lived here.

An aura brushed mine. I turned to see Jack Hickathrift standing in the doorway, dressed in tight, high-waisted trousers and a poet shirt. One hand had been on the knife at his belt, but he let go of it at once.

'Underqueen,' he said, with a deep bow. 'Your pardon. I thought it might be an intruder.'

'I feel like one.'

'I'm sure. This must be very strange for you.' He opened the door wider. 'Please, come through.'

He led me into the adjacent room, which had been the boudoir. The furniture was still in its place, if nothing else. I sat on the chaise, while Jack sprawled on the couch, leaving the upholstered chair empty.

'Do I hear another guest downstairs?' he asked, just as Eliza sidled into the room, pursued by her muses. 'Ah, the famous Martyred Muse. I've heard tales of your talent.' He took her by the hand and kissed it. 'May I offer you both a drink? I found a very fine brandywine at the Garden.'

Eliza perched beside him. 'I'd love one.'

Jack raised his eyebrows at me, but I shook my head. He glanced back at Eliza as he reached for the bottle.

'Now,' he said, 'what can I do for you, my queen?'

'Just checking in,' I said. 'How is I-4 treating you?'

'Very well. I spent last night in Soho, meeting the proprietors of local businesses. I thought I would encounter more resistance,' he admitted, 'but it seems anyone who *was* loyal to the White Binder has already left the section. Others seem quite glad he's gone.'

'Has there been any sign of him?'

'None,' he said, with a thin smile. 'I highly doubt I'd be alive if he were still anywhere close.'

'What about the other Seals?'

At this, Jack pursed his lips. He poured Eliza a generous amount of brandywine.

'When I came to the section, I found them in this building. They locked me out,' he said. 'I offered them shelter, as you requested, but Nadine refused. Fortunately, Zeke persuaded her to leave without violence. She said they were going to find the White Binder.' He passed Eliza the glass. 'Nadine was the one who plotted the destruction of the Juditheon, ostensibly to attract his attention. It seems she was spurred on by Slyboots, among others.'

That was why Didion and I had been the targets. Because we were his particular enemies.

'I see,' I said. 'Even they don't know where Jaxon is, then?'

'Apparently not. It appears he abandoned them.' Jack motioned to the vacant chair. 'And that this last-ditch attempt to summon him was in vain.'

Because he was with Scion, and clearly had no intention of returning.

'I still can't understand Nadine,' Eliza said. 'She was never this loyal to Jax.'

'According to my new sources in the Garden, the small resistance movement has already collapsed,' Jack said. 'And now there are no Seals left in Seven Dials, you have nothing more to fear, my queen.'

Nothing more to fear from Jaxon's supporters. And a little less to fear from Terebell.

'Thank you,' I said. 'It seems like you have everything under control.' I stood. 'If you need any more support, let my mollishers know. They'll make sure this is a smooth transition.'

'Absolutely,' Eliza said.

Jack kissed her hand again, lingering a little longer than before. 'Thank you,' he said. 'I trust we'll meet again soon, Martyred Muse.'

'I'm sure.'

She left with another winning smile.

Terebell would be pleased to know that there was no more threat from Seven Dials – I had, at least, obeyed her on this – but there was nothing else to celebrate. If Nadine and Zeke had found Jaxon, they might already be in the Rephs' clutches.

As I made to leave, Jack stopped me, reaching into his back pocket. 'I almost forgot, Underqueen. Zeke asked me to give this to the Red Vision,' he said, handing me a small envelope. 'You need not read it. It's a love letter.'

'You know it's considered impolite to read other people's mail.'

'I consider it my responsibility, as mime-lord, to know what transpires in this section.'

I tucked the envelope into my inner pocket, making sure it was buttoned in. It might give Nick a little comfort.

'Underqueen,' Jack said, and I looked up. 'I hope I don't presume too much by making you an offer.' I raised an eyebrow. 'All syndicate leaders have need of succour. The position of Underqueen is a taxing one. If you ever wished for a . . . private audience, you know where to find me.'

He was so close that I could smell the nutmeg oil on his skin, see an old scar on his forehead. I was perfectly aware that half the underworld would have killed to be on the receiving end of this offer. He really was shameless, right after flirting with Eliza in front of me.

He also wasn't who I wanted.

'Jack,' I said gently, stepping away, 'we hardly know each other. I'm flattered, but—'

'I understand.' Jack flashed me a smile, showing his dimple. 'You must already have a lover.'

'Yes. No. I mean—' I collected myself. 'I won't be taking you up on that offer. But I do appreciate your loyalty. And I never did thank you.'

'For what, Underqueen?'

I gave him the lightest kiss on the cheek.

'For putting your knife through a man's neck for me,' I said, and saw myself back out.

'We call the Swan Knight, mime-queen of IV-4. What matter do you wish to bring before the Underqueen?'

We were only halfway through the audience, and petitions from the syndicate were coming thick and fast. The gathered voyants parted to let the Swan Knight through. Redcap, a berserker, had thrashed her during the scrimmage; she used a cane to approach the stage. Her request was for money, to patch up a derelict in her section.

No surprises there, of course. Nine out of ten requests were for money.

We were in the basement of the Mill, where I sat between Glym and Wynn. A film of sweat covered my collarbones. I had promised to grant this audience, but I was desperate to be back on the streets, gathering information. I needed to know if the report was true.

I also needed to see Danica. She was still our best and only link to Senshield, and we couldn't stop looking for the core.

A soothsayer came forward and pleaded for food. Wynn promised that the Pearl Queen would help. Another petitioner asked me if his cell could be moved from Marylebone, as there was a new scanner in the district and nobody liked having to pass it every day.

'I know I'm a sensor, not at risk,' he said (I tried not to tense), 'but it makes us all nervous, Underqueen. The lower orders can't even go out.'

I said I would consider moving the cell to a neighbouring district. Others asked if I could do the same for theirs.

I imagined how much worse it would get if the fourth order really could be detected.

The final person to come forward was Halfpenny, the new mime-lord of II-5. Like the Swan Knight and Jack Hickathrift, he had been mollisher to a grey marketeer and taken control of his section after the scrimmage. He was heavily tattooed, with thick eyebrows he dyed marigold. We had exchanged a few words in the past.

Then I had broken his nose in the Rose Ring. And kicked him in the head for good measure.

'Underqueen,' he said nasally, 'the Glym Lord came to one of my cells last night and asked for any summoners to volunteer for an assignment. I sent one named Wayland. I wish to know where he is now.'

Glym glanced at me.

'I'm afraid he won't be coming back, Halfpenny,' I said. 'He was killed by paratroopers.'

Whispers broke out in the basement. A military word like *paratroopers* was not often heard in London.

Halfpenny folded his fleshy arms. 'What happened?' When I didn't answer at once, he pursed his lips. 'You said you'd be different from Hector, Underqueen. Wayland was an old friend. I'd like to know why he died.'

This was the first time anyone had challenged me in public. He had the right to do it, but my hands tightened on the arms of my seat.

'Halfpenny,' I said, 'I'm sorry for your loss, but I can't reveal the nature of all of our assignments. We're moving against a highly efficient and militarised empire. If anyone were to betray our strategies—'

'First you let the Jacobite walk free,' he cut in, to mutters from the audience, 'and now you've clearly baited Scion into attacking us, at a time when we're already under serious threat from Senshield. Why were there paratroopers in the capital, if not because of you?'

'Listen to this. You'd think the Underqueen was on trial,' Wynn said. 'Black Moth doesn't have to justify her methods to you, Halfpenny. You were happy enough to do as Haymarket Hector demanded without question or protest, but now Paige is Underqueen, you've discovered your tongue.'

Several voyants murmured agreements. Others, however, were clearly ruffled by the sight of a vile augur speaking with impunity at the side of the Underqueen.

'I did my best to change things under Hector,' Halfpenny said. 'In my section, at least.'

Wynn snorted. 'You worked for a grey marketeer.'

'I didn't know.'

'Binder wouldn't have risked our lives,' someone called from the corner. 'You betrayed him. Who's to say you won't turn your back on us, too?'

Silence ruled in the basement, broken only by a gasp.

I waited several moments, letting it deepen, before I rose from my seat.

'This syndicate,' I said, 'has existed for almost a century. Its leaders' power is passed not from parents to children, but between Underlords and Underqueens. Ours is an authority based not on the blood of our families, but the blood we spill in the Rose Ring. That blood was my promise that I would only ever do what I thought was best for voyantkind – and I promise you now that I would shed blood again for any of you. And I expect to, before this war is over.' I thought about saying more, then picked up my jacket. 'This audience is finished.'

My nape was burning as I left the basement. Halfpenny had been reasonable enough, considering I had got one of his friends killed.

Wynn and Glym followed me upstairs. The other commanders waited in the surveillance room, with the exception of Minty, who was in Grub Street, overseeing a corrected reprint of *The Rephaite Revelation*. I could tell from their faces that they had news. I locked the door and took my seat, trying to tamp down the rising consternation.

'Paige,' Maria said, 'it seems the report was accurate.'

Those few words punctured what was left of my confidence.

'I see,' I said.

'A whisperer was taken this morning. I knew him.' Tom sighed. 'His aura was as yellow as a lemon.'

Shock washed over me. I hadn't wanted to accept it, but now I had no choice. The sensors were exposed. That left a fraction of us who could roam London without fear of detection, at least by day.

And all because I had gone into the warehouse without ensuring that our information was reliable.

'Vance used my aura to improve Senshield.' I kept my voice low. 'We need to focus on damage control. And letting the fourth order know.'

If I told the syndicate the whole truth, many of them might blame me for our new vulnerability. If I lied, and they found out anyway, their reaction would be much worse. Either way, I needed them to believe – as I did – that revolution was now crucial to our survival.

'I have to warn the Unnatural Assembly,' I said. 'I should . . . tell them how Scion did it.'

'I wouldna do that, Underqueen,' Tom said.

'Tom, they have to know that they can trust me. If I lie to them—'

'You won't be lying. You'll be leaving something out, for the sake of harmony.'

'Perhaps you should take the rest of the night to consider this, Underqueen. We can't bring the Unnatural Assembly together during the curfew,' Glym said. 'It would be prudent to wait until sunrise.'

He had a point. I would only put them in more danger if I forced them outside now.

'Okay. I want them all at the Old Lyre at half past five, before Weaver can make any early announcements,' I said. 'I'll inform them that the sensors are in danger and hold a vote on what we should do next – go into hiding, or stay on the streets. Whatever the outcome, I'll have to square it with the Ranthen.'

'Never mind a vote. Those of us who are detectable *must* hide,' the Pearl Queen said. Maria gritted her teeth. 'Well, what else is there to do? Senshield is intruding farther and farther into our lives by the day. Personally, I have no desire to be pounced upon by Vigiles if I stray too close to a letter box. Let us not put pride over sense.'

'This is the Mime Order's decision to make. Together.' I sounded much calmer than I felt. 'I'll see you tomorrow. Be there at quarter past, if you can.'

They all nodded. Maria lit a cigarette as I left the room and took the stairs down to the tenth floor.

Before I could head farther down, Nick caught up with me. My muscles felt so spring-loaded with tension that I flinched when he touched my shoulder.

'Paige.' He let go. 'Sorry. Are you okay?'

'Fine. I just didn't—' I stopped when I saw his face. 'What is it?'

'I wanted to tell you in private.' He looked grim. 'Dani is gone.'

'Gone?'

'Every trace of her – clothes, equipment. No sign of a struggle.'

'That means nothing.' My heart pounded. 'Nick, she could have been detained.'

'I doubt it. They would have stayed in the hideout to lie in wait for her allies.'

If Danica hadn't been taken, she had left of her own accord. My first deserter, and it was Danica Panić, the last person in the world to run from a problem.

Just one more solid kick in the teeth.

'Eliza saw her earlier, but she didn't say anything,' Nick said quietly. 'I think what happened at the warehouse really shook her, Paige.'

The words dug out a hollow in my chest.

'That's our last link to Senshield gone,' I said. His face reflected my disquiet. 'Maybe it's time to approach the night Vigiles. Like Warden said, they want Senshield destroyed as much as we do, and they might have information. We can't give up on finding the core.'

'We'll have to be very careful.'

'You don't need to remind me.' I drew my coat closer. 'Tom confirmed the report.'

'I still don't see how your aura could have been used to expose the sensors. Vance clearly likes to manipulate her targets' emotions. What if she *wants* you to believe you're responsible, to make you blame yourself?'

'And what if she wasn't lying?'

Nick didn't reply.

'I'm going to inform the Unnatural Assembly tomorrow.' I glanced behind me, lowering my voice. 'I want to do it tonight, but—'

'Don't, Paige. If you're going to address the situation, you need to know exactly what you're going to say. Take this evening to think about it. And try to get some sleep,' he said gently. 'You don't look well.'

'I'm grand.'

'You're not a machine. Just give yourself a few hours.'

I wanted to argue, but he was right. My muscles ached from the lingering shock of my fall into the river. I hadn't washed or eaten properly in days. My wounds were hurting where I had forgotten to put on salve.

And there was someone I had to see. Something I needed to resolve.

'I'll go to Lambeth,' I said. 'Can you pick me up at half four?'

'I'll be there.'

'Okay.' I reached into my jacket and held out the envelope. 'Zeke gave this to Jack to pass on to you. He and Nadine have left Seven Dials.'

Nick took it with care, his brow tightening.

'Thank you, sötnos.' It went into his coat, close to his heart. 'Let's hope they don't run into any scanners. And that they've found somewhere warm.'

I didn't tell him that they might have gone to Jaxon. He would already have guessed.

'I said I would help Wynn polish her medical skills tonight,' Nick said. 'You rest, Paige.'

'I'll try.'

He walked into the shadows of the Mill. I eased up my hood and headed out into the snow.

6

HOURGLASS

It was almost curfew by the time I reached our hideout in Lambeth, drenched and shivering. Cully had driven me as far as the Old Tull, but I had gone the rest of the way alone, despite the snow. She needed some time to get indoors, too.

Lambeth East had been a stop on the secret Pentad Line. Out of curiosity, I had looked for any likely entrances to the tunnel between London and Oxford, to no avail. Even if I had found one, Scion would already have sealed it.

The safe house was a little Georgian place on Theed Street. I took off my jacket and boots. Once I had a fire going, I reached for the golden cord.

No reply.

I needed to see him before he left for the Netherworld. It could be weeks before he returned. To distract myself, I made supper and ate in the parlour, taking bite after small bite until I had scraped the plate clean. I went upstairs and ran a bath, lying in the hot water until my fingertips crinkled.

Had Danica gone to Scion with our secrets?

Had we walked into the trap because of her?

I was doubting everything I had once believed about the people closest to me. On the other hand, Danica might have just lost her nerve, and I couldn't blame her for running from Vance. She had been a child when Scion had invaded her country, just as I had been. She must have a healthy fear of anything related to the army.

I brushed my teeth and tended to my wounds. I could see why Nick had said I looked ill. My face was almost grey. Still, he had been right – being full and clean made me feel more alert than I had in a few days. Now all I needed was more than two hours' sleep.

I tried the cord again. Nothing.

Warden wasn't going to come.

Back in the parlour, I crawled on to the couch with a blanket, wanting to sleep by the fire. Beneath the pall of fatigue, I still felt the same cold fear that swooped through me whenever I thought of Jaxon, or saw a Vigile.

When the front door opened, I sat up, sensing a familiar dreamscape. Warden entered the parlour and lowered himself into the armchair.

I had given him my spare key for this house. Back when I had still thought I could shake the doubt Jaxon had planted.

'I didn't think you'd come,' I admitted. 'Was Terebell happy for you to see me?'

'I did not ask her for permission.' His gaze found mine. 'What do you need of me, Paige?'

Even now, I loved hearing him say my name. Loved the way it sounded on his tongue. He imbued it with singularity, as if I were the only person in the world who could ever possess it.

'The report was accurate,' I said. 'The scanners have been adjusted to identify the fourth order. The majority of our recruits are detectable now. I'll be announcing it to the Unnatural Assembly tomorrow.'

Warden was silent for some time. A few tufts of snow were melting in his hair.

'Until Senshield is fully portable, and fully operative in terms of the orders it can detect, the Mime Order can survive,' he concluded. 'You must focus on gathering and training recruits, preferably by draining them from the Vigiles' ranks. With you at the helm, I believe this revolution will recover from this loss and thrive.'

'You really believe that.'

86

'I always have.'

There was an open bottle of wine on the table (Nick, again). I reached for it.

Warden was right. Vance had dealt us a terrible blow, but we still had time. It would be a few weeks before there were enough scanners to end free movement.

'Let's just hope the syndicate doesn't find out that Vance used me,' I said, 'or I imagine I'll go the way of the last two Underlords.'

'The Ranthen will not allow that to happen.' He looked at me. 'You have decided not to tell the whole truth, then.'

'I wanted to be honest, but I think my commanders are right. It would only create discord.'

He made no comment. I took a wine glass from the cabinet before returning to the couch.

'Warden, I owe you an explanation,' I said, 'and I wanted you to hear it before you leave.'

'You owe me nothing.'

'I do.'

I filled the glass for him and handed it over. His eyes were almost human in their darkness.

'I've been avoiding you,' I said. 'I need to tell you why.'

I sat back down and looked at him. It took me a few tries before I began.

'When I saw him in the Archon,' I said, 'Jaxon implied that you chose me in Oxford on Terebell's orders. That wouldn't really bother me, but he made it sound . . . calculated. And that made me think that everything between us was a lie, that the Guildhall was only ever a way to cement my trust in you. That it was all just . . . bait.'

'Bait,' he said, a question in his tone.

'Jaxon also implied that you were ordered to ... seduce me, or something along those lines. To keep me under control.'

Warden narrowed his eyes a little.

'Terebell would never have approved of such a scheme,' he said. 'You know her position on flesh-treachery.'

'You could have invented or exaggerated that.'

'For what purpose?'

'To make me believe you were risking your neck to be with me. So I would do anything for you in return.' I shifted. 'Even if you got carried away with the act in the Guildhall, I wondered if Terebell had asked you to … entice me with the possibility of a relationship, at least, so I would fall for you.'

The admission hung between us for some time. Warden swirled the dark wine in his glass.

'And are you enticed?'

The fire was drying his hair. It brought out notes of darker brown that I had never noticed before.

'Maybe,' I said.

Warden never took his gaze off my face. Probably wondering how I had lost so many marbles in so little time.

'You became our associate by choice,' he said. 'Why should Terebell need to manipulate you?'

'No idea. Maybe she got used to humans being forced to follow orders in Oxford, and now she wants to make sure I stay biddable.' I rubbed the corner of my eye. 'I promise this all made sense in my head. It sounds absurd when I say it out loud.'

'I do not question you to mock your misgivings, Paige. Only to understand their roots.'

I tucked a curl behind my ear.

'Jaxon knows how to get to me. That was never going to change overnight,' I said. 'Not only that, but I lived with him for three years without knowing about his past. He must have been laughing behind my back when I told him about Oxford. Now I don't know who else I've been playing the fool for. And maybe it seemed too good to be true.'

'How so?'

'Well, not to put too fine a point on it, but you're a Reph, and I'm clearly not. And most people in Scion wouldn't consider me a catch.'

Who would ever look at her?

'So I have wondered why,' I said. 'Why you kissed me in the Guildhall.'

Warden was quiet for a while. I could tell he was contemplating my confession.

'You have heard other Rephaim call me a flesh-traitor. It is understandable for you to wonder why I would have chosen this path, if not for some ulterior purpose,' he said. 'It is also understandable for you to doubt those closest to you now Jaxon has shown his true colours.'

'Why, then?'

'Why did I choose you in Oxford,' he asked, 'or why did I kiss you on the night of the Bicentenary?'

I held his gaze. 'Both.'

'You may not like the answer to the first question.'

'Try me.'

Rephs didn't make a habit of disclosing their emotions. Warden had made oblique statements about his feelings towards me, but this was the first time he seemed to be volunteering information.

'At the oration, twenty years ago,' he said, 'there was a young man with auburn hair and black eyes, full of contempt. While the other humans kept their heads down, he alone stared back.'

'Jaxon,' I said quietly.

'He became Nashira's tenant that year. Her only tenant.'

'Nashira was his keeper?'

'Yes.' Warden paused. 'You looked at me the same way, twenty years later. You looked me in the eye, asserting yourself as my equal.'

I remembered that night all too well.

'I suspected, in the years to come, that he was the traitor. It tested my faith in all of humanity,' he said. 'Yet when I saw that glimpse of him in you, I sensed that you might have the courage to rebel. Terebell had taken an interest in you, but she did not order me to take you in. Quite the opposite. She thought I was a fool for bringing you into such close quarters.' His fingers tapped the arm of the chair. 'Of my own accord, I elected to take you into Magdalen. I knew that Nashira would try to steal your gift.'

'So you did it to protect me.'

'It was not a wholly altruistic act. If Nashira had mastered dreamwalking, she would have become far more powerful, making it difficult for us to revive the Ranthen.'

It was disturbing to hear him talk about Nashira. 'But you first chose me because . . . I reminded you of Jaxon.'

Warden didn't answer. I tried not to show how deep the words cut me.

'Paige,' he said, 'how close were you to Jaxon?'

'You know,' I said. 'You've seen my memories.'

'Not all of them.'

I considered. 'Mollishers are often closer to their mime-lords. They're lovers, sometimes, but Jax doesn't have any interest in sex. We talked a lot, but it was usually just about syndicate business. And he could be kind, but . . . only to keep me under his control.'

Warden rarely interjected, the way a human might to show continued interest in a subject. Neither did he look away from my face.

'Tell me,' he said, 'might he know about Dance upon Nothing?'

The memory I had shown him by choice. That I had trusted him to see.

'I never told him,' I said. 'Why do you ask?'

'What Jaxon said in the Archon plays upon certain aspects of your past and personality. He knows you are protective of your heart and dignity. He knows, most likely, that the first person you loved – or believed, for a short time, that you loved – did not return your feelings,' Warden said. I glanced away. 'Jaxon has poisoned your impression of me with great care. In your mind, I am now someone who might be making a fool of you, who cares nothing for you, and who only means to use your gift for his own gain – another of your fears.'

He understood so much about me, and I still knew so little about him.

'What he has done is insidious. Nashira must be pleased to have him back at her side,' he said. 'There is no way for me to prove to you that I am not what he claims. Not unless I publicly turn against Terebell, which would sow tension within the Ranthen. Perhaps that is what he expects me to do. To win back your confidence at the expense of our ability to work together.'

My skin turned cold as I listened to him. I seemed fated to flee from one set of strings to another, endlessly caught in a web of deceit.

'With one falsehood, designed to target what he sees as your emotional vulnerabilities, Jaxon has demolished the foundation that you and I have laid,' Warden said. 'Nine months, and your trust in me is wavering.'

If true, it meant that Jaxon had thought of everything. This was mental warfare. The only way to fight was to refuse to do what he expected.

To trust that Warden was my ally.

'I make no apology for refusing your request in front of the Ranthen. Only for the hurt it caused you,' Warden said. 'I would choose Terebell's orders over yours again – if it held the Mime Order together, and if it protected you. Having no choice but to hide what I feel for you; to withhold all warmth and support in public, in defiance of my instincts – this is the price I will pay for change. And we all must pay a price.' He looked into the fire. 'Jaxon may have left scars on my body, but I will not allow him to scar the alliance we have built together.'

A tingling started beneath my ribs.

'I should have told you sooner,' I said. 'I've let it eat away at me for weeks. I still don't know if this alliance can work, but it will take more than one lie to break my trust in you.'

'Do we have a truce, then?'

'For now.'

Weeks of dancing around the truth, and just like that, it was over. Now it would only take a step to bring us close enough to touch.

Instinct made me glance towards the door. I had heard him turn the key and draw the chain across when he arrived. Before I could stop myself, I moved towards him.

Our foreheads pressed together. As I searched the endless depths of his eyes, I let him frame my face. He still traced my features as if he wanted to decipher them.

'We shouldn't do this,' I murmured. 'Maybe it's best if we just . . . let it go.'

Warden offered no words of comfort. No white lie to make things easier.

After all, it *would* be best.

'The Mime Order would collapse if the Ranthen knew,' I said, even as my willpower deserted me. 'Everything we've worked for—'

He waited for me to continue, but I couldn't.

'I consider your company worth the risk,' he said into my hair, 'but the choice is always yours.'

I considered his face once more. I couldn't keep second-guessing myself. Jaxon was the liar, the snake in the grass.

Trusting Warden felt right, somehow. So did being in his arms. It was a feeling I couldn't deny, a certainty I could never explain. I just knew that I felt a relief beyond words, to be this close to him again.

I sought his lips first. The choice was mine.

Warden returned my kiss in kind. I melted into his embrace. Just for one night, I would forget the harsh demands of being Underqueen. I would let myself live in this interlude, where only we existed.

It was some time before I led his hands into my blouse. The kiss broke, and he met my gaze. When I nodded, he parted the silk from waist to throat. A chill spread over my stomach and breasts.

There was a low fire in his eyes as he took me in. I was perfectly still, trying to tell what he was thinking. After a few moments, his gaze flicked back to mine, and I nodded again. He traced my collarbone and jaw. His other hand glided over the seam in my side, where the skin was knitting back together. I linked my arms around his neck, cocooned by his aura.

A truce couldn't last when we were at war. For the time I had him to myself, I wanted as much of him as he would give.

Vance had reminded me of my mortality. I was tired of holding back from Warden. Tired of yearning to be close to him. Tired of denying myself. I cupped his face and kissed him deeply, as I had never dared before. As if he sensed the need in me, he tightened his embrace.

A soft ache bloomed between my legs. I felt my lips quake, the blood throbbing through my veins, as he lowered his head to where the wound tapered off, just shy of my breast, and kissed the delicate new skin. Once he had seen to my side, he worked his way down my body. His lips lingered on my stomach, making me shiver.

He went no farther. Not yet. That was for another night. Instead, he laid his head on my breastbone, as if he meant to listen to my heart.

It might be naïve, but I wanted to believe in this.

'Warden.'

'Hm?'

'You never told me why you kissed me in the Guildhall.' I combed my fingers through his hair. 'You only answered my first question.'

He lay still.

'So I did,' was all he said.

I let it go. It was enough that he was here. To know that he was with me.

The next kiss was softer. We shifted our positions, so my back was against his chest, and stayed like that in the light of the fire.

The room was an hourglass that hadn't yet turned. My heartbeat slowed, falling in line with his. When I was close to drifting off, Warden set his cheek against mine. He touched his lips to my jaw, where the welt was, and I threaded my fingers between his knuckles.

'There is one way that you might see proof that I am on your side. Something that would betray me,' he said, his voice a rumble in his throat, 'if anyone but you could see.'

I was so fire-warmed and drowsy, I couldn't think of what he might be talking about.

'What can I see?'

He only drew me closer. I tried to keep my eyes open, so I could savour these fragile hours. In the softened state that comes before oblivion, I imagined that this moment could be safe from time, like he was. I imagined that the dawn would never come.

'Denizens of the citadel, this is . . .'

My eyes opened, furred with sleep. The fire had gone out, leaving a chill on my skin. I couldn't work out what had woken me.

At some point, I had turned to face Warden. His arm was still around my waist, his hand on my back. Sleep had made his body heavy beside mine. I nosed closer to his chest, where it was warmest, and lifted the blanket over my shoulder.

'. . . matter of public security . . .'

I snapped upright, muscles tensed. It took me a moment to work out that the disembodied voice was coming from Nick's data pad, muffled by the cushion that had fallen on to it. With slack vision, I lifted it from the floor. Warden stirred beside me.

'*We must not be tempted by change, when change, by its very nature, is an act of destruction*,' Frank Weaver was saying. '*Mahoney's faction of misguided loyalists, known as the Mime Order, is now classified as a terrorist organisation under Inquisitorial law. It has shed the blood of Scion denizens and threatened the peace in our beloved capital.*'

I waited, not breathing.

'*However, all is not lost. Thanks to a recent development in Radiesthesic Detection Technology, our engineers were able to use Mahoney's own radiesthesic signature to recalibrate Senshield.*' My hands shook. '*Four of the seven known strains of unnaturalness are now detectable.*'

'Vance,' I whispered.

It was her. Weaver might be the one speaking, but I sensed her face behind his, her fingers knotted in his strings.

Scion had made the announcement before I could, and they had laid the blame at my door. If the syndicate believed it, they would never forgive me. I had never thought Weaver would reveal that a fugitive's aura had been used to improve Senshield – or that he would make an Inquisitorial broadcast during the curfew.

I should have insisted on speaking to the Unnatural Assembly hours ago.

'*To ensure that Senshield is used with the greatest possible efficiency, and to support internal security forces at this time*,' Weaver continued, '*I have no choice but to execute martial law, our highest level of security.*'

Warden lifted himself on to his elbows.

'*The First Inquisitorial Division of ScionIDE, our loyal army, is now approaching London. Its soldiers are led by the Grand Commander, who is determined to safeguard our capital before the New Year. Upon their arrival, martial law will be effective in the Scion Citadel of London until Paige Mahoney is in Inquisitorial custody. There is no safer place than Scion.*'

The broadcast ended, leaving the anchor to spin on the screen.

The short-lived warmth was torn from me. I snatched my blouse from the floor and left the pocket of heat in the room, desperate for air, needing the cold to shock me back to reality. When I flung open the front door, the night hit my body like a shout hits the ears. I leaned against the doorframe, clutching my blouse around me. The wind scalded my legs and cheeks.

Something was straining in my dreamscape. I could hear things I hadn't heard since I was six years old. The gunfire and screaming. The tortured cries.

Finn.

Warden stood in the doorway to the parlour. I took deep breaths, shaking a little.

'I need to see the high commanders, now. The syndicate won't survive martial law for long.' I towed the cold into my lungs, as if it could freeze the fear. 'You get the Ranthen. Find me as soon as you can.'

'Very well,' Warden said. 'Where will you meet the high commanders?'

'Battersea. I'll have to walk.'

'Let me escort you, at least.'

'It's fine. I'll sense any Vigiles before I run into them.' I grabbed my jacket. 'Anyway, that broadcast would have woken the whole citadel. I doubt I'll be the only person flouting the curfew.'

I strode past him, back into the parlour. I dug my phone out from behind the couch, where the shapes of our bodies were pressed, and buckled on my jacket and boots while Warden prepared for a séance.

Neither of us spoke again, even when I left.

In case of emergency, our meeting place was always Battersea Power Station. I ran through the snow, eluding cameras and squadrons of Vigiles, taking the rooftops when I could. Before long, I was squirming under the fence that surrounded the derelict – the skeleton of a massive, coal-fired station that had long since fallen out of use. Stars glistened above its four pale chimneys.

Memories gathered like crows in my mind. None of them were clear, but I had the sense of being surrounded, suffocated.

A few sets of footprints had already spoiled the snow. I found Glym, Eliza and the Pearl Queen inside, all with grave expressions. Behind them, Maria was slumped over a control panel. Her hair flamed against her pallid brow, and she was strangling a bottle with one hand.

'You were all at the Mill,' I said, out of breath. 'How did you get here before me?'

'A portent,' the Pearl Queen said. 'Shortly after you left, multiple voyants had a great sense of impending danger, including Tom and Nick. We thought it best to spend the night in Battersea.'

'Cully couldn't have driven you.'

'We borrowed two more cars,' Maria said hoarsely. 'Good thing we're all criminals, isn't it?'

'The others will be here soon,' Eliza said, her cheeks pink with cold. 'Well, maybe not Minty. She won't be able to get here from Grub Street.'

As it happened, Minty Wolfson arrived a few minutes later. By a stroke of luck, she had been staying the night with a contact in nearby Vauxhall.

Nick and Tom came next, followed by Wynn. For the first time since I had met her, she was armed. I could see the leather strap of a holster where her coat fell open.

'ScionIDE will crush the Mime Order,' I said. 'With Senshield, they'll root us out in days, and they won't be as easy to avoid as the Vigiles.'

'We might have a chance if we stay on the move. Or go to ground here as best we can.' Maria drank from the bottle. 'The First Inquisitorial Division has spent years stationed on the Isle of Wight. We know this citadel. Most of them won't.' She wiped her mouth with a shaking hand. 'This could be fine.'

She didn't sound convinced.

'It won't work. We can't hide in plain sight any more,' I said quietly. Her face crumpled. 'Senshield would have pushed us into hiding in the end. This just . . . forces us to take action earlier than we expected. We have to vanish.'

The silence that followed was painful, heavy with shock and grief. Never, in all of syndicate history, had voyants been forced to leave their districts, their homes, the streets. What I was proposing – what I was ordering – was an evacuation.

Even as I spoke, I was suddenly conscious of the æther, my sixth sense overpowering the others. Nick touched my arm, jolting me back.

'Paige?'

'Wait,' I said, and ran from the control room.

Scaffolding had been left to rot on one side of the power station, where property developers had been defeated by its age. I spidered my way up it with ease, ignoring the others' calls. A mass of dreamscapes was approaching from the south, moving at a regimented pace.

Surely they couldn't have got here so quickly.

Nick was in pursuit, navigating the vertical labyrinth. When I reached the top, I ran to the base of one of the chimneys and grasped the rusty ladder. Behind me, Nick heaved himself off the scaffolding.

'What are you doing?'

'I need to see.' I tested the ladder with my boot. 'Something's coming.'

'Paige, that thing has to be three hundred feet.'

'I know. Can I use your binoculars?'

His lips pressed together, but he handed them over. I slung them around my neck and climbed.

I moved like clockwork, past concrete scabbed with dirty paint. When I thought I was high enough, I turned to behold the star field of blue streetlamps and illuminated skyscrapers. I could see the bridges closest to the power station – two of the many that crossed the River Thames. The nearest was for trains, but the one beyond would normally be weighed down with traffic, even in the small hours. I took one hand off the ladder and lifted the binoculars.

A convoy of armoured black vehicles was thundering across that bridge. I almost stopped breathing when I saw the tanks among them. Each vehicle was flanked by armed soldiers. I couldn't see the end or the beginning of the convoy; there must have been hundreds or thousands of them, all on their way to subdue the capital.

My heart climbed into my throat. When a helicopter rushed over, I pressed myself against the ladder.

I descended as quickly as I could. 'Paige,' Nick said. 'What did you see?'

'A convoy, heading north on Chelsea Bridge.'

'ScionIDE.' His throat bobbed. 'They must be going to Westminster. They'll secure the Archon first, then work their way out.'

'Then we still have some time.'

We climbed back down the scaffolding. The others were waiting for us at the bottom.

'They're here,' I said. Minty lifted a hand to her mouth. 'We need to get our voyants off the streets, into every available hideout. Maybe some of the abandoned Underground stations, too.'

'Jaxon knows those places.' Eliza was holding her own arms. 'We need somewhere he's never been.'

'Damn it, *think*,' Maria barked. 'Where can we go?'

'There's always the Beneath.'

It was Wynn who had spoken. She was standing by a window, her hands in the pockets of her coat. As one, we all turned to look at her.

'The underground rivers. The deepest tunnels. The storm drains and the sewers,' she said. 'The lost parts of London.'

'Oh, Wynn, don't be an idiot,' Maria burst out. Wynn raised her eyebrows. 'The Beneath is the mudlarks' and toshers' territory. We all know they have no interest in dealing with syndies. They protect their kingdom of shit like it's a river of gold. Any time we've ever tried to push too far underground, they've driven us off.'

'Ruffians,' the Pearl Queen said.

Tom looked grim. 'Can we not fight our way in?'

'Fighting them would end in deaths,' I said. 'I'm not going to slaughter one community to save another.'

Yet going deep underground could protect us from Senshield, and from Vance. I imagined the soldiers knocking on doors, forcing people through the scanners, searching every derelict building.

'I'm afraid overwhelming the mudlarks and toshers simply isn't an option,' Minty said. 'The Beneath *is* their domain, beyond debate. Their right to the Beneath has been enshrined in syndicate law since 1978. And as you say, Maria, they protect it fiercely.'

'There must be some way to convince them. It might be our only way out of this,' I said. 'ScionIDE won't think to look there; even Jaxon will have no inkling. We could move around London *under* the streets, without activating the scanners. If the Mime Order could go where the soldiers can't follow—'

Wynn cleared her throat loudly.

'If I might finish speaking,' she said, 'I happen to know how we can access the Beneath without violence. Would anyone care to listen?'

Every head turned in her direction. Maria was good enough to look slightly embarrassed.

'The mudlarks worship the Old Father, the god of the Thames,' Wynn said. 'Jacob's Island sits at the mouth of a subterranean river called the Neckinger, which they consider sacred. When the syndicate imprisoned the vile augurs there, locking them out, they were furious. Every so often, they would try to break down the fence, or attack syndicate voyants in protest. This went on for a while.'

I had never heard about this. Danica had sometimes bought scrap from the mudlarks, but Jaxon had never done business with them.

'Finally, the Wicked Lady lost patience, and a young mudlark was thrown in with us. I spoke to their king through the fence, gained his trust. I promised Styx I would keep the child safe, and I did, for nine long years. In return, he promised me a favour. It so happens,' Wynn said, 'that I never claimed it.'

I didn't dare to hope.

'Wynn,' Nick said, 'are you saying you might be able to get us into the Beneath?'

Wynn stared hard at each of them in turn, and then at me.

'Know this, Paige Mahoney,' she said. 'If you had punished Ivy at all during that trial – if you had touched even a hair on her head – I would have left you all to rot, and done it gladly.'

The silence was absolute. When I could speak again, I said, 'Send word to the syndicate. We're going underground.'

THE GREAT DESCENT

1 December 2059

We sent out an alert to the Unnatural Assembly. *Gather supplies. Prepare to evacuate.* There was to be no discrimination – every voyant would be granted safe passage, starting with those who lived in I Cohort. Each cell would be given a meeting point. From there, someone would lead them into the Beneath.

If Wynn could still claim her favour. If Styx would allow us to share his domain. I was putting our lives in the hands of a complete stranger.

Scarlett Burnish had appeared to soothe the citadel.

The voice that read news and announcements, now asking all denizens to remain in their homes and await further instruction. So few were listening. These were Londoners – they had never experienced the ruthlessness of ScionIDE. They had spent their lives under a carapace of superficial freedom, with no idea that the soldiers would not tolerate any form of protest. That was why they were out in force on the streets, seeking answers from the Vigiles, who no longer seemed to be enforcing the curfew. Scion must have expected this chaos.

'*The Grand Inquisitor requests that all denizens return to their homes, allowing soldiers of the First Inquisitorial Division to establish themselves in the capital,*' Burnish said. '*By eight a.m. at the latest, all denizens should be indoors. There is no safer place than Scion.*'

Weaver had made his broadcast at four. This announcement gave us a narrow window of opportunity to leave the surface.

While the others were coordinating the evacuation, Wynn took me and Nick to the Old Toll, formerly known as Blackfriars Bridge. We followed her down a set of steps, out of sight of the main road.

'Wynn,' Nick said, 'where are you taking us?'

'To the mouth of the Fleet.'

'The what?'

'A lost river. Buried over the years, as London was piled on top of it.' Wynn kept marching. 'Scion won't be looking down there for criminals. Not for a while, in any case.'

She glanced over a low balustrade, down to where the Thames swashed against an outcrop of ice. I exchanged a worried glance with Nick.

'You can only access the entrance at low tide.' Wynn climbed over, on to a ladder. 'Paige, wait for a whistle. When you hear it, come down and join me.'

'Where are you going?'

She grabbed me by the collar and pulled me forward, so I had to lean over the balustrade. 'Look.'

I looked. Nick switched on his torch, but it took my eyes a moment to find the narrow entrance to a tunnel, hidden beneath the bridge.

'Wynn,' I rasped, 'we can't put the voyants in a *river* for months.'

'This is only one part of the mudlarks' and toshers' network. They use the Fleet and its storm drains to cross the citadel – just as we must, if we mean to evade Vance.' She made her way down. 'Wait there.'

It didn't take her long. She crossed the shingle on the riverbank and disappeared into the tunnel.

Darkness. That was what the syndicate now faced under my rule. Days, weeks, possibly months, buried in forgotten places. I had known that something like this would happen one day, ever since Scion first mentioned Senshield, but not this soon. Not like this.

'This could work,' Nick said, his breath clouding as he spoke. 'If the mudlarks and toshers can survive down there, so can the syndicate.'

'Let's hope so.' The wind lashed my face. 'It's our only chance.'

'Do the Ranthen know what's happening?'

'Yes. Warden saw the broadcast.'

The transmission screen across the river was static. Hildred Vance was a shadowy figure, rarely appearing before cameras – most denizens would have no clear impression of what she looked like. Perhaps that was a tactic, meant to frighten us. If Vance remained faceless, communicating only through her soldiers' brutality, she would be imagined as something more than human.

The whistle came sooner than I expected. Nick and I went down the ladder and ventured under the bridge.

Beyond the archway was utter darkness. Marbled water washed around our boots.

Two dreamscapes were here. Nick shone his torch, revealing a chamber of stock brick. The far wall was taken up by sealed iron doors. I never failed to marvel at how many parts of London had been left to rot in the vaults of history, unseen and unknown by most.

Wynn's dark eyes reflected the torchlight. The amaurotic beside her was unshaven and defiantly filthy. He wore an oilskin coat, a helmet, rubber gloves and high gumboots, winched up by metal clips on his belt. He also carried a long pole, which must serve as both walking stick and spear.

'This is the outfall chamber of the River Fleet,' Wynn said. 'And this is Styx, elected king of the mudlarks and toshers. Styx, I give you Paige Mahoney, Underqueen of the Scion Citadel of London.'

We regarded each other. He didn't look much like a king – but then, I probably didn't look like his idea of a queen, either.

'Wynn tells me that you wish to move the clairvoyant syndicate into the Beneath,' Styx said. His voice was throaty. 'I see no reason why I should grant this request. If not for Wynn, I wouldn't even be considering it.'

'Because there are soldiers in our citadel. And if you don't,' I said, 'my voyants' blood will be on its streets today.'

'I wouldn't mourn. Your syndicate has long been a festering wound on the face of London, almost since the first Underlord died. The syndicate held my child hostage for years. And it seems to me that you brought martial law upon yourselves.'

Nick opened his mouth to protest, but I stood on his foot.

'I promised Wynn anything for taking care of my child,' Styx said, 'but I can't allow you to share our sanctuary if I fear your people may harm mine. You syndies have never been kind, even when we coexisted. The waterfolk were here before your syndicate. Mudlarks combed the Thames in the days of Queen Victoria. Toshers crawled beneath the streets before London knew the word *unnaturalness*. You're the youngest criminals in this citadel, yet you brutalised us.'

'And I don't expect you to forgive us for it,' I said. 'I can only swear to you that it will not happen again on my watch. We'd be indebted to you, Styx. We don't know how to navigate the Beneath.'

'No. And it is deadly without a guide.' Styx leaned on his spear. 'I'm inclined to believe you, knowing you released the vile augurs. There are many sorts of outcasts in the Beneath . . . but the risks to us are great.'

'It wouldn't have to be a permanent arrangement,' I said. 'My voyants only need asylum for as long as it takes me to damage ScionIDE.'

'And you have a plan to do that?'

He sounded sceptical, as well he might.

'Yes,' I said. 'I do.'

It was almost true. I had the pieces of a plan, even if I had yet to slot them together.

'Styx,' I said, wading closer, 'I don't have time to negotiate with you. I need to get my voyants to safety – not tomorrow, but now, today.' My voice shook with the effort of staying calm. 'I'm asking you, one outcast to another, to let my people into the Beneath, so they won't have to face what's above. There are good people among them for every one that's done wrong. If money is what you want—'

'I've no use for money. We make enough from the blessings of the Old Father.'

'What can I offer you, then?'

'A life.'

I waited.

'A mudlark was slain by syndies in 1977,' Styx said. 'Cruelly slain, and tortured before.' Sunken eyes stared into mine. 'We require a life for the one that was stolen.'

'You want to execute a voyant for a crime committed almost a century ago?'

Despite my efforts, my voice cracked. For the first time, Styx grinned, showing rotten teeth.

'Much as I'd be curious to see if you would make that sacrifice,' he said, 'I'm not a tyrant, like some of your leaders. No, we claim one of your voyants as a resident of the Beneath.'

'To do what?'

'That's my business.'

Whatever it involved, it would be a life of darkness. A life in the filth of the underground tunnels. One person condemned to that.

One life to save many.

'Agreed,' I said.

Styx took a long knife from his pocket and held out a hand. Slowly, I offered mine. He sliced open my palm, then lowered both our hands into the brownish water, making Nick grimace. The cut stung ferociously. Rough skin pressed mine, squeezing my blood into the Fleet.

'The river witnesses this settlement,' Styx said. 'This day, after many days, our communities are reunited. Should you go back on your word, or should your people harm mine during their time here, we will drive you out, whether the anchor will hurt you or not.'

'Understood.'

'Good.' We rose, and he let go of my hand. 'The Beneath has many doors, doors to which Scion no longer has keys. You will be safe with us, so long as you obey our orders.'

'Just tell us what to do,' I said.

At quarter past seven, we met up with Maria and Eliza at Old Spitalfields, which had opened in spite of the curfew. Hundreds of amaurotics milled around the stalls, trying to get provisions before the Vigiles forced them all inside. For all they knew, it could be days before they were permitted on the streets again. Eliza was carrying an enormous rucksack, while Maria was handing out waterproof clothes and torches to some of her voyants.

'We're good to go,' I said to her. 'Did you find the Bone Season survivors?'

'Jos and Ivy are with us. Glym will bring Nell and Felix.' Maria tossed me an oilskin. 'Let's get the hell out of here. Where's our entrance?'

'Holborn,' Wynn said.

'I'll round up the other Firebirds,' Cully said. 'Dobrev, you go with Maria.'

'I'll call you,' Maria told her. 'Head back to the hideout until you hear from me.'

A few rickshaws and pedicabs were still offering rides, albeit for sky-high prices. Dobrev ushered us to a row of unregistered cabs.

The Inquisitorial broadcast was now playing on a loop between long drones from the civil defence sirens, with Burnish stating that all denizens should clear the roads for military vehicles. The soldiers must be on the move.

The cabs dropped us off by the Holborn Viaduct, a flyover bridge that crossed Farringdon Street, where our group would enter the Beneath. Cars were jammed bumper-to-bumper; pedestrians wove around them, rushing to get home by the deadline. Wynn gathered us beneath the bridge and took a strange sort of key from her belt.

'The entrance is that manhole.' She pointed it out. 'We can't let anyone see us go underground. Eliza, come with me to help lift the cover. Paige and Nick, when I signal, you follow.'

'No,' I said. 'Jos and Ivy first.'

I checked for cameras or obvious scanners, but there were none. Wynn and Eliza dashed across the street. Their heads dipped out of sight as they crouched beside the right manhole. When Wynn stood again and beckoned, Maria nudged Ivy and Jos forward.

Jos was swamped by his oilskin and mittens. He put on a brave face as Ivy pulled his hood over his brow and hurried him across the road. Wynn waited for them to climb into the shaft, then followed.

While she vanished into the pavement, cars began to reverse, their wheels mounting the kerb. Others veered away from the centre of the road, the way they did when an ambulance or fire engine needed to get through.

I didn't need to feel their dreamscapes to work out what was coming.

'Go,' Nick barked. I found myself running into the snarl of traffic, just missing a Scion cab as it backed into a lorry. Horns screamed in protest. Our boots pounded. I saw the manhole, its open lid, the ladder inside it. I tried to push Nick in front of me, but somehow my legs and shoulders were in the shaft, my hands colliding with the ladder. I clambered down, rung after rung, until I hit solid ground.

Eliza was next. A moment later, I heard a creak as Nick stepped off the ladder.

'Maria,' he called, 'get down here!'

Her silhouette was above us, her boots on the rungs. 'Dobrev, hurry—'

Ignoring the ladder, Dobrev dropped straight into the shaft, landing hard. He shouted to Maria in Bulgarian. Without hesitating, she reached up and closed the manhole cover – even though six of her trusted voyants were still out there, and Wynn had the key. The darkness was as good as a blindfold, but I sensed their dreamscapes above.

'No. Wait for us,' a muffled voice cried. 'Underqueen, Maria, please!'

'Run, damn it,' Maria gritted out. 'All of you, go back and find Cully!'

I grasped a rung. 'Maria, what are you doing?'

'They are too close,' Dobrev said. 'The soldiers—'

He was right. I sensed them. The convoy must be within sight of the manhole.

I closed my eyes, cold sweat on my brow. To do nothing would abandon them to the mercy of the soldiers. To lift the cover would compromise the only chance of survival we had.

'Leave them.'

My words rang. It took only seconds for the voyants' footsteps to retreat.

The convoy ploughed over our heads. The thunderstorm of wheels reverberated through the tunnel. My hands found a damp wall. I was a little girl again, trembling beneath a statue. All around the vehicles, single dreamscapes – foot soldiers – were moving at a slower rate.

One of them stopped near the manhole. Maria was motionless. I thought about ordering everyone to run, but one splash, one step, could give us away. After an eternity, the soldier returned to the convoy.

It was a long time before anyone moved. Nick turned on a torch, revealing the drawn faces of the group. Jos was tearful, Wynn very still, Ivy looking at me strangely. Eliza had both hands over her mouth. When the rumble of the convoy had softened, Maria slid down the ladder and switched on a torch of her own. The two beams revealed a cramped brick passageway. A musty smell invaded my nose, laced with something foul.

'So,' Maria said, 'this is the Beneath. Home, sweet home.'

You would never have guessed from her face that several of her voyants had been left behind.

'Why didn't you let them in?' Jos said, sounding choked. 'There was time.'

His confusion made my heart ache. Maria just handed her torch to Dobrev and groped in the pocket of her oilskin.

'I'm sorry, Jos. They weren't fast enough,' I said quietly. 'The soldiers would have chased us down here.'

'You wanted longer in Oxford.' His cheeks were damp. 'You shouldn't leave people behind just because they're not fast enough.'

'Well, we had to, kid,' Maria bit out. 'If we hadn't, the rest of us would have been killed. Including the Underqueen.' She took a cigarette out and stuck it between her teeth. Her hands were shaking. 'They know I would never have left them unless there was no choice.'

I believed it. Maria was one of the few members of the Unnatural Assembly who had gone out of her way to show her voyants that she cared about their welfare. Wynn caught her wrist before she could light up.

'Not here,' she said. 'Sewer gas.'

'Oh, lovely.' Maria chucked the cigarette away. 'My voyants will be fine. They can hide. Cully will bring them down when it's safe.'

Eliza crossed her arms, shivering. 'Can we really trust the toshers?'

'Yes. You've no choice, in any case.' Wynn eyed her. 'Those trousers of yours aren't waterproof. I hope you'll be warm enough.'

'Here's the river.' Maria shone her torch on greenish water. 'No sign of shit. Yet.'

'We're meeting our contact in the storm drain,' Wynn said. 'Follow me.'

The River Fleet coursed between these walls, a cryptic cousin of the Thames. We ventured into the dark, carrying what few possessions we had brought. Wynn chalked marks on the walls along the way.

This could be the beginning of the end. ScionIDE would leave no stone unturned. If a single entrance to the Beneath was discovered, we would find ourselves smoked out like a plague of rats.

Speaking of rats, there were plenty down here. They twitched under our torchlight. As we walked, my mind wandered. Slowly, a suspicion came to the surface.

'Senshield might not have been developed in isolation,' I said, thinking aloud. 'Maybe it was always meant to make ScionIDE more efficient.'

'Senshield detects, ScionIDE destroys.' Nick caught a wall for support. 'Warden was right about the Vigiles. They're about to be superfluous.'

'Not until the scanners are portable,' Maria said, 'which I imagine is on the cards.' She flicked her torch towards the wall, revealing the slime Nick had just put his hand in. He grimaced and removed it. 'If that *does* happen, then, yes, the Night Vigilance Division is doomed. Krigs don't work with unnaturals.'

We waded upstream against a gentle current. The water wasn't deep, but with the supplies weighing us down, it was a slog. Jaxon would pop a rib laughing if he ever got wind of this. The glorious descent into the sewers.

Wynn led us down a ladder, into the storm drain, which was just about dry enough to sit in. She sat on a ledge to catch her breath.

'One of the toshers will collect us from here,' she said. 'They're allowing us to take over one of the old crisis facilities. Scion built them in its early days, in case of war or invasion, but it seems they were forgotten when better ones were constructed.'

We could only hope.

'That sounds promising,' I said. 'Thank you again, Wynn.'

Ivy ran a hand over her short hair. 'Are they dry, these crisis facilities?'

Wynn poured the water from her boots. 'So they say.'

Nick rested his brow against his clasped hands. It wasn't hard to guess who he was thinking about.

Eliza dug into her rucksack and handed out packets of biscuits. We shared a canteen of water to offset their dryness. Jos had been bright-eyed with distress, but he soon dozed off against Ivy, who curled an arm around him. Dobrev elected to sleep, too, and didn't seem to care how filthy he got doing it. Parts of the tunnel were caked in what looked like used toilet paper, so I propped my head on my knees – which weren't much cleaner – and tried to clear my head.

Only hours ago, I had been lying with Warden in the light of the fire. It felt like a lifetime had passed since then.

Time moved strangely in that darkness. I had left my watch at the den, but it had to be past sunset now. One of the torches flickered out.

'Reminds you of the Rookery, doesn't it?'

Ivy was leaning against the bricks. The others had fallen asleep, leaving the torches on a ledge.

'Not really,' I said. 'The Rookery had fires, at least.'

'True. I didn't see it much.' She was staring at the ceiling. 'I'm still trying to work you out, Paige. I didn't expect you to leave those voyants just now, but . . . you didn't even flinch.'

'I wasn't *happy* to leave them. I did it to protect us,' I said quietly. 'I'm trying to protect all the people who are left. Who survived.'

She drew in a breath, deepening the hollows over her collarbones. 'Yeah,' she said. 'I know.'

My hand burned where Styx had cut it. I didn't sleep, but I pretended. I didn't want to talk if anyone woke up. My mind was too full of thorns. ScionIDE, Senshield, the bargain with Styx; Terebell, and how she might respond to this disaster – but most of all, Vance. That blank face, and the eyes that seemed to stare right through me. In a matter of hours, she had reduced me from a queen to a sewer rat.

The net was tightening.

I allowed myself a few deep breaths. I had to be rational. Not all of it was my fault.

Not all of it, but some.

And *some* was far too much.

Dobrev turned over in his sleep and knocked the second torch into the water, putting it out. The darkness was so thick that it seemed to seep inside me with every inhalation.

Hours must have passed before our rescuer arrived – a slender amaurotic with a lamp on her helmet, wearing the same uniform as Styx. Choppy auburn hair framed her face, which was splashed by a grape-stain birthmark.

Wynn stood. 'Styx sent you?'

The tosher nodded and motioned for us to follow. Nick woke the others.

It was a long walk. The crisis facility was over four miles away from where we had entered the Beneath. Some fortunate voyants would be led to it through the Underground, but it seemed my advance party would be taking a much harder path.

Our noses soon forgot the smell. The darkness was harder to bear. Jos was a trouper, as usual, but he was soon exhausted. Nick hitched him up on to his back.

The water rose past our knees, carrying waste I thought it best not to examine too closely. Every so often, more would rush in from else-where, chilling us. There was no way out if it came any higher, but the tosher didn't seem worried. She guided us in silence, only stop-ping to listen to the tunnels, or to pocket something from the water.

Wynn seemed just as comfortable. This had nothing on the squalor of Jacob's Island.

We cut through a chamber, out of the storm drain, back into the mainline. By the time we had scaled the ladder, we were all drenched to the bone. Maria braced herself against the wall and coughed up bile. The tosher stopped just ahead of us and signalled to Wynn.

'What now?' Nick said. His cheek was smeared with dirt. 'Wynn?'

'We can't go any farther upstream,' Wynn said.

Maria wiped her mouth on her sleeve. 'You're not telling me we have to go back out.'

'No.' She nodded to an opening in the wall. 'We have to go through there.'

The tosher handed her a torch, which she shone towards the pitch-black passageway. The sight of it made my throat close up. It was barely wide enough for Jos, let alone the rest of us. We were going to have to crawl, in single file, for as long as it took to reach the other side.

Wynn crouched beside the opening. 'Take this,' she said, offering me the torch. 'I can manage.'

She followed the tosher. Beside me, Nick was still as stone, transfixed by the prospect.

'It's all right,' I said to him. 'I'll go first.'

8

COUNTER PLAY

It felt like years that we were in that final tunnel, a pipe so cramped and black that it plagued me with persistent thoughts of being in a coffin. I could hear Eliza choking back sobs of disgust as we inched our way through congealed filth, following the bluish light of the headlamp. It was hard to remember – through the aching and the stench, and the sense that we were being suffocated – that daylight had ever existed.

When the tosher opened a grate, the nine of us tumbled into a pit, where murky water stagnated in a pool. Shaking with exertion, I towed myself on to a set of steps and lifted a heavy-eyed Jos out with me. He was dead on his feet.

Another tosher, who carried a signal lantern, met us at the top of the steps. Without a word, he led us down a passage, where the walls were grey and nondescript. We passed a door embossed with the word BATHROOM.

'Well,' I said, 'this is civilised.'

'Oh, yes.' Maria picked a string of tissue from her hair. 'Then again, everything seems civilised when you've just been getting friendly with other people's excrement.'

Another bathroom was just around the corner. As far as I could see, everything inside was functional.

'This is incredible,' I said. 'Why did we never know about this?'

'Not many do,' the tosher said.

He showed me a diagram on the wall, titled II COHORT DEEP-LEVEL CRISIS FACILITY. Two cylindrical tunnels ran parallel to one another, each split into an upper and lower deck to provide extra room, and they were linked at several points by smaller passages. Not only were there bathrooms, but there were also side tunnels for use as medical wings, canteens, storage rooms, and so on.

'This looks promising,' I said. 'Does anything work?'

'Showers, but don't overdo it. The water collects down below, and it won't go anywhere unless you get the pumps working,' the tosher said. 'I reckon the rest would function if there was power.'

'We were told that some of our voyants were already here,' Wynn said.

'Yeah. They were choosing their bunks, last I saw.'

'Bunks?'

'That's right.'

The tosher headed back to the staircase, leaving us to take in our surroundings. After losing half our group in the descent and wading through the dark for hours, good news was a much-needed surprise.

I set Jos down and stripped off my stinking oilskin. Alsafi might be able to help us get the power back on if we could get word to him.

'We should set up a meeting room for the commanders,' I said.

'And somewhere secure for you to stay, Paige,' Nick said quietly.

The brief exhilaration flickered out. I didn't need him to spell it out for me. Soon enough, the syndicate would be baying for my blood.

'There's a supervisors' post on the other end of the facility,' Wynn said. 'That should be secure.' She brushed past us. 'I'm going to see who else is here.'

Still plastered in filth, she hurried upstairs. For her sake, I hoped Vern and Róisín – her family – had made it down here. Ivy hesitated before following her, and Jos, who tended to go wherever she went, stumbled after them.

'Right,' I said to those who remained. 'Before we do anything, I suggest we wash.'

The suggestion was met with sounds of resounding approval. Eliza offered me a bundle of fresh, warm clothes from her backpack, which I took. If I had to face the music, I might as well do it clean.

Stained curtains divided the bathroom into eight shower cubicles, each of which contained a threadbare towel. I would have recoiled on any other day, but I was already coated in all manner of filth, so I steeled myself and undressed. As promised, the showers just about functioned. I excavated a bar of soap, which looked about a century old, and scrubbed myself raw, scouring under my nails and soaking my hair until the water I wrung from it was clear.

I patted myself dry with the corner of a towel, then pulled on a thermal shirt and grey woollen trousers. Not as impressive as the outfits I usually wore in front of the syndicate, but anything was better than the oilskin. I rinsed my boots and jammed them back on.

There was a water-spotted mirror by the door. With no greasepaint to mask the shadows under my eyes, I would have to appear before the syndicate with a naked face. I turned away from my reflection.

It was time to see my subjects.

We took the stairs to the upper deck. Distorted sounds echoed through the tunnel. Lanterns had been set on the floor, showing me that at least a few voyants had already found their way into the facility.

The relief curdled when I saw what was happening. Wynn was shielding Ivy, while Vern was locked in a brutal fight with a sensor, bloody at the mouth.

'Stop it,' Róisín was screaming. 'Leave him alone!'

They were surrounded. I flung pressure through the æther, scattering the knot of attackers. The sensor let Vern go and clapped a hand to her bleeding nose.

When they found the source of the disturbance, hatred filled their faces. I had almost allowed myself to believe that the discovery of this refuge would soften their fury, but I could see now that I had underestimated it.

Nick placed a hand on my shoulder. 'Paige,' he said, 'let's go to the supervisors' post.'

I brushed him off and went straight to Ivy, who was holding on to Wynn. Her free hand was pressed to her cheek. When I guided it away, I drew in a breath. A rough T had been sliced into her face. Jos was hiding behind her, shaking.

'Eliza,' I said, too quietly for the crowd to hear, 'get them to the medical wing. Bar the door.'

I rose and brazened out my subjects. Under those bloodthirsty stares, I wanted nothing more than to leave – but if I walked away now, if I showed them that I was afraid, I would lose all my power at once.

'Who,' I said, keeping my voice soft, 'is responsible for this?' Wynn cradled Ivy and wrapped her other arm around Róisín. Eliza ushered them out.

'I'll ask once more,' I said coldly. 'Who cut Ivy?'

'She's a traitor,' a voice said from the back. 'Let everyone remember it.'

'We don't want her down here. Let the soldiers take her.' The sensor spat at Vern and wiped angrily at her nose. 'Whose side are you on, Underqueen? First you don't punish the Jacobite when she was helping sell us on the grey market – then you bring the army down on us – *and* it turns out you've helped them change Senshield. You're worse than Hector ever was, and that's saying something!' Shouts of agreement filled the tunnel. 'Every sensor who's detained from now on – that's on you, Mahoney. Their blood is all over your dirty Irish hands.'

'Traitor,' someone bellowed. 'Traitor!'

'You showed them how to find us,' a whisperer shouted. 'It's all right for you, dreamwalker! So much *higher* than the rest of us, aren't you?'

'You're helping Scion!'

'Traitor!'

More of them piled on, delighting in my downfall. Somebody hurled a shard of rubble, catching my cheek. I restrained my spirit from flying at the perpetrator. Nick shouted at them to get back, but nobody was listening.

They screamed their wrath straight into my ears, so close that my face was freckled with spit, but I didn't flinch. *Tyrant. Murderer. Warmonger. Brogue. Traitor. Traitor. Traitor.* Their voices became Jaxon's voice; their many-headed rage, his vengeance. I would be damned if I took one step away, if I gave an inch. The syndicate had never bowed to cowardice.

'Nick,' I said, 'take Jos back to the lower deck.'

'If you think I'm leaving you—'

'Do it.' Before he could argue, I raised my voice to the mob: 'I don't have time for this. The only traitors here are those who threaten the peace. If you'll excuse me, I need to prepare this facility for the rest of the Mime Order – and thanks to this incident, it seems I'll need to cordon off a holding cell. The next person to spill blood in here will spend a month in it.'

I walked straight into the sea of bodies. When the first hand grabbed my arm, I threw out my spirit.

Nobody tried to touch me again.

I marched between the bunks with my torch, through multiple sleeping areas, past another medical room and signs reading KITCHEN and CANTEEN and STORAGE. When I reached the supervisors' post, I crashed through its door and closed it behind me. Inside was a transmission screen, a desk without a chair, and a bunk that folded down from the wall. I lowered the bunk and sank on to it, aching from the four-mile trek.

In the tunnel, the shouting continued for a while before dying down. My nails bit into the skin of my palms.

I couldn't be taken by surprise like that again. Law and order would be critical down here. I needed to rally my commanders and work out what to do next, but my confidence was running between my fingers.

This might have been the wrong choice. My army was made up of criminals – voyants who had spent years bearing grudges, fighting each other for money and turf. And now they were all on top of each other. In a confined space, where nobody could blow off steam, one flicker of resentment, one insult, could ignite a riot.

They were right to be angry. I had brought the anchor down on their heads. These voyants had gone without many things, but by trying to fight Scion head-on, as no syndicate leader had before, I had taken away the one thing that had sustained them: I had taken away the streets.

My cheek was throbbing where the rubble had struck me. I had to think, and quickly. We had somewhere to hide, but we couldn't last down here for ever.

The only way to free the Mime Order was for a group of us to get back out there and use every available resource to deactivate Senshield. The soldiers would still be there if we succeeded, but if they had no way to detect us, we could risk a return to the surface.

I wrenched my backpack open, rifling through it for the map of London. Maybe there was a pattern in the scanners' locations, or a military facility in the suburbs where they might be keeping the core – something, anything . . .

I stopped when I saw it. An envelope, nestled among my clothes, addressed to me. Inside was a note, hastily written.

Paige, as you'll know by now, I've left. I applied for a transfer to Athens. Scion approved it two days ago. I'm not the revolutionary type, and of you and Jaxon, you seemed like the easier person to run away from. No offence.

I would, however, like to leave you with a parting gift. It relates to Senshield.

Danica had never meant to stay with me, but it was clear that she hadn't betrayed me. I read on.

You may have noticed, over our years of cohabitation, that I don't like being outsmarted. Vance fooled you through me, which leads me to conclude that I bear some responsibility for the deaths at the warehouse. Apparently I have a conscience.

I traced the blur where the side of her hand had smudged the letters. She must have been deeply humiliated, to admit to any of this.

So I've spent my last hours in London doing better investigation. I discovered something – and this time, it's not false information. I made sure.

We all knew that, sooner or later, Scion would make a portable scanner. I was under the impression that they were still in the early stages of design. I was wrong about that, too. As you read this, handheld scanners are being manufactured for military use in a factory in Manchester, which is controlled by SciPLO. These scanners will be linked to the core, whatever or wherever it is. My feeling is that you'll want to pay a visit to Manchester, in the absence of better leads.

I could feel sweat forming on my upper lip. This couldn't be happening. Handheld scanners, sooner than we had thought. I imagined each soldier carrying one. An army that could see our auras.

I understand that you will need somewhere to start in an unfamiliar citadel, so here is one more breadcrumb. SciPLO records indicate that one of their former employees is wanted for theft. It might be a long shot, but if you can find Jonathan Cassidy, he may be willing to give you some insight into the manufacturing process.

I hope this makes up for my error. I'd say goodbye, but unfortunately for both of us, we will probably meet again.

I scrunched the note into my hand. This was more than a setback. It was a death sentence.

The door opened. I snatched up the knife in my boot, expecting to see a murderous voyant.

'Warden,' I said, lowering it. 'How did you get here?'

'Through the Underground, with the Glym Lord.'

He came to sit beside me and gently lifted my face. His thumb skirted my cheek and came away bloody.

'What happened?'

'The inevitable.' I pressed my fingers over the cut. 'This place is a pressure cooker. They won't last a month down here without killing each other. Or me.'

'You were right to call for an evacuation. So long as you find a way to replenish your supplies, the Beneath may serve you better than your original network of buildings,' he said, unruffled as ever.

'Fortunate that you had mercy on Ivy, or the Mime Order would have no haven. Your compassion has repaid you, Paige.'

'For the time being.' I held out the note. 'We won't be returning to the surface for a while.'

He read it, expressionless.

'If portable scanners haven't already been issued to the soldiers, they will be soon.' My voice was hoarse. 'This is all on me. If I had just disappeared after Oxford, none of this would be happening.'

'No.'

'You're telling me that martial law *isn't* in place because of me?'

'It is because of all of us. You do not fight alone.'

My jaw and throat were aching. Warden shifted off the bunk and crouched in front of me.

'Never allow yourself to believe you should be silent.' His voice rumbled from deep in his chest. 'Even if you had never become Underqueen, Senshield was on the horizon. You know this. It has been in development for a long time. The scanners might not have come so soon, but they would have come. There is no choice but to fight.'

A tear escaped. I blotted it with my sleeve.

'I should never have risked going to that warehouse,' I whispered, 'I helped make Senshield stronger.'

'Paige.'

I met his steady gaze, my eyes brimming. A moment later, I leaned into him, and he wrapped me into his arms. Even as his body warmed mine, I could feel myself starting to shake again.

'I didn't think it would be like this. I never thought they'd put soldiers in London,' I said thickly. 'Even Hector didn't fuck up this badly.'

'Hector made no preparations for Senshield.' He stroked my wet hair. 'You did right by your subjects by finding this place. Alsafi will restore the power. It will be all right, Paige.'

Alsafi.

Their double agent in the Archon.

Slowly, I regained control of my breathing. I drew back a little and looked up at Warden.

'If I were to put together a team,' I said, 'could Alsafi get them to Manchester?'

Warden seemed to consider this.

'I am no longer able to contact Alsafi directly,' he said. 'After I requested that he restore the power here, he told us to cut off further communication with him. The risk of receiving our messages has become too high. However, I believe he divulged the identities of certain humans in his network to Pleione. She may be able to arrange safe passage. If she is successful, you will have to choose someone you trust as your interim.'

'I didn't mean *I* would go. I'd send a team,' I said. 'The leader of the syndicate never leaves London.'

'Traditionally. You are not a traditional Underqueen.'

'Warden, I can't. If you think they're fuming now, they'll be murderous if I run away.'

'Consider the alternative. The Mime Order blames you for this state of affairs. While you are in their line of sight, their anger will remain fresh,' he said. 'Many will resist your orders out of resentment.' His gloved hands cupped mine. 'You broke from convention by turning on your mime-lord, Paige. You can do it again.'

He might be right. The time for tradition was gone. 'You'll stay now, and help us,' I said. 'Won't you?'

'No.'

I stared at him. 'Are you serious?'

'Now more than ever, we must have Rephaite support,' Warden said, his voice low. 'Terebell has no intention of changing her plans. And it may be best that the two of you do not see each other for a time.'

I could only imagine how enraged she must have been when she realised what Vance had done at the warehouse.

'We must also harvest alysoplasm, to help conceal your voyants on the surface,' he said. 'That means that we must hunt more Emim.'

'Fine.' I pulled away and stood. 'I need to speak to my commanders.'

'I also wish to speak to your commanders, if I may.'

'You don't need my permission.'

He looked at my face for a long time. I wondered if he could possibly understand the emotions bubbling through me – the bitterness and disappointment, the fear.

Even now, he wouldn't stay.

We took the parallel tunnel back to the other end of the facility, avoiding the bunks. I didn't want to get into the habit of hiding from my subjects, but it was safer if I let their tempers simmer down. As we passed one of the cross tunnels, the lights on the ceiling flickered, then glowed, and a bluebottle hum filled the facility.

'Alsafi.' I switched off my torch. 'He's quick.'

'He knew the need was pressing.'

'Is he sure Scion won't notice?'

'They abandoned this facility a century ago. It is forgotten,' Warden said. 'He will see to it that it remains so.'

I nodded.

'Thank you,' I said. 'For asking him to do it.'

'Hm.'

Our surroundings were a little more welcoming now. None of the bulbs grew too bright – Alsafi must be being cautious with the electricity – but they warmed the concrete and cast iron.

The others had claimed places on the lower deck, pairing up to share bunk beds. Ivy was sitting in silence on a bare mattress, while Jos was above her, fast asleep beneath two blankets.

'Paige,' Nick said from his bunk. 'Are you all right?'

'Fine,' I said. 'I see you found bedding.'

'Yes. A lot of it.'

'Good.' I spotted a bag on the floor. 'Whose is that?'

'Mine.'

I turned to see Tom and Glym, both a little worse for wear. It was Tom who had spoken, and he was grinning, if grimy. I was so relieved to see them that I embraced them both.

'Minty asked us to deliver a message.' Glym looked grave. 'She has decided against entering the Beneath. She would prefer to stay in Grub Street and assist us from there.'

I wanted to protest, but Minty Wolfson was the soul of Grub Street, and I couldn't imagine her anywhere else. 'And the Pearl Queen?'

'We've heard nothing from her.'

'Okay.' I tried to think. 'I'll get a message to Leon Wax. Our amaurotic network can help us find anyone who didn't make it down here.'

'Very good, Underqueen.'

Four out of six commanders, Warden, and both my mollishers. More than enough to decide on our counter play. I beckoned the others into an empty side tunnel, where someone had set up a table and chairs. Warden barred the door behind us before taking a seat.

'Time for us to plan our next move,' I said, 'because things are about to get much worse.'

'Worse,' Maria echoed. 'Than this.'

I handed her the note from Danica. She read it, scraping a hand through her hair.

'Portable scanners. For the soldiers,' she murmured. 'It's a damn good thing we did move underground.'

Tom took it from her and digested it.

'I know it's not good news,' I said as they passed the note around, their faces turning grimmer as they read, 'but it does give us a new lead on Senshield.' I raised my chin. 'I've decided to go to Manchester. If that's where portable scanners are being manufactured, we might be able to find out how and where they're linked to Senshield, which could lead us to the core. It's a chance, at any rate.'

Eliza shook her head. 'You seriously want to *leave*, now?'

'That would be unprecedented,' Glym said. 'No syndicate leader has ever left the citadel. It may not be a popular move.'

'I didn't become Underqueen to be popular,' I said. 'Tom, Maria – will you come with me?'

Tom grinned. 'I'm with you, Underqueen.'

'Absolutely,' Maria said.

It was risky to take two commanders away, but I sensed their skills would be the most useful. Tom was a powerful oracle who had lived outside London, while Maria had experience as an insurgent, as well as the sort of relentless energy we needed for this journey.

'Good. And Glym,' I said, 'will you be interim Underlord?'

There was an odd silence. Glym blinked, but dipped his head. 'You do me a great honour, Underqueen.'

I nodded. Glym was loyal and well respected, had been a syndicate leader for years, and didn't take any nonsense from the Unnatural Assembly.

'Your priority is to preserve life,' I said. 'Get the pumps and ventilation working. Send the higher orders to retrieve food and drink for the lower, and to liaise with Leon and Minty. Keep the peace. Above all, make sure the secrecy of this place isn't compromised.'

Warden had watched our discussion in silence.

'What did you want to say?' I asked him quietly.

He looked between my commanders.

'The Mime Order is an alliance between our two factions,' he said. 'You have all contributed your skills and knowledge to its continuation. Now, we wish to give something in return.'

'Oh, at last,' Maria said.

Warden gave her a sidelong glance. 'With Senshield now able to detect four of seven orders, all clairvoyants in this country – whether they yet know it or not – are in an extremely precarious position,' he continued. 'If ever the time was ripe to sway them to our cause, it is now. It would be advantageous to alert them to the situation in the capital and urge them to join the revolution.'

'And how do you propose we do that, given Scion's famous tolerance for freedom of information?'

Tom snorted.

'I suggest,' Warden said, undeterred, 'that we send a message through the æther, encouraging them to assist the Mime Order in its fight against Scion.' There was silence from us all. 'I take it you have all attended a séance at some point in your careers.'

Everyone nodded, including me. They were group invocations of spirits, requiring the presence of at least three voyants, conducted to glean information.

'Most séances are held in order to make contact with spirits,' Warden said, 'but they can also be used to amplify clairvoyant gifts. I propose that we hold one here. First, I would draw memories from any willing ScionIDE survivors, which will illustrate the threat the soldiers pose. Paige will enter my dreamscape and experience them with me. Immediately after, she will jump into an oracle.'

'Okay,' Nick said, frowning.

'This stage is theoretical, but I believe that Paige should be able to transfer the memories to the oracle, allowing them to be projected into the æther as a vision. The longer we can sustain the séance, the farther the message will travel. In order for it to travel far and wide, we will need most of the Unnatural Assembly.'

Maria folded her arms. 'Sounds great. Why haven't we been doing this all along?'

'You did not have a Rephaite with you.'

'True.'

I exchanged a silent glance with Warden. Even if he hadn't said it, he must be pinning his hopes on the golden cord to help us pull this off.

'Tell me,' he said, 'who here has had dealings with ScionIDE?'

'I'll share,' Maria said. 'My memories are nice and gruesome.'

'My experience was—' Nick wet his lips. 'I don't know if I want it made public.'

We all waited. And as I looked at my best friend, I slowly understood.

Nick once told me that Scion killed his sister, Karolina. I always thought she must have been hanged, like most voyants. Seeing his face now, I knew otherwise.

'Take mine,' I said to Warden. 'My memory of the Dublin Incursion.'

'You were too young,' Warden said. 'Those memories may not be clear enough.'

Nick circled his temples with his fingers. Throughout my time in the gang, he had gone out of his way to protect me, taking on the hardest work for Jaxon in my stead. I wished I could spare him this.

'Have it,' he said. 'If it will help other voyants understand, have it.'

'Let me do the projection,' Tom said, patting Nick on the back. 'I've a wee bit more experience in the art.'

Nick nodded.

'It is settled, then. If you can persuade the Unnatural Assembly to perform the séance,' Warden said, 'I will help you strengthen it.'

Tom grimaced. 'You dinna think the Assembly will all hold hands together, do you?'

'Oh, they will,' I said.

'They willna like it, Underqueen.'

'I might be wrong, Tom,' I said, 'but I don't think Scion will give half a damn whether they like it or not.'

9

THE COST

It took sixteen hours to gather enough of the Unnatural Assembly to perform the séance. They were scattered far and wide across the citadel – either making their way through the Beneath, or waiting to enter it.

While the toshers got them to the facility, the rest of us got to work on setting up our new home. We laid bedding on the bunks. A team was assembled to work on the pumps and the ventilation system. What food we had carried was stashed in the canteen area, ready to be distributed. All weapons were confiscated and locked away.

The work kept me too busy to speak to Warden. Sometimes we passed each other as we carried supplies between the sectors, and I would catch a glimpse of his face in the dim light, but I always avoided eye contact.

All the while, more voyants trickled into the facility. Some came through a passage that connected to the Underground, others through the sewers, and others still through a derelict building on the surface. We cleaned up the medical wing as best we could, pooling our supplies, and Nick and Wynn were handed the keys. Wynn immediately called me in and sat me down on a crate. Her hair was back in its fishtail braid.

'Let's see that hand. And your face,' she said. 'We can't have you dying of infection.'

The cut had long since stopped bleeding, but knowing me, I would tear it open if it wasn't stitched. Wynn laid my hand in her lap and took a small bottle of alcohol from her skirts. She tipped some on to the cut on my palm, then dabbed a little more on my cheek.

'Thank you,' I said. 'Are you all right, Wynn?'

'We're used to poor treatment by now,' she said. My palm smarted. 'Paige, you must choose someone for Styx. He won't forget about your bargain.'

'What will he do if I don't send anyone?'

'He'll go to Scion. The toshers take vows very seriously,' she said. 'That's why he cut you. Once the river has witnessed your oath, you're bound to it. If you go back on it, there's no reason for him to protect us.'

'Would you be opposed to me sending a vile augur?'

'Not if they were willing.'

'And if they weren't?'

She slowed in her work. 'That would depend.'

I let her clean my wounds in peace for a while. Once she was satisfied, she plucked a needle from her cardigan and washed it in the alcohol.

'Wynn,' I said, 'you've seen that the voyants still despise Ivy.' Her face tightened. 'It could cause a lot of trouble while you're down here. They're crying out for blood.'

Wynn looked up sharply. 'Don't you dare.'

'I won't make her go.' I lowered my voice. 'I just want to give her the option. She might be safer with the toshers than she is in here.'

'Styx demanded a life. Not a year or a month, Paige.'

'I will get her out,' I said.

'How?'

'However I can. She won't stay there for ever.'

She returned her gaze to my palm, her jaw tight. The needle shoved into my skin.

'You know how frail she is,' she said, with unusual softness. 'She doesn't sleep. And you ought to see the scars her keeper gave her.

She has been punished more than enough for what she did.' Her shoulders pulled back. 'Ivy is like a daughter to me. All the Jacob girls are. Send her, and I'll go to Scion with our whereabouts myself.'

'Wynn.' I grasped her wrist. 'You'd kill all the vile augurs in here, as well as the rest of us.'

Her lips pursed. She cut the thread and enfolded my hand in a clean bandage.

'I don't know what I'd do. You know I've no love for this syndicate, Paige. My loyalty was only ever to you.' She secured the dressing. 'Go on, now. I have another patient.'

Her face had turned to stone. I left.

As it turned out, the next patient was Ivy. She waited outside the door with Róisín, who seemed to have taken on the role of bodyguard.

'Paige,' Ivy said. I walked away. 'Paige?'

It would sate their bloodlust to give Ivy to Styx, and it would keep her out of danger. Every minute, I expected to hear that someone had snapped and taken *justice* into their own hands. I feared it.

Ivy was a survivor, but while I was in Manchester, I wouldn't be able to protect her. I wanted to see her settled in a safe place – somewhere where she could mend, where she would be surrounded by people who cared about her. That place clearly wasn't here. If she was ever going to reach it, she had to last for the next few weeks.

For now, the decision would have to wait. It was time for the séance.

I joined my mollishers in the cross tunnel, all three of us silent and tense as we waited. So far, thirty members of the Unnatural Assembly had made it to the crisis facility. All of them had been summoned to an empty stretch of the upper deck, where there was enough room to form a circle. Their voices mingled in the darkened space. They must have come willingly, but even so, I had no idea what sort of reception awaited us.

'Nick,' I said, watching his closed face, 'you don't have to do this.'

His gaze was distant. 'It's time I faced it.'

A few more mime-lords and mime-queens trailed into the chamber. I watched them, still out of their sight. No sign of the Pearl Queen.

When the three of us stepped into the tunnel, their voices slammed into me like a wall – shouts for me to explain myself, for evidence of any plan to get rid of the army. Eliza and Nick moved straight in front of me, calling for order.

Spirits quavered nearby, ready to attack. When one of the new mime-queens punched Jimmy O'Goblin, I brought them all to heel with my spirit. A wave rolled through the æther and broke against their dreamscapes.

They quietened, their expressions wary. *They need to be afraid of you, or they will never respect you*, Glym had told me, the second time we met after the scrimmage. *All you have to do is show them what you can do, if you choose.*

Several of them had souvenirs from the scrimmage: scarred faces, burns, missing fingers. Others had more recent wounds. I spotted Jack Hickathrift, who smiled at me.

'The Underqueen,' Nick called.

I stepped forward. Eliza and Nick flanked me, both forming spools for my protection.

'Members of the Unnatural Assembly,' I said, 'as you're all aware, we are facing a crisis on an unprecedented scale. With the execution of martial law and the increased presence of Senshield, I have had no choice but to order the syndicate into the Beneath.' A few mutters followed, but I was holding their attention. 'After years of threatening us with Senshield, Scion has not only installed hidden scanners across the citadel *and* recalibrated the technology, but combined the threat of it with the presence of their army, ScionIDE.'

'Because of *you*,' Ark Ruffian snarled.

'Get to fuck, dreamwalker!'

'We should have never let you have the Rose Crown,' the Fifth Sister shouted. 'Binder had his faults, but he would never have let *this* happen!'

Others chimed in with their agreements. My commanders were at the back of the gathering, weapons at the ready, but I had warned them not to leap to my defence. I needed to handle this on my own.

'Pipe down, the lot of you, and listen to me,' I ordered, speaking over the uproar. 'We have received intelligence that there's a Senshield manufacturing hub in Manchester. I intend to go there myself, along with Tom the Rhymer and Ognena Maria. We are hopeful that we'll be able to gain crucial information about the power source of Senshield. And when we find out what that power source is, I vow to you, we will destroy it.'

The reaction was immediate and livid. 'How do you expect to do that?'

'Ah, so that's how it is – scarpering at the first sign of trouble!'

'Putting other citadels in danger, too, are we? Going to expose *more* voyants to Scion?'

And so on, until the Glass Duchess snapped, 'Shut up and let the woman speak!'

Gradually, the commotion died down.

'This was always going to happen,' I said, fighting to keep my cool. 'Hector denied it, and so did every leader before him, but now we know that the only way out of this is to resist. Scion has just used me as their excuse. They've used *us* as their excuse, because they are *afraid* of us. They've been afraid of the power of the syndicate from the beginning, the potential for voyants to unite against them. That's why Senshield exists. That's why we're here. If ScionIDE is allowed to remain, armed with portable scanners, they will not rest until they have stamped out the voyant way of life. If we are to survive, we *must* fight.' I pointed upward. 'Up there, Scion is preparing to wage war against us. For once in our lives, let's give them a taste of their own fucking medicine.'

Something I'd said had reached them. A smattering of applause went through their ranks.

'You wish to declare *war* on Scion, in this weather?' the Heathen Philosopher blustered, one eye magnified by his monocle. 'The Unnatural Assembly is an administrative body that facilitates the felonious activity of worthy clairvoyants. Certainly not one with the capacity to declare *war*.'

I was beginning to appreciate Hector's restraint in not killing the whole lot of them.

Scion declared war on *us*,' I said, my voice growing stronger, 'the day they put their first voyant on the gallows. They declared war on *us* the day they spilled the first blood on the Lychgate!' Cheers. 'You are the clairvoyants of London, and I will not see you extinguished. We are going to reclaim our streets. We are going to seize our freedom. They made thieves of us – it is time to steal what's ours!'

The words stemmed from a place in me I hadn't known was there. More cheers, louder. Calls of support.

'You've got some cheek, brogue,' Slyboots sneered, and they died down. 'None of us signed up to be soldiers.'

'I did,' Jimmy O'Goblin slurred.

'Jimmy, with all due respect, sober up or hush it,' I said. Jeers followed. (Jimmy jeered along with them, then looked confused.) 'I know the odds are daunting, but we have the æther on our side. We can fight our way back to the surface, because we have the means to do so. As the Ranthen have shown us, we can *all* use our clairvoyance against the amaurotics. It's a matter of unlocking our potential. Of trusting the very source of knowledge that binds us together.

'If the White Binder had become Underlord, he would have made you into an army, too – but not one that fights for freedom. You would have been an army of cat's paws and puppets, spreading word of the anchor. You would have survived,' I said, 'but at what cost?'

'Rubbish,' Slyboots shot back. 'Binder would have found a way to make it work.'

'Mind your tongue, Slyboots. I know you helped the Silent Bell destroy the Juditheon – and if memory serves, you were also bosom friends with the Winter Queen, one of the grey marketeers, who is still missing. I do hope you don't share the same sentiments.'

He opened his mouth to argue, but Glym clipped his ear. 'Speak to your Underqueen with respect,' he said, 'or you will not have a tongue to mind.'

'You've got no right to give us orders,' the Ferryman said. He was a wiry, white-haired augur, someone I knew only by sight. 'You've never known hardship, girl. You're a dreamwalker, not to mention the daughter of a Scion scientist. You were chosen by a wealthy mime-lord, who you betrayed for power. Give me one reason I should go to war for you. You're the one who brought this down on us.'

Dark muttering followed his statement. I tried to muster the words to counter it, but it was like trying to pour from an empty bottle.

'Leave her be,' Tom growled.

'Oh, she talks a good game, but I'd like to see her spend one day in the gutter. And she left Ireland quickly enough when—'

'Stop,' I cut in. 'I'm not asking you to go to war for me. Not yet. I'm asking you to *wait* for me. And once I return, I'll be asking you to defend yourselves.' I paced before them, looking many in the eye. 'When I became the ruler of this syndicate, I expected some backbone. I expected to see that unquenchable desire for *more* – the desire that drives this underworld. It's what I've seen in all our eyes – the eyes of gutterlings, pickpockets, all of us – since I first chose these streets. Years of oppression never crushed it, that flame that has led each of us to resist an empire that strives to destroy our way of life. Even if we've acted on it in the shadows, everything we've done, in the century the syndicate has existed, has been a small act of rebellion, whether daring to sell our gifts for coin or merely continuing to exist, and to profit.' I stopped. 'Where is that desire now?'

Silence answered me.

'You've always known your worth. You've always known that the world owes you something, and you meant to take it, no matter the risk,' I said. 'Take it now. Take more.' Applause. Jimmy punched the air. 'I will not allow this to be our extinction. Today, we descend. Tomorrow, we rise!'

This time, there were roars of approval. They really were a fickle bunch. Halfpenny clapped, even if he didn't speak. In the midst of it all, unheard by most of them, the Ferryman spat on the concrete floor.

'I'll not follow a brogue to my death,' he said.

He offered a mocking bow before he left. My stomach flurried, but only his mollisher followed him. I pressed on.

'It's time to tell other voyants in this country about the Mime Order's cause,' I said. 'Right here and now, we are going to perform a new kind of séance, taught to us by the Ranthen. We're going to send a message to the voyants of Britain, which will spread through the æther as a vision, as far and wide as we can send it. At the end, they will see *this*.'

I motioned to a section of wall, where Eliza had painted our call to arms.

THEY CAN DETECT FOUR ORDERS NOW.
HOW LONG BEFORE THEY SEE US ALL?

WE NEED EVERYONE, OR EVERYONE LOSES.
NO SAFE PLACE. NO SURRENDER.

A black moth flew beneath it.

Warden emerged from the shadows and came to stand beside me, towering above them all. Spring-heel'd Jack let out a nervous snicker.

'Form a circle,' Warden said, 'and join hands.'

Spluttered protests and hoots of laughter followed this command.

'I'm not holding *her* hand,' somebody said, making Mary Bourne look wounded.

'By all means,' came the reply, 'stand beside a person whose hands offend you less.'

Maria took a box of candles from her pocket, while I clipped on my cannula and checked my can of oxygen. Painfully, like children cajoled into playing together, the Unnatural Assembly shambled into what could arguably be described as a circle. Some clasped hands with casual ease; others shuddered at the prospect of touching their neighbour. As Nick and Eliza came forward, Warden reached for my hand.

Our fingers interlocked. The worn leather of his glove pressed against my palm, soft between my knuckles and beside my inner wrist. Nick took my other hand, while Tom took Warden's, and the ring was closed.

The Unnatural Assembly stood in silence together, waiting for the æther to open around them.

I had never imagined that I would see this in my lifetime.

Warden murmured in Gloss. The candles grew brighter. One by one, spirits were drawn to the ring, where they basked in an unbroken chain of auras. Nick and Maria had taken salvia; both were swaying on their feet.

'Tom,' Warden said, 'the message. Hold it in your mind.'

Tom squinted at the graffiti, mouthing the words. Maria's head rolled forward, but she kept hold of the hands on either side of her.

'Now, Paige.'

I closed my eyes and jumped.

Warden had invited me into his dreamscape many times. By now, the path was familiar – weaving between the red velvet drapes, crossing the ashes to his sunlit zone, where I joined his dream-form and grasped its hand, echoing our position outside. Now that no one else could hear, I gave him a message.

'Meet me at midnight,' I said. 'On the lower deck.'

His dream-form nodded.

The golden cord vibrated with a force that was almost violent, pulled like a tightrope by our proximity in a single dreamscape. As we stood there, thin smoke rose in front of us, slowly twisting into pictures. And then I was inside a memory that wasn't mine.

He is searching for her in the forest, buried to his ankles in snow, holding up a lantern from the storehouse. This was Nick. I couldn't explain how I knew. I was seeing through his eyes, feeling as he must have felt, but still an observer. *Eight sets of footprints snake between the trees, veering away from the path. The sound of his heart fills his ears like a drum.*

A new memory. *The gun must have been heavy at first, but now it is as much a part of her arm as a muscle. She releases it only to ransack the other woman's pockets. Blood cascades down her chin and soaks the neckline of her shirt. Her hands never shake when she searches a corpse, but this one is different. This one is Roza.*

'Yoana!'

Her hands sift through wet tissue and fabric and bone, picking out two precious bullets, slick with blood. One she must save for herself, one for Hristo.

Survival first. Pain later.

'It's over,' Hristo says. 'All they need is a formal surrender. We'll go to the border, to Turkey—'

'You can try.' The district is ablaze around them. All she can hear is the rattle of gunfire. The English soldiers are almost upon them. 'I had my chance to leave,' she says. 'Sit with me, Hristo. Let's go to hell with a little dignity.'

She lights her last cigarette, her hands gloved in blood.

Hristo kneels in front of her. 'If you won't try,' he says, 'I must. My family—' He squeezes her wrists. 'I'll pray for you. Good luck, Yoana.'

She hardly notices him leave, knowing she will never see him again. Her gaze falls to the gun.

Back to Nick. I was rooted in place, unable to stop watching.

Now there are more footprints than eight people could make. He runs. A patrol has come through this part of the forest.

In the clearing, the tents have been torn down. A sign gives notice of their execution.

She is curled on her side by the ashes of their campfire. Håkan is nearby, prostrate, his coat drenched in rust. Their hands reach across snow. Between them, the bottle is undamaged, the bottle they must have bought in secret, the bottle of wine with a Danish label. He gathers her body into his arms and screams like a dying thing.

Warden released me, and the memory evaporated.

'Go, Paige.'

My spirit fled.

I woke gasping for air. Nick was on his knees, his hand crushing mine. I jumped again, tearing from my body, leaping into Tom. I launched myself into his sunlit zone, where his dream-form reached for mine. Contact between two spirits was deeply intimate, but there was no time for embarrassment. The moment we connected, I knew Warden had been right. The memories arced between us like lightning, travelling along the golden cord, allowing Tom to see them.

Now all we had to do was hold on.

As soon as I landed back in my body, Tom gritted his teeth and projected the memories. The vision hit the Unnatural Assembly, and all of them drew in their breath. Instead of the dream-like way in which Warden experienced memory, I saw them like pages in a flick book. The forest and the burning street smothered my vision.

'Hold the circle,' Warden commanded.

The memories repeated over and over, faster and faster, lifted away from us by the spirits, until all I could see was the moth and the message. It held for a while, long enough to be remembered.

At last, we all fell down.

Night and day didn't exist in the Beneath, but the séance had exhausted the Unnatural Assembly. The lights turned off, allowing them to sleep. I had already noticed the division in our ranks. Most of my supporters had clustered on the lower deck, while those who spoke against me were on the upper. All I could do was hope that Glym would be able to unite them.

I sat on the vacant bunk beside Eliza's, gazing into the blackness. The thought of leaving now, when I was just about holding on to their loyalty, was hard to stomach. Even harder to stomach was the knowledge that Nick, who was asleep or pretending to be, had spent the last few hours in his bunk, ignoring anyone who spoke to him.

His private memory had been used as fuel. As propaganda. His little sister's murder.

'You're going to give me to Styx.'

The voice was hoarse. Light flickered from the end of a torch.

'I overheard you talking to Wynn.' Ivy was sitting cross-legged on her bunk. 'I want to do it.'

Wynn had covered the wound on her cheek with a square dressing.

I didn't say anything.

'She doesn't want to see it, but you know I won't last long down here. Someone will cut my throat when I'm looking the wrong way. The only reason they haven't killed me already is because you've been here,' she said. 'So it has to be me. For all our sakes.'

I breathed in through my nose.

'If you stay with us,' I said, 'then you'll be killed. But if I send you, Wynn will betray us to Scion.'

'There is another way.'

The new voice had an Irish accent. Ivy aimed the torch. Róisín was awake, watching us from her bunk. Her lip had puffed up since the attack.

'I know the toshers. I used to talk to them through the fence,' she said. 'I like Styx, and I'm in better shape than Ivy. Send me.'

'Ro,' Ivy started.

'You're in no fit state to be crawling through tunnels. You'll give me to Styx,' she said to me, 'and Wynn will accept it without question, because I'll tell her I'm going of my own free will.'

'They won't let you. This is my responsibility. It was *my* crime.' Ivy's voice cracked. 'Besides, Paige needs to punish me, or someone else will.'

There was a pause before Róisín said slowly, 'They *will* see you punished. You'll be officially chosen, and then I'll offer to go in your stead. But, Ivy, the one person here that Wynn won't stand to lose again is you. She suffered enough the first time.'

Ivy buried her head in her arms. 'I don't know.'

'You need to decide by tomorrow,' I said. 'The Glym Lord will announce that he's stepping in as interim Underlord in my absence. He'll also need to announce who is being sent to Styx. I'll have him say that Ivy Jacob has been sentenced to a life in the Beneath for her crimes against the syndicate. Róisín, you'll come forward and insist that you take her punishment. And, Ivy, you will act as if seeing Róisín sent in your place is a far higher price to pay than going yourself.'

I had never heard myself sound so callous. Ivy stared at Róisín, then flung me a bitter look.

'I won't have to act,' she said, and turned over.

I dropped my gaze, clenched my jaw. Róisín watched the lump beneath the blanket for a while.

'She'll understand,' she said to me. 'Wynn, I mean. All she's ever wanted is for us vile augurs to be able to make our own choices. I've made mine.'

She laid her head back on the pillow. I rose from the bunk and walked into the darkness, holding my jacket around myself.

Relief warred against self-disgust. I had been ready to send Ivy. Barely a month of being Underqueen, and I was already becoming someone I didn't recognise. Someone who would punish a person who was already broken. Someone who would do anything to achieve her aims.

Only a tissue of morality now set me apart from Haymarket Hector.

Warden was waiting for me in a deserted sleeping area. I sat on the opposite bunk and set my torch down on the mattress.

'Pleione has made the necessary arrangements. You leave from Euston today, at half past six in the evening,' he said. 'The contact will meet you outside the oxygen bar on Judd Street.'

'Thank you.'

My fingers ran over the bandage on my hand.

'Lucida will be here by morning. She will ensure the Glym Lord is accepted as your interim, and that no further violence occurs.' Warden paused. 'I make the crossing to the Netherworld at dawn.'

I only nodded in response. The two bunks were so close that our knees almost touched.

Sweat coated my nape. I had practised these words all day, but couldn't let them out. I couldn't even look at him. I would only lose the will to do this.

'The other night, I made a mistake,' I said eventually. 'I should have called the Unnatural Assembly right away, to tell them about Senshield being able to detect the fourth order. So they could hear it from me first. So I could frame it to our advantage.'

My words were too clear in the silence of this place, a silence untouched by the din of the citadel.

'I could have got there before Weaver,' I continued. 'But I let myself be persuaded to wait until morning, because I wanted to see you. I wanted to be selfish, just for a few hours. Those hours put Weaver ahead of me.'

His gaze burned on my face.

'I'm Underqueen, and you're . . . a distraction I can't afford.' It took effort to keep going. 'I swore to myself that I would sacrifice everything if it meant I could take down Scion. If it meant that voyants could be free. We can't let the Mime Order fail, Warden, not after what we've been through to get here. We can't put it in jeopardy.'

'Say it.'

My face had been hidden behind my hair. Now I lifted it.

'You said change had a personal cost for all of us.' I looked him in the eye. 'You are what change will cost me.'

We sat there for a long time. I already wanted to take it back; with difficulty, I stopped myself. It seemed like a lifetime before he spoke again.

'You need not justify your choices.'

'I wouldn't choose it. Not if it wasn't necessary. If it were different—' I looked away. 'But it isn't.'

He didn't deny it.

Jaxon had been right about words. They could grant wings, or they could tear them away.

Words were useless now. No matter what I said, how hard I tried to articulate it in a way a Reph could understand, I would never be able to express what it would do to me when I surrendered him to the war we had started, or how much I had wanted our stolen hours to continue. I had thought those hours would be my candles, as our days grew darker. Points of light, of fleeting warmth.

'Perhaps this is for the best,' Warden said. 'You already dwell too deep in shadows.'

'I would have gone into the shadows for you,' I said. 'But I . . . can't allow myself to care about you this much, not when I'm Underqueen. I can't afford to feel the way I do when I'm with you. We can fight on the same side, but you can't be my secret. And I can't be yours.'

When Warden finally moved, I thought he was going to get up and leave without saying anything. Then, gently, his hands clasped mine.

If I ever touched him again, he would be wearing gloves. It would be in passing. By mistake.

'When I return,' he said, 'we will be allies. Nothing more. It will be . . . as if the Guildhall never was.'

It should have been a weight off my shoulders. My life was already too dangerous. Instead, I felt hollow, as if he had taken something from me that I had never known was there. Before I could stop myself, I embraced him, burying my face in his neck.

We sat with our arms around each other, holding too tightly and not tightly enough. Once we left this place, there would be no more talks beside the fire. No more nights spent in his company, when I could forget the war and suffering that loomed on the horizon. No more dances in derelict halls. No more music.

'Goodbye, little dreamer,' he said.

I almost voiced my answer. Instead, I pressed my forehead against his, and deep in his eyes, a flame was kindled. As his thumb grazed my jaw, I committed the way his hands felt on my skin to a hidden vault in my memory. I wasn't sure which of us brought our lips to the other's first.

It lasted far too long for a farewell. A moment. A choice. A mirror of the first time we had touched this way, behind the red drapes in the nest of the enemy – when danger had been everywhere, but a song had still been rising in us both. A song I wasn't sure that anything could silence.

Our lips parted. I breathed him in, one more time. I stood up, turned my back, and walked away.

PART TWO

ENGINE OF EMPIRE

10

MANCHESTER

3 December 2059

The train glided across the snowbound English countryside. Not that we could see any of it – the four of us were hidden in a small baggage compartment – but Alsafi's contact had given us a satellite tracker, allowing us to watch the progress of our journey.

The contact had smuggled us into Euston, straight on to a non-stop train to Manchester. Another ally would take us to a safe house. Alsafi had done well to build this small network of humans.

In the end, I had decided to take Eliza on the journey. She and Tom had long since fallen asleep, but Maria and I were alert.

'So,' Maria said, keeping her voice down, 'the plan, such as it stands, is to locate this person Danica thinks can help us—'

'Jonathan Cassidy,' I said.

'—locate the factory where the portable scanners are being produced, and find out how it's done. That's it?' she prompted. 'That's the plan?'

'Well, it's a start. If you want to dismantle something, you should know how it's put together. There must be a point at which an ordinary piece of machinery is converted to an active Senshield scanner.' I rubbed my raw eyes. 'Look, we don't have any other leads. We might unearth some information about Senshield's core, at least.'

'Let's hope so.' She peered at the tracker. 'And let's hope Danica got her facts straight this time, or we could find ourselves walking into another trap.' The light from the screen tinged her face with blue. 'There's some information in here about *enclaves*, but I don't understand it.'

I took it from her and tapped a tiny symbol of a house on the screen. ENCLAVE, the tracker read. LOOK FOR BLACK HELLEBORE.

'He's using the language of flowers,' I realised. 'Black hellebore points to the relief of anxiety. We might be able to find shelter and supplies where it grows.'

Alsafi must have been preparing for an emergency like this for a long time. Interesting that he spoke the language of flowers, the secret code the syndicate had used from the beginning. I had despised him in Oxford, but his work was turning out to be vital to our survival.

While Maria dozed, I occupied myself by studying the Republic of Scion Britain on the tracker. The territory covered the places that had once been called Scotland and Wales, which were no longer recognised as separate countries; *England* and *Britain* were used almost interchangeably by Scion. The island was divided into eight regions, each of which had one citadel, which acted as its regional capital – though all bowed to the will of London. The surrounding areas were peppered with towns, villages and conurbations, all under the yoke of Scion outposts. We were headed into the North West region, to its citadel – Manchester, centre of industry.

It had been ten years since I last left London. It had kept hold of me for so long.

I nodded off against the side of the compartment for a while, my hand still curled around the tracker. Everything that had happened over the last few days had left me hungry for sleep.

And I didn't want to think about Warden. I couldn't afford to overthink my decision, or to crack in front of the others. It was done.

The train came to a sudden halt, jolting me awake. Maria took the tracker from my unresisting hand. When she saw our location, she stiffened.

'We're still forty miles away.'

'*Denizens of Scion, we apologise for the delay in your journey to Manchester. This is Stoke-on-Trent.*' I pressed my ear to the wall, straining to hear the muffled voice. '*Under new regulations imposed by the Grand Commander, all Sciorail trains from London are now subject to regular inspections. Please accommodate the guards as they move through the train.*'

My heart pounded. Had Vance snared us again already?

Maria shook the others awake. We gathered our belongings and crept towards a sliding door, which would allow us to steal away without the guards seeing. I reached for a lever marked EMERGENCY DOOR RELEASE. As it pushed outward and glided aside, letting in an icy gust of wind, I glanced out of the compartment, searching for oncoming trains. Mercifully, there was no one on the other platform.

'Now,' I whispered.

The guards were getting close; I sensed them. Eliza turned and swung her legs on to a short ladder, which took her down to the ballast between the tracks.

Footsteps slapped along the platform, and I caught a snatch of voices. '. . . why Vance thinks they're going to be here.'

'Waste of time.'

I went next, followed by Tom. As Maria got out, she grabbed at the door for support, causing it to slide shut.

'As soon as they leave,' I breathed, 'we get back on.'

We edged a little farther down the track, shivering in the frigid air. When the guards entered the baggage compartment, we all pressed ourselves against the train and grew still, waiting for one of them to look out and see us. Finding nothing of interest, they soon retreated, muttering about paranoid krigs and pointless work. I motioned to Maria, who reached up to grasp the door – only to find that there was no handle. The only thing there was a finger-print scanner. We were shut out of the train.

Shit.

As the guards left the platform, a whistle sounded in the station. The train was moving. We didn't have long before we were exposed. I beckoned frantically to the others. Tom pulled Maria away from the door. We sprinted back the same way the train had come, into billows of snow, while our ride left Stoke-on-Trent without us.

We kept running, our boots crunching through ballast. Only when we were a fair distance from the station did we slow down to catch our breath. We helped each other over the fence, on to the street, and clustered beneath a bus shelter, heads bent to see the tracker. I brought up a map of our location, which offered up morsels of data about Stoke-on-Trent. *Status: conurbation. Region: Midlands. Nearest citadel: Scion Citadel of Birmingham.*

'We can't stay here for long,' I said. 'Outlying communities are too dangerous. They're much more observant than people in the citadels.'

Maria nodded. 'We'll have to walk.'

Eliza was already shivering. 'In this snow?'

'I walked across countries to get to Britain, sweet. We can make it. It wouldn't be the most insane thing we've done this week.' Maria peered over my shoulder at the tracker. 'It's almost fourteen hours on foot to the centre of Manchester. Probably a little longer, in this weather.'

'There's an enclave between here and there.' I tapped the tracker. 'Let's head there and ask for help. Maybe they can get in touch with whoever was meant to meet us in Manchester.'

'Good idea.' Maria patted Tom on the back. 'Can you make it that far?'

Tom had a slight limp from an old injury to his knee. 'There's no other choice,' he said, 'unless we mean to stay here and wait for the Vigiles to find us in the morning.'

I adjusted my winter hood so only my eyes were uncovered. 'Then let's stretch our legs.'

Although Stoke-on-Trent was quiet in the small hours, it put me on edge. Even a notorious fugitive could be anonymous in the capital of Scion, but not in settlements like these. It reminded me of Arthyen, the village where I had first met Nick. Its residents had been on a permanent quest to sniff out unnaturalness in their neighbours.

We stole through the streets, passing darkened shops, small transmission screens, and houses with the occasional lit window. Maria went ahead to scout for cameras. I only managed to relax a little when the streetlamps were far behind us and we were out in the countryside. It wasn't long before we crossed the regional boundary, which was marked by a billboard reading WELCOME TO THE NORTH WEST.

For a while, we risked the road, which had been gritted. We passed a derelict church and a lone oak. Tom found a sturdy branch to use as a staff. To distract myself from the blistering wind, I started counting stars. The sky was clearer here, and the stars burned far brighter than they did in London, where the blue haze of the streetlamps watered down their light. As I strung those broken necklaces of diamond together, trying to find the constellations, I wondered why the Rephs had taken the stars' names as their own.

I wondered why he had chosen *Arcturus.*

After a lorry gunned past us and blared its horn, we ducked under a barbed-wire fence into the fields, where snowdrifts were piled like whipped cream. More snow was falling, catching in my lashes. We had the tracker, but it was so disorienting, with the black sky above us and white as far as the eye could see below, that we finally risked switching on our torches. The world around us was drained of colour, flickering with snowflakes.

'I can't wait to advertise the Mime Order to the n-northerners,' Maria bit out through chattering teeth. '*Join Paige Mahoney for unexpected rambles through snow and shit.*'

I chased white powder from the tracker again. 'Nobody s-said the revolution would be glamorous.'

'Oh, I don't know. I like to think that in the great uprisings of history, they had beautiful d-dresses and decadence to go with the misery.'

Tom managed a chuckle.

'If my Scion History class on the French had it right,' I said, through numb lips, 'the dresses and decadence were p-part of what caused those uprisings.'

'Stop spoiling my fun.'

We passed a row of pylons, steel goliaths in the frozen sea. The power lines above us were so laden with ice that some of them almost touched the ground. I reached into my jacket, where I had stashed some of the precious heat packs Nick had given me, and handed them out to the others. When I cracked one, warmth filled my fingertips.

The conditions had one advantage: they stopped me thinking about anything but keeping warm. They stopped me thinking about Warden, and whether I had made the right choice. Thoughts like those would lead me down a darker path than the one I walked now. Instead, I envisioned a glorious bonfire and promised it would be waiting for me at the end of every field we crossed, over every wall and fence we encountered. Before long, my muscles were aching, I could no longer feel my toes, and I was so caked in snow that the black of my coat and trousers had been engulfed by white.

We followed a country lane for a while, heads bowed against the perishing wind. I trudged on, blinking snow from my lashes.

'I need a break soon.' Eliza could barely get the words out. 'Paige, are we close?'

'Almost there.' My winter hood muffled my voice. 'Keep going.'

The enclave turned out to be a thatched cottage at the edge of a tiny village called Dyrne. As we approached it, shining our torches, I made out the white flowers on its windowsills.

'There,' I said. It was the first time I had spoken in hours. 'Black hellebore.'

Maria squinted. 'Where?'

Eliza pulled down her scarf. 'You know black hellebore is white, don't you?'

'Of course. N-nothing makes sense.' Maria stomped ahead. 'These people had better have hot chocolate.'

Dyrne was silent at this time of night, only two windows lit. The few parked cars were buried under snow. I peeled off my gloves and blew on my fingers.

Something pricked at my sixth sense, stopping me in my tracks, as Eliza circled around to the front of the cottage. I had the sudden notion that I had been somewhere like this before, though I was certain I had never set foot in the North West. There were no spirits. Not one. A warning beat in the pit of my stomach: *stay away, stay away.*

That was when Eliza let out a scream. It jolted adrenalin through my veins, giving me the strength to draw my revolver and run over with Maria. We found Eliza beside a fence, one hand pressed over her mouth. The snow in front of her was marbled with blood.

We stood before the wreckage of a human being. The ribcage was torn open, and most of the left arm was missing, but the face remained intact.

Shock made my ears ring. The victims had been decapitated, dismembered, thrown and mauled. Their remains littered the village, covered by a shroud of snow. From the state of the bodies, they had been lying here for some time.

'What did this?' Maria muttered.

I turned my back on the slaughter. 'Buzzers.'

'Let's bury them.' Tom swallowed. 'Poor bastards.'

'We don't have time to *bury* them, Tom,' Eliza said, her voice cracking. 'It could come back.'

Tom traded a look with Maria, who was clutching her pistol. It wouldn't help. They might have learned a little about the Buzzers from *The Rephaite Revelation*, and now they knew what they did to flesh – but they had no idea what it was like to be in their presence. Eliza did.

My boots sank to the ankle as I followed my instinct to the edge of another field. When I found the source of my unrest, it took all my nerve not to run at once. I dug through the snow with gloved fingers, revealing a perfect circle of ice – too perfect to be naturally occurring.

This was where the monster had come through. The Ranthen knew how to close the doorways to the other side, but it was an art they had never shared with their human associates.

'We have to leave,' I said. 'Now.'

Even as I said it, a chilling scream echoed over the snowdrifts. A sound exactly like the cries that must have risen from this village when the creature came, a sound that grated along my spine and raised every hair on my nape. Eliza grabbed my arm.

'Is it close?'

'I can't sense it.' All that meant was that it was slightly more than a mile away. 'It will come back here, though, to its cold spot. Come on. Come *on*,' I barked at Maria, who seemed rooted in place.

So we pressed on through the fields, away from the village of the dead.

Nashira had told us that Oxford had protected the amaurotic population from the Buzzers. *Oxford served as a beacon, drawing the Emim away from the citadels*, Warden had told me later, confirming it. *Now it has been abandoned, London will tempt them next.*

London and elsewhere, it seemed. Perhaps the Buzzers were testing the waters, hunting near rural settlements before they attacked larger ones. Warden did believe they were intelligent, to some degree.

I had never wanted to believe that Nashira was right – that by rendering Oxford useless, I had put lives at risk. That Warden and I might be responsible for the deaths of everyone in Dyrne.

'Paige,' Maria said, 'can it possibly be a coincidence for the Buzzers to have attacked that village, of all places?'

'I've had worse luck in my life. I think this sort of thing is happening more than we realise,' I said. 'Scion must be covering it up.' I put my gloves back on, breathing out in a puff of fog. 'The next enclave is four hours away.'

'Then let's keep moving.'

An hour later, we were crossing yet another field, leaden with exhaustion. It felt as if splinters of glass were slashing me across the eyes. It was only fear of the Buzzer that kept us moving, but it stayed off my radar. It hadn't caught wind of us.

We heard the car coming from a long way off. The engine sounded like the death rattle of a rusty tractor, so it was unlikely to be Scion, but we couldn't take any chances. Wordlessly, we made for the hedgerow that ran alongside the road and hunkered down behind it. Minutes later, the glow of headlights dappled our faces.

The car pulled over. It was a small urban runaround, coated in soot. I told myself it was just turning – until the door opened, and a figure emerged.

'Paige Mahoney?'

I tensed.

'Hello?' A muttered curse. The stranger tramped across the road and peered over the hedgerow. 'Look, I can see your position on my tracker. If you don't come with me now, you'll be on your own out here.'

He spoke with a rolling accent I had occasionally heard at the black market. At first, I stayed put. Vance was laying traps for me, and I had no intention of running into her net again. But there was only one dreamscape – no Vigiles lying in wait, no paratroopers above. When I rose, a torch glared in my direction.

'Ah, good. Found you,' the voice said. 'Get in, quick. We don't want to run into a patrol.'

The word *patrol* got the others moving. I squeezed into the back of the car with Tom and Eliza while Maria swung herself into the front.

The bespectacled man who had rescued us was probably in his mid-twenties, with curling black hair and dark brown skin, smattered with freckles and small moles. A few days of stubble coated his jaw.

'Underqueen?' he said. I nodded. 'I'm Hari Maxwell. Welcome to the North West.'

'Paige,' I said. 'These are my commanders, Tom and Maria, and Muse, one of my mollishers.'

'Your what?'

I searched for a suitable alternative. 'Second-in-command. Deputy.'

'Ah, right. I can call you Paige, can I? You don't expect *Your Majesty*, or anything?'

Paige is fine,' I said.

I had thought this network was made up of amaurotics, but Hari was voyant. A cottabomancer, specifically – a rare and interesting type of seer, able to scry with bowls of wine.

'Sorry,' he said to Eliza. 'What was your name, again?'

Eliza was already heavy-eyed. It took her a moment to realise Hari was talking to her. 'Oh, me?' she said. 'Muse.'

'Doesn't sound like a real name.'

'I only tell my friends my real name.'

Hari grinned and turned the car, yanking the gearstick. The engine retorted with a coughing fit.

'Sorry to leave you stranded for so long. I got here as soon as I could, but it took me a while to get access to your location, once I realised you weren't on the train,' he said. 'What happened?'

'There was a spot check at Stoke-on-Trent,' I said. 'We had to get off.'

'How did you get all the way here, then?'

'On foot,' Maria said, 'hence the dejected-snowman look we're all modelling.'

Hari let out a breath. 'I'm dead impressed you walked all this way, 'specially in this weather. If you'd waited in Stoke, I would have come to pick you up.'

Eliza sighed. 'You mean we didn't need to walk for hours?''

'We didn't know that.' I peeled off my gloves. 'What have you been told, Hari?'

'Just to help you however I can. Circinus only contacted me yesterday.'

'Circinus?'

'The network.'

'You should know that one of its enclaves has been destroyed. We meant to ask for help in Dyrne, but everyone in the village was dead.'

'Dead,' Hari repeated. 'Did Scion get to them?'

'In a manner of speaking,' Maria said hoarsely.

'Right.' Hari let out a slow breath. 'I'll send a contact to Dyrne in the morning. Thanks for letting me know.'

I nodded. 'How did you get involved with Circinus?'

'A bloke from London approached me last year, asking if I wanted odd jobs. I'd just have to be willing to flout Inquisitorial law. No idea who runs the operation, and I don't get orders very often, but it pays well. We should be in Manchester by two,' he added. 'You all get some kip, if you want.'

He turned up the heating. Eliza leaned against Tom and closed her eyes, while the rest of us stayed awake.

The spot check had set us back by a few hours, and there was no time to lose on this mission. Sooner or later, Vance would begin to wonder why the scanners weren't detecting as many voyants as she had anticipated, and she would make it her mission to root them out.

'Hari,' I said quietly, 'does *SciPLO* mean anything to you?'

It was a while before he answered.

'Yeah,' he said, and cleared his throat. 'Means something to everyone here. Stands for Scion: Processing Line for Ordnance.'

'Ordnance,' Maria repeated. 'Weaponry?'

'Right. Anything that can kill you, SciPLO makes it. Guns, ammo, grenades, military vehicles – anything that isn't nuclear. Don't know where they handle that.'

This was promising. It fitted with what Danica had said. Senshield was a military project, after all.

'Okay,' I said. 'What about a Jonathan Cassidy, wanted for theft?'

'Doesn't mean anything to me,' Hari said, 'but I can do some digging for you. Anything else you want to know?'

'Are you aware of a link between SciPLO and Senshield?'

'No, but I've never worked for SciPLO, so I might not be the best person to ask.'

'Do you know anyone who does?'

'Not personally. Funny you should come here asking about it now, though,' he said. 'They've just introduced quotas in the SciPLO factories. The workers used to be able to sneak out the odd weapon and sell it in the Victoria Arches – our black market – but now the whole trade has dried up. I never wanted a gun myself, but a lot of the Scuttlers carry them, just in case they run into the Vigiles.'

Maria put her boots up on the dashboard. 'Scuttlers?'

'The local voyants.'

'I've heard of them,' I said. 'Do they have a leader?'

'Yeah. We don't have a big syndicate like yours. We just have the Scuttlers, and the Scuttling Queen.' He glanced at me with full-sighted eyes, taking in my red aura. 'By the way, was it you who sent those visions?'

So they *had* reached Manchester.

'Not me,' I said. 'Tom.'

Hari shook his head in awe, smiling. 'You must be the best oracle in Britain, mate.'

Tom chuckled. 'I had some help.'

For the rest of the journey, I questioned Hari about SciPLO. Fortunately, he was happy enough to talk. He told us that the arms industry had been based in Manchester for decades, with SciPLO manufacturing weapons for both the Vigiles and ScionIDE. It had always been secretive, but particularly so in the last year, when production had increased exponentially. Many employees were now forced to do eighteen-hour shifts, six days a week, and faced execution for attempted theft or industrial espionage – which included talking to their own families about their work.

Hari knew very little about what went on inside, but reassured me that somebody would be willing to share the information I needed. I had the distinct feeling that Hari was an optimist.

The fields soon gave way to the Scion Citadel of Manchester. High-rise apartment blocks filled the outskirts, stern and monolithic. As Hari drove farther in, a greyish smog appeared, choking the streets; you could hardly see the dim blue of the streetlamps through it. Jerry-built houses huddled in the shadow of gargantuan factories, which vomited dark smoke. An industrial chimney had fallen, crushing a small dwelling.

Every surface I could see was wallpapered with layer upon layer of soot. Most denizens wore a mask or respirator, as did the Vigiles, who had them built into their visors. That would work to our advantage.

'Hari,' I said, 'do you have Senshield scanners here?'

'Not yet. You have the prototypes in the capital, don't you?' Hari said. 'Are they as bad as they sound?'

'Worse. And they're not prototypes.' I glanced at him. 'You don't seem worried.'

'Ah, I doubt they'll bring them up north for a while. It's people in the capital that Scion cares about. Weaver wants them to feel safe.'

A humourless smile touched my lips. 'People don't feel safe up here?'

'Well, let's see how you feel. If you end up believing there's *no safer place* than Manchester.'

He stopped the car. Above us, I could just make out a rusted sign reading ESSEX STREET. The snow had been swept on to the pavement and trampled into slush.

When I opened the car door, the back of my throat burned. With my sleeve over my mouth, I followed Hari into a cookshop on the corner, the Red Rose, which promised traditional food from Lancashire. He led us through a dark interior, up a flight of stairs, and through an unmarked door, into the apartment above.

'Welcome to the safe house.' Hari drew several chains across the door. 'Don't go back outside without a respirator. I've got a few spare.'

He showed us to our rooms. While the others were placed on the second floor, with Maria and Eliza sharing the larger room, I was shown to the attic.

'And here's yours,' Hari said. The floor creaked underfoot. 'It's not much, but it's cosy. Bathroom's down the hall if you want a wash. I'll contact the Scuttling Queen for you.'

'No need for that.' I dropped my backpack on to the floor. 'We might want local help at some point, but we should start searching for—'

'You can't do anything here without being introduced to her.'

'What if I do?'

Hari blinked. 'You can't.' When I raised my eyebrows, he shook his head, looking uneasy. 'She needs to know what's going on. If she finds out the Underqueen of London is on her turf without her permission, there'll be trouble.'

I supposed I would expect the same, were our situations reversed. 'How quickly will she get back to you?'

'I'm not sure.'

'I can't wait long, Hari.'

'I wouldn't rush her, if I were you.' Seeing my expression, he sighed. 'I'll try my best.'

'Thank you.'

He closed the door. The attic had a small bed, an alarm clock, and a lamp. I left my outerwear to dry over the radiator and sat beside it, warming my fingers. Every joint in my body felt stiff and rusted.

We needed to be out searching for Jonathan Cassidy, or sizing up the factories, trying to locate the one that made scanners. Then again, there must be sighted Vigiles in Manchester. It was probably best to wait until sunrise.

I still hoped that the Scuttling Queen would answer Hari quickly. I had already grown too accustomed to power – to being able to walk where I chose without announcing myself. Here in Manchester, I had no such privilege.

Something made me focus on the golden cord. For the first time in months, I couldn't feel Warden. Usually I was aware of him in the same way I was aware of my own breathing, not noticing it unless something was wrong.

Eliza appeared with two mugs of tea, steering my thoughts away from him.

'Hi,' she said. 'Mind if I join you?'

'No, but don't you want to sleep?'

'I need a hot drink first.'

I patted the floor in invitation. We huddled up to the radiator, sipping the tea.

'Paige,' Eliza said, 'the village. Is that going to keep happening now?'

'Unless the Ranthen find a way to stop it. Or Scion opens their next prison city in Paris.' I blew on the tea. 'Until then, we're caught between being killed by monsters or ruled by tyrants.'

'Great.' She pressed her feet against the radiator. 'I was thinking about the séance the whole way here. You never told me you saw ScionIDE.'

'When I was six, in Dublin. I don't remember much of it.'

'I'm sorry.'

'I'd have shown you, but you heard Warden. I was too young for the memory to be useful.'

'I guess he knows what he's talking about. Jax never wrote that much about oneiromancy.'

It occurred to me that Jaxon might have learned about oneiromancy *from* Warden, by observing him. It wasn't mentioned in the first edition of *On the Merits of Unnaturalness*, but it had appeared in later ones. He must have done plenty of research on the new kinds of clairvoyance he encountered in Oxford. Never a man to waste an opportunity.

'Warden's . . . interesting, isn't he?'

I glanced at Eliza. 'That's one word for him.'

'You must have ended up getting quite close to him. Living with him for six months.'

'He's a Reph. There's only so close you can get.'

She was watching my face intently. When I didn't elaborate, she looked away.

'Paige,' she said, 'why did you choose Glym to be interim Underlord?'

'I thought he was the right person for it.'

'He's great, but . . . shouldn't it have been one of your mollishers supreme?'

The words sank in. I had broken with another syndicate tradition, and I hadn't even thought about it. Now I understood why Glym had been surprised. It must have seemed as if I didn't trust my own mollishers.

'I didn't mean to snub you.' I touched her shoulder. 'I thought Glym would be fair, but hard. It's what they need in the Beneath.'

'You don't know what my approach would have been. I started off in the pits of the syndicate,' she reminded me. 'I know how tough you have to be.' It was my turn to look away. 'It took all the nerve I had to leave Jax at the scrimmage. You know how much I owe him.'

'I do.'

'But you also made me realise that he was just like the dealers who used me when I was a kid. I saw that you wanted justice for everyone, not just those you deemed worthy. So I chose you.' Her eyes were full. 'Don't take that for granted, Paige. And please, don't underestimate me.'

She must have had to muster a lot of courage to say this. I shifted closer.

'Eliza,' I said, 'I'm sorry.' I released my breath. 'It's not that I didn't think you could do it. Maybe I just wanted to keep one of my best friends close.'

'As you should.' She nudged me. 'I know how much you have on your shoulders. I just want you to know that you can still trust me. With anything.'

I could see from her face that she needed me to understand this, to acknowledge it, but I did trust her. I always had. Maybe I had spent too much time around Rephs, forgotten how to show what I was feeling. Before I could say anything else, Hari appeared in the doorway.

'No one is more surprised than me,' he said, 'but the Scuttling Queen will see you today. Seems she might be willing to move at your pace, Underqueen.'

After the slog through the snow, everyone needed to warm up and sleep. I allowed it, safe in the knowledge that I had already made some progress. The Scuttling Queen would see me at three in the afternoon – later than I hoped, but earlier than I had expected. Until then, we could get some rest.

I tried, as I had tried for weeks. The chill had sunk too deep. Instead of sleeping, I slid into a restless doze, stirring every so often, shivering under the quilt. It was morning by the time I passed out, and when I woke, it was almost noon. Still exhausted, I forced myself out of bed and went to find a shower.

The bathroom was an icebox. I washed in a hurry, then dressed in grey trousers, a rib-knitted black jersey with a roll neck, and a body warmer. My hair was a lost cause, a knotted briar after hours in the wind, and I knew from experience that brushing it would cause mayhem. As I reached the bottom of the stairs, Hari elbowed his way through the door with a paper bag in hand.

'Ah, good.' He shut the door with his heel. 'Here's something to eat. You must be starving after that walk.'

I followed him into the kitchen, which was small and dim, like all the rooms.

'Sorry it's so cramped. I've had one guy in here for a month,' he said. 'He's wanted for painting a caricature of Weaver on the Guildhall.'

He snorted with laughter as he set down a few cartons. Inside mine was a pastry, a spoonful of mushy peas, and thick-cut chips, cooked in beef dripping. It was only when I smelled it that I realised I was famished.

'Got you some lunch,' he said. 'If you're hungry.'

'Thank you.' I sat down. 'How much was it?'

'You're all right. My treat,' he said. 'The network covers me for most expenses, anyway.'

'If you're sure.' I rubbed sleep from my eyes. 'Hari, what time do night Vigiles come on duty here?'

'About six, usually. I'll have you all back here by five.'

Hari sat opposite me. As we ate, I noticed the corner of a penny dreadful, poking out from under the Daily Descendant.

'*The Rephaite Revelation.*' I brought it across the table, tracing the illustration on the front. The story I had published to warn the syndicate about the Rephs and Buzzers, which the Rag and Bone Man had edited to glorify the Sargas. 'I didn't know it had made it up here.'

Hari gulped down his mouthful. 'The voyant publishers in Withy Grove got hold of a copy and printed their own. People loved it. Then they reviewed it in the *Querent,* and since then—'

'The what?'

He swept aside some unopened mail, showing me a saddle-stitched booklet with a coffee ring on the cover. 'It's a penny paper,' he said. 'Scion is trying to stop it spreading, but it keeps coming back.'

The headline was printed in the old blackletter script. SECOND VIGILE REVOLT ON THE HORIZON AFTER SHOCKING ORACULAR IMAGES FROM THE MIME ORDER, it blared. In smaller print: THE QUERENT SAYS NO TO KRIGS IN MANCHESTER! NO TO SENSHIELD IN OUR CITADEL!

'Vigile revolts,' I murmured.

'The first one was only small, to be honest. A handful of our night Vigiles turned on the factory overseers a few days ago. Didn't last long – they were all hanged,' Hari said, 'but there are rumblings of more to come.'

'Why?'

'They heard about the Senshield expansion in London and thought they were going to lose their jobs. They won't be needed if Senshield spreads. And if they aren't needed, well.'

He drew a line across his neck. I handed back the newsletter. Warden had been right; the Vigiles *were* ripe for revolution.

Regardless of how long such a tense alliance would last, we might be able to call upon them without fear of betrayal – especially if we told them that Senshield was about to become portable. That would be the death knell for their employment. And for them.

Tom came into the kitchen with Maria, who drew up a chair. Her hair was back in its usual pompadour style, and she had painted a ribbon of blue across each eyelid.

'Hari, do tell us,' she said. 'Who is this mysterious Scuttling Queen?'

'Aye. Last I heard, it was a Scuttling King.' Tom cracked open a carton. In the grey light of morning, he looked his age, his face gaunt and grey. 'Attard, wasn't it?'

'Yeah, Nerio Attard,' Hari said. 'His family have led the voyants of Manchester for a few generations. He tried to set up a Council of the North a while ago, to bring more of us voyants together, but Scion killed him a couple of years back, so it ended up not happening. Roberta, his daughter, took over as Scuttling Queen. She has a younger sister, Catrin – the muscle – but she was detained a few days ago.'

'For what?' I asked.

'She helped the Vigiles stage their uprising. Apparently she'll hang this week.'

'Right.' I paused, thinking. 'Do you think the Scuttling Queen would be open to cooperating with me, even if it's just by sharing information?'

'Maybe. I don't know her that well.' He eyed his watch before shovelling in a few more mouthfuls of food. 'We'll go to the Old Meadow now. Better to be early than late.'

I looked to Maria. 'Where's Eliza?'

'Still asleep, I think.'

She wouldn't want to miss this meeting. While the others got ready, I went up to the second floor and knocked. When there was no answer, I went in.

Eliza lay unconscious, her lips dark. I rushed to her side. Finding no ink or paints to hand, the muse had made her scratch a face into the wall with her nails, leaving her fingertips bloody. I checked her airways, as Nick had taught me, then cleaned up her hand and covered her with blankets.

The æther takes as often as it gives, people said in the syndicate. It was true. My nosebleeds and bouts of fatigue; Nick's migraines; Eliza's loss of control over her own body. We all paid a price for our connection to the spirit world.

'She all right?' Hari asked when I returned.

'An unsolicited possession. She'll be fine,' I said. 'Your wall, not so much.'

He frowned before handing me a respirator.

I saw the world through glass eyeholes. The mask was uncomfortable, but it would keep me anonymous. I laced my feet into snow boots and zipped myself into a hooded puffer jacket with a thick fleece lining.

There was no curfew in Manchester. We could go out after dark, though we had to stay alert for night Vigiles. Still, I was glad to be moving by day. I followed Hari from the cookshop at a distance, the others walking close behind me. When we reached a main road, we squeezed into an elevator labelled MONORAIL OF SCION MANCHESTER, which hoisted us up to a station platform.

It took less than a minute for a train to arrive. It must have been sleek once, but now it was worn and soiled, rattling on the track. I stepped over the gap and took a seat in the carriage. Maria sat beside me and picked up a copy of the *Descendant*.

The others removed their respirators. Taking advantage of the invisibility mine afforded, I took a good look at the people around us. Only a few of them wore everyday clothing. One was clad in the crisp red of those who worked in essential services, but he stood out; most were in black or grey boiler suits. Black was for skilled personnel, but I didn't know what grey signified. Only two of the passengers wore the white shirts and red ties that filled the Underground every morning in London. Hari nudged me and tapped the window.

'There.'

I turned to face the dirty glass behind us. At once, I realised what he meant.

A factory.

Its walls towered over the nearest dwellings, black and cold as the night sky, dwarfing the monorail. SCIPLO was painted vertically down one side of the building, with a white anchor beside it, each letter gargantuan. Its employees, whose grey uniforms almost blended with the smog, filed in and out through titanic gates. Each pressed their finger to a scanner before entering or leaving. There were at least ten armed Vigiles at the gates, another six patrolling the street outside, and I had no doubt there would be more within those walls.

'Terrible life they have in there.' Hari shook his head. 'The work fucks you up, if it doesn't kill you. They handle dangerous materials for long hours and not much money – plus, they get fined for the slightest thing. Most have to shave off their hair so it won't get caught in the machinery.'

Tom shook his head, his brow furrowed.

'They've started beatings since the quotas were introduced. If you don't meet your target, you'll know about it in the morning.' Hari nodded to where a squadron of Vigiles was escorting several workers. 'Even the kids don't escape it.'

I tensed. 'They have children working in there?'

'Kids are cheaper. And small enough to clean under the machines.'

Child labour. It wouldn't be tolerated in London, though enough children washed up on its streets and ended up working for kidsmen for scraps.

'Since you want to find out more about SciPLO, you could try and get one of its employees to talk – if the Scuttling Queen gives you permission to do your investigating, that is – but it won't be easy.' Hari pushed his glasses up his nose. 'Might be an idea to visit Ancoats. A lot of factory workers live in that district. Mostly Irish settlers.'

I watched the factory until it was out of sight.

We crossed a bridge over the River Irwell. Dead fish floated like balloons on the water.

After a while, the factories and foundries gave way to warehouses. Soon enough, we were stepping off the train and down a stairway to the street. As my boot hit a manhole, I thought again of the Mime Order, all of them relying on me. I needed to persuade Roberta Attard to let us conduct our investigations in peace. Didion Waite had once described me as an 'ill-mannered, jumped-up little tongue-pad' when I tried to charm him, which didn't seem to bode well for our meeting, but Attard and I were both leaders of our respective communities. That had to count for something.

In the shadow of the track, letters on an archway declared this district to be the Old Meadow. The meadow itself was little more than a scuff of grass, encircled by a wrought-iron fence. In the feeble glow of a streetlamp, a group of children kicked a ball to one another, watched by a greyhound. One of them whistled as we came closer.

'You here to see the lady?'

Hari pocketed his hands. 'Tell her I'm here, will you?'

She threw the ball and took off across the grass. 'Give us a fiver, Hari,' one of the boys wheedled. He was missing his front teeth and a chunk of fire-red hair. 'Just for some grub.'

Hari opened his wallet with a sigh 'You ought to be at the factory, you. You'll starve.'

'Ah, sod the factory. I've done enough scavenging.' The boy held out a hand. Half of his index finger was missing. 'Do us a favour, mate. I don't want to be crawling under those machines again.' When Hari threw a coin, he caught it with a grin. 'You're a good bloke, Hari.'

'Get that dog some grub, too. Where'd you even find him?'

'The McKays' house, where the chimney fell. He didn't have anywhere else to go.'

Tom shook his head. 'Poor weans,' he muttered. 'Just look at them.'

'Yeah,' Hari said sourly. 'Just look at how much of my hard-earned money I give them.'

'Are they all orphans?'

'Yep.'

I watched the scene through my respirator. In London, I had never seen a child with missing fingers. Dockland workers and syndies, but never children.

Soon enough, the girl was back. 'Come on, then,' she said to us. 'The lady will see you now.'

II

A TALE OF TWO SISTERS

4 December 2059

Our guide led us deeper into the Old Meadow. I had walked in the worst slums of London, but they were always hard to see.

This one was devoid of all but silent life. A lone man lolled on a step, staring at nothing, while two elderly women swept ash from the pavement. Tom's face grew tighter with every step.

'She's never in one place,' Hari told us. 'She has a few retreats, and you never know which one she'll choose.'

She was sane, then. That was a decent start.

We passed under a great plane tree, which had somehow endured the pollution for long enough to grow to a remarkable size. It still wore a few brown seed balls, but the flaking bark was blackening, losing its hard-fought battle with the air. In the next street, ramshackle houses were jammed together like teeth on a jaw. The girl pointed at a door with a tarnished keyhole. When Hari knocked, it was opened by a sensor. Yellow cloth covered his nose and mouth. We followed him into a tiny parlour, where a fire burned low, illuminating a woman.

Six feet tall and broad-shouldered, Roberta Attard, the Scuttling Queen, was a formidable presence. Her aura marked her as a capnomancer. Must be useful to have smoke as your numen in these conditions.

'Hello, Hari.' Her voice made me think of sawdust. 'And you must be the Underqueen.'

She sounded wary. When she turned to me, I saw that her skin was the sepia of shadows in old photographs, her lips mulberry red. Tight black curls erupted from beneath a cap, which was angled to allow her fringe to cover most of her left eye. At first glance, I would have said she was in her early thirties. I removed my respirator.

'And you must be the Scuttling Queen,' I said.

'Two queens of thieves in one citadel,' she said. 'Scion must be petrified.'

There was a moment of sizing each other up. Attard studied my face, lingering on my jaw. Her cheeks were a patchwork of thin scars.

'I thought you'd be alone,' she said. 'Who are your friends?'

'These are two of my high commanders, Tom the Rhymer and Ognena Maria.'

Tom took off his hat. 'I've heard a tale or two of your father, Scuttling Queen,' he said warmly. 'It's an honour.'

'Cheers,' she said.

There was nowhere for us to sit, so we all remained standing. Attard wore a blue neckerchief, white trousers, and several belts, each with a polished buckle and sheaths for her many knives. Her boots had wooden soles.

'I trust you understand why I wanted to see you,' she said. 'I had a feeling you'd be on the move after that . . . vision. Didn't realise you'd come all the way up to the North West, though.' She closed her eyes, as if the pictures were still unfolding in front of her. 'Let's cut to the chase, Underqueen. What do you aim to do in Manchester?'

'We're here to investigate Senshield,' I said. 'With the view to destroying it.'

Attard huffed a laugh. 'You're not serious.'

'I didn't travel two hundred miles to tell jokes.'

'You're still a fool.'

'We could use allies while we're here,' I said. 'I'd be grateful if you could ask your people to accommodate us as best they can, and to provide assistance if we need it.'

'If you mean to scare us into joining you, you're out of luck,' Attard said. 'From what I can tell, ScionIDE are in Britain for the sole purpose of snuffing out your movement. They'd only move into this region if they found any trace of that movement here. If *you* were spotted here. By helping you, we'd only be signing our own death warrants.'

'They've started in London,' I conceded, 'but Scion wants to eliminate all organised clairvoyance in Britain. If we're going to survive what comes next, the first thing we need to do is stop Senshield.'

'There is no *we*, Underqueen.'

'Oh, come on. You'll have it on your streets within a year,' Maria said. 'It detects four orders now. You and I are both augurs, Attard. We know the risk. Are you just going to wait for it to catch you?'

Attard stiffened. It was clear she wasn't accustomed to people speaking to her like this.

'There's no sign that they're going to build them here,' she said, her tone even. 'If they do, we plan to map their locations and avoid them. That's how my father always did it. Stay out of Scion's way.'

'And how did that go for him?'

'Maria,' I said quietly. Attard pursed her lips. 'Scuttling Queen, with all due respect, I'm not sure how you'll be able to stay clear of *portable* Senshield scanners. If you have a way, I'd like to hear it.'

'I don't know what you're on about,' Attard said. 'What portable scanners?'

'Scion is building a handheld version of Senshield in the SciPLO factories,' I said. 'That's why I'm here. I need to see them for myself, to work out how they're being powered. If we can locate and neutralise the core—'

'I've not heard of portable scanners being made in Manchester. Where's your evidence of this?'

'I have an insider in my employ.'

'Unless I see proof, I'm not buying it,' was the curt reply. I had the feeling she wouldn't accept a crumpled note from Danica as proof. 'Either way, my voyants aren't going anywhere near those factories. Nobody in this citadel would be stupid enough to try a break-in, not even with your visions filling their heads. These people already know fear, Underqueen. They live and breathe it every day.'

'The factory bosses,' Tom murmured.

Attard nodded. 'The overseers.'

'Who leads them?'

'Emlyn Price, the Minister for Industry. We call him the Ironmaster,' she said. 'He usually lives in London in his fancy townhouse, but he's been up here for a year now. Even brought his spouse and kids with him. They're in a gated community in Altrincham.'

'And the people working under him don't want to fight back?' Maria raised her eyebrows. 'They don't want to stop living in this hell?'

I had always liked Maria for her willingness to give anyone a tongue-lashing, but I could sense she was riling Attard.

'I wouldn't know,' Attard said, staring her down. Maria folded her arms. 'None of my Scuttlers work in the factories. That's exactly why my family created the network – so voyants could stay out of them. So they wouldn't get so desperate for money that they were forced into industrial labour. We steal our money. We earn it with our gifts.'

'I understand, Scuttling Queen,' Tom said gently. 'I used to work in a factory myself, in Glasgow. I ken what it's like.'

'It's worse than you remember.'

'I'm sure it is,' he said. 'But surely we should at least investigate what the Underqueen suspects. If it's true, it has implications for us all.'

'Maybe. I still can't let you do this.' She thumbed the buckle of one of her belts. 'You're not going to break into a factory, potentially bringing Vance down on us, on the off-chance that you'll be able to find out how Senshield works. I won't have my people die for a pipe dream.'

I sought her gaze. 'People like your sister?'

'Do not talk to me about my sister.'

Her voice now held a razor edge. I glanced towards Hari, who shook his head.

'Just so I understand,' I said, 'are you saying you won't allow us to stay?'

'Oh, you can stay, Underqueen. Stay as long as you like,' Attard said. 'Just don't try getting into one of those factories, or I'll send my Scuttlers after you. And you won't much like that.'

I tried to think of how someone else would handle this situation. Nick would ask her questions, try to get to the root of her reluctance to fight, but I didn't have time for that. Wynn would demand to know why she was refusing her duty of care to her people, but that would get her back up. Warden was both soft-spoken and forthright in a confrontation. Coupled with a pair of chilling eyes I didn't have, that tended to get people to listen to him.

In the end, I could only do things my way.

'If we don't act now, no voyant will be able to go outside without fear of arrest,' I said. 'Sooner or later, the Scuttlers will be forced into hiding.' I stepped forward. 'Help us. Let us do what we need to do here. Just one soldier, with *one* portable Senshield device, could devastate your community.' I was about to snap. 'My syndicate has been forced into lockdown. It will get worse, and soon, if we don't fight back now. We never thought it would happen to us. We ignored it for months, and now we're paying for it.'

Attard drew in a deep breath.

'You're a leader. It's your responsibility to protect the Scuttlers,' I said. 'Do you want to see them buried alive?'

'Don't you swan up here and question my ability to lead, Londoner.' She fixed a hard stare on me. 'I have the means to protect my voyants. If we don't get involved in this mess, Vance won't come.'

Maria sighed. 'Try to stop lying to yourself.'

'You're the one lying to yourself if you think provoking Vance is going to bring you peace.' She cast a scathing glance over Maria. 'You sound Bulgarian. How did rebelling turn out for you?'

Maria shut her mouth, but the look she gave Attard was murderous.

Attard turned back to the fire, her jaw tight. Everything we knew was changing, washing away the safety of tradition, and her solution was to stand and wait for it to pass. She would be waiting a long time.

'Cause any trouble, and you'll live to regret it,' she said, a soft note of finality in her voice. 'I have more support than you know, Underqueen.'

'Then I guess we're done here.' I inclined my head. 'Good luck. Truly.'

Roberta Attard said nothing as we left.

'She's just like Hector,' I fumed to the others, once we were back on the monorail. 'Does she really think the trouble's going to stay in London?'

'There were hundreds like her in Bulgaria,' Maria said. 'Even after Scion took Cyprus, they denied the warning signs.' She blew cigarette smoke out of the window. 'Some people believe that if they keep their heads down and stick to their safe routine and trust that nothing bad will befall them, then it won't. They see things happening to others, but they think they're different; they're special; it could never happen to them. They believe that nothing can get better, but also that nothing can get worse. They're cowards, in one way, because they won't fight, but they're also brave, because they're willing to accept their lot in life. *Glupava smelost*, we called it. Foolish courage.'

My boot tapped out a furious rhythm. Part of me didn't blame Attard for wanting to avoid Vance, but it didn't help the Mime Order.

'Hari,' I said, 'there must be someone else who can help us get into a SciPLO factory.'

'She's right about the security, you know,' Hari warned. 'You'd be mad to try and get into one of those places.'

'Would you help me if I kept trying?'

Hari sank deeper into his jacket. 'As a voyant of Manchester, it's generally safest if I obey the Scuttling Queen,' he said, 'but I'm not a Scuttler. She just gives me the odd bit of money to help me run the safe house.'

'Is that a *yes*, then?'

He considered for a minute. 'Circinus paid me to help you however I could,' he concluded. 'I guess what she doesn't know won't hurt her.'

Maria patted his shoulder. 'Good man.'

The Red Rose was full to bursting by the time we got back to Essex Street. The place had a homely smell of gravy and nutmeg and coffee, tinged with the pervasive reek of smoke, which clung to the patrons' clothes. A whisperer with braided hair was serving the food, calling out orders in a musical voice. Sensing her aura stiffened my resolve. If she were in London, she would be at risk of detection.

We found a peaky Eliza in the safe house. 'Hello,' she croaked. 'Did you see the Scuttling Queen?'

'Yes,' I said. 'She won't help us.'

'Shit.'

Tom hung up his hat. Without another word, I went up to the attic and sat on the windowsill.

Sallow grey mist swirled past the glass. I stared into it, allowing my mind to wander.

When you dream of change, it shines bright, like fire, and burns away all the rot that came before it. It's swift and inexorable. You cry for justice, and justice is done. The world stands with you in your fight. But if there was one thing I had learned in these last few weeks, it was that change had never been that simple. That kind of revolution existed only in daydreams.

Someone knocked on the door. Tom the Rhymer's grizzled head appeared a moment later.

'Everything all right, Underqueen?'

'I'm fine,' I said.

'Don't blame yourself, lass.' He stepped inside, his weight listing on to his good leg. 'Hari has some business at a local place, which the criminals of Manchester apparently frequent. I thought we could go along with him and try asking after this Jonathan Cassidy.'

'Sounds good.' I got up. 'Are *you* all right, Tom?'

'Still a wee bit tired after the long walk, and that séance.' He hesitated. 'I still don't understand how it was possible. I felt— Well, forgive me, Underqueen, but I felt like there was more to it than Warden was telling us.'

I sighed. 'Tom, if there's one thing I can tell you about Rephs, it's that there's always more to it than they see fit to tell you.'

Hari's den of criminals turned out to be a supper room called Quincey's. It was a slender building on a street corner, with a dirty terracotta façade and windows that fluttered with candlelight. It was nearly dawn, but if the silhouettes were anything to go by, the place was packed. A gaunt costermonger was selling bread rolls and soup from a cart nearby.

Inside, the walls were dark and tiled, and an amaurotic was playing 'The Lost Chord' – a blacklisted song I'd always loved – on a piano. Each note strained to be heard above the chatter. Somebody threw a handful of nails at the performer (tough crowd), but he sang on regardless.

It was warm enough to make the windows sweat. Hari took us up a floor, shepherded us into a booth, and held out a wad of cash.

'Courtesy of the Scuttling Queen,' he said. 'A token of her gratitude for your . . . cooperation.' I was about to decline, but Maria snatched it. 'I've got to speak to one of my suppliers. Keep your heads down.'

The others unmasked, but I kept my respirator on. I wasn't fool enough to bare my face here.

'I'm starving,' Maria said. 'I'll get us something to eat.'

'If you can, ask around about Cassidy,' I said. 'Just be subtle about it.'

'As if I'm ever anything but.'

She elbowed her way to the bar while I sat with Eliza and Tom, observing our surroundings. A transmission screen was showing a local game of ice croquet, the national sport of the Republic of Scion England. Jaxon had never let us follow it in the den ('utter frivolity'), but Nadine would often watch matches at Oxidate. It was an amaurotic obsession in London, but many of those watching here were voyant. When the Manchester Anchors scored a point, half the spectators groaned, while the others shouted in triumph and pounded each other on the back.

'Paige,' Maria said, when she returned (I could barely hear her over the commotion), 'I spoke to the bartender. Jonathan Cassidy was known for selling weapons on the black market. SciPLO eventually caught him red-handed. He escaped on the way to the gallows and is rumoured to be in hiding, but no one knows where.'

'Naturally,' I said. 'Any useful information about him?'

'He's bald, amaurotic, and always wore a rag over his face. That's all,' she said. 'Helpful, I know.' She squeezed into the booth next to Eliza. 'I asked about the SciPLO factories. Apparently there are seventeen of them, all focused on munitions. And there's no reason Scion should have spent the last year mass-producing munitions . . . unless they're planning another incursion.'

'Or they're trying to arm all their soldiers with the scanners,' I pointed out.

'I highly doubt they would need *seventeen* factories to do that. Either way, we should stay here and take them out.'

'The factories?' Tom said, squinting at her. 'All seventeen?'

'Yes.'

'Right,' I said, deadpan. 'And how do we do that?'

Maria flicked on her lighter. 'I'm a pyromancer, Paige.' She beckoned a spirit, and it carried the flame to the end of her cigarette. 'I promise you, I can manage a little arson.'

Eliza pushed down her hand. 'Maria, there are *rotties* in here. What are you doing?'

'Nobody cares, sweet. Look.'

She nodded to a nearby table, where a seer was sitting with a crystal ball. GENUINE UNNATURAL, a sign proclaimed. OUTCOMES OF ALL CROQUET GAMES REVEALED. The unnatural in question was surrounded by eager amaurotics, none of whom appeared to be reporting her.

We stopped talking while a waitron laid out our food, along with chipped mugs of hot chocolate. 'What I'm saying,' Maria continued, once he was gone, 'is that if we can't get into the factories—'

'We're not burning anything down,' I said. 'If we destroy the factories, we destroy any clues that could lead us to the core.'

'Do you have any better ideas?'

I surveyed the room again. 'We have to find Jonathan Cassidy. Dani wouldn't have given me his name if she didn't think he could help.'

'We could also contact Catrin Attard,' Maria said.

Eliza tilted her head, and I explained: 'Roberta's sister, condemned to hang. If she helped the Vigiles revolt, she's clearly willing to resist Scion.'

'I doubt the Scuttling Queen would like that, Underqueen.' Tom glanced over his shoulder. 'We shouldn't disrespect her wishes on her turf.'

'We can't quibble over turf any more, Tom.'

'She could drive us out if she finds out we're poking around. Besides, by all accounts, Catrin is under lock and key.'

I rubbed my temple. If we were going to infiltrate SciPLO without dying in the attempt, it would have to be carefully planned.

'I have an idea about where we can find Cassidy,' I said. 'It's a long shot, though.'

'This whole revolution is a long shot,' Maria reminded me. 'Is it the Victoria Arches?'

'No, though we can look there, too.' I paused. 'Hari mentioned a district called Ancoats. Apparently a lot of Irish workers live there.'

Eliza frowned. 'So?'

'Cassidy is the anglicised form of an Irish surname.'

Her expression cleared. 'Like yours.'

'Yes. If he's hiding in Ancoats, the people there might reveal his location to one of their own.'

'Good thinking,' Maria said. 'Shall I search the Arches?'

'If you can.' I sipped my drink. 'Tom, while we're gone, I want you to chat to some factory workers. Eliza, you find out if Catrin Attard is still alive, and if so, where she's being held. And whatever you do, make sure Roberta and the Scuttlers don't catch you.'

Between all these lines of investigation, we had to find something that could nudge us a little closer to unlocking the secret of Senshield. If not, and I returned to London empty-handed, I doubted I would be Underqueen for long.

12

FORTRESS

I allowed myself to be coaxed back to the Red Rose for the night. I would have liked to go straight to Ancoats, but Tom warned me not to go out after dark, and Eliza backed him up. We could avoid sighted Vigiles in London, but none of us knew Manchester.

I soon regretted my decision. At six in the morning, a local voyant called Hari, warning him that a random inspection was being carried out on the nearest factory. That meant Vigiles. Even if these ones couldn't see our auras, they would be more hostile and observant than usual. Hari refused to let us out until they had left the district.

I paced around the attic as the morning wore on, consumed by frustration. The clock became a source of mockery. Every second was another second the Mime Order was trapped, and so far, our mission had gone nowhere. I couldn't imagine how Nick and Glym were holding up.

At noon, I lost patience and went to find Hari, knocking on the door to his room. 'Hang on a mo,' he called, but I was already through.

'Hari, we really have to—'

I trailed off.

Hari was sitting up in bed. Beside him was a dishevelled Eliza, naked as the day she was born. When she saw me, she made a hasty grab for the sheets, her cheeks burning as red as my aura. I raised my eyebrows.

'Underqueen.' Hari fumbled for his glasses. 'Sorry. Is everything all right?'

'Fantastic. If you're . . . finished,' I said, 'would you mind checking to see if we can leave?'

'Yeah, course.'

I retreated sharpish. Eliza let out a mangled groan that sounded like *never live this down*.

I should have learned not to barge through closed doors. That habit had landed me in hot water plenty of times while I was collecting money for Jaxon. I envisioned him smoking a cigar in the Archon, chuckling as the army brought London back to heel.

In the kitchen, I piled on layers of warm clothing while I waited for the others to emerge. Hari finally strode in, wearing a fresh shirt and a sheepish expression.

'The inspection just ended,' he said. 'You can go now, if you like.'

'Good.' I fastened my jacket. 'We should be back in a few hours.'

'I'll be working. Just come to the counter and I'll give you the key.'

Maria and Eliza joined me in the hallway, and we left for the monorail station together, walking through a drizzle. While we waited for our respective trains, Eliza kept shooting me sidelong glances. As soon as Maria was gone, she faced me, looking rueful.

'Sorry, Paige.'

'You don't need to apologise,' I said. 'I'm not the sex patrol.'

'No, but I shouldn't get distracted.'

'I don't remember anyone distracting you before the scrimmage. You still managed to do your work for Jaxon well enough.'

'True.' She cracked a smile. 'Don't do anything reckless out there. You have a bad habit of not coming back when you get on a train.'

'When do I *ever* do anything reckless?'

She gave me a sceptical look. I stepped on to my train before she could answer.

The sky must never be blue above Manchester. I watched the citadel through the window, taking in the flickers of activity beneath the monorail track. When the train rounded a corner and jounced past another SciPLO factory, I leaned forward until my breath misted the glass. A small group of workers were gesturing at the Vigiles beyond the gate.

This place was on a knife-edge.

As the train pulled away again, my thoughts inevitably drifted towards Warden. I still hadn't felt so much as a slight tug from the cord. I must not be able to sense him while he was in the Netherworld.

The Ranthen would be searching for Adhara Sarin, to persuade her that I was capable of leading the Mime Order against the Sargas. Perhaps they had already found her. But when she asked for evidence of my skill as a leader, Warden would have nothing to give her. Not yet. He believed in me so utterly, and I had given him so little in return.

Thinking of him made a sharp pain flare in my chest. The silence on his side of the cord was unsettling, as if I had lost one of my senses.

Ancoats slumped in the shadow of the largest SciPLO factory in Manchester. I descended from the monorail and trekked through the snow, my head stooped against the wind, grateful for the protection of the respirator. As I wandered past the cramped dwellings – all infested with dry rot, small enough that I could have reached up and touched their roofs – I passed a scrawl of orange writing on the stonework: MAITH DÚINN, A ÉIRE. Seeing the Irish language in Scion jarred me, then filled me to the brim with home-sickness for the place I hadn't seen since I was eight.

The people here moved like sleepwalkers. Most wore factory uniforms and blank expressions. Others sat in doorways, wrapped in filthy blankets. A young woman was among them, arms wound around two small boys, cheeks blotched with tearstains.

I asked for Jonathan Cassidy in the local shops. I was met with averted eyes and denials. As soon as I had left the last shop – a haberdashery – a sign reading CLOSED appeared in its window.

I had been a mollisher for long enough to know when people were hiding something. It was tempting to take off my respirator and prove I wasn't a bounty hunter, but there was no guarantee that I would be safe here.

My search finally brought me to a cookshop, perched on the corner of Blossom Street. Its door had no window or handle. Shrivelled paint named it *Teach na gCladhairí* – House of Cowards, in English. Strange name for a cookshop. A yellow-bellied eel twisted on its sign.

A wilted bouquet of must and cigarettes awaited me inside. Paintings of stormy landscapes cluttered the walls, which were covered by peeling floral paper. I drew my hood down and sat at a round table in a corner. A bony, sour-faced amaurotic barked at me from the bar.

'You want something?'

'Just a black coffee,' I said. 'Thanks.'

She stormed off. I replaced my respirator with my scarf. Within a minute, the waitron had banged down a cup in front of me, along with a dish of soda bread. The coffee looked and smelled like vinegar.

'There you go, now.'

'Thank you.' I lowered my voice. 'I wonder if you could help me. Do you have a patron by the name of Jonathan Cassidy?'

She gave me a dirty look and stalked back to the bar. Next time I should show my wallet.

There were several patrons nearby, all sitting on their own at small tables. For appearances' sake, I picked up the greasy menu and scanned it.

'You should try the stew.'

I glanced at the amaurotic who had spoken. He had come in after me, and had just been served. 'Sorry?'

'The stew.'

I eyed it. 'Is it good?'

'It's grand.'

It was tempting, but I couldn't linger. 'Not sure I trust the cook, to be honest,' I said. 'The coffee smells like it should be on chips.'

The man chuckled. Most of his face was obscured by a peaked hat. 'You from Dublin?'

'Tipperary.'

'That's quite an accent you've got. You must have left a long time ago.'

'Eleven years.' I could hear my lilt thickening as I spoke. 'Where are you from?'

'Galway. Been here two years.'

'And I suppose you don't know anyone called Jonathan Cassidy, either.'

'I do. In fact,' he said, 'I've heard he's in this very place.'

I looked away, then back at him, realising.

'Glaisne Ó Casaide,' he said. 'I shed my first name when I came here, but I couldn't bring myself to cut all ties. I'm sure you know the feeling, Paige Mahoney.'

I sat very still, as if even the slightest flinch could make him reveal my identity to the rest of the district. This man might be a fugitive, but there wasn't always honour among thieves.

'Very good,' I said, keeping my composure. 'How did you guess?'

'A woman from Tipperary, covering most of her face, seeking out someone wanted by Scion. Doesn't take a genius. But I won't tell.' He turned to look out of the window. 'We all have our secrets, don't we?'

When I saw the other side of his face, I only just kept my expression in check. The cheek around his jaw had rotted away, showing blackened gums and absent teeth.

'Phossy jaw. You get it working with white phosphorus,' he said. 'Can't go to a hospital. One of the many downsides of not having the correct Scion settlement paperwork, along with the poor wages. And they wonder why I started a little business on the side.'

As he spoke, more of the inside of his mouth showed. I glimpsed the pink flesh of his tongue.

'I heard a young woman was asking about me. Supposed you must have good reason,' he said. 'When the haberdasher pointed you out, I followed you in here. So, what do you want?'

This was my chance. With a quick glance around the room, I joined him at his table.

'I know you worked for SciPLO. I was told that portable Senshield scanners are being made in one of those factories,' I said under my breath. 'Is it true?'

It was a long time before he gave me a nod.

'Establishment B. That's where they do all work related to Senshield in Manchester, as far as we can tell,' he said. 'Unfortunately, you won't get an eye-witness account, if that's what you're after. When you're assigned to that place, it's a life sentence. The labourers eat, sleep and die behind its walls.'

'They *never* come out?'

'Not since a year ago. They're usually conscripted from other factories without warning.' He spooned a little stew into his mouth. 'No one goes in or out. Even the venerable Emlyn Price rarely emerges, though I've no doubt he's free to come and go. He's based there.'

The Minister for Industry himself. Now we were on to something. This reeked of military secrecy.

'If nobody comes out,' I said, 'how do you know that's where they handle Senshield?'

'Why else would a factory be turned into a fortress?'

I had no answer. 'Have you ever heard anything about how Senshield works?'

'If I had that information, I would already have sold it. Thanks to Price, that secret is locked inside Establishment B. Even the Scuttlers don't know exactly what goes on in there, and they know most things that occur in Manchester.'

'You're amaurotic. How do you know about the Scuttlers?'

'Can't avoid them. Roberta doesn't trouble us, but she won't help us, either. She minds her own. Her sister, on the other hand—'

Disgust oozed into every crease of his face.

'I take it you're not fond of Catrin,' I said.

'No. She's a nasty piece of work.' He used the bread to mop up the last of his stew. 'Nerio didn't choose her to be his successor, so she finds other ways to feel powerful. If I had a penny for every time she's come to Ancoats, demanding money for *protection* from the very same thugs she employs to torment us, I'd be a wealthy man.'

'Does she do this in every district?'

I schooled my expression as I spoke. Catrin was racketeering. A long-established practice in the syndicate I ruled.

'Likely,' Ó Casaide said, 'but she had a long rivalry with a Scuttler from Dublin. She won the final confrontation, but he got in a good swing before she stabbed him in the gut. Scuttlers use their belts to fight, you know. Since then, she's punished us for the Irishman who scarred her face.' His brow darkened. 'She'll be hanged at Spinningfields tomorrow, and good riddance.'

Catrin sounded like trouble. Hector would probably have loved her.

It disturbed me that I wasn't ruling her out as an ally.

The waitron thundered past with a bowl of gruel. 'I saw some workhands protesting outside one of the factories,' I said. 'Do you know who leads them? Are there any key players here but the Attards?'

'Those are just random outbreaks. They've been happening more and more since Price introduced the quotas.'

'Price sounds like the root of the misery here.'

'He's a bastard. Things were bad before him, but not this bad.'

Emlyn Price had come to Manchester a year ago, which coincided with both the increased production of munitions *and* the acceleration of Senshield. With that level of responsibility, he must report to Vance.

'Thank you,' I said. 'You've been very helpful.'

I had got what I had come for. I started to rise, ready to return to the others and tell them that Establishment B was our target, when I found myself sinking back into my chair.

'You left Ireland two years ago.' I kept my voice low. 'What has Scion done there since I left?'

Ó Casaide pulled the peak of his cap slightly lower. 'You got out a long time ago. I'm thinking you remember it as it used to be. The Emerald Isle.' He barked out a laugh. 'What a load of shite.'

'I saw the start of the Molly Riots. I was in Dublin.'

He was silent for some time.

'You left around 2048, I take it,' he finally said. I nodded. 'Just in time. After they hanged the riots' leaders, the other rebels went to one of four massive labour camps, one in each of the provinces of Ireland. Then they were joined by anyone with a strong back – anyone who wasn't necessary to keep the country running in other ways. I was in the Connacht camp for three years, cutting down trees for nothing but bread.'

The words were going in, but I couldn't make sense of them. I had known that most of the country was under Scion rule, but not this. Never this.

'Took me far too long to escape. I reached the coast and stowed on board a ship carrying lumber to Liverpool. Then I made a living for myself here,' he said. 'For a time.'

He kept eating. The room was tilting on its head. They were using forced labour in Ireland, my homeland, to fuel the engine of empire.

'I don't understand,' I managed. 'On ScionEye, they've always talked about the Pale. I thought—'

'You thought that was the only area Scion had full control over. It's a lie they tell their denizens, so they can convince everyone that we brogues are violent. There is no Pale. Scion controls Ireland.'

The next question was one I shouldn't ask. I shouldn't taint my memories. I should keep my childhood in a glass box, where nothing could stain it.

'Did you—' I stopped, then: 'Did you ever hear of Feirm na mBeach Meala?'

'I didn't.'

'It was a family dairy farm in Tipperary,' I said, already knowing that he would shake his head. 'The owners' names were Éamonn Ó Mathúna and Gráinne Uí Mhathúna.'

'They would have lost it,' came the clipped reply. 'All livestock was requisitioned. Scion prefers factory farms.'

My grandfather had always been opposed to factory farming. His animals had been treated gently. *Quality over quantity*, he would say as he bottled milk. *Rush the cow, spoil the cream*. That farm had been their life.

'Thank you,' I said. 'For telling me.'

'Not a bother.' The man patted my hand. 'I wish you luck with what you're trying to do, Paige Ní Mhathúna, but it's best you don't think about Ireland any more. There's a reason this cookshop is called by the name it is.' He turned away. 'All of us left loved ones in the shadow.'

Manchester rushed past the window, a mural of grey shapes against the sky. I sat alone on the monorail, listening to the sound of my own breathing through the respirator.

The birthplace of my memory was gone. I should have known that Scion would have no mercy on Ireland. I pictured soldiers marching through the Glen of Aherlow, setting fire to everything they touched.

The wind scourged my face as I got off the train. My ribs felt broken, as if they could no longer hold my shape. I had left, and my grandparents had stayed. Even if they weren't dead, losing the farm would have killed them inside. I forced myself not to think of them dying in a camp, or trying desperately to live off the land.

I would become stone. For the people here, for my grandparents, for myself. I would shatter Scion, as they had shattered the country I loved, even if it took me every day of the rest of my life.

And I *would* begin here. No matter the cost.

Darkness had almost fallen again by the time I got back to Essex Street. The Red Rose was stifling and crammed with people, most of whom were engrossed in another game of ice croquet, sporting waistcoats stamped with MANCHESTER ANCHORS or MANCHESTER CONQUERORS. Seeing me, Hari beckoned me to the counter. I accepted a mug of tea, along with the key to the safe house, and trudged up the stairs, leaving flecks of snow in my wake.

Tom was waiting for me. 'Any luck, Underqueen?'

'Yes.' I took off my respirator. 'We need to get into SciPLO Establishment B.'

I relayed to him what I had learned. He stroked his beard, eyes narrowing.

'They're going to great lengths to keep what happens in there a secret,' he said. 'Why?'

'A *portable* Senshield has to be kept under wraps. If the night Vigiles knew for sure that they were about to become obsolete, Scion would be dealing with more than a few small revolts. Vance clearly wants to arm all the soldiers with the scanners, then axe the NVD.'

'Maybe you're right. Well, nice work,' he said. 'I didna have any luck on my end. I dressed like a beggar and waited outside Establishment D. I couldna get many of the workhands to talk, but those that did said nothing unusual happened in there. The Vigiles drove me off after a while, so I went to Establishment A. Same result.'

'That's because there's nothing to know,' I said, 'unless you work in Establishment B.'

He smiled grimly. 'And nobody comes out of there to tell the tale.'

Maria and Eliza returned as he spoke. The former had searched the Victoria Arches, finding only numa and blacklisted records, while the latter had visited Withy Grove, where the *Querent* was based. While the penny paper was sympathetic to our cause, they had the same ethos as Grub Street – revolution only through words – and could offer no useful information about Catrin. I updated them on what I had learned, then told them to get warm and have something to eat. I needed space to think.

In the attic, I sat alone and marked two locations on a map. The first was that of SciPLO Establishment B, which was in the adjacent section of the citadel. The second was that of Spinningfields Prison.

For a long time, I sat in the dark, considering my options.

Leaving aside the botched raid on the warehouse, this would be our very first heist. There was information in that factory, and I meant to steal it.

First, I needed to get inside. I was a dreamwalker, capable of moving through walls and locked doors, but my weakness – my need for oxygen – put me on a time limit. Even after training with Warden and practising by myself, I still couldn't stay in a host body for long.

I would have to go to the factory in person. To do that, I would need local help, but the Scuttlers – the dominant gang – were off the table.

Catrin Attard was eager to oppose Scion, if her short-lived union with the Vigiles was anything to go by. As a member of the Attard family, she would likely have the support and resources to get me into SciPLO Establishment B. There were a lot of good reasons to approach her, but she was about to get acquainted with the end of a rope.

Catrin and Roberta Attard. These sisters were like two halves of Hector – one with his bloodlust, the other with his unwillingness to change.

Terebell would want me to do whatever it took to find and deactivate Senshield. Something in that factory would lead us there. I felt it.

I got up and paced the room. As I passed the window, a flash of bright purple caught my attention. A Scuttler was on the other side of the street, watching the safe house. Her neckerchief was vivid even in the smog.

Roberta. She had sent her people to keep an eye on me, and she didn't care if I knew it.

A burst of resolve had me tipping the contents of my backpack on to the floor, searching out my oxygen mask. Despite the injury it had suffered during the scrimmage, my gift had sharpened over the past few months. I might be stronger than I thought. There was one way to find out.

I had learned a hard lesson at the warehouse, going in without any evidence but what Danica had overheard. This time, I would make certain that we weren't walking into a trap.

I knew the physical location of Establishment B, but it took a while to find it in the æther. When I was sure I had the right place – crammed with dreamscapes, their defences thinned by fatigue – I took hold of the first person I encountered.

A warren of machinery surrounded me. Everything was washed in the glow of a furnace. The smell was atrocious: a hot, iron stench, as strong as if the walls were bleeding. And the *noise*. A deafening cacophony vibrated through my teeth. I was a morsel in the mouth of hell.

My host was soaked in sweat, standing in front of some kind of production line. Nearby, several people were working with hammers. I couldn't quite make out what they were striking, but this was clearly a real factory, not another dummy facility. A good start.

I cast my eyes around for any trace of ethereal technology. It always took a while for my vision to clear after a jump, but I could just see an armed Vigile, standing guard in a doorway.

'Password.'

I started. A second Vigile had appeared to my right.

'Password.' A respirator muffled their voice. 'Now.'

One of the other workhands slowed. When I only stared in shock, the Vigile grasped my shoulder. 'Come with me.' They looked to the other Vigile. 'Commandant, suspected unnatural infiltrator.'

'I'm sorry,' I said faintly. 'I've forgotten it.'

He shoved my host away from the workstation. At last, the blinding panic kicked in. I threw off my borrowed flesh and soared back into my own body.

I clawed off the oxygen mask, gasping.

Scion had found a way to stop me accessing their buildings. I should have expected this, after I had walked into the Archon in a stolen body, bold as brass, and threatened the Grand Inquisitor. Now they had patched that gap in their armour. All they had to do was be vigilant. If anyone behaved strangely, Scion could ask for a password. If the suspect couldn't give it, they might well be possessed.

I felt naked. My gift was the one weapon I had known I could use to hurt them.

This had to be Vance, with Jaxon as her advisor. He knew I couldn't access my hosts' memories. He also knew the signs of possession: vacant eyes, nosebleeds, jerky movements. I still hadn't mastered my gift. I pulled off my sweater and breathed, letting the sweat cool on my skin. My host would have fallen as I left her. Her lapse in memory might be put down to the heat, or exhaustion. We still had to act quickly, before Scion put even more security in Establishment B.

I joined the others in the kitchen, where they were sitting around the table, sharing a homemade butter pie that Hari must have brought up. As soon as Eliza saw me, she knew.

'You've been dreamwalking.'

I nodded and took a seat, setting off a throb in my temple.

'I want to release Catrin Attard. Hear me out,' I added, when Tom grimaced. 'We need help getting into Establishment B, and I've just discovered that I can't dreamwalk inside.'

Eliza frowned. 'Why?'

'Scion almost caught me doing it just now. The Vigiles were prepared.'

Maria hissed in a breath. 'Shit.'

'I don't think they realised it was me,' I said, 'but they'll be suspicious. We need to go ourselves, and fast.'

'And I take it you have a plan.'

'Establishment B is guarded by Vigiles. We know that Catrin has friends among them. This is our moment to ask for their support,' I said. 'If ever they were going to rebel, now is the time. I'm going to make Catrin an offer. If she helps us get into the factory, I'll break her out of prison.'

'You're lucky Glym's not here,' Tom muttered.

'I never ruled out working with the Vigiles,' I said. 'If anyone has any other ideas, let's hear them.'

Tom and Eliza both stayed quiet, as I'd known they would. This was the only lead we had.

'Burn it down?' Maria said hopefully.

This was what I got for trying to build an army out of criminals.

Spinningfields Prison, like all places where death was common, was easy enough to find. While my spirit was still supple, I jumped into the guard in the watchtower, who was midway through his cup of tea when I occupied his dreamscape. The hot drink spilled over his thighs.

The interior of the prison was designed to resemble a clock, with the watchtower at its heart, surrounded on all sides by five storeys of cells. I heaved my new body from its chair, panting with the effort of doing this for a second time, and descended from the watchtower, careful to avoid the guards.

The stairs to the gangways quaked as I stepped on to them. I walked past voyants and amaurotics, silent and malnourished, many with signs of flux poisoning. A whisperer was rocking in the corner of one cell, hands over his ears.

As I searched, I tried to make my stride more fluid, my expression more alive, but I could see just from my shadow that I was moving about as naturally as a malfunctioning automaton. Something to work on.

I stopped when I sensed a capnomancer. A woman lay on the floor of her cell, her feet propped on the bed.

'I thought I got a last meal,' she rasped.

When there was no reply, she looked at me. Her skin was tinged with grey, and she had flux lips.

'Ah, you're probably right.' Her laugh was sharp. 'Wouldn't want to throw up on the gallows.'

A down of dark hair covered her scalp, short enough to expose a small tattoo of an eye on her nape. When she sat up, the light from the corridor reached her face. That face was all I needed to confirm her identity. A tress of scar tissue stretched from her hairline to her jaw, obliterating her left eye. The right one narrowed.

'Must be a slow night for you.' Catrin cocked her head. 'You know, even for a rottie, you are dull as lead. Did I ever tell you that?'

'ScionIDE is coming,' I ground out. 'I hear you're the best chance of getting Manchester to do something about it.'

'What is this?'

'An opportunity.'

She gave a shout of laughter.

'Keep your mouth shut, Attard,' someone bellowed. 'Some of us want to sleep.'

'You'll have time for that when you're dead,' Catrin sang back, making laughter echo down the corridor. Her smile faded. 'An opportunity, you say?'

'You have friends in the NVD. I want you to help me break into one of the factories,' I said. 'As a condition of your release, I also want you to stop intimidating the people of Ancoats. In return, I'll walk you out of this place. You can kiss the gallows goodbye, Catrin Attard.'

Catrin still looked as relaxed as anything, but her good eye was like an iron rivet. Under the bravado, she must fear the noose.

'I'd heard the new Underqueen was a dreamwalker,' she said. 'Somehow I doubt there's more than one.'

'There isn't.'

'You must really need a hand if you've come to me, not my big sister.' Her smile returned. 'On second thoughts, I bet you did ask for her help, and she turfed you out on your arse.' I said nothing. 'Even if I agree to your demands, I might not keep my word. You don't know what I'll do when I get out of here. Must be terrifying for you, dreamwalker. Not being able to control everyone all the time.'

'You don't know what I can control. You don't know where or when I could reach you,' I said. 'And this offer has a time limit, Catrin.'

'Funny,' she said. 'So does my life.'

She lay on her back again. I waited.

'I'll help you,' she finally said. 'Seeing as you'll be sparing me the noose, I could just find it in my heart to leave the brogues alone. But if there's one thing we Scuttlers must have, it's vengeance. I warn you that if you release me, there will be trouble between me and Roberta.'

'Why?'

'I saw her standing there when I was arrested, *watching*. I shouted for help and she turned her back, knowing what I'd get for treason. Maybe it's time I showed this citadel that Daddy made the wrong choice.'

'You have issues, Attard.'

'And you don't?'

I had to smile at that.

Catrin Attard stood. 'So,' she said, grasping the bars, 'if I promise to be *very* good, how do you plan to get me out of here, Underqueen?'

'Just do exactly what I say.'

13

THE IRONMASTER

Spinningfields Prison may have been cleverly designed, but it didn't have half the staff it needed. I escorted Catrin out while the other guards' backs were turned and delivered her to Maria and Tom, who were waiting near the entrance. Catrin accepted a coat from Maria and told us to take her to the Barton Arcade.

'I'll need to stop at a call box,' she said. 'If you want help from the Vigiles.'

'Certainly,' Maria said. 'Just don't try anything, Attard.'

Once they were out of sight, I dropped my host and returned to my body. It would draw attention to Spinningfields, away from Establishment B.

Eliza and I took the monorail to Deansgate, where Catrin had already let the others into the Barton Arcade. The disused Victorian building was made from white stone, cast iron, and glass, evoking a conservatory. At least, the stone might *once* have been white, just as the glass might *once* have shone, had they not been buried under decades of industrial filth. Several of the panes were cracked, while dead wisteria climbed up one of the domes, strangling its metal skeleton.

When I stepped into the building, Catrin was waiting by the door. 'The famous Paige Mahoney.' She sounded out of breath. 'Not quite as menacing as you seem on the screens, are you?'

'I'm on a tight schedule here, Attard,' I said. 'Let's skip the theatrical introductions.'

'Fine by me.' Her respirator covered most of her face, but I heard the smile. 'And who's this?'

'Her second-in-command,' Eliza said, lifting her chin.

'How fancy.'

She cocked her head, beckoning us farther into the hideout. From the look of it, this had once been a small retail gallery, presumably for the overseers and anyone else with more than two pennies to rub together. Faded shopfronts promised fine perfumes and jewellery.

Along with Tom and Maria, a stranger awaited us, silhouetted against the moonlight that shone in through the roof. When he saw Catrin, he embraced her.

'Cat,' he said, his voice thick. 'I thought you were a goner.'

'Nah. You can't get rid of me.' Catrin drew back, turning to us. 'This is Major Arcana, my contact in the Night Vigilance Division. Major, this is Paige Mahoney, Underqueen of London.'

It was exactly what I had wanted from her, but I found myself stiffening as he came closer. His mouth and nose, like mine, were hidden by a respirator.

'Paige Mahoney,' he said. 'An honour.'

I didn't return the sentiment. I could bear the idea of working with Vigiles if it moved us closer to Senshield, but old instincts weren't easily quelled.

'Tell me, Major,' I said, 'do you still hunt your own kind?'

'Not any more. Cat persuaded me to desert.' His creased brow softened when their eyes met, reminding me uncomfortably of the way Cutmouth had looked at Hector. 'And I had my reasons for joining the NVD. One was Roberta Attard. Under her, the Scuttlers won't adapt to change. And we all know change is coming now.'

'I wonder if you'd still be on the other side if machines weren't coming for your job.'

'Maybe I would. It gave me a full stomach and somewhere to sleep,' he said evenly, ignoring Tom's dark look. 'Many voyants feel their only real option is to remain in the ranks. If I can help you destroy Senshield for the sake of their livelihoods, I will.'

They must have a close bond, these people who had traded their integrity for borrowed years. Catrin touched his arm before she paced across the floor.

'You let me out, Mahoney, so you must want to raise some sort of hell in this citadel,' she said. 'The question is . . . what sort of hell?'

'I told you,' I said. 'I need to get into a factory.'

'Which one?'

'Establishment B.'

She looked from face to face, as if one of us was going to crack a smile and admit to the joke. 'You've got ambition, brogue,' she remarked. 'What do you think you're going to find in that place?'

'Portable Senshield scanners.'

She snorted, but Major Arcana breathed in, making his respirator whirr.

'We're trying to find Senshield's core,' Eliza explained, 'so we can destroy it. Paige thinks if we see exactly how the scanners are being manufactured, we might be able to pinpoint the location of what powers them. It might even be inside Establishment B, if we're lucky.'

I doubted that, but we could hope. We were overdue some luck.

'Portable scanners. We saw this in the cards,' Major Arcana murmured. 'Ace of Swords. The exposure of truth. You are the one who comes with the blade . . . to cut away the shadows Scion wove around us.' He stared at me for a long moment, then blinked, as if breaking from a trance. 'All the years of loyalty we gave them, and for what?'

Catrin drew Major Arcana towards her. 'I'm sure the Major would love to help you,' she said to me, 'but I have one condition.'

'There are no conditions, Attard,' I said. 'I released you in exchange for your help.'

'And now I'm negotiating, like any good daughter of Nerio Attard.' Catrin offered a wolfish smile. 'I want to come with you. That's my condition. I'd like to help liberate voyantkind from Senshield.' She saw my jaw tighten. 'Of course, I *could* just go to Roberta and tell her what you're doing. I'm sure that will go down well.'

I should have known our bargain couldn't be so easy. If Catrin Attard joined us, I could already tell she would be a liability.

'Major,' I said, turning to him, 'you don't need Catrin's approval to help us. If you think the Ace of Swords pointed to me, why not follow your instincts?'

'I'd do most anything to get rid of Senshield,' Major Arcana said, 'but I won't go against Cat.'

The corner of her mouth quirked. I had to wonder how these two had met – the conflicted Vigile and the daughter of Nerio Attard, who now stood together, firmly allied. As much as I disliked the idea of her coming with us, I saw no choice but to accept.

'Fine,' I said. That smile crept back to her lips. 'But you follow my orders to the letter in there, Catrin.'

'Oh, but of course, Underqueen.'

We planned the raid by moonlight in that derelict arcade.

Major Arcana had a contact who had been stationed at Establishment B since October. At six in the morning, when the shifts changed, she would let our team through the gate, allowing us to access the factory through its kitchen.

'The next step will be locating the portable scanners,' I said. 'There must be some sort of storage room.'

'Or the loading bay,' Tom said. 'That would be our best bet. Find out where they're kept before they're shipped.'

I nodded. 'Stealth will be crucial. We don't want to run into Emlyn Price.'

'Paige,' Maria said, 'you dreamwalked inside. Were the employees wearing respirators?'

'Not that I saw.'

'Then you can't come in with us. A uniform isn't going to hide your face.'

It was true. My presence would blow the whole operation. I wanted to go in for selfish reasons, so I could feel as if I was making a difference. I had led the charge into the warehouse for the same reason, which had given Scion their deadliest advantage in years. Any leader worth her salt would learn from her mistakes.

'Fine,' I said. 'We'll compromise. I'll come into the complex with you, but I won't go into the factory itself. I'll stay hidden near the door while you search for the scanners, in case you need backup.'

'I'll stay with you, Underqueen,' Tom said.

'I have to go now, to see my old colleague,' Major Arcana said. 'Meet me outside Establishment B at quarter to six.'

'Let's hope my sweet sister doesn't find out about this,' Catrin chimed in, 'or she'll ruin our chances.'

'Let's hope you don't do that, either,' I said curtly.

'We might disagree on how to run a citadel, Paige Mahoney, but we agree on one thing.' She made for the door. 'Senshield can do one.'

We spent our last remaining hours making the infiltration team look as much like factory conscripts as possible. Fortunately, Catrin and Maria already had short hair. We considered shaving Eliza's for authenticity (she blanched at the suggestion, but didn't complain), eventually deciding against the razor. Plenty of labourers did risk keeping their hair, and it was unlikely to arouse suspicion. Instead, we dirtied it with grease and bound it at the base of her skull.

As we concealed our weapons, I told the team what little I knew about ethereal technology, including the fact that they might be able to sense it in the æther. Other than finding evidence of the core, their priority was to steal a portable scanner so we could examine it elsewhere.

Just before six, we met Major Arcana outside the massive brick wall that surrounded Establishment B. Through the gate at the front – the only way in – I could see that the building was of the same design as the others: black metal, hard angles, a few square windows on the second floor, and a door that had to be ten feet high. It was a bleak design, brutally utilitarian, constructed with no thought for beauty.

'My contact will be along shortly. She's persuaded some other disgruntled Vigiles to leave their posts for a few minutes,' Major Arcana said. 'They won't come out on our side, but they'll look the other way. I'll be waiting in the van. Good luck.'

Catrin pulled him in for a kiss before he left. His form was swallowed by the smog.

We waited, backs against the wall, out of sight of anyone inside. I tried to ignore the moil in my stomach. This time, I was certain we had come to the right place. Every whisper in this citadel had pointed me here.

Moments passed. I thought no one would come for us, that the contact had been apprehended – until someone pressed their finger to the scanner on the other side of the gate.

Our abetter was a slight woman, who ushered us inside without a word. Unlike street Vigiles, she wore no body armour and carried no firearm, though she did have the standard-issue helmet with a visor. Her only visible weapon was a truncheon. She led us out of sight of the main entrance and past a corrugated metal door. At any moment, I expected to hear a shout or be blinded by a searchlight, but it was still dark enough to obscure our movements, and no one challenged us.

When we reached the entrance to the kitchen, the Vigile snapped up her visor, allowing me to glimpse her dark brown eyes and skin. She looked into a retinal scanner, unlocking the door.

'The night shift is just ending,' she told us, speaking for the first time. 'When the workers leave their sleeping quarters for the day, blend in as best you can.' Her visor slid back into place. 'I can give you twenty minutes, at most – after that, I have to clock in to the barracks. Anyone who doesn't get back on time will be trapped inside.'

Twenty minutes. That wasn't nearly enough time for the team to search the whole place. It was frustrating that I had to stay hidden, but Maria was right. My face was too famous.

'Understood,' I said to the Vigile. 'Do you know where the portable scanners are stored?'

'Afraid not. You're on your own there.'

Eliza stepped into the darkness first, touching a nervous hand to her hair. Catrin followed. As Maria went after them, I grasped her arm.

'Don't take your eyes off her,' I said against her ear, nodding at Catrin.

'Naturally.'

'Tom and I will wait for you here. Remember, *anything* you can find out is useful.'

She gave me a nod and disappeared inside. The Vigile closed the door.

'I have to return to my rounds,' she said to me and Tom. 'Stay out of sight. You won't find every Vigile sympathetic to your cause.'

'Thank you,' I said.

She marched away. Tom and I hunkered down to wait behind an industrial waste repository. These could be the longest twenty minutes of our lives.

'I trust that Catrin about as far as I could throw her,' Tom muttered.

The wind howled against the cheap fabric of my boiler suit, chilling my ribs. 'I trust most people about as far as I can throw them,' I admitted, 'but if we're going to win this war, we need most people.'

We stayed close to one another for warmth, keeping an eye on his wristwatch. A lifetime seemed to pass between each click of the second hand.

I wasn't made to stay behind.

After five minutes, two more Vigiles passed, but neither of them checked behind the waste receptacle. Eight minutes. Ten. Fifteen. Sixteen. By eighteen, I was getting nervous.

'Underqueen,' Tom murmured. 'If they don't come in time—'

'We are *not* leaving here without one of those scanners.'

I had hardly finished speaking when three chimes rang out from inside the factory, each note climbing higher than the last.

'*SciPLO Establishment B, this is the Minister for Industry,*' said a cold voice. '*An intruder has been detected. Security protocol is now in effect. All doors to the factory floor and loading bay will close in thirty seconds. All personnel, remain at your stations, and report any unauthorised individuals to a Vigile or overseer. Failure to do so constitutes high treason. Remember, the safety of your assigned machine is paramount.*'

We stared at each other. At any other time, Tom would be advocating caution, but not where Maria was concerned. My attention snapped to the æther. I found their dreamscapes at once, not too far from us.

'Follow me,' I whispered.

We rushed towards our entrance, through the empty kitchen, ending up in a wide passageway with an immensely high ceiling. Fluorescent lighting illuminated its concrete floor from one end to the other. All signs indicated that this was the passage that led to the sleeping quarters.

A low-pitched grinding came to my attention. A massive internal door was closing on our left, sliding downward on its rails – the way to the factory floor, our means of reaching the others. Beyond it was the furnace I had seen when I had dreamwalked in that room; I could feel its heat on my face already, infernal and suffocating. We broke into a dead run, our footfalls drowned by the roar and hammer of machinery. My palms slammed into the door just as it closed.

'Damn it.' I stepped back, staring up. 'There has to be a way to release the doors.'

'There will be.' Tom was panting. 'In the overseers' office. On the upper floor.'

Footsteps were approaching from our left. Vigiles.

In silent agreement, we separated. Tom made for the nearest door, while I turned right, into an offshoot of the central passageway. It was a dead end, but a freight lift presented me with a way out. I mashed the button to call it, certain that, at any moment, a squadron of Vigiles would round the corner and riddle me with bullets. When it arrived, I got in, breathing hard. The doors slid closed.

I sent the lift to the third and highest floor. It trundled upward, jolting my stomach. Every heartbeat was a solid punch, each reminding me that it could be the last. I was in a Scion building, breathing the same air as a high-ranking official, and all the doors were closed. It took all my willpower to keep the panic restrained.

When the lift opened, I sidestepped into a corridor. Off-white walls and a vinyl floor, like you might find in any office block. A sign reading ADMINISTRATION. Minimal lighting. Pressing myself into a corner, I nudged my focus to the æther. Tom was very still, and farther from me than anyone else – he must be hiding in the basement. Maria and Eliza were together. If their proximity to most of the other dreamscapes was anything to go by, they remained on the factory floor, presumably undetected.

It was Catrin who had given the game away. I should have known she would be the one to put the assignment in jeopardy.

She was close to me. Very close, on this floor. Three unfamiliar dreamscapes clustered around her. I reached into my boiler suit, drawing a knife from its sheath on my holster.

Price would be up here.

At the end of another corridor, I was faced with a door marked OVERSEER, flanked by two small windows. When I looked through one, the first person I saw was Catrin, bleeding from a fresh wound to her temple. Her wrists were strapped to the arms of a chair. A Vigiles stood on either side, each grasping one of her shoulders.

Someone was standing in front of her, hands flat on the table that separated them. Catrin looked up, and her gaze darted to me. I tried to get out of sight, but her interrogator had already turned. I found myself facing a man who could only be in his twenties, not much older than me, wearing the uniform of a Scion official.

Price.

It was too late to hide. The Ironmaster took me in with piercing grey eyes, lighter than mine. His hair was dark, his skin smooth and pale, and he wore gold cufflinks.

'Paige Mahoney.' He sounded almost friendly. 'I never expected someone so . . . exciting.'

14

OPERATION ALBION

'Let me in, Price.'

'Now, why would I possibly do that?' His voice was muffled by the glass, but I could hear him well enough. 'I appear to be very secure in here. Let's keep a door between us, shall we?'

His bodyguards had their guns trained on my chest. Several knives lay on the table in front of him, no doubt taken from Catrin.

'I'm the hands-on sort,' I said.

'So I hear.' Price lowered himself into a chair. 'I know you tried to enter the factory earlier today. I commend you for your bravery, coming here in your own skin.'

Without warning, I possessed the man beside him. Through the glass – and my new eyes – I saw my body reel before collapsing like a house of cards. The other bodyguard aimed his pistol at my host, but I had already jumped into him, leaving the first Vigile to collapse in my wake.

Price swam back into view. I swayed on the spot, adjusting to my fourth host in as many hours. It was disturbing, how quickly I was getting used to this sensation.

I didn't have long before I needed to get back to my own body. As soon as my new fingers worked, I used my truncheon to crack the other Vigile over the head, making sure he would stay down. Catrin huffed a laugh.

'Now we can talk, Price,' I said. 'Face to face, as it were.'

'Indeed.' Price dredged up a smile 'What is it you'd like to say to me, Paige?'

I hadn't intended to interrogate anyone this morning, but now I was here, I would find out as much as I could. And if he was going to talk, Price had to believe I was capable of murder.

'I know you're manufacturing portable scanners here. You're going to tell me where they are,' I said. 'You're going to tell me how they're connected to Senshield's core. And then you'll tell me how to disable it.'

It was a shot in the dark; I didn't expect the reaction. Price gave me an incredulous look, then let out a peal of boyish laughter. I stared at him, unnerved.

'Wait,' he said. 'You don't think they're connected *here*, do you?' 'He shook his head. 'Oh, dear. Somebody really has got her facts muddled. You didn't honestly believe that by sneaking into this factory, you *had* Senshield, did you?'

I waited, my heart thumping.

'The *portable scanners*, as you call them – the ones we make here – are deadly, yes, but not yet equipped with ethereal technology.' Price was savouring every syllable. 'I'm afraid you've only found one link in the intricate chain of Senshield. The scanners are activated elsewhere.'

If he wasn't telling the truth, then he was very convincing. Still, a little more persuasion couldn't hurt. I stepped forward and shoved the gun against his head.

'Where?' I said.

'And to think, the Grand Commander genuinely believed you were a threat,' Price said. 'I've always admired Vance for respecting her opponents' intelligence, but I imagine this will disappoint her.' He smiled. 'She suspected that you might come here, you know.'

That was how they had been ready for me. The famous intuition of the Grand Commander. Vance had warned them that Paige Mahoney was sniffing around Senshield; that this facility was one of her potential targets. She had taught them what to expect from the enemy.

'I'm disappointed in her, too,' I said. 'If she'd prepared you better, I wouldn't be holding a gun to your head.'

Catrin was observing the conversation with interest, as if she were watching a play. Aside from the cut head, she was no worse for wear.

'Paige,' she said, 'mind getting these things off me?'

Keeping my gun aimed at Price, I unfastened one of the restraints. Catrin dealt with the other herself. She stood and rubbed her wrists before reclaiming one of her knives from the table. As she turned to face Price, I spied a glint in her eye.

'Well, here he is. Emlyn Price, the Ironmaster. The man who turns blood into gold. You're quite the legendary figure around here,' she said. 'One might say you're the king of this citadel.' She lifted his chin with one finger. 'Well, we all know what happens to kings here in Scion.'

Price, to his credit, didn't appear to be afraid. His mild smile stayed exactly where it was.

An oracular image suddenly filled my vision. Tom had sent me a crystal-clear picture of a keypad, followed by a glimpse of stencilled letters spelling LOADING BAY.

He would only have sent me this if he needed urgent help. Either the loading bay was our way out, or Tom had found some evidence of Senshield. Maybe both. But the door needed a code.

Shit.

'You see this scar on my face?' Catrin was saying to Price. The vision faded. 'Hard to miss, I know. My friend Paige would like to know where Senshield's core is. If you don't start talking, I'll give you a matching one. What do you say to that, Price?'

'You can torture me for as long as you like,' was the calm reply, 'but I promise you, all you will draw from my lips are falsehoods.' He looked back at me. 'We prepared for all eventualities.'

What happened next knocked the smile off his face. Lightning quick, Catrin brought up her arm and rammed her knife straight through the back of his hand. I flinched inside. Price stared at the blade, embedded just below his knuckles, before he let out a roar of agony.

'Where is the core?' I asked.

'Liverpool,' he managed. 'It's in Liverpool.'

'Is it?'

I forced myself to keep my eyes on him. He was just another puppet, another cog in the machine. When Catrin wormed the blade deeper, he made a sound that twisted my gut.

'Cardiff,' he bit out. 'Belfast.'

'Enough,' I said sharply. 'We have no way of knowing if he's telling the truth.'

'Oh, I know.' Catrin let go of the knife. 'I'm just having fun.'

Price stared at his hand, panting. The blade pinned him to the table.

He had been ready for this, too. Someone like Vance would expect her employees to be willing to suffer – even to die – to protect her military secrets. That didn't mean the Ironmaster had no weaknesses. And not all secrets needed to be drawn out with a knife.

I unlocked the door and occupied my own body, waking to an intense headache. When I returned, stepping over the crumpled form of the bodyguard I had used to get in, I pulled up a chair and sat down opposite the Minister for Industry. Blood ran from his nostrils as my spirit probed the edge of his dreamscape.

'Let's go back to the scanners,' I said. 'I know they're in the loading bay, but we need you to give us the code to get in. Don't make me ask twice, Minister.'

'Once again,' he said, 'I'm afraid Vance is a step ahead of you on that front.' Sweat varnished his forehead. 'There is only one code to open the loading bay. Entering it incorrectly will destroy its contents.'

The first response this stirred in me was fear, but it faded as quickly as it came.

'I don't believe you,' I said.

'Why?'

He sounded genuinely curious.

'Because Vance wouldn't destroy huge quantities of her own equipment. She clearly protects her assets,' I said. 'Besides, we all know how urgently she wants these scanners in her soldiers' hands. There's also the matter of *how* the contents would be destroyed. I doubt you have a procedure that involves blowing up the loading bay, risking the entire facility. Vance isn't that wasteful.'

'You're shrewder than I gave you credit for. Already a little less naïve than you were,' Price said, his voice strained. 'You and Vance are similar, you know. She also learns from the enemy, and from her own mistakes.' Blood was seeping from his hand. 'If you were on our side, perhaps she would have been your mentor.'

'I'm done with mentors.'

'Now, now, don't slide into arrogance. Even Hildred has mentors.'

I studied his face. If his watering eyes were anything to go by, the pain was getting worse.

'I'd like to talk less about Vance,' I said, 'and more about the code, Minister. If you think you won't tell me, I assure you, you will. It's hidden in your mind, where Vance thinks it's safe. Fortunately for me, I know all about minds. We voyants call them *dreamscapes*.'

'You can't access my memories.'

'No, but I can see things.' I clasped my fingers and leaned across the table. 'Let me demonstrate.' I pushed my spirit against him again, dipping into his dreamscape. A vein bulged between his eyebrows. 'You feel safest in a garden, where you can escape from the pollution. There are foxgloves and roses, and a winding path, and at the centre of it all is a bird bath, sheltered by oak trees. You often see it in your dreams. Your beautiful home in Altrincham.'

His breathing was getting shallower.

'Impressive,' he said, 'but we all know what you can do, dream-walker.' He dropped his voice to the softest whisper. 'The Suzerain has told us in detail.'

'Your family feels safe there, too, I imagine,' I said. 'You must miss them when you're here. Are they waiting for you right now, Minister?'

The tiniest flicker of apprehension crossed his face. His pupils were constricted.

'I want the code. If you don't give it to me, I promise you this,' I said. 'When I leave here, I will go straight to that beautiful garden, and I will kill your wife and children. You will come home and find them dead, and you'll wonder why you didn't just hand over the code. A few little numbers. Vance will never even have to know.'

Somehow, I kept my voice under control. Price glanced at his unconscious bodyguards, beads of sweat glistening on his forehead.

'I don't think you would, Mahoney,' he said. 'You're not a born killer.'

'Killers can be made.'

A few long moments passed in absolute silence. Slowly, Price extended his uninjured hand towards a control panel. His spousal ring glinted as he pressed a flat grey button labelled DOOR RELEASE.

'There are two codes. One to enter the loading bay from the factory, and the other, from outside,' he forced out. 'The code to the internal door is 1801. The code to the external one is 2608.'

'Thank you.' I stood, committing the numbers to memory. 'Catrin, with me.'

'You're just going to leave him?' Catrin asked. 'He'll alert Vance.'

'She already knows.'

Price didn't contradict me. I took a gun from the nearest bodyguard and checked it for bullets, then walked away from the Minister for Industry. I didn't breathe again until I had rounded the corner.

I wasn't only shaking because of the possession. Price had believed me. He had looked me in the eyes and seen someone who could murder innocents. I had almost believed my own threat, in that moment – and in my ability to carry it out if he denied me what I wanted, which he had, after everything. I still didn't know where the scanners were activated.

Perhaps I should have pushed him harder, but I could not allow myself to become a monster. I could not allow anyone else to look at me and see a budding Hildred Vance.

I was halfway back to the freight lift when I heard gunshots, and a dreamscape faded, stopping me dead. A few seconds later, I started to run.

By the time I reached the office, Price was dead. Blood had sprayed everywhere, across the table and the carpet, pooling around the Ironmaster. Catrin Attard stood over his body, holding the gun that had killed him.

'You—' I gripped the doorframe, white-knuckled. 'What the hell have you done?'

'He had nothing else to offer.'

Her calm demeanour was unsettling. This wasn't a hot-blooded killing.

'This was your aim all along,' I said, cold all over.

Catrin nodded. 'Arcana and I have wanted to bump Price off for a while, but this was the first time we saw an opportunity. And the perfect scapegoat if it all went wrong.' She gave me a smile. 'Big risk, assassinating an Archon official. If the response on the streets is fear and anger, I can blame you. No one even has to know I was here. But if it's deemed heroic, I'll make sure everyone knows I'm the one who rid Manchester of the Ironmaster.'

I couldn't speak.

'You wait and see, Underqueen,' she said. 'The Scuttlers will rally behind me. I'm the true heir, regardless of what certain external parties have decided. I'm the one who's willing to do what's necessary for this citadel. In a few days' time, I'll be Scuttling Queen.'

'You've lost your mind,' I said. 'Vance will have revenge on this entire citadel for what you've done.'

'She would have come here in the end. Now the Scuttlers will be ready.' Her smile widened, showing teeth. 'Now, don't look at me like that, Paige Mahoney. Who did you kill for the Rose Crown?'

I shook my head, disgusted with myself for not anticipating this, and left her with the corpse.

As I broke into a run, I tried to smooth out my breathing. Price had been wrong about me. I was still naïve, still the woman who had walked into that trap in the warehouse. I should have trusted my gut, used Attard to get us into the factory, and then forced her to wait outside.

I had to make this worth it. We didn't have long until someone found the body and reinstated the security protocol.

The freight lift took me back to the lower floor. When I emerged, I could already see there would be enough confusion to cover our escape. The Vigiles clearly had no idea why the doors had opened again without a word from the Ironmaster.

I slipped through the door Tom had gone through when we separated.

I found the others hiding near the vast door to the loading bay. Without pausing for breath, I tapped in the code.

'That was too close,' Eliza said. 'Where's Catrin?'

'Leave her.' I ducked under the door as it began to open. 'We don't have time.'

The others followed me. On the other side, I keyed in the same code, sealing us in. Maria threw a switch. A flicker crossed the length and breadth of the ceiling before stark lights thrummed to life.

The loading bay was large enough to accommodate several heavy goods vehicles. Large crates were piled everywhere, stacked in tidy units so high they almost touched the ceiling. Several amaurotics raised their hands when I pointed my stolen gun at them.

'Underqueen,' Maria said.

She sounded strange. I joined her beside a crate, the lid of which was slightly ajar. We hefted it aside and made our way through layers of packaging before we got to the final container.

Inside was a rifle.

For a heartbeat, I just stared at it, uncomprehending.

'Guns.' My mouth was dry as sandpaper. 'No. The scanners must be here, they *must*—'

'They are.' Maria passed me a sheet of laminated paper. 'You're looking at one.'

I took it with icy fingers.

It was a diagram of a weapon called the SL-59. Its components were sparsely labelled, but the diagram clearly showed a small compartment under the scope of the rifle, designed to hold some kind of capsule. A capsule labelled RDT SENSHIELD CONNECTOR.

It took me a while to understand, then to accept, what I was seeing.

Maria lifted the rifle with care. 'It seems like an ordinary gun,' she observed, 'except for this.' She tapped the empty compartment. 'Once the connector is in place, you have an inbuilt Senshield scanner.' Her brow creased. 'I just . . . don't understand this.'

'You do,' I said. 'You just don't want to believe it.'

Scion had always tried to create an impression of peace. They had relied on that impression for two centuries – to prove to their denizens that the system worked, that they were safer than anyone else in the world. It was a silent bargain they made. *Let us remove the unnaturals around you, no questions asked. In return, you will be protected.*

A gun-mounted Senshield scanner heralded a new age. Martial law had never been intended to be a temporary measure while they dealt with the Mime Order. No, Scion intended to declare all-out war on unnaturals.

And now had a way to fight us – to kill us – without any risk of collateral damage.

'Paige,' Eliza said. 'Look at this.'

She indicated a label on the lid of a crate. Above the Senshield symbol and the data, there was a destination. I ran my finger over the precious letters, the reason we had infiltrated this factory.

ATTN: H. COMM. FIRST INQ. DIVISION
PRIORITY: URGENT
PROJECT REF: OPERATION ALBION
SHIP FROM: SCIPLO ESTABLISHMENT B, SCION CITADEL OF
    MANCHESTER, NORTH WEST REGION
SHIP TO: CENTRAL DEPOT, SCION CITADEL OF EDINBURGH,
    LOWLANDS REGION

'Edinburgh. That must be where they're connected to the core.' Eliza loosed a breath. 'This is it.'

The feeling in my heart wasn't quite hope. It was hard to feel hope in a room filled with war machines, with danger closing in. I looked again at all the towers of crates, at the level of organisation and preparation that Scion had attained over the years, while we had occupied ourselves with mime-crime and ignored the growing shadow.

There was only one way to stop it now.

Maria reached into the crate. 'Quickly Grab one each.'

We fumbled with the weapons, wrapping them in our coats. Suddenly the alarm sounded again, making us all flinch. Bands of red light arced through the loading bay.

'Now might be a good time to mention that Catrin killed Price,' I said hoarsely. 'I imagine we're about to feel the consequence of that.'

'Come on!' Tom was already by the exit. 'Underqueen, hurry. What's the code?'

'2608,' I shouted.

He didn't need to hear it twice. The internal door was opening again. We crossed the loading bay at speed, weighed down by our plunder.

Maria ducked under the external door. Tom was on the other side, holding it open with nothing but his own strength. Sweat poured down his face as he forced his shoulder against it. Someone must have overridden the code. Eliza scrambled under next, almost losing the rifle.

As the Vigiles entered the loading bay and opened fire, Tom let go of the door. I threw my rifle ahead of me and slid through the gap, into the snow, just before a teeth-rattling crash of metal against concrete. I gathered up the rifle as Tom hefted me to my feet.

The factory gate was ajar. Our contact had given us one more chance to escape. We ran, our boots crunching through fresh snow. When a Vigile sprang out on our left, Maria threw a knife into his thigh. Tom slowed, panting heavily, as we closed in on our exit.

'Tom—' I pulled his arm around my shoulder. 'Come on. You can make it. Just a bit farther.'

'Leave me, Underqueen,' he rasped.

'I won't do that.'

More gunfire from behind us, along with the alarm. Maria flung the gate open. A few more desperate, staggering steps, and we were through, into the van that waited on the corner. It was only when Major Arcana slammed his foot on the accelerator that I realised who was in the front seat, still drenched in the blood of Emlyn Price.

Catrin Attard caught my eye in the rear-view mirror.

'Pleasure working with you, Underqueen,' she said, taking in the rifle I was hugging to my chest. 'Glad to see we both got what we wanted.'

15

THE GRAND SMOKE

6 December 2059

Another day, another journey.

This time, we were on our way to the Lowlands.

After Catrin had dumped us in Essex Street, Hari had helped us escape from Manchester. It was best that he didn't know exactly what we had done, or Roberta might think he had been involved, but he knew something had happened. He had wished us the best of luck, kissed Eliza on the cheek, and passed us to someone else from Circinus. Now we were stowed in the back of an armoured Bank of Scion England vehicle, bound for Edinburgh.

Sweat pearled on my neck and forehead. I stayed close to the stolen rifles, like an animal guarding its young.

Catrin might work to protect her people if Vance retaliated, or she might just continue the cycle of violence that had left her with that scar. I had no way of knowing. I might not even live to see what I had done to Manchester.

'Tom,' I said hoarsely, 'does the Lowlands have an organised voyant community?'

Tom had been quiet since our escape. I heard him take a deep breath before he spoke.

'Not in Glasgow,' he said. 'I . . . did hear of a group in Edinburgh that sheltered voyants from Vance, back in the day, led by someone called the Spaewife. If they're still there, they might help us.'

His voice was slower than usual. 'You don't sound good, old timer,' Maria said. 'That little adventure hasn't tired you out, has it?'

'I'm fine, hen. Just need a sleep.'

I couldn't imagine ever sleeping again. My head was heavy, my thoughts mired in fatigue, but all I could think about was Vance. Her face was engraved on my vision. It floated in the darkness, disembodied and all-seeing, like something a dose of flux would summon. I felt too watched to close my eyes.

Vance would soon realise the rifles were gone. That was more than enough to confirm her suspicion that I was going after Senshield, and for her to pick up our scent. Even if she tried to intercept us in Edinburgh, I saw no choice but to keep trying to find the core.

I only hoped that it couldn't be moved.

Eliza drifted off first, followed by Tom, whose sleep was restless. I lay on my side with my head pillowed on my arm, trying not to think about how many crates had been in that loading bay.

A rustle of movement came on my left, accompanied by the glare of a torch. Maria was unwrapping one of the guns.

'I didn't get a chance to examine this properly in the loading bay,' she said, by way of explanation. Her fingers skimmed over the barrel. 'SL-59. *S* is for Scion. The second letter is usually the designer's initial.' She inspected the gun. 'Ah, there it is. Lévesque.'

'Who?'

'Corentin Lévesque, a French engineer. I know him by reputation.'

'And aside from the space for a Senshield . . . connector, there's really nothing unusual about the gun?'

'Not that I can see.'

The next step had to show us how the scanners were linked to the core. At last, that puzzle would be solved. I lowered my head back on to my arm – and despite the fact that Hildred Vance still hovered before me, her face like a portent, I drifted into a fitful sleep.

The Scion Citadel of Edinburgh, regional capital of the Lowlands, was cloaked in coastal fog. After the industrial haze of Manchester, the air here almost tasted sweet – but it was also colder, chilled by wind from the North Sea. Our driver handed me a key and told us where to find the safe house.

The streets were quiet this evening – which was fortunate, given what we were carrying. There were no skyscrapers here. It was an opium dream of a time long past; a city of bridges and crumbling kirks. Mist laced around the old stone buildings, which had rooftops crowned with snow. Edinburgh was sometimes called the Grand Smoke, and now I knew why – there were chimneys everywhere, so it seemed as if we were walking through a cloud. The citadel was carved into the unruly Old Town, where the labourers and service workers dwelled, and the more expensive and modern New Town.

On a ledge of volcanic rock, a decaying fortress knelt on the skyline of the citadel. 'Edinburgh Castle,' Eliza observed. 'They say it's haunted by the spirits of the Scottish monarchs.'

I glanced at her. 'You read Jaxon's history books, too, did you?'

'Every one. Jax taught me to read with those.'

Jaxon still eluded me. It was all too easy to think of him as the enemy, the traitor. Yet this was a man who had taught an orphaned artist to read. She hadn't needed to know her letters to earn him money.

Our little party trudged up the lamplit stairways that slipped behind and between the houses. 'It's good to see Scotland,' Tom said hoarsely. His face was losing colour. 'Just need . . . a lie-down.'

Maria rubbed his back. 'You're getting too old for this.' His laugh was more of a wheeze.

We pressed on through the citadel – past a train station, across a bridge, and up a narrow street. Chandleries and apothecaries, cutlers and wigmakers, bakeries and bookshops all nestled together on the stony incline.

The safe house was in an alleyway halfway up, blocked off by an iron gate. When she read the gold letters above it, Eliza tilted her head.

'Anchor Close.' She sighed. 'Is this a joke?'

'Best place for a safe house,' Maria said. 'Who'd dare put rebels in Anchor Close?'

The gate let out an agonised creak. The safe house was up the flight of steps beyond. Its windows were shrouded by curtains, their sills capped with moss, and a lantern sputtered beside the door. The smell of mould snaked from inside.

The decoration was as melancholy as the exterior. Claret walls patterned with floral designs, coated with decades of grime. Furniture that looked as if a pennyweight could break it. Some dusty numa were piled on a table, guarded by a ghost, which drifted sullenly away from us.

As we shuffled into the hallway and shucked our coats, Tom began to wheeze. I reached for his hand. Cold as marble.

'Tom,' I said, 'how are you feeling?'

'The leg is . . . giving me trouble. I'll live, Underqueen.'

The words left him breathless. I squeezed his arm.

'I'm taking him upstairs,' Maria said, her tone clipped. 'Does anyone have painkillers?'

'Yes,' Eliza said. 'I'll bring them.'

As Tom mounted the stairs, leaning hard on the banister, I caught Maria by the sleeve. 'It's not his leg,' I said quietly. 'Something else is wrong.'

She stiffened. 'How do you know?'

'He's not getting enough oxygen. I know the signs.'

'Do you have your mask?'

I handed it over, along with a fresh can of oxygen. She followed Tom upstairs, and Eliza went after her.

As I put down the heavy rifle, my sixth sense tingled. There were three other dreamscapes here. How had I not noticed?

I pushed the nearest door open. Beyond was a small parlour, where Nick and Lucida were sitting on armchairs by a fire – and in the corner, watching the flames dance in the hearth, was Warden.

'Hello, dreamwalker,' Lucida said.

Nick got to his feet and offered a weak smile. I wrapped my arms around him. 'You're freezing, sötnos,' he said, holding me close. 'Are you okay?'

'I'm fine,' I said, 'but how did you find us?'

'Tom sent a vision of Edinburgh. I got the sense he was asking for help.'

'Circinus assisted us in taking a train from Inquisitors Cross,' Warden said. 'They also pointed us to this safe house. We hoped you would be sent here, too.'

'Good timing,' I said.

Warden nodded. Our gazes held for a moment too long.

'I'm happy to see you all,' I said, 'but you should be in the Beneath.'

'It's okay. Terebell sent reinforcements,' Nick said. 'Pleione and Taygeta are there.'

I relaxed a little. Taygeta Chertan was one of the Ranthen who had arrived to support me at the scrimmage, who had apparently been going steady with Pleione since before their arrival to Earth. She was just as intimidating as Terebell, with a penetrating stare and a sharp tongue, which made her perfect for keeping the syndicate in line.

'That's good.' I studied his face. 'How do things stand'

Nick breathed out. What little joy had touched him when he saw me was already gone.

'It's bad,' he said. 'We need to get them out of there. For all our sakes.'

If he didn't want to give me specifics, it must be hell in the crisis facility.

'I'm working on it,' I said. 'Did Ivy go into the Fleet?'

'Glym announced that you'd sentenced her to join the toshers to protect the syndicate, which renewed a certain degree of support for your rule. They've haven't forgiven you,' he said, 'but they feel a little more warmly towards you now than they did a few days ago.'

They had been ready to eviscerate me a few days ago, so that wasn't saying much.

'Róisín came forward after the announcement,' he continued. 'She expressed concern for Ivy's health and offered to go in her stead, which most of them grudgingly accepted. She was due to leave when we realised Ivy was gone.' I raised my eyebrows. 'One of the toshers said she'd asked him how to find their king, then gone into the sewers with food enough for a few days. She left this on her bunk.'

He passed me a scrap of cigarette paper. The note was written in a spiky, quaking hand.

You can't save us all, Paige.

'It's not a pleasant thought,' Nick murmured, 'but I don't think there was another way, Paige.'

Against my will, I remembered those dark, oppressive tunnels. The dead silence, broken only by the drip of water.

'Not one that kept her alive.' I pocketed the note. 'I'm going to get her out of there. I'll give Styx whatever he wants when I'm back.'

'Róisín went after her. For now, they have each other. Once Senshield is gone, you'll have enough power to bargain for their lives.'

'And a few more supporters, I hope.' I glanced at the two Rephs. 'I take it you found Adhara Sarin, and that's why you've been allowed to return.'

'Yes,' Warden said. 'Terebell is attempting to forge an alliance with her, assisted by Mira and Errai. Given the situation in London, she elected to send the rest of us back.'

'Which leaves us free to help you,' Nick said. 'What did you find in Manchester?'

I almost didn't want to burden him with this, but I couldn't lie.

'Dani was right,' I finally said. 'They *are* manufacturing portable scanners.' I retrieved one of our prizes from the hallway and laid it on the table. 'Only . . . they're not quite what we expected.'

Nick came to join me at the table. A moment later, Warden and Lucida followed.

'This is—' Nick swallowed. 'You're saying *this* is equipped with Senshield?'

'It will be,' I said. 'Once it's activated.'

'Nashira is preparing for war,' Warden said.

I looked up at the sound of his voice. Nick turned to face him. 'War with who, exactly?'

'Clairvoyants.' Warden cast a detached look over the rifle. 'This version of the scanner gives Scion a means of slaying unnaturals without risk of collateral damage. If it came to physical combat with the Mime Order, they would be able to fight back without injury to amaurotics.'

'So they can keep saying *no safer place* to amaurotics,' I said, 'while leaving no safe place for us.'

'Yes.'

Nick closed his eyes. 'Do I want to know how you got this, Paige?'

I told them about our search for Senshield in Manchester – my attempt to negotiate with the Scuttling Queen, my visit to Ancoats, the uneasy agreement with Catrin and Major Arcana, the heist, and the assassination. By the time I was finished, my throat hurt from talking.

'I keep thinking you can't do anything more dangerous.' Nick pinched the bridge of his nose. 'How you got out of that factory alive . . .'

'Vance may turn her attention to Manchester now,' Warden said.

'She'll punish Manchester,' I said quietly, 'but she'll come here in person. By now, she knows where I'm going.' I held my hands close to the fire. 'We should look for the local voyant community, if it still exists, and ask them how to find the depot where these rifles are activated. Even if they don't know, it's a good idea for us to connect with them, in case we need help while we're in Edinburgh. Hopefully the visions reached them.' Nick nodded. 'Once we've found—'

'Nick.'

Maria was in the doorway. There was none of the usual good humour in her expression.

'A word,' she said.

With a slight frown, he followed her. When I heard their footsteps, I faced the two Rephs.

'Be honest,' I said. 'Do you think Adhara is likely to join us?'

'Adhara has grown accustomed to exile,' Warden said. 'She will only join the Ranthen if she sees a compelling reason.'

She must not see one yet. I couldn't really blame her. Apart from leading the rebellion in Oxford, all I had done so far was rip the syndicate from under Jaxon and start its transformation into an army of disgruntled criminals. I could claim no significant victories against Scion.

'I still hope to give her one,' I said.

'We hope the same,' Lucida said. 'For now, you ought to rest, Underqueen.'

'No time for that. I doubt Vance rests.'

Upstairs, I deposited the hideous guns on a bed. Their weight sent up a cloud of dust. Two burner phones and a charger waited on the windowsill, presumably donated by whoever owned the safe house.

'Paige.'

Nick stepped into the doorway, wiping his hands on a cloth. As soon as I saw his face, I knew something was very wrong.

'Tom,' I said.

'He's dying, sweetheart.'

The cloth was bloody.

'He can't be,' I murmured. 'How?'

'You couldn't have known. Tom made sure of it,' he said. 'He took a bullet when you left the loading bay. I'm amazed he's lasted this long.'

'He was holding the door open for us, so we could escape the factory. That must be when—' I released an unsteady breath. 'Can I see him?'

'Yes,' Nick said. 'He asked for you.'

He led me across the landing to another door. Inside the little room, Maria was hunched in a chair, her head cradled in her hands.

Tom lay in a bed that was far too small for him, his hat on the nightstand, his shirt peeled open. His broad chest was stained by plum-coloured bruising, bundled beneath his left pectoral. His eyes cracked open.

'Underqueen.'

'Tom.' I sat on the edge of the bed. 'Why didn't you say anything?'

'Because he's a stubborn old fool,' Maria said thickly.

'Aye, and proud.' His wheezing breaths turned into a cough, and Maria rushed to pour him water. 'I didna want to slow you down, Paige. And I wanted to see Scotland again, one last time.'

I stroked the back of his hand with my thumb. Perhaps I would have kept my silence, too, if I had thought I might see Ireland again.

'I worked in a factory in Glasgow in my younger days, before I went south. I saw what Scion would do for their metal.' He was turning greyer by the moment. 'I just . . . couldna bear to see it still happening, all these decades later. It had to end. It all has to end.'

Maria tipped the water to his lips. Tom took a little and leaned back into the pillows.

'Paige, I dinna want you to watch me snuff it, but I have a last favour to ask of you.' His face creased into something like a smile. 'Just a small one. Bring Scion down.'

'I will,' I said quietly. 'I won't stop. One day, they'll call this country by its name again.'

He managed to lift a big hand to my cheek. 'That's brave talk, but I can see in your eyes that you're doubting yourself,' he said. 'There's a reason we accepted you as Underqueen, and there's a reason Scion has been trying so hard to find you. They know they canna control someone with a flame like yours. Don't ever let them put it out.'

I pressed his hand.

'Never,' I said.

With the death of Tom the Rhymer, I lost one of my most faithful commanders. One of the few kind and honest people in the syndicate.

We had so little time to mourn him, or even to absorb his passing. Vance would soon be on her way. I sat beside Maria on the roof of the safe house, and she lit a roll of blue aster.

'He was a good man. A gentle soul,' she said. 'When I arrived in London, he showed me the ropes of the syndicate.' She took a drag, her gaze distant. 'So it begins again. I lost many friends to the Balkan Incursion. At least Tom knew what we were really fighting. The Rephs.'

'Thank you for sharing that memory,' I said. 'That can't have been easy.'

'No,' she said. 'But sometimes it doesn't hurt to remember.'

She tilted her face into the light rain.

'In 2039,' she said, 'Scion launched its assault from Cyprus, marching first on Greece. In 2040, they came for Bulgaria.'

'How old were you?'

'Fifteen. Along with my friend Hristo, I left my hometown of Buhovo and joined the youth army in Sofia. That was where I met Rozaliya Yudina, the woman in the memory. She was charismatic, free-thinking, single-minded in her search for justice – rather like you,' she said. 'Roza was amaurotic. She convinced us that we all had to fight, even if we weren't voyant. She was adamant that any organisation that labelled one group of people as evil would eventually do the same to others. That to treat any one person as less than human was to cheapen the very substance of humanity. Training was rigorous, and we knew our chances were small, but for the first time in my life, I was free of my father, free to be who I truly was. Yoana Hazurova – not the son he had never loved.

'When ScionIDE approached Sofia, we made our own cannon. We took the guns of dead police, stole them from the soldiers' camps. We did everything we could to defend our capital.' She inhaled deeply. 'The battle lasted ten days, after which Scion overwhelmed us, and the Prime Minister issued our surrender. Hristo fled to the Turkish border; I highly doubt he got there.'

'You picked up a gun in your memory.' A drop of rain iced my nose. 'You weren't going to use it on the soldiers.'

'Ah, you noticed,' she said. 'Back then, we didn't know how Scion would punish those who fought back, but I guessed. Unfortunately, the gun jammed. The soldiers beat me almost to death, then threw me into prison.' Her face tightened. 'Several years later, the new Grand Inquisitor of Bulgaria forced prisoners into heavy labour. That was when I managed to escape. I fled on a boat across the Black Sea, then spent months travelling across Europe, determined to find a large community of voyants. London's underworld embraced me.' Smoke plumed from her roll. 'We didn't last long, I know. But with every friend lost and home burned, we fought harder.'

'What kept you going?'

'Rage,' she said. 'That was my fuel. Sometimes people are only moved to action when they see others suffering – when the blood of innocents is shed. But they also need to see people standing, Paige.'

'And who decides who suffers and who stands?'

'You have to stand. We *must* get rid of Senshield. If you return to the capital with a dead commander and no evidence that you've damaged the core—'

'I know.'

Nothing would protect me then, Underqueen or not. Loyalty would sour to hatred; even my allies among the Unnatural Assembly would abandon me. ScionIDE would steamroll us all.

Time was of the essence, now more than ever.

'Maria,' I said, 'did Tom say where that voyant group was based?'

'Yes. The Edinburgh Vaults.'

'Any idea where they are?'

'Off a street called the Cowgate, which lies beneath South Bridge,' Maria said, 'but the entrance is hidden, and he wasn't sure where.'

'I'll go now. You . . . have a rest, if you need it.'

'No. I'll take Eliza and scout for information about the depot elsewhere.' She dropped the roll and ground it out underfoot. 'Vance will already be ahead of us, but let's not let her get too far.'

Back in the house, I unearthed a map of Edinburgh and spread it on a table. The Rephs had gone out, presumably to find some unsuspecting voyants to feed on.

Underneath my exhaustion, fear was building. Eight hours had passed since we left the factory. For all I knew, Vance was already here.

Nick came down the stairs, looking as tired as I felt. 'Where are you going, sötnos?'

'To find the Edinburgh Vaults. Tom thinks—' I stopped. 'Tom thought they were a hideout for a voyant group that's been here for decades.' My finger skated across the map, over the latticework of closes and wynds that branched off the Grand Mile, then south a little, landing on the Cowgate. 'He said they were close. Are you coming?'

'Of course.' Nick reached for his coat. 'But dare I ask if the depot is on the map, so we can avoid having to ask the local voyants for help finding it?'

'That would be too easy.'

I zipped up my puffer jacket and buckled my boots. A clock was ticking somewhere in the house.

'Nick,' I said, 'we . . . never spoke about the séance. About your sister.'

He turned away from the firelight as he buttoned his coat, obscuring his expression.

'It happened in Småland, where my family had moved from Mölle,' he said. 'I went home to see Lina for her birthday. The night after we celebrated, she snuck out to camp in the forest with her friends, against our parents' wishes. She had bought some bottles of Danish wine on the black market, so they could toast with alcohol, like they'd heard people did in the free world. When our father realised, he sent me after them. Hours too late.' He drew in a long breath. 'There were soldiers on patrol in the forest. Birgitta Tjäder stationed a lot of them in Sweden, ostensibly to protect Inquisitor Lindberg. According to the official notice of death we received from Tjäder, Lina and her friends had been using the wine to induce unnaturalness. Håkan, her boyfriend, was the eldest. He was fifteen.'

I had met Birgitta Tjäder in Oxford. Her reign of terror was notorious – she saw the slightest infringement of Inquisitorial law as high treason – but I couldn't imagine what sort of mind would perceive a group of kids drinking wine as deserving of the death penalty.

'I'm so sorry, Nick,' I said softly.

He nodded.

'I'm glad we did the séance. Now Lina is in many voyants' memories,' he said. 'Tjäder reports to Vance. Whatever we can do to hurt her is worth the risk.'

Just then, I sensed the cord and glanced up. Warden was in the doorway, his eyes green from a feed.

'Paige, Nick,' he said. 'On behalf of the Ranthen, I extend my sympathies for your loss. Tom will not be forgotten.'

'No. We'll make sure of it.' I straightened. 'Do you know Edinburgh, Warden?'

'Not as well as I know London, but I had cause to visit during my time as blood-consort.'

'Have you heard of the Edinburgh Vaults?'

'Yes.' He looked between us. 'Would you like me to take you there?'

16

THE VAULTS

Even in our dire straits, I could appreciate the beauty of the Old Town. Its motley buildings were charming, spires and rooftops clambering high, as if they were all trying to outmatch the nearby hills. The evening sky was like a finger painting, coral and amber with smudges of cloud. Warden led us up the flight of steps outside the safe house, past a smear of white graffiti reading ALBA GU BRÀTH. A cry for a lost country.

'Paige,' Nick said under his breath, 'what's going on between you and Warden?'

'Nothing,' I said quietly.

It wasn't exactly a lie. Nick looked like he wanted to ask more, but Warden had stopped, letting us catch up with his long strides.

I had thought I was acting as I always had around Warden in public, but something had betrayed me to Nick. As we fell into step, I was too aware of my expression, my posture, my tone of voice.

'I'm glad you made it back,' I said. 'Did you run into any Buzzers?'

'Yes.' He offered me a small vial. 'We harvested alysoplasm. I do not know if it will conceal you from Senshield, but you ought to have it.'

'Thank you.' I pocketed it. 'When were you last in Edinburgh?'

'Eight years ago.'

'I hadn't realised you ever left Oxford.'

'Only on rare occasions, with a chaperone,' he said, 'but now and then, Alsafi was chosen to guard me. Only then could I take my fill of a city.'

It had only been a couple of days since I had last seen him, but I had missed his voice. His presence was reassuring, even if he was avoiding my gaze. I couldn't quite meet his, either. I knew it would hurt if I did.

The steps led up to the Grand Mile, where cast-iron streetlamps burned from the fog – clean fog, the breath of the sea. Beneath our boots were broad, piebald cobblestones, sheened by rain. Restaurants and coffeehouses were filling up with evening trade, their patrons gathered by outdoor heaters, hands clasped around steaming glasses.

Some way along the street, a squadron of day Vigiles was on patrol. Fortunately, Warden could pass as human in fog as thick as this, though he was taller than everyone else on the street. We shadowed him down an incline, into a slum that sprawled beneath a bridge, darkened by a canopy of laundry. The smells of cooking and sewage mingled in the smoky air, and tattered Irish flags – green, white, and orange – were draped across the bridge.

It was forbidden to display the old Irish tricolour under any circumstances. The Vigiles must rarely come through here. Families huddled around outdoor fires, warming their hands, while a wizened man lifted clothes from a barrel and wrung them through a hand-operated mangle. A sign above his head read COWGATE.

Another corner of hell for the brogues. Scion had let a handful of us escape the terror of the invasion, but any who came after had been left to rot.

My father had known our position. It was only his job in Scion that kept us from a place like this. Even before we had left Tipperary, he had drummed it into me that I should never speak my first language, not even in private. I should bury the stories my grandparents had told me. I should be an English rose. I should forget.

He had been trying to protect me. I could forgive him, but it didn't mean that any of it had been easy to bear. There was no reason we couldn't have remembered our past, and our dead, in the privacy of our home.

Nick touched my shoulder. 'Paige.'

'I'm fine,' I said, and kept moving.

Warden waited for us in a street that splintered off the Cowgate. I felt his eyes on my face, but I turned mine into a mask.

'The South Bridge Vaults,' he said. 'Also known as the Edinburgh Vaults.'

The entrance was a slender archway. It resembled the entrance to a wynd – no one would think it was anything else – but I suspected we would never have found it on a map. An overpowering stench came wafting out. We all stepped back, coughing.

'Fish oil,' Warden said. 'The tenants burn it for light.'

The passageway was so dark, it was as if a hole had been cut out of my vision. I ducked in.

Inside, it was worse than I could have imagined. No daylight pierced these corridors of stone. The ceiling was low and curved. I kept one hand on the wall, my boots scrunching through oyster shells and rat droppings.

Stale draughts raised gooseflesh on my arms, but the cold wasn't what made this place so oppressive. Every pore of æther here was choked with spirits. Most were ghosts or shades, but I sensed poltergeists, too.

Water dripped from the ceiling, forming pools in the corners. Every so often, an oil lamp would shed queasy light, giving us a glimpse of the Vaults' amaurotic inhabitants, who slept inside cramped alcoves, curled around their few possessions. A few children sat by a tallow candle, playing games with bottle tops and making cats' cradles with string.

'I don't see any auras,' Nick said.

The ceiling dipped lower as we left the lamps behind. I felt the brick outline of another archway and eased my hand into the blackness. Another draught scuttled up my arm, lifting every fine hair.

'Wait.' I moved into it, feeling a smoother wall, made of plywood. 'There are dreamscapes somewhere below. I think there's—'

The wall gave way beneath my hand, and my boot plunged into nothing.

Some merciful reflex made me twist instead of toppling forward, sparing my head as I crashed down a slope. I was slithering into an abyss, heels and hands tearing at stone, gasping the air that rushed up to meet me. Rough brick nicked my cheek. More grazed my hip and thigh before my left side smashed through wooden boards. I fell with them, slammed into a hard floor, and rolled to a painful halt among the fragments.

For a long time, I didn't move, fearing I had broken something. When the golden cord vibrated, I gritted my teeth and pushed myself on to my elbows.

'Dreamer!'

I took a deep breath to call back. Dust shot into my nostrils, and I sneezed. As soon as I got to my feet, my head cracked against stone, flooring me again.

'*Bloody* shitting fuck—'

'It sounds as if she is alive,' Warden said.

I directed a dark look towards the ceiling. 'I'm fine, Nick,' I called. My hand scraped against the nearest wall. 'But I can't see a thing.'

A sliver of torchlight flashed past, giving me a glimpse of the boards I had come through. A sign reading TYPE E RESTRICTED SECTOR lay among them.

'Perfect.' I leaned against the wall. 'I always wanted to die alone in a Type E Restricted Sector.'

'What?' Nick shouted.

'It's a Type E—'

'Paige, you know that means the structure is unstable! Why aren't you panicking?'

'You're panicking enough for both of us,' I sang.

'Stay there. And don't move a muscle.'

Silence descended as Nick and Warden went to find a safe way down. The utter lack of light was disorienting.

Well, I wasn't just going to sit here, whatever Nick said. I rose with caution, navigating with my hands. From what I could tell by touch, I was in a narrow tunnel. A short distance from where I had fallen, what felt like wooden barrels formed a line along one wall. I might be able to scramble back up the slope, but it was steep and damp, the darkness deep enough to drown in.

As I searched blindly for another way out, my sixth sense demanded my attention. I felt the voyants' dreamscapes before I heard their footsteps. There was just enough time for me to shroud my face with my scarf again before they came into the tunnel.

The walls ran wild with tongues of firelight, making the shadows flicker. When a flaming torch swung towards my face, I shielded my eyes against the heat.

'Dè tha sibh a' dèanamh an seo?'

Finding myself at knifepoint, I raised my hands. The man was a medium, short and skinny, with a bony face. There must be little need to hide your identity down here. I listened carefully to what he said next: 'A bheil Gàidhlig agaibh?'

I lowered my hands. The language sounded very much like Irish, but the words weren't quite what they should be. I thought he was asking me what I was doing here, and whether or not I spoke . . .

Of course. Gàidhlig, the old language of Scotland, long since banned by Scion. It had the same roots as Irish, but that didn't make me fluent.

'Táim anseo chun teacht ar dhuine éigin,' I said, speaking slowly. *I'm here to find someone.*

The knife lowered by degrees. 'Spaewife,' the man called, 'we've found a brogue. Think she might be wanting to join us.'

Tom had mentioned that title. The leader of Edinburgh's voyant community.

At the other end of the passageway, five hooded voyants had gathered, each carrying a lantern. The woman at the front, who was wrapped in a twilled shawl, had the aura of a cartomancer. Her salted black hair was cut into a bob, and her dark, close-set eyes narrowed at the sight of me.

'How did you get in here?' she said in English. 'Who told you about the false wall?'

'No one. I just . . . found it.'

She eyed the shattered planks. 'A painful discovery, no doubt.'

'I need to speak to the leader of the Edinburgh voyants,' I said. 'Are you the Spaewife?'

She looked me up and down without comment, then spoke in soft Gàidhlig to one of the others and walked into the gloom. Two more augurs grasped my arms and escorted me through the passageways.

In another small chamber, oil lamps sputtered in every nook and cranny. A group of vile augurs sat around a rough triangle of bone, hand in hand, spirits dancing between them. Other voyants were sitting or lying in deep alcoves – laid with minimal bedding – or eating from cans. Most of them were deep in conversation, their voices raised to fever pitch. I caught a familiar name and stopped dead.

'What's that about Attard?'

The nearest voyants stopped talking. The Spaewife placed a hand on my back.

'We've just had news from Manchester,' she said. 'I suppose you haven't heard.'

'Roberta Attard, the Scuttling Queen, is dead,' another medium told me. 'And you'll never guess how.'

One of the osteomancers chuckled. 'Dinna make her guess.'

'She was murdered,' the medium said. 'By her sister.'

I must have been escorted to another vault, but I didn't remember moving my feet. Next thing I knew I was sitting down, and someone was offering me a drink that looked like honey and smelled like clove.

'You're all right, now.'

My hands were like ice. I wrapped them, finger by finger, around the glass.

'You're very pale all of a sudden,' the cartomancer said. 'I hope Roberta wasn't a friend of yours.'

'Catrin—' I cleared my throat. 'How do you know that Catrin killed her?'

She let go of my shoulder and sat on a cushion opposite me. Her hooded attendants stayed close.

'The news came to us this morning,' she said. 'Catrin Attard had joined a Mime Order raid on a factory and killed the Minister for

Industry, the man they call the Ironmaster. Roberta confronted her, and the two of them ended up fighting for leadership of the Scuttlers.' She shook her head. 'Terrible thing to happen. Roberta was a good woman, by all accounts. She wanted the best for her people.'

I sat in weary silence, numb.

An Underqueen should consider this purely in strategic terms. In those terms, perhaps this was progress. Catrin was a warmonger. With her sister gone, she could prepare the voyant community to rise against Scion. This was war, and war was ugly.

Yet the knowledge that my actions had killed Roberta, even if it hadn't been my intention, was stomach-turning. Catrin would have done it brutally and in public, to prove she was the one their father should have chosen – the one who would do anything for the Scuttlers.

She had warned me. She had said there would be trouble between them. In two days, I had turned the Manchester underworld on its head, and I had no idea what would become of it.

'On you go.' The Spaewife nodded to the glass in my hands. 'Hot toddy. Always makes me feel better.'

For the time being, I had to put Manchester behind me. Now was the time to reveal why I was here. When I raised my head to address the Spaewife, I caught sight of the wall behind her, where photographs had been arranged.

In one of them, a family of three stood in the mist, with rugged hills in the background. One was a thin woman with a careworn face; the other, a man in an oilskin, smiling in a way that didn't reach his eyes. Between them, they held a small girl with the same black hair, a ribbon fluttering.

And even though I had met her many years after this photograph had been taken, I knew her.

'Is that Liss Rymore?'

'Aye.' The Spaewife studied me. 'And who might you be?'

After a moment, I lowered my scarf, revealing my face. The hooded voyants exchanged glances before looking back at me.

'Goodness me,' the Spaewife muttered. She clasped her shawl around her shoulders. 'Paige Mahoney.'

I nodded.

'You were in Manchester, then,' she said. 'You led the raid on the factory.'

'I wanted to steal a military secret from Scion. What I found led me here, to Edinburgh,' I said. 'I'm very close to uncovering it, but I need local allies. If you want to save your voyants from Senshield, I'd appreciate your help.'

'Did you send the visions, too?'

'A friend of mine did that. An oracle.'

'And you let Catrin Attard kill the Minister for Industry.'

'Catrin made her own choice,' I said. 'What she did to Price, and to Roberta – that was not on my orders.'

One of the other voyants suddenly grasped her arm. 'Wait, Spaewife.'

He spoke too quickly for me to follow, but one word got my back up – *fealltóir*, an Irish term, used during the Molly Riots to refer to the handful of Irish people who had assisted Scion.

'I'm no traitor,' I said curtly.

The Spaewife raised her eyebrows. 'You have Gàidhlig, do you, Underqueen?'

'Gàidhlig or no, she ought to prove her claim,' the bearded man beside her said, looking askance at me. 'You might be one of Vance's spies, for all we know. Someone who only *looks* a great deal like Paige Mahoney.'

'Don't be a fool. The Underqueen is a dreamwalker,' the Spaewife said to him. 'Have you ever seen that sort of red aura?' (Apparently the whole of Britain knew about my gift.) 'Besides, she knows my Liss.'

She reached up to the wall of photographs and traced the one with Liss in it. For the first time, I saw the resemblance.

'I'm her aunt,' the Spaewife told me. 'My name is Elspeth Lin.' She returned to the cushion and poured herself a drink. 'You ken my niece, then?'

We could have gone to my aunt in Edinburgh, but my father was too proud to ask for help.

The truth would hurt, but I had to tell it. It wasn't fair to leave her with false hope.

'I'm sorry you have to hear this from a stranger, Elspeth,' I said. 'Liss is . . . in the æther.'

Her smile receded.

'I feared she was lost,' she murmured. 'I read my own cards a few weeks ago, and I drew Four of Swords. I saw Liss in a pool of blood.' She took a tarot deck from inside her shirt. 'I saw you, too, Paige. A great wave washed around your feet, and dark wings lifted you away. This card represents both a beginning and an end. Answering a call.'

She shuffled through her deck and passed me a card titled JUDGEMENT. It showed a fair-haired angel sounding a trumpet, surrounded by billows of smoke. The grey dead rose from their graves, lifting their hands, while high waves reared against a pale blue sky.

'A powerful card,' she said. 'You're going to make an important decision. Very soon.'

I held it for a long while. Readings always troubled me, but perhaps it was time I faced my future.

'You must tell me what happened to Liss,' Elspeth said. 'Tell me it was swift, at least.'

My throat seemed to grow smaller. 'Do you know about her parents?'

'I assumed. Arthur stopped writing to me.'

'He and Imogen died of lung fever. Liss was arrested,' I said. 'Scion sent her to serve in a . . . penal battalion. When I was sent to the same prison, Liss helped me adjust. She was kind.'

'That sounds like her.'

Elspeth waited. I wasn't sure how I could possibly explain Oxford.

'I was with her,' I said, each word strained. 'I said the threnody.'

Elspeth closed her eyes. I took a slug of the drink.

When all I had wanted was to kick and scream, Liss had given me the strength to bite my tongue and play the game. It still hurt that she had never left Oxford. She had wanted to go back to Scotland, to the clearing in her dreamscape.

'I see.' Elspeth breathed in. 'We canna truly grieve for those who've gone. Not before we've fought to change the world that took them. If you were a friend to someone as sweet and good-hearted as Liss, that gives us all the more reason to help you.'

I handed back the Judgement card.

'Liss did an ellipse reading for me before she died,' I said. 'Perhaps you could help me understand it.'

'Aye.'

When Elspeth presented me with the deck, I took her favoured numen from her hand with care. It was a sign of great trust and respect for a soothsayer to allow a fellow voyant to handle their connection to the æther. I laid out the six cards in order: Five of Cups, King of Wands inverted, the Devil, the Lovers, Death inverted, and Eight of Swords.

'An ellipse spread uses seven cards,' Elspeth said.

'The last card was lost.'

'Ah.' She traced the cards. 'Liss was a prodigy. Even when she was a bairn, she could handle a deck and see visions. Have you worked any of these out, Paige?'

'The first two, I think.'

Five of Cups was my father in mourning, presumably for my mother, who had died shortly after I was born. The inverted King of Wands had to be Jaxon, referring to the power he had once had over me.

'That makes sense. Your past and your present,' Elspeth said. 'The third card would have indicated your future at the time of the reading.' She picked it up. 'The Devil.'

'Liss said it represented hopelessness and fear, but that I'd chosen it myself,' I said. 'That it represents someone I can escape, even if I don't know it.'

Elspeth held the card up to the light.

'You're moving against Hildred Vance. She's certainly a force of hopelessness and fear, and it seems she was in all our futures,' she said darkly, 'but I doubt many people would give in to her by choice.' She scrutinised the card, as if the Devil might reveal its identity to her of its own free will, if only she looked hard enough. 'Notice the other figures below. The Devil looms over a man and a woman.'

She flipped it to face me. The Devil was as sinister as its name implied, with its downturned mouth and staring white eyes. Two naked figures were on either side of the pedestal, bound to it – and by extension, to each other, by a silver chain.

'The two figures closely resemble the couple in the Lovers card, which comes next,' Elspeth said. 'They could almost *be* the Lovers. Look closely. The Devil controls them. Manipulates them.'

The words left a fine sweat on my brow. For the first time, a possibility occurred.

The Devil could be Terebell. Both Warden and I were chained to her: Warden by his loyalty, me by a need for her support. We were also bound to each other by a chain, albeit a chain of gold.

'The Lovers have a witness, too.' Elspeth pointed to a winged figure above the man and woman. 'Someone is always watching this couple.'

Liss had given little detail on the Lovers, except that it would show me what to do. *I can't see anything, but there's tension between spirit and flesh*, she had told me. *The card has weight. This will be a pillar of your life.* I hadn't understood her at the time, but I had since collided with a lover – or someone who might have become one, at least.

As a Reph, Warden was neither pure spirit, nor flesh. We had always felt watched, knowing the consequences of discovery. If he represented the path I should be taking, then by trying to distance myself from him, by telling him we had to part, I had gone astray; I had turned my back on the counsel of the cards.

And yet he could so easily be the Devil himself – or a puppet in its service, keeping me chained.

Was he meant to be my lover or my downfall?

'The way I see it,' Elspeth said, 'you must follow the path of the Lovers. Stay close to the person you think the card might represent, and make sure you've identified that person correctly. If you stray from whoever it is, I suspect you'll be vulnerable to the Devil.' She gathered the deck back together. 'I hope the answers soon become clear to you, Paige.'

My brow was knitted. Once again, I had more questions than answers.

I shook myself. I couldn't dwell on this when I was getting so close to Senshield.

Not when another devil could be watching us, preparing to cast another net around me.

'There's a reason I came searching for you all.' I looked between the voyants. 'I need to know how to find the Edinburgh Central Depot.'

Elspeth's expression was guarded. 'Why?'

'Because I want to deactivate Senshield. And I think the key is in there.' She pursed her lips. 'You'll not find the depot on any map,' she said, 'but those of us who live here know fine well where it is. You'll find it in Leith – a military district beside the port, off limits to most denizens. Don't try to get in. You'll wind up dead or captured.'

These days, just going outside put me at risk of winding up dead or captured. If I let that daunt me, I would never do anything.

17

BLOOD AND STEEL

Nick and Warden eventually found me, after making their way through a convoluted network of tunnels. We emerged from the Edinburgh Vaults, into the light of a low sun, which had banished the fog and now glared off the snow. I was armed with a pistol from Elspeth, whose voyants had been able to build up a cache of weapons over many years, stolen from vehicles bound for the depot. She had promised us assistance, supplies, and somewhere to hide, should we need it while we were in Edinburgh.

As we returned to the safe house, I pictured the faces of people I'd seen, suffering under Scion. The Mime Order, entombed in the Beneath. The factory hands, tired and beaten. The Irish, ostracised. The night Vigiles, threatened by a technology that might destroy us all.

Yet now I thought of others, too – the living and defiant. Elspeth Lin, who might be the last member of a family Scion had torn apart, resolved to keep fighting. My high commanders in London. The Ranthen. The friends who had refused to let me do this on my own. I didn't know if we could stop the machine, but a fire had started deep within it. Even the smallest flame could raze the strongest house.

Eliza and Maria awaited us in the parlour. From their frustrated expressions, their investigations had been fruitless.

'Paige,' Eliza said. 'Did you find the voyants?'

'Yes,' I said. 'They'll help us.'

'And the depot?'

'It's in Leith. We should go now.'

Lucida narrowed her eyes. 'When *was* the last time you slept, Underqueen?'

'I'm fine.'

Maria was already digging out the tracker. 'Yes,' she breathed. 'Look at what happens when you try to zoom in on Leith.' She showed me the screen. The district appeared as a nebulous smear on the coast, not too far from the middle of Edinburgh. 'Scion doesn't even want its own satellites to see what's going on there.'

'All the more reason for us to go. Eliza, you didn't have a proper chance to recover from the possession in Manchester,' I said. 'We need someone on the outside if we get into trouble. Would you prefer to stay here?'

'I can do that,' she said. 'Just be careful, Paige.'

As evening fell, we made for Leith. Instead of an Underground or a monorail, Edinburgh had a system of automated trams that ran round the clock. While the Rephs went their own way, the rest of us found a tram towards Leith and took seats at the back, away from other passengers. We got off at the terminus, where Lucida and Warden waited.

A fence divided Leith from the rest of Edinburgh. All I could see beyond it were more buildings. I spied a camera jutting from a wall and backed into the shelter of a doorway, reading a red sign on the fence.

WARNING

SCIONIDE MILITARY ZONE

ACCESS IS RESTRICTED BY THE GRAND

COMMANDER IN ACCORDANCE WITH

INQUISITORIAL LAW. USE OF DEADLY FORCE IS AUTHORISED.

'We're going in,' I said.

Maria looked mystified. 'How?'

I lifted an eyebrow.

'Ah,' she said, with a smirk. 'Of course.'

The nearest guard was alone. It took me more time than I wanted to worm into his dreamscape, and he made a hell of a fuss as I overcame his defences, but I managed to keep my claws in him for long enough to walk him to the gate and open it. I was getting better at this.

As soon as she could fit through, Maria charged forward and knocked the guard out with the butt of his own gun. I returned to my own body just as Nick was carrying it into the facility. Warden and Lucida stepped through before the gate closed with a hiss behind us, sealing itself with a throb of red light.

Nick set me on my feet. We were inside a military district, edging through the darkened streets that must lead to the depot. Warden and Lucida moved ahead of us, ready to silence any soldiers that appeared, while Nick kept an eye out for cameras and scanners. With every step, a feeling that we were being watched crept up on me. Probably my rising paranoia about Vance.

'Paige,' Maria said, 'I feel I should know more about your gift. Did I need to knock the guard out?'

'Let's not take any chances.' I kept my voice as low as hers. 'My hosts usually fall unconscious after I leave, but it seems to depend on the person. And they don't stay down for long.'

'Noted.'

Despite the cold, my nape was damp. A wrong move here could get us all killed. I sensed people in the buildings, but no one seemed to be on the streets. This section of Leith must be solely administrative, a smokescreen hiding the real secret.

I was proven right when we came to a ten-foot concrete wall. On top of *that* was another fence, crowned with metal spikes, adding another nine or ten feet to the height of the barrier. A few more signs warned that deadly force was authorised.

'Somebody give me a boost,' I said.

'Wait. Let me go first.' Maria tied her coat around her waist. 'Warden, you're the tallest. Mind giving a lady a leg-up?'

Warden glanced at Lucida, who was visibly scandalised. Maria, blissfully unaware of the Rephs' aversion to contact with humans, gave him an expectant look.

'I will,' Nick said, and cupped his hands.

Nick was strong, but he couldn't hoist Maria quite high enough. She made one grab for the wall that almost unbalanced them both, causing Nick to swear through his teeth and lower her.

'Sorry.' Maria grinned at Warden. 'Has to be you, big man.'

A hysterical urge to laugh seized me. Lucida didn't seem thrilled by this state of affairs, but we weren't in a position to debate it. Warden lifted Maria with ease, letting her stand on his shoulder. She caught the top of the wall and scrambled up.

In the moments she was out of sight, I didn't breathe. I half expected to hear a gunshot, but her head soon popped over the edge.

'Come on,' she whispered.

Warden gave me a nod. I stepped on to his palm, then his shoulder. He held my calf to steady me, sending a shiver up to my back as I reached for Maria. She took both my hands and some of my weight. My boots scraped on the smooth wall, seeking traction. When I was up, Maria patted me on the back.

'Take a look, Underqueen,' she said, a little hoarsely. 'Just try not to scream.'

I hunkered down on my stomach and crawled right up to the fence. What I saw beyond it, I knew I would never forget.

Hundreds of tanks formed perfect columns in front of a black warehouse, surrounded by armed soldiers. Even in my darkest moments, I could never have imagined that a force of this magnitude really existed.

The people of Edinburgh must have no idea that they shared their citadel with so many war machines. This was what the factories were generating in Manchester; what human blood had been shed to create.

Warden appeared on my right. His eyes flamed as he took it in. Nick joined us and dug out his binoculars. He absorbed it all for a couple of minutes, then handed them over, ashen. I focused on the nearest unit. The soldiers' armoured backs were emblazoned with SECOND INQUISITORIAL DIVISION. And I could see now that the SL-59 rifles they carried had a thin strip of white light along the barrel.

The scanner-guns had been brought here from Manchester as ordinary firearms. Now they were pieces of ethereal technology. They really were activated here.

In the darkness beyond the floodlights, the iron hulls of warships were just visible. One emptied soldiers down a gangway, while two others drank them back in.

'Second Inquisitorial Division,' I murmured, reading their armour again. 'That's the overseas invasion force, not homeland security.'

Images knifed their way to the front of my mind. Placards held towards the sky. A blaze of copper hair and gunfire as Finn turned to meet his doom.

The soldiers had worn plain clothes in Dublin, to take us by surprise, but they had been from this division.

'The last incursion was in 2046,' Maria said. 'Scion is overdue another.' Her face was bloodless. 'This is how Vance means to commemorate the New Year. Some free-world country has fallen into the shadow of the anchor, and now its time is up.'

I looked to Warden. 'Did the Sargas ever talk about any more invasions?'

'They aim to establish total control over humans,' he reminded me. 'I did not hear of any specific targets, but nowhere on Earth will be spared.'

We stayed there for a long time, taking in the immensity of our enemy – the tanks, the artillery, and the soldiers moving around it all, like clockwork.

'Wait.' Nick was peering through the binoculars again. When he lowered them, his features tightened. 'Helvete. It's Tjäder.'

Maria snatched the binoculars before I could. A moment later, she lowered them.

'And someone else.' She glanced at me. 'Someone you'll be delighted to see.'

I took the binoculars from her unresisting hands.

They were walking away from one of the warships, flanked by soldiers. I remembered Birgitta Tjäder from Oxford – pale and glacial, with high cheekbones. Her thick hair was braided and wound at the back of her head, and she was garbed in light armour, carrying a helmet under her arm. Tjäder was best known as the Chief of Vigilance in Stockholm, but these days, she also commanded the Second Inquisitorial Division.

The feeling evaporated from my limbs when the lights threw the second person into sharp relief. The official beside Tjäder was an arrow of a woman, who barely came up to her shoulder. Even from a distance, I knew her. The white hair, the Reph-like lack of expression, those abyssal black eyes – eyes that swallowed information, letting no morsel escape. The last time I had seen this face, it had been on the screen in the warehouse, and I had been helpless in a net.

Hildred Vance, the woman destined to conquer the world for the Rephs.

Finally, I was seeing her in the flesh.

This time, she wasn't just going to toy with me from a distance. This time, she had come to collect me herself.

Like most Archon officials, she wore a tailored suit and a high-collared cape with a crimson lining. As I watched her, her gaze flicked upward, and it seemed for all the world as if she was looking straight at me. I backed away, nausea unfurling in the pit of my stomach.

'We have to move.'

Nick tensed. 'What's wrong?'

Vance had already turned back to Tjäder, but I was shaken.

'She knows we're up here.' I swallowed. 'She was staring right at me.'

'Everyone thinks that when they see her,' Maria said. 'It's just her eyes, sweet. She looks at the entire world as if it means nothing to her.'

I drew a steadying breath.

'We can't search this place,' Nick said. 'It's too dangerous.'

'The core could be there,' I said under my breath. 'The scanners might be activated right inside that warehouse. I'll be damned if all this was for nothing. I'm taking a look in there, even if I have to possess one of those murderous bastards to do it.'

'You *can't*, Paige. Scion was ready for your possessions in Manchester. If the soldiers realise—'

'I will go,' Warden said.'

The rest of us stared at him.

'You're not serious,' I managed. 'Even if you could get through the barrier—' He took hold of the fence and pulled two of the bars apart, creating a large enough gap. The rest of that sentence died on my tongue. 'Warden, you are not going in there. As Underqueen, I order you not to go in there.'

He never took his eyes off the depot. 'Permission to disregard your orders, Underqueen.'

'Permission not granted,' I hissed. 'Permission categorically denied.'

'Paige, we don't have a choice,' Maria pointed out. 'If we leave now, we lose our chance of finding out what powers Senshield. This is what you've wanted to do from the beginning. The only way to help the Mime Order.' She grasped my arm. 'We're all in this with you. We're all willing to stand.'

Warden stayed where he was, waiting.

It made the most sense for him to go. If he was shot, he would survive. In the unlikely event that he was captured – which would require Scion to have poppy anemone to hand – he was fast and strong enough to escape. He had the element of surprise if someone saw him, giving him enough time to react. He could also move in silence through the guarded building.

In short, he was a Reph, and that made him better for this mission than any of the humans.

'Permission granted,' I said.

Almost in one movement, he was through the fence and over the edge of the wall. Maria crawled through the gap and looked down, holding her hood in place.

For the time Warden was gone, I stayed prone on the concrete, keeping close to Maria and Nick. Here on the coast, the wind was callous. I watched Tjäder and Vance disappear into the vast warehouse, the soldiers stopping to salute the Grand Commander.

I didn't want Warden in there. The thought of him near Vance was sickening. I cleaned the mist from my watch and saw the seconds click away, trying not to imagine the soldiers emptying their guns into him.

He would come back. He must come back.

I would not consider what would happen if he didn't.

A gloved hand appeared on the wall, making us all flinch. A moment later, Warden came into view, holding something in the crook of one arm.

He joined us on the other side of the fence. I let out my breath. 'Did anyone see you?'

'If they had,' he said, 'I presume that we would know of it.'

'Is the core there?'

His gaze met mine.

'No,' he said, 'but I found this.'

He presented me with a heavy rifle. It was an SL-59, just like the ones we had stolen from the factory, but with a single, crucial difference. This one had been activated. The white stripe glowed along its barrel.

'Perhaps this is best explained at the safe house,' Warden said.

'You saw something.'

'Yes.'

He took the gun back.

'We'll meet you back at the safe house,' I said. 'Let's take a closer look at this thing.'

The guard was still unconscious when we rushed past him. Getting out of the district was easier than it had been to get in, but we broke into a run as soon as we cleared the fence. Suddenly, the sheer recklessness of what we had done was catching up with me.

We parted ways with the Rephs and took a tram to Waverley Bridge – one of two over the valley that divided the Old Town from the New Town. Rain soaked us to the skin as we returned to Anchor Close.

Eliza was sitting on the couch, wrapped in a duvet. When she saw us, she breathed out.

'There you are.'

'We're okay,' Nick said. 'Are the Rephs back?'

'They're doing a séance upstairs. Warden . . . left the gun on the table.'

The rest of us moved to stand around the rifle. Maria was the first to touch it.

'An activated SL-59,' she said. 'Our new worst enemy.'

She skimmed a finger along the thread of light. Once she had detached the magazine and scrutinised the bullets, she handled the weapon with practised ease. Even knowing it was empty, Eliza tensed when it was pointed at her.

'Sorry, sweet,' Maria said. 'I need a voyant Senshield can detect. The gun itself still seems unremarkable, so I assume it's the scope that's—' She peered through it. 'Ah. There it is.'

She let me look. Through the scope of the SL-59, the world had no colour, but Eliza was surrounded by a faint glow, which had to be her aura.

'May I?'

Warden had materialised with Lucida, who seemed to be his shadow now. Maria shrugged and handed him the scanner-rifle, which he examined.

I had never seen a Reph hold a firearm; the sight was strangely unsettling. After a minute of silent contemplation, Warden removed the scope and took a capsule from beneath it, snapping a tress of wire. The white light ebbed, and the gun was just a gun again.

'I found no evidence of a single core in the warehouse,' he said, 'but these were being added to the guns.'

He held out the capsule, showing us. It was silver and shaped like an almond, about the size of your average painkiller.

'Right,' I said, perplexed. 'Is that an ethereal battery?'

'No,' Warden said. 'There is no spirit inside it.'

'Can I take a look?'

Warden handed it to me and returned the gun to the table. The capsule was softer than I had expected, with a little give.

Following my instincts, I pressed it between my finger and thumb. After a moment, it ruptured, releasing a tiny burst of molten light. Lucida let out a hiss of Gloss.

'What—' Eliza stared. 'What is that stuff?'

'Ectoplasm.' I ran it between my fingers. 'Reph blood.'

Handling it drank the warmth from my skin. The æther glittered around me, making me light-headed.

Warden looked down at the ectoplasm, eyes burning. His face was hard in a way I had rarely seen it.

'This is not an ethereal battery,' he said. 'What it is, I cannot say, but I can make some observations.'

'Please do.'

'The ectoplasm is molten and luminous. Usually, a certain amount of time outside of our bodies will vitrify it, extinguishing its properties. When that process occurs, it darkens. This has not.'

Nick frowned. 'Why?'

Warden paced around the gun. We all waited for his judgement, watching him.

'As you know, Paige, Nashira is similar to a binder,' he said, 'though far more dangerous. She can not only control voyants' spirits, but turn them into fallen angels, stealing the gifts they had in life.'

'What the fuck,' Maria said, 'is a fallen angel?'

'I'll tell you later,' I said.

'Let us suppose that Nashira found a voyant who was especially sensitive to the æther,' Warden continued. 'And let us suppose that she bound their spirit to an object with her blood, as many binders can.'

'An object,' I said. 'You mean . . . a scanner?'

'Yes.'

'Jaxon said his blood was like ethereal glue,' Eliza said, her brow creasing. 'He used it to bind the muses to the den.'

Warden nodded. 'By installing each scanner with a capsule of her own ectoplasm – and I believe it to be hers – Nashira could theoretically link them to one of her angels, instilling each one with its gift.'

Nick was starting to look curious. 'Jaxon couldn't attach one spirit to *many* places.'

'Nashira is a Reph,' Eliza pointed out. 'That makes her a sort of . . . super-binder, right?'

I couldn't think straight. Perhaps it was because I hadn't slept properly in a while, but I was starting to feel dangerously close to losing it.

'To put it simply,' Warden said. 'A fallen angel is no ordinary spirit. A shade or ghost would likely be too weak to power many scanners, if any, but an angel or a breacher could. That is my supposition.'

'That's quite a supposition.' Maria breathed out. 'You lost me, my friend, but I commend your intelligence.'

'I can explain it again, if you wish.'

'No, thank you. My brain is melting.'

'I'd usually trust your intuition,' I said to Warden, 'but I don't believe this of Nashira. Would she really let lowly humans take pints of her blood and put it into hundreds, maybe *thousands* of scanners?'

'Perhaps.' Warden looked back at the gun. 'Her ambition knows no bounds. She would go much further than other Rephaim.'

'Does that mean—' I couldn't face this possibility. 'Does that mean the core is one of her angels?'

'If so, where would it be kept?' Maria said. 'Here in Edinburgh?'

'The spirit could be anywhere.' Warden paused. 'But if I were to make an educated guess, I would say it is most likely with Nashira.'

My legs could no longer take my weight. I sank into a chair.

'So we have to destroy her,' I said softly. 'That's the answer.' I let out a faint laugh. 'You know, I really thought I was getting close. For a whole three days, I actually believed I could save the Mime Order.'

'Paige,' Warden said, 'there may be another way to detach the spirit from Senshield. In any case, this is is only conjecture.'

'We need more than fucking conjecture,' I snapped. 'We thought we'd find the core in the depot, but all we have is guesswork and another fucking gun. I nearly killed us all in Manchester – I *did* kill Tom, not to mention Roberta – and for what? For this?' I held up the light on my fingers. 'No. That's it. It's over.'

Nobody spoke. I turned away from their eyes, feeling my own fill with heat.

'Paige,' Maria said, 'this journey was always a shot in the dark, but—'

'Wait,' Eliza cut in. 'Do you hear that?'

We listened. A message was coming through the public address system.

I pulled my hood up and went back outside.

Snow brushed my face. It was the middle of the night – not the usual time for Scion to be making public announcements, but Weaver had broken that mould. When we reached the top of the steps, we found ourselves at the edge of a small crowd of people. The vast transmission screen on the Grand Mile was full of Hildred Vance.

'. . . *Grand Inquisitor has heard your calls for fair and equal treatment of all criminals who pledge allegiance to the Mime Order,*' she was saying. '*Tonight, as Grand Commander, I hope to demonstrate to you the benefits of martial law.*'

Vance stared into Edinburgh. Scion officials usually addressed the public with a white background behind them, but she was quite clearly outside. Behind her, I recognised the Gothic monument on Inquisitors Street, just across Waverley Bridge.

She was letting me know she was here, in the citadel.

'*Two days ago, we received intelligence that Paige Mahoney, leader of the Mime Order, had escaped the capital and travelled to the North West to spread her violent message of contempt for Scion,*' Vance said. '*I have a message for Paige Mahoney. She cannot insult the anchor with impunity.*'

The voices around us drowned out her next words.

'. . . *execution will be carried out immediately, in accordance with martial law. So perish all the anchor's enemies.*'

Her face disappeared, replaced by a white screen. When the broadcast returned, the feeling drained from my face.

It wasn't the sight of the executioner. It wasn't the golden sword in his hands, poised high for the kill. It was the man whose neck was on the block, hands shackled behind his back. A man who seemed so much older than he had when I had last seen him, with his bloodshot eyes and scruffy beard and threads of silver in his hair.

LIVE: EXECUTION OF COLIN MAHONEY, the screen informed the country. UNNATURAL PROGENITOR AND TRAITOR.

Don't scream.

That sliver of survival instinct came out of the ringing in my head. Screaming would let everyone know I was here. Nobody else cared about Cóilín Ó Mathúna. Nobody was left. Nick was speaking to me, grasping my shoulders, but I couldn't tear my gaze from the screen. Every bead of sweat, every quiver of his lips, was so clear that I could almost believe I was there with him on the Lychgate, waiting.

There had been times when I needed my father, and he had looked away. When I had held out my arms, and he had turned his back, refusing to see me. But now, in his final moments, I felt more like his daughter than I ever had. I remembered our very last night at the farm, eleven years ago. He had carried me into the fields and shown me the sky, where meteors were darting over Ireland.

Look, seileán. He had sounded lost in a way I hadn't understood. *Even the sky has learned to weep.*

When the sword came down, I didn't close my eyes. I owed him that much.

To see what I had done.

I don't remember how I got back to the safe house. I have a dim memory of my tongue prickling, and a sense that I was floating. As I drifted in and out of consciousness, my thoughts shattered into ruby and gold, a labyrinth of thorns with no escape. Somewhere in the twisting darkness, I heard my grandmother singing a lullaby in Irish. I tried to call to her, but the words fell straight out of my mouth and broke at my feet, their wings useless.

When my eyes opened, I was underneath a blanket on the couch, and the hearth was full of embers. I watched them glimmer for a long time.

I was an orphan now. My father and I hadn't spoken properly in years – there had been too much pain between us – but I had never forgotten him. He was the embodiment of a simpler world. We could have reconciled after all this, when he understood that I had only ever been fighting to make our lives better. Whatever happened, I had always known I had a family to return to at the end.

'We do not have time to delay.' A glassy voice. 'Why has she still not moved?'

'She's grieving,' Nick said. 'Colin was the only family she had left. Don't you have parents, Lucida?'

'Rephaim are not offspring.'

I heard a sigh.

'If we're going to do this, someone needs to make sure she doesn't follow us. Paige won't let us risk our lives if she's not doing the same.'

'I'm coming with you this time,' Eliza said. 'I want to prove to her that I can hack this.'

They shushed each other as I shifted, my head throbbing. I had almost drifted off again when a cool hand touched my forehead.

'Paige?'

Nick was crouched beside me. With a heavyeyed nod, I sat up and drank from the mug of tea he offered.

'I'm so sorry, sweetheart.'

'It was always going to happen. From the moment I left Oxford,' My throat was raw. 'I . . . should feel worse than this.'

'You're in shock.'

That must be why my hands were steady. That must be why I felt burned through.

'Colin loved you,' Nick said, his voice soft. 'I saw the way people ostracised him at work, but he stomached it all to protect you, sötnos.'

I nodded again.

Maria and Eliza came into the parlour. Eliza sat beside me and squeezed my hand, while Maria sat in the armchair. At first, I wanted to shrink away from their sympathetic expressions. I had killed my father, not Vance. I was the reason he was dead, unworthy of their compassion.

But no. I couldn't allow myself to think like this. Scion had started to demolish my family before they had even known my name, starting with the Imbolc Massacre. I could have tried harder to rescue him, but it wasn't my hand that had wielded the blade.

'We might not be able to kill Nashira,' I said. 'But we *can* kill Vance.'

'No. That's exactly what you *mustn't* try and do.' Maria held down my arm. 'This is another move in her game, the game that started in Fulham. You've come too close to her secret. Now she wants you gone.'

I tried to make myself listen. All I could see was the blood on the sword.

'You've impressed her. She wasn't expecting a nineteen-year-old woman without any military training to evade capture for as long as you have,' Maria went on. 'Now she's going to try to draw you out for the last time.'

Nick placed a hand on my shoulder. 'How?'

'That broadcast was clearly pre-recorded. She was standing right next to a landmark. That was intentional. She wants Paige to go there, hungry for vengeance. That's where she will have set up the next trap.'

It took effort to hold my body still.

'Why kill him?' My eyes felt parched. 'Why not keep him alive to blackmail me?'

'Perhaps because she was no other use for him. Or there's another move to come,' Maria said. 'This is just what she did to Rozaliya. First, she clouds your judgement. Then, once you're vulnerable, she strikes. You need to stay calm, Paige. You need to defy her expectations.'

My fist closed, blanching my knuckles.

'We're not going back to London with nothing to show for it,' I said. 'I want to destroy those scanners.'

'That's exactly what we were thinking. We can set fire to the warehouse.'

I gave her a weary look. 'Are you a pyromancer or a pyromaniac?'

'Come on. Just this once,' Maria said, her gaze hungry. 'Fire leaves no evidence. Fire is our friend.'

It would send Vance a message, even if it failed. Even if it was a desperate plan – one I would never have sanctioned under ordinary circumstances.

'Fine.' I wasn't in the frame of mind to argue. 'Burn it down.'

Maria gave a little crow of triumph.

'How will we get close enough to cause this great inferno?' asked Nick, who had been listening. 'Leith is guarded to the hilt, if you remember correctly.'

'Lucida or Warden can help, and Elspeth might be willing to send a few voyants as lookouts.' I made to get up. 'I'll tell her the plan, at least.'

'Paige.' Maria grasped my arm. 'You can't go.'

'I'm Underqueen. If this is our last stand—'

'Paige,' Nick said, 'you just lost your father. You're the most wanted person in Scion.'

'And you're too susceptible to Vance,' Maria added gently. 'If she tries to manipulate you now, you might not be able to fight it. We're all in agreement, sweet. You need to be as far away as possible from all of this.'

I could tell from the others' faces that they would brook no argument. My gaze shifted to Warden.

'Fine,' I said. 'I'll go to the hills, stay out of the way. I won't even be able to see or hear the transmission screens. Warden, will you come with me?'

'Good idea,' Nick said, looking relieved. 'You shouldn't go by yourself.'

I could tell that Warden was trying to work out why I had chosen him over one of the others. It would be our first time alone together since our agreement. Finally, he nodded.

'Very well.'

'Excellent.' Maria slotted her guns into their holsters. 'Come on, then, team. Let's give Scion a night to remember.'

18

VIGIL

Warden and I went on foot through the rain, taking a few provisions. We were making for the hills behind Haliruid House – once a royal palace, now the official residence of the Grand Inquisitor in the Lowlands. The others had already left for the warehouse in a state approaching fevered excitement. After days of whispers and machinations, they were finally going to destroy a Scion building – or try, in any case.

Haliruid Park was thick with pine trees. We hiked around them and up the rough-hewn hills, belted by a bitter wind. Neither of us said a word.

The higher we ascended, the thicker the fog in my breath. By the time we reached a good vantage point, the cold was starting to break through my gloves, even my snow boots. My thermals sealed in some body heat, but my face was turning numb.

We made camp below an overhang, sheltering from the rain. The dry space beneath afforded us a clear view of the citadel. I took out some canned heat and placed it between us.

'Do you have a lighter?'

Warden reached into his coat and handed one to me. I lit the alcohol in the can, setting a blue flame.

Our vigil began. I was supposed to be safe from Vance up here, but she was waiting for me in the citadel, preparing to spring her trap. I couldn't imagine what it would be this time. All I knew was that it would be designed to result in my capture, and in turn, my eventual death. She had no intention of letting me escape this place.

Above us, the sky was a chasm, a mouth that threatened to swallow the earth. Up here, I could almost pretend that only he and I existed.

There was a tight weight in my stomach. My father and my failure, knotted together.

'My condolences for your loss, Paige.'

I shifted, if only to stop myself freezing in place.

'I don't know if *loss* covers it,' I said. 'He was taken.'

Warden looked at me, then away. 'Forgive me. Some . . . subtleties of English still elude me.'

'People do say it. It just doesn't make sense.'

We were associates now. I was Black Moth, Underqueen of the Mime Order, and he was Arcturus, Warden of the Mesarthim. Both of us committed only to the cause.

The last thing I should be doing was pouring out my heart to him.

'The clearest memory I have of my father is from when I was five,' I said. 'He'd been in Dublin for a while, and I'd been counting down the days until he came back to Tipperary. Every morning, I would ask my grandmother how long it was until he was home. I would sit at the kitchen table with her and draw pictures for him. Eventually, he came back. I sensed him. Even when I was very young, I could feel dreamscapes. Not as well as I can now, but well enough.

'So I knew he was coming,' I went on. 'I waited for him at the boundary of my grandparents' land, until I saw the car. I ran to him. I thought he would pick me up, but he pushed me away. *Get back, Paige, for pity's sake.* I was so little; I didn't understand why he wasn't happy to see me . . . I still loved him, for years. I tried. And then, at some point, I just . . . stopped trying.'

Warden watched my face.

'I'm sure Nick is right, and he loved me,' I said, 'but he didn't know how to show it. I don't think I reminded him too much of my mother, or anything like that. I just think he knew I was unnatural, and it frightened him.' I held my fingers over the flame. 'Sorry. You don't have to be my grief counsellor.'

'Our agreement did not make me indifferent to you, Paige.'

The wind dried my eyes.

'I know how your mother died,' Warden said, 'but not her name. That does not seem right.'

I hadn't spoken it aloud in years, not having any need.

'Cora,' I said. 'Cora Spencer.'

The only dead member of my family who hadn't been killed by Scion.

'You feel that you are not as angry about your father's death as you should be.'

'He was all that was left of my family,' I said. 'I should be grief-stricken, or . . . consumed by the need for revenge, like Vance wants me to be.'

'I cannot tell you how to feel. I am no one's son. What I will tell you is that you cannot force yourself to mourn. Sometimes, the best way to honour the dead is to simply keep living. In war, it is the only way.'

The ensuing silence was heavy, but his words did ease the strain.

I thought of the cards. The Devil, the Lovers. He could be either of them, or both, or neither.

'You knew what I was feeling,' I said. 'Do you always know?'

'No,' Warden said. 'On rare occasions, I have some sense of your feelings. A glimpse into your mindset. It soon fades. Whatever the golden cord is, it remains an enigma. As do you.'

'You can talk. I've never met someone so wilfully cryptic.'

'Hm.'

I looked in the direction of the sea, where the warships floated. Wind rushed through our shelter, chilling my neck. The conversation had distracted me from what I had to do.

'You should rest,' Warden said. 'We have nothing to do but wait.'

'I won't sleep. It's too cold.'

'You are welcome to my coat.'

I looked at him, shivering. 'Don't you need it?'

'Not for warmth. It would invite unwanted interest,' he said, 'were I to be without a coat in these conditions.'

Even my knees were shaking. He looked as composed as always, so I nodded. When he passed me the coat, I draped it over my jacket, trying not to notice the faint scent of him that clung to its lining.

'Thank you.' I held it around me. 'I'd heard Scotland was freezing, but this is something else.'

'Hm.'

The silence closed in again, like the tide. His coat helped, but I still wouldn't sleep. Not with Vance this close.

She was out there, somewhere in the night, waiting for me. It was only a matter of time.

'This is it.' I wet my chapped lips. 'How long did we last against the anchor? Three months?'

'This is not the end, Paige.'

The wind tossed my hair across my face. I huddled deeper into his coat.

'Warden, there's a reason I asked you to come up here with me.' I managed to look him in the eye. 'First, I wanted to say that I'm sorry.'

His expressions had never been easy to read, but the shadows made it impossible.

'Sorry for what, Paige?'

'Adhara Sarin will only support the Mime Order if it has strong leadership. I wanted to prove that I was the leader you needed – that I could change things – but I failed.'

My thumb circled the old scars on my palm. I couldn't bring myself to watch the fire die in his eyes again.

'You believed in me,' I said. 'Right from the start, you believed I was the one who could lead everyone out of Oxford; that I was the one who could lead the Mime Order. Even I ended up believing it. But I failed them, and I failed you. So when we get back—' I made myself say it: 'I'm going to give up the Rose Crown. And I want you to choose someone else to be your human associate.'

Warden said nothing. I held my head up.

'I won't leave you in the lurch. I'm not going to abandon the Mime Order,' I said, 'but I've proven that I'm not the person you need to lead it. You need someone who can win the voyants' support after this, someone who can achieve a strong enough victory against Scion to convince Adhara of their worth. Maria is probably your best bet. She understands war, and she gets on well with most of the Unnatural Assembly. She's reckless, though. If not her—'

'Paige.'

'—Eliza would do well. She knows London, and she's stronger than she realises. There's Glym, too, if he wants to continue. And Nick. He survived Tjäder in Stockholm. He'd make you proud. Any of them would.'

Warden didn't move. I chanced a look at him, trying to understand his expression.

'Paige Mahoney,' he said, 'I never thought that you, of all people, would prove worthy of your yellow tunic.'

I was too drained to be hurt.

'You're right,' I said. The cold made it harder to speak. 'I am a coward. I . . . left them.'

'Who?'

'My family. Do you know what Scion did to Tipperary?'

His face didn't change. 'I thought you knew.'

'No,' I said, with a bleak laugh. 'It doesn't matter. I know what I have to do. If the Mime Order is going to have a chance, I have to abdicate.'

The shadows set his eyes on fire.

'Fool,' he said softly. 'Do you think so little of yourself?'

'Call me a fool again,' I said, just as softly.

'Fool. Vance has made you doubt your strength, but you have endured worse than her.'

I looked up at him, taking him in.

'I did not let you give up your memory of ScionIDE for the séance,' he said. 'If you are willing, I want you to step into it now.'

'Why?'

'Because it is time you remembered.'

'I did remember.' My voice tightened. 'You made me.'

'Not all of it.'

He was right. In Oxford, I had only heard the first gunshots before the memory stopped dead. I started to shiver again, my heart pounding.

'I want to face it,' I whispered. 'I just . . . don't know if I can.'

'You survived it once before. And this time, you are not alone.'

The golden cord vibrated with our proximity, pulled taut as a string along the long neck of a violin. He was the bow, and I was the music. His aura intertwined with mine as we moved close enough to touch.

'The memory will be fragmented,' he said. 'I have no salvia.'

'Then how can you do this?'

'It is an aid. No more.' Warden held my gaze. 'Do I have your permission?'

In answer, I let myself fall against him, my head listing on to his shoulder. He waited for my nod before he reached into my past.

Golden light filled my vision, and the taste of copper sickened me. I was no longer in Edinburgh. The ground fell away, and I was swan-diving through time and space, pulled over the Irish Sea, and then—

And then—

Kayleigh Ní Dhornáin in Dublin, auburn hair under the sun. Finn, my cousin, deranged by grief, howling as he disappeared. And me, left behind, alone in the crowd, with no one to protect me.

Kay. A sob in my ears, my own sob. *Kay, wake up, please wake up—*

The Irish flag all around, falling down. A man, both hands above his head, shot dead dead dead. The crowd set on fire, devoured from within, a monster with many heads, each one roaring. An airless crush of bodies, pressing from all sides, like jaws. Mouths that scream, hands that shove. The smell of iron, everywhere.

Mercy, have mercy. Pushing. *Please don't hurt me.* Molly Malone, the bronze statue, the cart. *Help us.* Crawling past the bloody flowers, under the wheelbarrow. *Get away.* Just enough room for a child in the shadows. *Please someone save my baby, save her.*

Now I was petrified in the present, gaze still halfway in the past, both in Edinburgh and Dublin. Warden knelt with me, grasping my arms.

Paige, he said, his voice distant. I couldn't move, but I could feel him. *I am with you.*

Don't leave me.

A toy in the blood. The silence around it. A girl, stiff and cold as a doll, all alone. Nobody left but Molly to see her. The streets too still, too quiet, no breath. This is her first sight of death.

A giant, looking at her, fire in its eyes. Surely a dream, like the tug on her senses, telling her where to go, towards life. Her aunt on the other end, clutching her close. The last desperate run to the car, and then nothing.

Flowers at their funeral, wildflowers on empty graves. All too careful to speak to the youngest. Hasn't spoken since that day – day she was brought home dripping red, drawing nightmares. The first time she speaks, it is at the grave.

Finn, I'm going to make them pay.

Warden framed my face between his hands as my eyes opened again. The sleep-dealer was deep within the dark vaults of remembrance.

Listen to me, Paige. My father. *We have to change our names.* His features were a blur, distorting. *Paige, it's not enough. At school, pronounce your name differently. You make it sound like an English name.*

A Dhaid, scanraíonn an áit seo mé.

We don't speak Irish any more.

I was falling into a whirlpool of memory, towing Warden to Ancroft with me. My fingers were nerveless, but I could hold on to him.

He was still there. I wasn't alone.

Here comes the brogue. A crowd wrapping back around her, a bear trap. *Go back to your swamp, boglander.* Another cruel word, a sentence, a curse. *Ancroft isn't for kerns. Don't want the likes of you in our school.* An older girl shoving her, parents in the army, in Ireland. *Where's your red hair, Molly Mahoney? Wash our soldiers' blood out, did you, did you?*

Year after year, pummelled by hatred, until she is cold steel. One day she will show them the fire she still holds, fire that burns her skull with rage. One day she will haunt them to the grave.

One day I will show them what it means to be afraid.

Reels of recollections, tapestries of colours, unravelling. Somewhere among it all, I could move again, kicking free of the current. The golden cord burst into flame, and—

—darkness—

Water purling over stones, mirror-still and crystal clear. No reflec tion; only a steep drop to the deep below, and a bed of stainless pearls.

Nothing lives.

Everything is.

Cloud forest. Emerging-place. His instinct always guides him here. Above, always twilight – blue hour, time of the Netherworld. Time without time.

Silhouettes of trees in the mist, taller than any tree on Earth. Nothing living here, and nothing dead.

A new stranger, dancing under the glow. Dark hair on sarx; the lilt of their bodies. Her name is a song on his lips, a name not tamed by a fell tongue. Terebell and Arcturus, names they will bear when war has begun.

Beyond the veil, mortals sleep. When their lives end, the gods are waiting. Here mortals descend, free of pain, free of sickness, yet still they wander, lost. They pine for a place where a falling sun puts them to sleep, where hunger never ends, where the ground waits to be fed with flesh—

I wrenched free of the memories and lurched to my feet, backing away from Warden until our auras ripped apart. Sweat and tears bathed my cheeks. Voices echoed through my ears; I tasted fear, smelling the blood and smoke. The nightmare was over, but all of it was real.

'Paige.'

My throat was a clenched fist. Every sinew of my body felt tight with terror.

'Warden,' I said, 'what was that?'

'You chose what to see.'

'I remember everything. I saw—' A single tear ran to my jaw. 'A Reph. In Dublin.'

'Gomeisa Sargas was there to bear witness to the Incursion,' Warden said. 'Since then, Hildred Vance has been his most reliable weapon.'

My young mind must have closed down, burying the memories deep. The streams of death, so great in number that the gutters had run red. Babies and children killed with the rest. From under the statue of Molly Malone, I had watched the soldiers check the bodies, knowing that if I moved an inch – if I let out one sound – I would be among them. Butchery orchestrated by Hildred Vance, with Gomeisa Sargas pulling every string.

And it would happen again.

Any day now, it would happen again.

The tears kept coming. I breathed as evenly as I could, dabbing my eyes with my sleeve.

'I saw you,' I said. 'In the Netherworld.'

His eyes flickered. 'The golden cord must have allowed you to mirror my gift.'

'You were dancing with Terebell.'

'She was my partner, long ago.'

I was too numb to absorb it, but part of me had known. There was no other reason for her to be so protective of him, to be so intimate with him. She wasn't like that with any of the other Ranthen.

'Why aren't you with her any more?'

Warden looked back at the citadel. 'It is not wholly my tale to tell.'

There was a tender pressure at my temples. 'I didn't realise that you thought in Gloss,' I said. 'I know I couldn't have understood your voice or thoughts in my body, but with the golden cord, my spirit could make sense of it. It was like hearing . . . a song I used to know—'

I buckled against him. Warden caught my arms, steadying me, and we knelt on the ground, facing each other.

'All of this has already happened.' My voice cracked in a way I couldn't stand. 'I can't let Vance do it again, I can't—'

'You are still here. So is the Mime Order.'

I found myself leaning into him. His embrace was tight enough to warm me, but not so tight that I couldn't pull away, as I should. As I must.

'Why did you want me to remember Dublin?'

His hand came to the back of my head.

'Because you needed to remember. To remember why you must be Underqueen.' His voice rumbled through both of us. 'You have known what it is to be a citizen of the free world and a denizen of Scion. A Londoner and a daughter of Ireland. A survivor of Oxford. A mollisher of Seven Dials. You understand all that is at stake in the war to come, and why it is necessary. You know what it is like to live beyond Scion as well as within it. You know what mortals would endure if the Sargas were ever to conquer this world.'

'Other people have survived them.' I gripped his shirt. 'I'm not your only choice, Warden. I told you this before.'

'No one else in the syndicate has your history with Jaxon Hall. Only you watched Nashira kill a child because you refused to be her weapon.' His gaze was inescapable. 'You *burn* to destroy Scion. To avenge all that has been done to you. To undo the world they fashioned and reshape it. The Ranthen chose you. I chose you. Most importantly, you chose yourself. On the night of the scrimmage, you decided that you, not Jaxon, were the one to lead the syndicate.'

I had no argument to offer. The dive into my memories had taken all my strength.

Warden hitched his coat back over my shoulders. I pressed myself against him, letting him stroke my damp curls. Neither of us stopped the other. We stayed like that until the little flame in the tin went out, lashed by wind and rain.

'Whether or not I decided that,' I said quietly, 'it doesn't change the fact that we've failed.'

'You have risen from the ashes before. The only way to survive,' he said, 'is to believe you always will.'

The motion of his gloved hand on my hair steadied my breathing. I held him close, letting his warmth take away the pain of the past, just for one fragile moment. I wanted him all over again, wanted him with an intensity I had never known, but I couldn't act on it. Nothing had changed. So I slid myself from his arms, feeling as if I was tearing a seam. I picked up the lighter and tried to ignite the alcohol a second time, but it stayed cold.

The silence between us was fraught with unspoken words. When I looked at him again, his eyes were afire.

'Paige.'

'Yes?' I said softly.

A quake in the æther made me tense. I turned slowly to face Leith.

The disturbance was far away – too far for my spirit to reach – but stealing closer by the moment. The æther filled with the softest, fluttering tremors. Like the ripples from a footstep near water, or birds unsettled by a gunshot.

Warden noticed my tension. 'What is it?'

My heartbeat marched to a new drum. I could hear nothing but that call to arms behind my ribs.

Something was coming.

19

OFFERING

.

My burner phone rang in my pocket, I scrambled to pull it out, forcing my numb fingers into action.

'*They're marching,*' Maria said. '*The army. They're marching on the citadel.*'

'What?' I stood. 'Did they see you?'

'*It had nothing to do with us. We never even made it to—*' Her voice faded, then returned: '*. . . get out of here.*'

I clutched the phone tighter. 'Where are you?'

'*We'll meet you on Waverley Bridge.*'

She hung up.

'Shit.' I shoved the phone into my pocket. 'The soldiers are marching on Edinburgh. Why the hell would Vance send them into the citadel now?'

Warden touched my cheek, seeking my gaze. 'Remember what Maria said. You must assume that, whatever Vance is planning, however large the scale, however grand the aim – everything she does will be aimed at you.'

I stared back at him, swallowing my dread. For thirteen years, I had buried the Dublin Incursion beneath my poppies, locking it in a strongbox where I could never truly see. I had been a child, suffocated by fear. Every memory I thought I'd had was a mockery of the true violence I had seen – violence that would never end if Senshield remained active.

We might yet stop it.

And I thought I might know how.

'Warden,' I said, 'if I jumped into Vance, and you used me as a conduit, do you think you could see her memories?'

'You should not enter her dreamscape.'

'If you want me to be a leader, I suggest you follow my orders, Arcturus.'

His face was still a mask, but his eyes glowed.

'It may not work,' he said. 'But we can try.'

I might have known he would help me. I pressed his hand in mine, full of words I couldn't say.

We made our way back down the hill and ran between the pines. It was starting to rain. As I sprinted beneath the branches, adrenalin crashed through me, erasing all the pain from my old wounds. I came to life in the arms of fear. Some would suffer. Some would stand. Either way, Hildred Vance would surrender the information I had chased across the country.

Hildred Vance, who had killed my father. Hildred Vance, who had overseen the fall of Ireland.

At the edge of Haliruid Park, I skidded to a stop, unable to believe what I was seeing. A huge crowd of people had amassed before the gates of Haliruid House – hundreds of them, gathered around a fountain on the driveway, all of them shouting at the Vigiles and brandishing signs: KEEP THE WAR MACHINES IN LONDON, NOT THE LOWLANDS. VICIOUS VANCE. DITCH THE DEPOT. NO MORE BOMBS IN BONNY SCOTLAND. Among them were black moths, splashed on to placards and held up high.

A protest.

Where had this come from?

The roar of the crowd was extraordinary. Warden stayed close to me. I pulled up my scarf and backed into the shadows beneath the pine trees. I had sensed Vance's dreamscape at the depot; I could find it again. I dislocated and searched for her.

'She's close,' I said.

'Close enough?'

I opened my eyes. 'Yes.'

NVD vehicles screamed to a halt outside Haliruid House. When a commandant got out, one of the protestors hurled a swollen balloon at him. It exploded like a blister, and the offal inside oozed down his riot shield.

'Butchers,' the protestor screamed.

A driver emerged. Without a word, she shot the protestor, who doubled over like a jackknife. The Vigiles raised their guns, but now another crowd was pouring around the side of the building. I had to focus, to tune out the noise. I leaned against Warden and tore free of my body, vaulting first into the æther, and then – like a stone skipping across water – into Vance's dreamscape. A chamber of white marble, with a high ceiling and a grand staircase. Clean, elegant lines.

Vance stood at the very top of the stairs. She saw herself exactly as she appeared in the mirror, down to the last line on her face. No evidence of a conscience. Like any amaurotic, she had no way of seeing her own dreamscape, or consciously taking control of her dream-form. Her spirit was a grey, machine-like thing, dealing with threats as best it could. I ran to meet it and wrestled it to the floor.

'You,' it hissed.

Its jaw moved as if on a hinge. An amaurotic shouldn't be able to make their dream-form speak.

'Me,' I whispered.

I was too far away from her to unseat her spirit from? her dream-scape. All I could do was grasp it.

Her dream-form trembled, setting off an earthquake in her mind. Someone must have trained her to defend herself, but I was used to overcoming voyant spirits. An amaurotic's – even that of Hildred Vance – was easy to suppress. I took hold of its head, only to see that my hands were coated in blood.

The golden cord went taut, connecting Vance to Warden. I felt myself straining under the pressure as he used me to bridge the physical distance between them. The ancient power of his gift surged through me, like electricity through a conductor, so strong that my dream-form began to shake, too. When it stopped,

I shoved Vance away. I had touched the pure essence of the woman whose orders had slaughtered thousands.

My silver cord was lifting me away when Vance seized me. Black eyes gaped at me, two glossy brooches.

'I will kill them all,' it warned. 'Give yourself up . . .'

I twisted away from her. As I fled, the threat resounded in my ears. She was capable of anything.

I shot back to Warden's dreamscape, just in time to glimpse the memory for myself. And there it was, frozen in his mind: the power source, the core of Senshield, my own personal grail – the end of the road. Mechanical, yet beautiful. A light sealed in a globe, beneath a pyramid of glass.

A spirit, trammelled and harnessed. Ethereal technology in its most powerful form.

And I knew where it was being kept.

Back in my own body, I sat up, gulping in huge breaths. 'Did you—' I tried again: 'Did you feel it?'

His eyes scorched. 'Yes.'

A gasping laugh escaped me. 'Warden, that was the core. It's real.'

I had never quite believed that this half-baked quest would be successful; that I would really discover where the core was. Now I had seen.

Now I knew.

The core was locked in the most secure building in the Republic of Scion. It was inside the Westminster Archon, back in London. I had come all the way here, only to have to return to where we had started. I didn't care. It had been worth it.

Because I knew something else, too. Something Vance's memory had betrayed, like a fracture in her armour. It was a fear she couldn't shake, and that no amount of money could repair.

Senshield was not indestructible. There was a vulnerability. I could feel that anxiety eating away at her, like rust through iron.

It was all I needed to know.

We had to meet the others. Pushing our way past bewildered denizens and protestors, we moved at speed through the streets of the Old Town. A few hours ago, the streets had been calm; now a protest had started in the middle of the night, seemingly at the drop of a hat.

A familiar sense of unease was stealing over me. When we reached a vantage point, I stopped.

'What *is* this?'

The Edinburgh Guildhall was burning from the inside out. Tongues of flame whipped from its windows. Its clock face was red, indicating the highest level of civil unrest, and a vast banner had been draped over its façade. Letters taller than a Reph: NO SAFE PLACE, NO SURRENDER.

In front of it, Inquisitors Street was a bottleneck. Hundreds of people were caught between the Vigiles in front of the inferno and the weight of other human beings. They were being herded from all sides, like animals in a pen. Others were climbing on to the Gothic monument to get out of the crush, or trying to reach the honeycomb of Old Town. The night was full of cries and shouts for help.

I stared at the tableau unfolding before my eyes.

The others waited on the bridge. Nick was supporting Eliza. Lucida, wearing a hood, went straight to Warden and spoke to him in Gloss.

'Eliza.' I stopped beside her. 'What's wrong?'

'She's been shot,' Maria said.

'I'm okay.' Sweat glazed her brow and throat. 'It's just a scratch.'

I knew from Nick's face that it wasn't.

'One of the soldiers saw us,' he said. 'We almost ran straight into them on our way to the depot.' His pupils were full stops. 'I need to treat her.'

'We did our best,' Maria said grimly, 'but this is it, Paige. We can't take on the soldiers.'

Eliza made a strangled noise and pressed a hand over her side.

'We're going,' I said. 'Are the stations open?'

'They're open, but—' Maria motioned to the crowd. 'We don't have any choice. Even if we can't get on a train, we can use the tracks to leave the citadel. Let's get the fuck out of here, either way.'

Nick grasped one of Eliza's arms. I took hold of the other and checked that the Rephs were still with us before we slipped into the horde.

The Underqueen's great descent, followed by her great retreat. Rose Crown or not, in this throng I was as powerless as I had been in Dublin as a child.

'Dreamer,' Nick shouted against my ear, 'can you—' His lips kept moving, but the roar drowned him out.

'What?' I shouted back.

'Are ScionIDE close?'

With so much chaos, it was almost impossible to concentrate on my sixth sense. I dislocated. With my hearing subdued, I drifted to the edge of my hadal zone. I could sense the æther for up to a mile, but I didn't need to go half that far to feel the legion of dreamscapes.

I snapped back, heaving.

'Paige.' Nick leaned closer, white breath mingling with mine. 'What is it?'

'They're here.'

Rain drummed on the streets around us, plastering strands of hair to my face. Nick wrapped one arm around Eliza, tucking her close to his chest, and used his free hand to clasp mine. Maria shoehorned her way between two men and reached for Eliza, too. Behind us, the transmission screens changed from public safety announcements to images of the street, as if to show us the folly of our actions. The public address system activated with three chimes, and Scarlett Burnish's voice boomed through the citadel.

'*Martial law is now in force in the Scion Citadel of Edinburgh. ScionIDE soldiers will neutralise any denizen who resists the imposition of Inquisitorial justice. The powers of both the Sunlight and Night Vigilance Divisions are now vested in the commandants of ScionIDE. All denizens should cease seditious activity and return to their homes immediately.*'

Panic. I remembered it – the taste of it, the smell of it – like it was yesterday. The crowd jostled and heaved. A wave of movement undulated from one end of the street to the other, passing from person to person, knocking them back like dominoes in a line.

'Alba gu bràth,' someone bellowed. I was flattened against a stranger, and Nick's weight pressed on me until my lungs ached. He braced his shoulder against the nearest protestor, growling with the effort of holding a breathing space open for both of us. I felt for Warden, reaching through the rain. I thought he was gone, that he had left me, until a gloved hand took mine.

Shouts rose, calling for people to get out of the way, to go home, to do what Burnish ordered. Scarlet light shot from a flare; projectiles cartwheeled overhead. Somewhere in the confusion, a child was crying.

Then I heard it.

Footsteps. Perfectly, regimentally synchronised. Over hundreds of heads, I beheld the vanguard, riding on horseback. Birgitta Tjäder was at the front, leading the mounted soldiers.

'*Martial law is now in force in the Scion Citadel of Edinburgh. Defiance will be viewed as sympathy with the preternatural entity, the Mime Order. Substance SX will be deployed to disperse sympathisers.*'

Substance SX. I knew exactly what that was. It had left a scar on everyone it had ever touched.

'It's the blue hand,' voices screamed. 'Let us out!'

Ahead of me, I could just make out Maria climbing over a temporary barrier, into the station. Eliza looked over her shoulder as she followed.

'Paige, come on,' she croaked. 'Stay with us.'

Nick clung to my hand so tightly it hurt. Shoulders and heads banged; backs clapped against chests. More Vigiles were moving towards us, along with the black stallions, each bearing a military commandant. Their body armour, combat helmets and heavy weapons made the Vigiles' seem like toys. Even their horses wore armour. The knot of people tightened around me, as it had in Dublin.

In Dublin . . .

A thought pierced the panic.

All of this has already happened.

I saw the Gothic monument. A bittersweet smell spiked the air, making my head spin – but it had already been spinning, like a lathe, turning over the realisation, fashioning it into an idea.

Above the street, two ScionIDE helicopters were circling us all like birds of prey. White light beamed down, blinding me for an instant. If they saw me, they would take me to Nashira, to the Archon . . .

Martial law will be effective in the Scion Citadel of London until Paige Mahoney is in Inquisitorial custody.

An airless crush of bodies, pressing in on me from all sides.

All of this has already happened.

Mouths that scream, hands that shove.

Everything she does will be aimed at you.

In that moment of not seeing, I saw everything as if from a great distance. I knew what I had to do. It was the only way to save us all. The only way I could rise from the ashes.

Nick was still holding my hand, but he wasn't prepared for what I did next.

I broke his grip with one brutal tug, cut through a line of people, and ran.

Sweat and rain dropped melting crystals on my skin. The people closest to the blaze would boil in their own body heat before the soldiers reached them. I was nearing the thickest part of the crowd when I sensed Warden in hot pursuit. He was too fast – the only one, apart from Nick, who could certainly outrun me. I dislocated my spirit with violent force, throwing pressure through the æther, making a few people cry out.

The golden cord sent harsh vibrations through my bones, my flesh, through the whole of my being. My nose leaked blood.

'Get back, Warden,' I called.

He didn't. I turned fully to face him, grasped my revolver, and took aim at his chest, stopping him. The tang of metal seeped down my throat.

'Don't try to stop me. I mean it. I will put a bullet in your heart.' My voice shook. 'And I don't care if it doesn't kill you. It will give me enough time.'

'You cannot stop this, Paige,' Warden said. 'No matter what you do.'

I jerked the gun higher. 'One more step.'

'Nashira will not let you go once you are in her clutches,' he told me. 'She will chain you in the darkness, and she will drain the life and hope from you. Your screams will be her music.'

As he spoke, I could have sworn I heard some echo of emotion, of fear, in the very depths of his voice. I might have thought it was on the verge of breaking, if he hadn't been a Reph. He held out a hand, his eyes blazing.

'Paige.'

Something in the way he said my name almost disarmed me.

'Please,' he said.

I stepped away from him. 'I have to.'

'If you expect me to stand and watch you hand yourself to the Sargas, you will have to empty that gun into me,' he said, softer. 'Do it.'

Blood ribboned from my chin to the hollow of my throat. Slowly, I drew back the hammer.

'Shoot, Paige.'

My lips trembled. I steeled myself. A bullet would only slow him down; it wouldn't kill him.

It didn't matter.

I lowered the gun. Warden nodded, but I didn't go to him. Instead, I pulled off the necklace he had given me, the Ranthen heirloom that had saved me after the scrimmage, and threw it towards him.

Then I ran.

The golden cord throbbed as I sprinted away from him, moving faster than I ever had, a stitch gnawing into one side of my waist. Warden came straight after me. Just as his footsteps caught up, I threw myself headlong into the next wave of people, ducking under arms, shoving past shoulders and hips with all my strength, crawling between legs when there was no other way through. I was more agile than any Reph, and even with his talent for blending in, it would take him time to whittle a path through this nightmare without creating another swell of panic.

He didn't understand, because he only saw the past, not the future.

He couldn't see what I was going to do.

There were too many people around me. I wrenched up my revolver and fired.

Although the soldiers were close, mine were the first gunshots this street had heard tonight. Screams and pleas were offered up. My palms shoved against sweating backs. I forced my way through, suffocated by the heat, snarling 'move' into the storm of human voices. I fired again, and suddenly there was a path to the front – and just like that, I was on the transmission screens.

The cameras were tracking me now. The woman with the gun, the violent protestor. Flashes blinded me, stripping people to nothing but silhouettes, searing rings of white on to my eyelids. Faces were contorted, monstrous in their fear.

'I'M PAIGE MAHONEY! DO YOU HEAR ME?' I shouted. 'I AM PAIGE MAHONEY! I'M THE ONE YOU WANT!'

The golden cord rang like a bell. The first gas shell soared towards us and ruptured.

'STOP!'

Blue mist swirled from the cracked egg of metal. Howls of agony ripped through the din as the chemical agent clawed towards us, bruising the night, its smell overpowering. I tore the red scarf from my face, letting it flutter to the ground, and threw down my hood, showing my hair. I broke through the front of the crowd and thrust up my arms before the burning Guildhall, clenching my hands into fists.

'I'M PAIGE MAHONEY!'

This time, I could hear myself. Rain drenched my clothes, dripped from my hair.

Smoke drifted between the people and the soldiers, and everything grew still, almost dream-like; all screaming ceased, and all cries ebbed away. Dull pain pounded at the base of my skull as silence descended. The commandants kept their weapons pointed at us.

And there was Vance astride her stallion, leading them. Her eyes locked on to mine. Beside her, Tjäder raised a hand, and one soldier dismounted.

This had to work.

It had to, or everything would end.

The commandant was little more than a silhouette. A helmet gleamed in the light of the fire. There was burning red where eyes should be, and a gas mask covering the rest. I was shaking uncontrollably, but I didn't lower my arms. I was small and I was endless. I was hope and I was fading.

I would not show fear.

The soldier lifted his rifle against his shoulder. In the crowd, someone cried *no*.

It was too late to go back. My heartbeat slowed. I stared down the barrel. I would not show fear.

I thought of my father and my grandparents. My cousin. I would not show fear.

I thought of Jaxon Hall, wherever he was. Perhaps he would raise a glass to his Pale Dreamer.

I thought of Nick and Eliza, Maria and Warden. There was no way for them not to see.

I would not show fear.

The soldier levelled his rifle at my heart. My arms dropped to my sides, and my palms turned outward. A last breath escaped me, blanching the air.

A great wave washed around your feet, and dark wings lifted you away.

INTERLUDE

The Moth and the Madman;
or, the Sad Calamities of War

by Mister Didion Waite, Esq.

O, Readers of Scion, you may well have heard
of a legend'ry Figure of good Written Word –
his Title, *White Binder*, his Name, Jaxon Hall –
who answers no Summons and suffers no Fool.
Ah! the Mime-Lord almighty of old MONMOUTH
STREET was the Picture of Poise from his Hair to his
Feet!
Observe his good Humour, behold his long Stride,
so spotless a Man must be all LONDON's Pride!
But would it surprise you to learn, faithful Reader,
why just such a Fellow could not be our Leader?

One ruinous Year, this Wordsmith decided
that all Voyantkind should be cruelly divided.
Some called him a Genius! Some called him mad,

some whispered his Writing was terribly bad
(and verily, *Didion Waite's* was far better,
superior down to each amorous Letter) –
but all seemed to love him, and after those Trials,
he ruled, drenched in Absinthe, from sweet SEVEN
DIALS.
O, and even as Binder sought seven great *Seals*,
he grew deaf to his Gutterlings' wretched appeals!

When cruel, od'rous *Hector* was found with no Head,
this good Mime-Lord fin'lly sprang up from his Bed.
He danced in the ROSE RING and fought for the Crown
and his Enemies, great and small, were cut down.
But close to the End, with a Victory certain,
a daring young Challenger swept through the Curtain!
And lo, who was she, but *Black Moth* arising,
and O, but her Face was most dev'lish surprising!
The famous *Pale Dreamer*, the *White Binder's* heir,
the Dreamwalker Traitor, a scand'lous Affair!

She struck down her Master with Spirit and Blade,
but to spare us from Bloodshed, her own Hand she stayed.
And to wondering Ears, this Brogue told a Tale
of the Anchor's Façade and what lies 'yond Death's Veil.
Monsters stood at her side! Voyants cried *Underqueen!*
and they called her the Thaumaturge never yet seen.
'Twas on that fair Evening, with Freedom our Lust,
that the Might of THE MIME ORDER rose from the Dust.
The *Binder*, incensed, to the Archon set forth,
and the *Dreamwalker Queen* took her Voice to the North.

And O, what a Spectacle! O what a Show!
Alas for the Unnaturals! Where now shall we go?
For two hundred Years we have fumbled like Fools –
we have feathered our Nests and woven our Spools!
Shall we hide in the Night, where Dread will soon find us

or stand against Doom with the Æther behind us?
Alas, when the *Dreamwalker* gave up her Throne,
her Subjects were stranded in Darkness alone,
and whispered that *Weaver* should bring them her head –
but now, when we need her, our young Queen is dead.

PART THREE

DEATH AND THE MAIDEN

20

TOMB

If this was the æther, it was different from how I remembered it. Pain radiated from a damaged place. I was a child in a red, red field. Nick called to me across a sea of flowers, but the poppies were too tall, and I couldn't find my way to him.

There was the spirit among the petals, reaching for my arm, whispering a message I couldn't understand. When I held out my hand to her, it was Arcturus Mesarthim who took it. I was a woman, the pale rider, the shadow that brought death. The night showered my hair with starlight. He danced with me as he had once before, his skin too hot on mine. I wanted him beside me, around me, within me. So I reached for him, but his teeth tore out my heart.

He ebbed away. The amaranth had grown in my mind, too. As I bled, Eliza Renton spun in a green dress beneath a tower. Lightning lashed its highest turret, and a golden crown fell to the earth and shattered.

The tower loomed in a not-too-distant future, obscuring the sun. And somewhere, Jaxon Hall was laughing.

Each exhalation echoed through my skull, into the emptiness. I had thought this was the æther, but I felt the millstone of my body, smelled the sweat on living skin. There was sand on my teeth, paper on my lips.

Blood thundered in my ears. I had no memory of where I was, what I was doing here, what I had been doing before.

Just below my breastbone was a second heartbeat – thick, grey, deep within my body. It sharpened as I tried to sit up, only to find that I couldn't. The only sound I could produce was a rasp. In a panic, I arched my back and pulled my arms forward, grinding my wrists against bracelets of metal. I was . . . chained. My hands were chained . . .

She will chain you in the darkness, and she will drain the life and hope from you. I shivered as I remembered his voice, his hand outstretched, offering me safety. *Your screams will be her music.*

White light scorched the backs of my eyes. I sensed the ancient dreamscape before I heard the footsteps.

'Good evening, 40.' I knew that voice; it dripped with an arrogance no mortal could attain. 'The blood-sovereign welcomes you to the Westminster Archon.'

No.

When my eyes adjusted to the light, I recognised the Reph, with the pale hair of the Chertan family. At once, my spirit leaped from my fragile dreamscape and slammed against the layers of armour on his mind, but I didn't last long before I stopped trying. Red lightning flashed between my temples, drawing a weak groan from my throat.

'I would not advise that. You have only just emerged from a coma.'

'Suhail,' I croaked.

'Yes, 40. We meet again. And this time,' he said, 'you have no concubine to protect you.'

A drop of water fell on to my nose, making me blink. I wore a black shift, cut off just above the knee. My wrists and ankles were chained to a smooth board. Another bead of water splashed on to my forehead, dripping from the metal pail suspended above me. My chest heaved.

'The Grand Commander has asked me to inform you that your pathetic rebellion amounted to nothing,' Suhail Chertan said, speaking over my quickening breaths. 'And that your friends are all dead. If you had surrendered earlier, they would be alive.'

I couldn't listen. It wasn't true. It could *not* be true. I lifted my head as much as I could.

'Don't think you've won, Reph,' I whispered. 'While we speak, your home is rotting. And so will you, when you have to slink back to the hell you belong in.'

'Your prejudice against Rephaim surprises me, given your lust for the concubine. Or should I say,' Suhail purred, 'flesh-traitor.' Water trickled into my hair. 'The blood-sovereign has forbidden me from causing any enduring damage to your body, but . . . there are ways to inflict pain.'

He paced around me. I writhed against my chains, but the first round of struggling had already exhausted me.

'No need to be frightened, Underqueen. After all, you are the ruler of this citadel. Nothing can touch you.'

I hated myself for shaking so violently.

'Let us begin with an easy question,' Suhail said. 'Where *is* my old friend, the flesh-traitor?'

We like to think we're brave, but in the end, we're only human. My hands became fists. *People break bones trying to get off the waterboard.*

'I will ask you once more. Where is Arcturus Mesarthim?'

'Try your best,' I said.

His gloved hand reached for a lever.

'You sound thirsty.' Suhail loomed over me, blocking out the light. 'Perhaps the Underqueen would care for a drink. To celebrate her short-lived reign.'

The board tipped backward. Gently, almost reverently, he covered my face with a cloth.

Suhail extinguished the lights as he left. I was limp on the board, drenched and shuddering and covered in vomit, unable to so much as lift a finger. My shift and hair were soaked with freezing water. As soon as his footsteps could no longer be heard, I dissolved into rasping sobs.

He had asked me many questions. About the Ranthen and their plans. About what I'd been doing in the Lowlands. Who had helped me get to Manchester. Where the Mime Order had hidden. What I knew of Senshield. He asked if someone in the Archon was helping me. He asked how many of the other Bone Season survivors were alive, and where they were. Endless questions.

I had said nothing, betrayed nothing. But he would be back tomorrow, and the next day. And the next. I had expected torture, and I had expected to be able to withstand it, but I hadn't expected to be so weak that I couldn't use my gift at all, not even to give myself a moment of relief from the pain in my body. The coma must have corroded it; it had certainly left my dreamscape paper-thin.

Sleep called to me. I kept my eyes open, telling myself to focus, to concentrate. I couldn't have much time before they executed me. A few days, at most.

Step one: survive the torture.

Suhail soon came back. Even after the first time, I wasn't prepared for ice-cold water to flood my mouth and knife its way into my stomach. For the fear that made me fight my chains until my wrists were raw. For the screams I couldn't control, even when Suhail told me I was a yellow-jacket, even when I knew that screaming would crack open the sluice gates in my throat. For my body to retort with bouts of vomit. I drowned on dry land over and over, a dying fish flopping on a slab.

Suhail became nothing but the hand that poured. He told me to forget my name. I was not Paige here. I was 40. Why had I not learned the first time?

Sometimes he would touch my forehead with a sublimed baton, which had the same effect on my spirit as a cattle prod. As I cried out, the deluge came again. He whispered to me that this interrogation would do no harm, that there would be no physical destruction to my body, but I didn't believe it. All my ribs felt splintered; my stomach was bloated with water; my throat seared from the acid in it. Whenever he left, I fought to keep my eyes open.

Staying alive was physically strenuous. Breathing was no longer a reflex, but an effort.

But I had to live. If I didn't live for just a little longer, everything I had done to get here – all of it would be for nothing.

Day and night were now water and silence. There was no food. Just water. When my bladder was full, I had no choice but to let the warmth seep out of me. I was a vessel of water, nothing more. When he returned, Suhail reminded me of what a sordid animal I was.

I hoped, every minute, that the others wouldn't try to save me. Nick might be foolish enough. They had faced odds almost as daunting when they had got me out of Oxford, but there was no way they could infiltrate a fortress like the Westminster Archon.

Whenever Suhail tired of tormenting me, I imagined how they might attempt a rescue. The scenarios I envisioned always ended in a spray of blood. I pictured Nick dead on the marble floor, a bullet through his temple, never smiling again. Warden chained and brutalised in a room like this one, held in a permanent state of torture, denied the mercy of death to escape it. Eliza on the Lychgate, like my father.

The next night, or day, Suhail fed on my aura as he worked.

A Reph hadn't fed on me in a long time. Blind panic made me haul against my fetters until the muscles of my neck and shoulders burst into flame. The double blow to my system left me so weak that once it was over, I could hardly cough out what had worked its way into my lungs. When Suhail took the cloth off my face, his eyes were the red of embers.

'Do you truly have nothing to say, 40?' he said. 'You were more vocal in Oxford.'

I used the last of the water in my mouth to spit at him. His hand collided with my cheek. Pain staggered up my face, and my head seemed to vibrate with the force of the impact.

'What a great pity,' he said, 'that the blood-sovereign wants you unspoiled.'

A second blow knocked me out.

When I woke, I was face down in a cell. Concrete floor, blank walls, and no light.

Suhail had really done a number on me this time. I could feel that I was badly bruised around my left eye, and my cheek was hot and swollen.

A cup of water sat beside the cot. It took me a long time to drag myself across the concrete and pick it up, and longer still to lift it to my lips. The first sip made me gag. I tried again. And again. Dipping my upper lip into the glass, I let the water soften the broken skin. Then more. Just the tip of my tongue.

At once, I retched into my arm. My throat closed in anticipation of the flood.

No. The water could be spiked. I crawled away from it and lay on my back, holding my aching stomach. They would not turn me into a mindless automaton.

When I didn't drink, they sent in a Vigile with a needle. Something that gave me temporary amnesia; I suspected, in lucid moments, that it was a potent mix of white aster and a tranquilliser.

Step two: resist the drugs.

After that needle punched into my muscle, I couldn't remember how to dreamwalk; couldn't even remember that I was able to do it. As if the drug had washed my knowledge of my gift away. When it was in my blood, all sense of identity and purpose collapsed, leaving my mind void. When the dose wore off, another Vigile arrived to top it up.

And so a pattern began – a cycle of sedation.

A constant thirst vied with my new fear of water. I would be taunted by thoughts of plunging, ice-cold pools, of crystal depths, of that stream I had glimpsed in Warden's memory. I wasn't sure if it was the drugs, or if I was hallucinating out of dehydration.

The next day, they took me into another room and allowed a squadron of Vigiles to beat me in lieu of the waterboard. With each blow, they asked questions. *Where are your allies? Who's been helping you? Who the fuck do you think you are, unnatural?* If I didn't answer, another kick came, along with a mouthful of spit and foul words. They wrenched my hair and broke my lip. One of them tried to make me lick his boots; I fought back viciously, and in the fray, another of them grabbed my weak wrist too hard. From the way the commandant hauled me away at once, the sprain hadn't been intentional.

No one used my name. I was only 40.

After the beating, I lay for hours in my stupor, cradling my wrist. When I finally surfaced, someone was standing in the doorway. I shrank away from the torchlight.

'You only have yourself to blame, 40.'

A familiar voice, to go with the face I now recognised. So much colder than it had been when I first met him.

'Carl,' I rasped. 'How are you?'

'Don't use that name.' Carl Dempsey-Brown stepped towards me. 'Were your three months of supposed freedom any better than Oxford, in the end?'

'I had some fun along the way.' I tried and failed to sit up. 'You hate me for burning it down, don't you?'

'You wanted to leave so badly. Well, here you are,' Carl said, 'in a cell where you have to shit in a bucket. You truly went up in the world.' I gave him a joyless smile, cracking my lips again. 'The last person in this cell was your father. The one you got killed. Did you know that, 40?'

I couldn't think about my quiet, weary father being locked in here, kept in his own filth.

Carl could only be my age, yet he was making a concerted attempt to look older. He had a trim beard now, and styled his hair more carefully. A few ballistic syringes of flux were tucked into his belt.

'You're lucky they haven't killed you yet,' he said. 'It won't be long.'

I directed a blank look at the ceiling, hardly able to open my puffy eyes. 'Did you get promoted?'

'Rewarded, for my loyalty. I'm a Punisher now.'

'Good for you. Still a rat.'

'Speaking of loyalty,' Carl said, ignoring the barb, 'you know they caught the concubine, don't you?' I grew very still. 'Oh, yes. A few days ago, while you were in the basement. Handed himself over, apparently, so you could live.'

His presence had stopped the Vigiles from injecting me. My spirit stirred.

'He's an idiot, of course. The Suzerain won't let you get away a second time,' Carl said. 'You should be grateful, 40. She's giving you a chance to die for a good cause, before the world gets any worse.' He sniffed. 'And it will get worse.'

He dabbed his nose on his sleeve. When he found blood on the silk, he backed straight into the wall.

'Stop,' he gasped. 'You're not allowed to—'

I already had him pinned, with a needle half an inch from his bare eye. He gaped as he recognised his own syringe, plucked like a boiled sweet off his belt.

'Commandant,' he screeched.

A set of keys clinked near his waist. I grasped them with a shaking hand.

A Vigile came bursting through the door. I attacked her with my spirit, or tried to, setting off an explosion of pain behind my eyes. No effect. Knowing I had lost this round, I rammed the syringe deep into his arm, making him squeal, before a dart bit my neck. The floor slammed into me.

They had Warden. I rocked on my haunches in the corner, damp with sweat, my fingers flexing in my greasy hair. How could he be so stupid? He couldn't have thought that Nashira would agree to an exchange. She wanted both of us. Always had. Or was this another lie?

I reached for the cord, but there was no answer. I couldn't feel him anywhere.

Rephs couldn't die, but they could be destroyed. Perhaps Nashira had no more use for him. Had given him a slow end.

No. They didn't have him, couldn't have him – Carl was lying. This was Vance again, trying to derange me. She was going to use every weapon in her arsenal to ensure I was a shell.

She must think Warden was my true weakness, then. Not Nick or Eliza.

The Vigiles had left the viewing slot open. I craned myself up, my body aching in protest, and peered between the bars. My cell looked out on to a junction in the tunnels, where the Vigiles would sometimes stop to talk during their rounds. A transmission screen ran on the wall, showing my photograph above a scrolling ribbon of news. PAIGE MAHONEY SLAIN IN EDINBURGH. There was no more threat to security.

Slowly, I sat and leaned against the wall. With my eyes closed, I recalled the heart-pounding moments before the gunshot. The smell of the blue hand.

And I wondered if Vance believed I was beaten. If she thought her strategy had worked.

It had come to me in a flash: the crowds, the smoke, the soldiers, the screams. It was a stage set, all that chaos; a psychological trap, just like the one she had used against Rozaliya – this time on a far grander scale.

There, on the streets of Edinburgh, Vance had recreated the Dublin Incursion, just for me. All the elements had been there. An ordinary street thrown into disarray, the army, the protestors, a demonstration that became a massacre. All arranged by the Grand Commander.

She had built a real-life flashback, with Edinburgh as the stage and many of its people as the unwilling actors, swept up in the deception. But one thing was necessary before she could guarantee my breakdown and surrender: she needed me to be unstable, in a state of rage and grief. That was why she had murdered my father on screen.

I was to be a child again, lost on the streets in a stampede.

I was to believe that by sacrificing myself, I could prevent that day in my childhood from repeating itself.

Clever. And extraordinarily cruel. She was willing to use innocents in her mind game, to let buildings burn, to endanger hundreds just to catch one.

It might even have worked, had Warden not shown me that memory of Dublin. In doing so, he had left it fresh in my mind. The cues which should have tipped me over the edge had been too obvious; I had recognised the tableau for what it was. Props on a stage. An imitation.

That was when I had realised.

If Vance captured me, she would take me to the Westminster Archon and bring me before Nashira – Nashira, who, if Warden had been right, controlled the spirit that powered Senshield.

All I had to do was stay alive for long enough to get to it.

21

SKINS OF MEN

The Westminster Archon wasn't designed to promote sleep. Every hour, the five bells in the clock tower would ring across London, and the clash of their tongues would tremble through the walls.

Days I had been entombed in my cell, with only a bucket to relieve myself in.

A cloud now lived inside my brain, thickened every so often by a Vigile with a syringe. They were keeping me as little more than a corpse. There was a period of clarity when the dose wore off, during which I received my meal. I was expected to use that time to eat and drink before another needle made me lose the use of my fingers.

They had to bring me before Nashira. She would want to see me before my execution, to rub salt into the wound.

While I was with her, I doubted I would be sedated. In the absence of other options, I would have to try and end her with my spirit. It would be madness, but if I couldn't find the place the spirit was kept and release it, all that was left to do was to destroy its master.

Sweat trickled down my face. Nashira feared my gift; that was why she wanted it so much. I could do it.

I must do it.

'. . . just keeps going up. Martial law is here to stay.' Two Vigiles were passing my cell on their rounds. 'Where are you tonight?'

'Lord Alsafi asked me to stand guard in the Inquisitorial Gallery. I'll be with them this evening.'

I raised my head.

Alsafi.

I hadn't counted on him being here. I might not need to face Nashira at all. If I could get my message to him – the knowledge I had of Senshield, gleaned from Vance – he might be able to act on it sooner than I could. He might be able to find and release the spirit.

Easier said than done when I didn't even have a scrap of paper.

My meal clattered into the cell. I crawled to it and scooped up the slop with my fingers.

Trying to destroy Nashir had to be a last resort. While I could still think, I tried to decode the image of Senshield that Warden had stolen from Vance – a clear globe with a white light in it. It did have a physical casing.

I thought harder. Above the globe had been a second glass structure – a pyramid, reflecting the glow. Beyond that pyramid, I had glimpsed the sky, so it had to be some kind of roof. All I had seen, apart from that, were the pale walls in the room. I didn't know enough about the layout of the Archon to find it by sight.

Alsafi could be my eyes.

Except there was no time, and no way to get to him. At any moment, I could be taken to my execution. If I had been stronger, I would have tried to speak to him in his dreamscape, but I was at my lowest ebb; Vance must have meant to weaken me so badly that I couldn't use my gift. In a sense, she had succeeded. I couldn't dreamwalk. Not even a foot out of my body.

But she had forgotten, or didn't know, that I could use my gift in other ways. She didn't know that I could return to my rawest form: a mind radar, able to detect ethereal activity without lifting a finger. And now, for the first time in days, I did.

Even shifting my focus to my sixth sense was agony. This should be second nature . . . I had survived physical weakness in Oxford.

I could do it here. Finally, I submerged myself, letting my other senses wind down.

My range had been damaged, but I could feel the æther. And it didn't take long for me to pick up on the turbulence in the Westminster Archon.

The core *was* here. I had been right.

As I lay in the black hole of my cell, I kept track of the dreamscapes in the Archon. Vance often went from one side of the building to the other. Sometimes I fixated on her for hours, trying to work out where she stopped most. She spent a good portion of her day in one place – an office, most likely.

Footsteps sounded outside. The Vigiles were back from their rounds. I had absorbed as much information as I could about the shifts; these two were my most regular guards.

'. . . going to be a long one on New Year's Eve.'

'Can't say I mind. Extra pay. Speaking of which, I might put in a request for nights next year.'

'Nights?' A short laugh. 'You not telling me something?'

Their shadows moved beneath the door.

'These new scanners.' Hushed tones. 'As soon as they're operational, the rumour is the unnatural lot will be obsolete. All Okonma has to do is sign the execution warrants, and they'll swing.'

A rubber sole tapped on concrete.

'I was thinking of handing in my notice,' the man said. 'Martial law is going to be hell for us. Extra hours, seven-day weeks. They're even going to dock our pay so they can give more to the krigs. We'll be drudges.'

'Keep it down.'

The drug was clouding my thoughts again, a siren song to oblivion. I pinched the delicate skin of my wrist, forcing my eyes open.

'You seen all these outsiders in the building? Spaniards, I heard. Ambassadors.'

'They were with Weaver in his office all day.' A light rap on the door. 'Who do you reckon they're keeping in there?'

'It's Paige Mahoney.'

'Right, nice try. She's dead.'

'You saw what they wanted you to see.' I heard the view slot open. 'There.'

'The unnatural who took on an empire,' the woman said, after a pause. 'Doesn't look like much to me.'

Time passed. Meals came. Drugs came. And then, one unexpected day – if it was day, if day existed any longer – I was woken with a splash of water, dragged up from the subterranean vault, and pushed into a cubicle.

'Go on,' one Vigile said.

I stumbled away from the shower. The taller Vigile slammed me into the tiles.

'Clean yourself. Filth.'

After a moment, I did as I was told.

I was thinner. My skin had a grey undertone that could only have come from flux. Bruises, blue and purple and pear-green, marked the injection sites on my arms; my legs were badly discoloured from the Vigiles' boots and fists. A blackberry stain fanned out below my breasts, where a ring-shaped wound sat just under my sternum.

A rubber bullet. It must have been. I stood there like a manne-quin, my legs shaking under my weight.

After giving me no more than a minute to shower, the Vigiles slotted my arms into a clean shift and took me out of the cubi-cle. Soon concrete gave way to bloodshot marble, painful on the soles of my feet. My head spun like a carousel as they steered me through the Archon, along sun-drenched corridors that hurt my tender eyes. Slowly, I became more alert. My feet slewed on the floor. This was it. The last walk.

'No,' a Vigile said, noting my feeble attempts to resist him. 'You're not dying yet.'

Not yet. I still had time.

Somewhere in the Archon, music was booming. It grew louder as the Vigiles manhandled me up flights of stairs. 'Death and the Maiden' by Franz Schubert.

A plaque on a heavy door read RIVER ROOM. One of the Vigiles knocked and pushed it open. Inside, honeyed light poured through windows overlooking the Thames, slicing between red brocade curtains. It gleamed on marble busts and a glass vase of nasturtium.

I stopped in my tracks. His waistcoat was the same red as those curtains, sewn with complex foliate patterns. He didn't look up from his book when he spoke.

'Hello, darling.'

My legs wouldn't move. The Vigiles took hold of my arms and bundled me into the opposite seat.

'Would you like her restrained, Grand Overseer?'

'Oh, no need for that sort of tomfoolery. My erstwhile mollisher would never be so foolish as to run.' Jaxon still didn't look up. 'If you wished to be even modestly useful, however, you can remind your underlings to bring the breakfast I ordered twenty-six minutes ago.'

The Vigiles' visors concealed most of their faces, but I heard one of them mutter something about 'bloody unnaturals' as they exited the room.

An unruly stack of paper sat on the table to my left. Between us was a silver teapot on a lace tablecloth. A surveillance camera was reflected in its side.

Jaxon finally set his book aside. *Prometheus and Pandora* was printed down the spine.

'Well,' he said. 'Here we are, Paige. How things have changed since our last meeting. How far you have wandered.'

I took a good look at him. His face was slightly pinched, and a hint of grey had crept into the roots of his hair. He had lost at least a stone since I had last seen him.

'So,' I said, 'am I here so you can twist the knife? One last laugh before the end?'

'I would never be so crass.'

'Yes, you would.'

Even his smirk was somewhat diminished. Whatever his title, he was a human among Rephs. Even if he was their ally, he would never be their equal – and if there was one thing Jaxon despised, one thing that would eat away at him, it was being anyone's inferior. This must be slowly killing him.

'Before we have our heart to heart,' he said, 'I want to ask you something. Where did you move my syndicate?'

Well, at least he had got straight to the point.

'ScionIDE has noticed a conspicuous absence of voyants on the street. This gives rise to the assumption that they have been relocated. But where?' He reclined in his chair. 'I confess to frustration. London is my obsession, a place I believed I knew in exhaustive detail – yet somehow, you have found them a way to elude the anchor. Enlighten me, Underqueen.'

'You don't really think I'd tell you.'

I sounded calm, but shivers were shooting through my body. His gaze raked over me, taking in my wretched appearance.

'Very well. If you mean to play coy,' he said, 'we will have to find another topic of conversation. Your turn.' When I didn't speak, he smiled in a way that jolted me back to Seven Dials. 'Come, now, Paige. You were always insatiably curious. You must have questions . . . questions that are burning up your mind as you lie there in confinement.'

'I don't know where to begin.' I paused. 'Where are Nadine and Zeke?'

'Quite safe. They came to me after you expelled them from Seven Dials. Speaking of which,' he said, 'did you really put Jack Hickathrift in charge of my section?'

'I did.'

'A popinjay with bedroom eyes and nothing in his skull. Fascinating choice, darling. Well, never mind,' Jaxon said, steepling his fingers. 'The longer he sits in Seven Dials, the longer I can dwell upon the way I will dispose of him.'

'I'm not here to talk about Jack. I asked about Zeke and Nadine,' I said coldly. 'If they're in Sheol II—'

'Sheol II is not quite ready. You did sink your claws into the others, though, didn't you? 'he added. 'Danica, usually so pragmatic – though I hear she's fled the citadel. Clever woman. Nick and Eliza – they proved themselves to be great *admirers* of yours.'

I lifted an eyebrow. 'Jealous?'

'Not particularly. If the footage I saw from Edinburgh is anything to go by, they have received their just deserts.'

They had to be alive. They had to be.

Jaxon leaned towards me and touched the coil of black at the front of my hair. It was all I had left of the dye he had given me to disguise myself when I had returned from Oxford.

'A memento, darling?'

'A reminder.' I pulled my head back. 'That I once let you control me.'

'Oh, you flatter me, Pale Dreamer.'

A soft knock came, and a line of personnel entered, carrying in the Grand Overseer's breakfast. Ever the epicure. French toast with berry compote, teacakes and whipped butter, then a silver tureen of cream, a pot of coffee, a dish of curried hard-boiled eggs and fresh, crusty bread. Jaxon waved the personnel away.

'*Every revolution begins with breakfast*,' I quoted as they left. 'Is this your revolution, Jaxon?'

'I was under the impression it was yours. A failed revolution,' he said, 'but you tried.'

'I expected to see more of you. You were full of fighting talk when I saw you in the Archon.'

'I came to the conclusion that there was little point in starting a war game with you. I knew the syndicate would tear you to pieces of its own accord, if Vance didn't destroy you first.' He assessed me with those pale eyes. 'Did you really think you could oust Scion with nothing more than a band of criminals? This is real life, Paige, not a pipe dream.' He poured cream into a cup. 'Eat. Let me tell you a story.'

'About what?'

'Me.'

'Jax, I don't have long to live. I really don't want to spend my last days hearing about you.'

'Would you rather lie about in a cell, lamenting your doomed love for Arcturus Mesarthim?'

'Don't be ridiculous.'

'Paige, Paige. I *know* you. Nashira told me all about your *embrace*,' he said. 'You may not care to admit it, but your heart is as soft as your façade is ruthless.'

'Let's not make rash judgements, Jaxon. You of all people know how hard my heart is.'

'True. I imagine he's been useful to you. I would probably choose a cold-blooded Rephaite myself, had I the time or inclination to pursue a star-crossed love affair.' He added coffee to the cream. 'Now, let us begin. The tale of a humble young man, stolen from the streets. No doubt you heard many whispers in Oxford.'

I didn't argue any more.

'When I was not much younger than you, I began writing the pamphlet that would one day change my life. *On the Merits of Unnaturalness*, the first document to carefully divide the orders of clairvoyance and rank their superiority. I hope you haven't been insulting me by thinking that the Rephaim dictated it,' Jaxon added. 'The work, the research, the hours of pondering and agonising, the *genius*, are mine.'

The record player switched to a soprano rendition of 'Drink to Me Only with Thine Eyes' – another blacklisted song. One rule for Jaxon, another for everyone else, apparently.

'It soon attracted the attention of the Rephaim, most likely because so much of *On the Merits* was correct. I was arrested for the creation and distribution of seditious literature. After a brief detainment in the Tower, I was transported to Oxford, where I became a pink-jacket after demonstrating my abilities as a binder. My number was 7. I suppose the Ranthen still call me by it.'

'No,' I said. 'They call you the arch-traitor.'

He chuckled. 'I never thought Rephaim were capable of such histrionics.'

I thought of the cold scars I had felt on Warden, the ones that still caused him excruciating pain, and loathed Jaxon all the more.

'Show me,' I said quietly. 'Show me your brand.'

'Why?'

'Just show me, Jax.'

Jaxon Hall never missed an opportunity to grandstand. With a smile, he removed his waistcoat and shirt, showing the pale skin of his chest. Two of his boundlings' names were scarred on to his lower ribs, and a third near his collarbone. When he stood and turned, my hands tightened on the arms of the chair. The rawness had long since disappeared, but the numerals on the back of his shoulder were all too legible.

'Are you satisfied?'

I forced myself to nod. I had never really doubted it, but the brand was the final proof.

'The discomforts of Oxford were tolerable, in exchange for the fruits of knowledge.' Jaxon returned to his chair and drew his shirt back on. 'Nashira, who took me under her wing, confirmed many of my observations about the seven orders. She taught me more. About Rephaite gifts. About *my* gift. I fell wildly in love with her mind – her deep understanding of the æther, her hunger to comprehend it entirely. I confess to being easily seduced by knowledge.'

'You make a lovely couple.'

'She certainly favoured me, despite my mortality. I became a red-jacket without having to lift a finger against the Emim.' He buttoned the shirt. 'A week later, I was granted the position of Overseer and moved to Kettell Hall. Life was altogether rather pleasant.'

'So you betrayed the Ranthen to make sure it stayed that way.'

'I betrayed the Ranthen in order to survive,' he said. 'I soon heard whispers of revolt. I could either help Arcturus Mesarthim, or betray his plans to Nashira. The only one of those two that guaranteed my survival was the latter.' He returned his cup to its saucer. 'Naïveté is a fatal flaw in immortals, and Arcturus was abysmally naïve about human nature.'

'He wasn't by the time I got there.'

'Yet you charmed him into trusting you. He must have been terribly disappointed when he discovered who you were. The heir,' he said, 'of his nemesis.'

'Don't flatter yourself, Jax. A nemesis is an equal.'

'You must think very highly of him. It seems my warning fell on deaf ears.'

'You're full of shit.'

'Believe whatever you will.' He pressed his fingertips together. 'I reported my findings. You know what happened next. A little . . . *lesson* was taught.' His tongue caressed the word. 'The Ranthen traitors were left alone for days with the spirit of the Ripper.'

I must have misheard him.

'The Ripper,' I echoed.

'Delectable, I know. One of her fallen angels – the poltergeist you faced at the scrimmage – is the very spirit we have hunted for a century.' He looked back at the window, so the light fell on his face. 'I am almost tempted to write and tell Didion, but no. Far more amusing for him to search in vain for the rest of his days.'

No wonder Warden and the Ranthen hadn't trusted me.

No wonder if they still didn't.

'You monster,' was all I could say.

Jaxon held up a finger. 'Survivor. Traitor. Marionette, yes – but not monster. This is what humans *are*, Paige. Only the Sargas can regulate our insanity.' His hand returned to the arm of his chair. 'Do you remember what Nashira said about me in November – how long it had been since she had last seen me?'

'Of course I remember. She said that you had been estranged from her for twenty years.' I served myself a coffee of my own. (Might as well die with caffeine in my veins.) 'Trouble in paradise?'

'In a manner of speaking. She wanted me to be her Grand Overseer, given my talent for spotting powerful voyants. Someone to guide the red-jackets,' he said. 'I was allowed to leave Oxford, but only as a Scion employee. I was to make a regular payment of interesting prisoners.'

'A regular payment.' I paused. 'The grey market.'

'Very good. I was its architect.'

'The Rag and Bone Man—'

'—is an associate,' he said. 'I let Nashira believe I would obey her. Then, one night, I escaped, shedding my old form. A skilled backstreet surgeon created this face.' He pressed a finger to one cheek. 'I needed wealth to achieve my dream of taking Seven Dials. I kept in touch with Nashira through calls to Winterbrook, promising to continue my work, but refused to meet again in person.'

'How did you get your hands on I-4?'

'I reported its mime-queen and her mollisher, who were detained within a day. Then I announced myself to the Unnatural Assembly,' he said. 'I settled in Seven Dials. Seven for my number. Seven for my name. I employed the Rag and Bone Man to assist me with my payments. He extended our network somewhat, as you learned in the weeks preceding the scrimmage.'

'Then why build the Seals?' I asked. 'You had your grey market. Were you planning to send us all to Oxford for extra money?'

'Every mime-lord needs a gang.'

'You're no ordinary mime-lord.'

He fell silent, gazing out of the window, the remnant of a smile on his lips. It wasn't difficult to piece it together.

'You *did* plan to send us there. Some of us, at least. You arranged my arrest.' I could hardly get the words out. 'You kept Nick busy so he couldn't take me home, so I'd have to get the train on my own. You arranged for there to be a spot check on that line. When I got away, you told me to stay at my father's apartment. Then you tipped them off.'

'Imaginative, Paige, but incorrect. Why would I want you taken? Remember' – he lit a cigar – 'it was I who rescued you.'

He was still looking away. My hand slid to the table and liberated a piece of paper from the stack.

'Who, then?'

'Hector,' Jaxon said. My fingers worked quickly, rolling the page. 'He alerted Scion when you stepped on to the train. I understand that it was out of spite towards me. Our Underlord was asking for more than his fair share of profits from the grey market, and I denied his request. So he took my prized mollisher and pocketed the money he received from Scion for you. The Rag and Bone Man later, at my behest, arranged for him to be slain by the Abbess. I was originally going to have him removed by cleaner means – a nice gunshot, perhaps – but for his greed, I ensured his death was rather bloodier.'

Hector.

All that blood in his parlour, all those mutilated bodies – all because Jaxon had wanted vengeance for the theft of his most cherished possession.

Me.

'And that cleared the way for you to be Underlord,' I said. He inclined his head.

'At the time of your arrest, I was no longer working for the Sargas,' he said. 'They had finally grown vexed with my refusal to play the game by their rules. They cut off my considerable salary, which hurt – I had grown used to finery, and to power. And yet,

I saved your life. I put myself in considerable danger to do so. It was when *you* betrayed *me* at the scrimmage – only then that I decided to return to my makers. Not only to continue my lifestyle, before you accuse me of avarice, but to continue my education.' Smoke pirouetted from between his lips. 'We can learn from the Rephaim.'

He finally looked back at me. The roll of paper was already up my sleeve.

I had no guarantee that anything he said was the truth, but his story held together.

He might have saved my life, but that didn't mean he cared about me. He cared about his own pride. He knew he had been the envy of other mime-lords and mime-queens for having a mollisher of my rarity. No doubt I had been worth a lot of money – money Hector had taken.

'If all I'll learn from them is how to be like you,' I said, 'forget it.'

'It is too late, Paige. You are already like me.'

'If you'll excuse me, Grand Overseer, I'd like to go back to my cell,' I said. 'I find myself missing the quiet.'

As I stood, Jaxon snapped upright and hooked a finger under my chin, freezing me. He coaxed me close, so I could smell the cigars and sweetness on him.

'In that case, I will come to my reason for bringing you here. There was a reason, beyond stories,' he said, very softly. 'Nashira is about to present you with your execution warrant.'

I had expected it, but I still turned numb.

'I suppose this is goodbye, then,' I said. The slightest tremor crept into my voice, in spite of myself.

'Not necessarily. There is a chance that I can secure a stay of execution.'

'How?'

'You could be very useful to the Sargas, Paige. I have told them that you might be persuaded to join this side of the conflict, under my instruction. I will be Grand Overseer in Sheol II, personally selecting voyants for the new city.' He didn't break his hold on my face. 'Come with me to France. I will offer myself as your mentor.

You can retrain as a red-jacket, and study to become my successor. Just as it should be.'

'And Nashira would agree to this.'

'I believe she would.' His grip tightened. 'Think of it, Paige. Mime-lord and mollisher, together again. There is so much more I can teach you about clairvoyance, so much for us to learn together. And think of the alternative. Your gift – your beautiful, singular gift – in her clutches.'

'She'll have it in the end,' I said. 'Dead or alive, I'll be used as a weapon. Better that I face it now.'

'You must stop being so *noble*, Paige. It will not save you,' Jaxon said. I couldn't escape his eyes. 'You can convince yourself that you are nothing like me. Tell yourself that you are the black to my white, the queen that stood on the right side of the board. But one day, you will be faced with a choice, as we all are. One day you will have to choose between your own desires, your own darkest impulses, and what you know to be right . . . and it will harden you. You will understand that all of us are devils in the skins of men. You will become the monster that lives inside us all.'

I started away from him. This wasn't the first time that his words had sounded like a prediction.

The Devil.

Had it been me all along?

Was it the devil in myself – the devil deep beneath my skin – that I was meant to resist?

On the surface I was composed, but my insides were a jigsaw of conflicting thoughts. Like a moth, I was drawn to the light that he offered. I was afraid of the humiliation and pain that Nashira would put me through. I was afraid of losing myself to that pain, of losing my mind to it.

I could say yes, with a view to escape. I had played his games for more than three years; surely I could play for longer. But Nashira would have considered this. She would have devised some way to keep me under control.

And I knew Jaxon too well.

'I find it hard to believe that Nashira agreed to this without the promise of something in return,' I said.

'Tell me where the Mime Order is.'

This time, I would listen to the cards. If I agreed, I would be making a deal with that devil inside.

'Not a chance in hell,' I said. 'Not if you offered me anything in the world.'

'You disappoint me.'

'The feeling's mutual. You once said, in *On the Merits*, that we had to fight fire with fire to survive,' I said. 'Did you lose your nerve, Obscure Writer?'

His face closed as he released me. 'All I lost was my naïveté. I have always had the best interests of our kind at heart.'

'How is it in our interest to work for the Rephs?'

'They need us. We need them. You were going to start a fruitless war, and war will not improve conditions for clairvoyants, Paige. What we need now is a time of stability and cooperation.'

'Have you said as much to your employers?'

'The Republic of Scion is not at war.'

'I saw the depot, the factories,' I said. 'The Second Inquisitorial Division *is* preparing for war, and I won't flatter myself by thinking it was all for me. Who are they invading?'

For some time, he gazed out at the sparkling Thames.

'Scion has long had a tenuous understanding with the free world,' he said. 'Scion tolerates them, and in return, they tolerate Scion, in spite of occasional incursions.'

I waited.

'We are hosting ambassadors from two European free-world countries in the Archon,' Jaxon said. 'Weaver has invited them here to demonstrate the advantages of Senshield, to persuade them that it will identify unnaturals in their countries with infallible accuracy, in the hope that those countries will peacefully convert to Scion. If they do not . . . well. Let us say that my hopes for peace may be scotched in the short term.'

As I realised what he was implying, my stomach clenched.

A knock came at the door. Jaxon turned back to me.

'Our time is up. Nashira will make you a final offer,' he said. 'If you wish to live, take it. Think of yourself.'

'Grand Overseer,' a voice called.

Suddenly I was full of pity, of sorrow, of grief for the man he might have been. I went to him and touched his cold face, imagining what it had been like once, before the knife had given it a new shape.

'You know,' I said, 'to see the White Binder reduced to nothing but a boundling, a pawn on someone else's board . . . I really am disappointed.'

'Oh, you may think me the pawn on this particular board, but I am playing on many others. And mark my words, we are nowhere close to the endgame.' The sun gilded his eyes. 'Even so, it seems that, in my brief time as a pawn, I have taught you one very valuable lesson, O my lovely. Humans will *always* disappoint.'

22

ULTIMATUM

Jaxon had confirmed it. Scion was ready to expand its empire again, just as we had feared.

The Vigile outside my cell had mentioned Spaniards.

Spain was their target. Spain, and possibly Portugal, if there were ambassadors from two countries here.

I didn't know much about the free world, but I knew Scion had promoted the virtues of its system globally in the hope that other territories would join the fold of their own free will. It had worked on Sweden. *Join us*, they would say, *and rid your country of the plague of unnaturalness. Join us, and you can keep your people safe.* Some countries, like Ireland, had been taken by force – but it would be easier, cleaner, if they could avoid costly invasions altogether.

Of course, Scion had many hurdles to overcome if it meant to convince the rest of the world to embrace the anchor. Every government with sense would be wary of a rising, militarised empire. Some would have moral concerns about its methods, though Scion had always taken care to conceal the beheadings and hangings from the outside. Others might not believe clairvoyance existed, and even if they did, they might fear that innocent people would be mistakenly identified as unnaturals. Nadine and Zeke had mentioned that being one of many concerns about Scion in the free world.

Now, however, Scion had the perfect answer. They had Senshield. Why shouldn't they take control, they would ask, if they had a foolproof method for winnowing the unnaturals from the innocents – a way of removing dangerous individuals from society?

Senshield.

It always came back to that.

The ambassadors being here must be a final test of the water. The guns would be kept secret, but if they showed an ordinary Senshield scanner to the Spanish – if they proved how efficient Scion was about to become – and their targets *still* refused to join the fold, then, only then, did they mean to invade.

The Vigiles herded me back to my cell and administered my drugs. In the precious seconds before my wits left me, I hid the roll of paper under the mattress of my cot.

If Nashira meant to see me today, there was a good chance Alsafi could be with her. He had never been far away from her in Oxford. And it might be my chance to tell him – somehow – what I knew.

When the drug wore off and my food arrived, I retrieved the paper and huddled close to the door so I couldn't be seen through the viewing slot. When I was certain no Vigiles were about to come through, I forced a small cut open, where they had struck me with a truncheon, and used the blood to scratch three words on to the paper.

COLCHICUM RHUBARB CHICKWEED

By the time the Vigile returned, the note was hidden. I was water-boarded for ignoring my meal.

Alsafi was fluent in the language of flowers.

Colchicum: *my best days are gone.*

RHUBARB: *advice.*

CHICKWEED: *rendezvous.*

It was evening by the time I was dragged out of the basement again. Now it was dark, there was more activity in the Archon. We passed faces I recognised from the news. Ministers in black suits, their crisp white shirts buttoned up high. Vigiles and their commandants. Scarlett Burnish's little raconteurs in their red coats, tapping notes into their data pads, preparing to report their lies. Members of the Inquisitorial courts, gliding across the marble in steel-buckled shoes and hooded cloaks lined with white fur. Some stopped to stare and whisper. I was clearly not as dead as some of them had thought.

Scarlett Burnish herself was at the end of one corridor, immaculate as ever, holding a sheaf of documents. She wore a sculpted velvet dress with a complicated lace collar, and her hair rippled down to the small of her back, with the top layer braided like a net.

With her was a woman I had glimpsed on ScionEye. She was petite and doe-eyed, possessed of a small, upturned nose and skin so pale it almost glowed. Her dark hair was piled up on her head and threaded with rubies, and her gown – crimson silk and ivory lace – fell in tiers to the floor, leaving her collar bare for a necklace of rose gold and diamonds. The layers of the dress didn't quite conceal the swell beneath.

'You look very well, Luce. How many months is it now?' Burnish was saying.

'It will be four soon.'

I remembered now. Luce Ménard Frère, spouse and advisor to the Grand Inquisitor of France.

'How lovely,' Burnish said, all smiles. 'Are your other children looking forward to it?'

'The younger two are excited,' Frère said, smiling back, 'but Onésime is very unhappy. He always thinks a new baby will take his maman away from him. Of course, when Mylène was born, he was the first person to be cooing over her like a little bird.'

They stopped talking as my guards marched me past. Frère placed a hand on her abdomen and spoke in French to her bodyguards, who formed a barrier in front of her. Burnish raked me up and down with her eyes, bid farewell to Frère, and strode from the corridor.

I was led into a final passageway. Above two double doors at the end was a plaque spelling out INQUISITORIAL GALLERY. Just before we went through it, I sneaked the roll of paper from my shift to my hand.

The sheer size of the place hit me first. The floor was red marble, as it was in most of the building. An ornate ceiling stretched high above my head, where three vast chandeliers were laden with white candles.

The walls at either end of the hall were hung with official portraits of Grand Inquisitors from decades past, while the side walls were covered by frescoes. To my left was a giant depiction of the establishment of Scion, with the First Inquisitor holding up the flag on the banks of the river and shouting to a euphoric audience; to my right, the first day of the Molly Riots. I stared up at the images of the monstrous Irish, with their bloody flags, and the soldiers of Scion, painted in lighter tones, who held out their hands as friends. A plaque underneath read ERIN TURNS FROM THE ANCHOR.

A rosewood banqueting table was the centrepiece of this magnificent hall, and a grand piano stood in one corner. Nashira Sargas sat at the head of the table. Gomeisa, the other blood-sovereign, was on her right, in a black doublet, staring at me with his sunken eyes. On her left was an empty chair, and beside that sat Alsafi Sualocin.

Jaxon sat opposite him, smiling, like we were having breakfast again. He couldn't just leave me in peace.

Vigiles were stationed on both ends of the hall, armed with flux guns. I recognised a few of their faces from Oxford. One of my guards lifted her staff and rapped it on the floor.

'Suzerain, I present to you the prisoner, XX-59-40,' she said, 'by order of the Commandant-at-Arms.'

'Seat her,' Nashira said.

I was taken past the other guests and deposited in a high-backed chair between her and Alsafi, with Gomeisa opposite.

Another guard reached for his handcuffs. 'Should we restrain the prisoner, Suzerain?'

'No need. 40 is aware that poor behaviour here will result in additional time on the waterboard.'

'Yes, Suzerain.'

The close call stole my breath. If I had been cuffed, they would have seen the note.

I placed my hands in my lap, out of sight of the rest of the table. As the guards bowed and retreated, Nashira took a good look at me, as if she had forgotten what my face was like. Her corrupted aura was a smoking fire, suffocating mine. Her five spirits were all here, including the poltergeist I recognised from the scrimmage – the poltergeist that had tortured Warden.

She had never had just five. The sixth – the most powerful – was elsewhere in this building. It would have been kept here, far away from Oxford, while engineers and Rephs alike worked out how to build Senshield.

I dropped my gaze to the gold-rimmed plate in front of me. Every muscle was rigid. I dared not even glance at Alsafi, who was close enough to touch.

Once I left this hall, I might never get near Nashira again. Perhaps I should just carry out my original plan, and try my best to push her spirit out – yet I already sensed that I had been mad to think I could. My gift was stronger than it had been the last time I faced her, but that dreamscape was wrapped in the chainmail of centuries. In my weakened state, barely out of my stupor, I would never do it.

'Well,' I said finally, when the silence had outlasted my nerves, 'this is an unexpected reunion.'

'You will not speak without permission from the Suzerain,' Alsafi said.

His voice was so close that I almost flinched.

'You have had quite a journey since we last met, 40,' Nashira said. 'The raid of a well-protected factory in Manchester, an Archon official murdered, and the infiltration of a depot kept secret and secure for decades, all in a matter of days. I am impressed by your persistence, if nothing else. You must have thought you had come very close to unlocking the secret of Senshield.'

I tried to keep my face blank. One wrong glance, one uneasy shiver, and she might guess that I was still trying.

From behind my hair, I risked a glance at the Suzerain. As usual, Nashira was dressed in black, slashed with gold at the sleeves, her bodice crusted with drops of amber. Her long hair was bound at the side of her neck, as bright as brass, spun into soft waves.

'I understand why it became your target,' she said. 'Of course, it was always a doomed endeavour. The core is indestructible.'

Liar, I thought.

Across the table, other blood-sovereign didn't say a word. Gomeisa, Warden of the Sargas.

He was unquestionably the most disturbing of the Rephs. None of them looked old – they were ageless creatures – but Gomeisa had a bone structure that lent a certain gravitas to his features, haunting them with cruel insight. Deep hollows lay beneath his prominent cheekbones. His eyes glowed in their sockets.

He had plotted the massacre in Dublin, giving Vance and Bell their orders.

He had murdered Liss Rymore.

'You were wise to give yourself up,' Nashira said. 'Now, the war and bloodshed the Mime Order wanted to bring to these isles will be avoided.'

Under the table, I reached for Alsafi, finding his thigh. His hands had been clasped on the table, but now he sat back, just a little.

'22,' Nashira said, 'will you not perform for us?'

I turned to look behind me. One of the red-jackets from Oxford was standing nearby. It took me a moment to focus on his face.

To see that his lips were sewn closed.

'You may remember 22,' Nashira said to me, expressionless. 'His duty was to secure the Residence of the Suzerain after your rabble fled. Sadly, he allowed a Ranthen assassin to breach the walls.'

I did remember. He had been at the summer feast. He bowed and sat dutifully at the grand piano.

Out of sight, a gloved hand touched my wrist. I pushed the note from between my fingers, into his grasp.

'Perhaps,' Jaxon said, lighting a cigar, 'we should tell Paige about Sheol II, Suzerain.'

My heart quickened. Nashira gave Jaxon the smallest nod; he offered a gracious smile in return.

'You should know,' he said to me, 'that despite your rebellion, the Rephaim still mean to protect us, just as they promised in 1859.' His cigar glowed. 'To that end, they are building a new prison city in France, to deal with the threat of the Emim. So you see, the Suzerain has mended the mess you made in September. And now that you have been . . . removed, the Mime Order will not interfere.'

Across the room, 22 had been playing a parlour song. Gradually, almost imperceptibly, the notes took a different form.

Just two verses, heavily embellished, disguised so you might miss it if you didn't know it well.

It was 'Molly Malone' – but not the original melody, the one most people here would know. It was the one the rebels had used in mourning, which was slower and darker. We had sung it in memory of Finn and Kay. For a fleeting instant, I was reminded of everything Scion had taken.

'Enough of this charade,' Gomeisa said, cutting off the music. 'It is time to inform 40 of her fate.'

Ice crept into my fingertips.

'Yes,' Nashira said, her eyes like uncut emerald in the gloom. 'The time for . . . persuasion is over.'

My body became too aware of its blood.

'XX-59-40, we have given you numerous opportunities to save yourself. It is clear to us that you are beyond reform; that you will not recant your support for the Ranthen; that you remain wilfully ignorant of the threat posed by the Emim. Keeping you alive would be a mockery of Inquisitorial law.' She beckoned one of the Vigiles, who unravelled a handwritten document and set it down in front of me. 'In ten days' time, on the first of January, you will be executed here, in the Archon.'

The document was a death warrant, signed by the Grand Judge. My gaze skimmed over it, picking out words like *condemnation* and *abomination*. Jaxon's hand tightened on the top of his cane.

'Your spirit will remain with me,' Nashira said, 'as my fallen angel. Perhaps you will learn, then, to obey.'

My ears were ringing now. Somehow, after months of defying Scion, I had never really expected to see this document. My father must have been presented with the same.

'Shall I escort the prisoner to her cell, blood-sovereign?' Alsafi said. I tensed.

'Soon. I would speak to her alone.'

There was a pause before the other three stood and left, along with 22, who was marched out by Vigiles. His small defiance, unnoticed by everyone but me, was over. As Jaxon followed them, he gave me a pointed stare that urged me to reconsider.

When the doors closed, and it was just the two of us, there was silence for a long time.

'Do you think human beings are good?'

The question rang, cool and clear, in the vastness of the gallery.

This had to be a trap. Nashira Sargas would never ask for a human's opinion without an ulterior motive.

'Answer me,' she said.

'Are Rephs *good*, Nashira?'

Outside, the moon was waning. Her posture was almost placid, fingers interlocked.

'You were reared, from the age of eight, in the empire I created,' she said, as if I hadn't spoken. 'You see it as captivity – internment – but it has sheltered you from crueller truths.'

I wanted to run from that cut-glass voice, the poisonous spill of her aura in the æther.

'I wonder if you have ever heard of a witch trial,' she went on. 'In the past, they were quite common. Anyone could be accused of sorcery and executed, with or without evidence of a crime. Those found guilty would be drowned or burned; many were tortured into confessing.'

'Sounds familiar,' I said.

'Hardly. In those times, executions were often far more imaginative than they have ever been in Scion. For the crime of high treason, such as yours, a criminal would be hung until almost dead, before his entrails were torn out before his waking eyes. His body would then be quartered, and his head set upon a spike to rot. The spectators would cheer.'

I had thought myself inured to violence.

'No Rephaite,' she said, 'has ever committed such a brutal act against another. And never would.'

I swallowed. 'I seem to recall you threatening to skin another Rephaite.'

'A threat is not an act. I have hurt Arcturus for his own good, but I would never be so grotesque.'

'Just grotesque enough to mutilate him.'

She didn't seem to think this worthy of comment. His scars, his pain, meant nothing to her.

'Before I was blood-sovereign, I dwelled in a great observatory, allowing me to see your world. As centuries passed on Earth, I watched the human race,' she said. 'I learned that humans have a mechanism inside them – a mechanism called *hatred*, which can be activated with the lightest pull of a string. I saw war and cruelty. I saw slaughter and slavery. I learned how humans control one another.

'When we arrived in your realm, I used the stores of knowledge I had saved from the observatory – including the knowledge of how intensely you can hate. It was painfully easy to turn the tide of loathing towards *unnaturals*. That was how Scion was born. An empire built on human hatred, meant to shape and control it.'

There was so little feeling left in my body that I was almost unaware of it.

'I have done nothing to you that you have not done to your-selves. I have only used humankind's own methods to bring it to heel. And I mean to continue.' Nashira rose and walked past one of the paintings, towards a window at the other end of the room. 'You may think I am your enemy. The Ranthen may have told you so. They are blind.'

Her shadow moved across the floor. I couldn't take my eyes from her silhouette.

'When he endeavoured to help humans before, Arcturus was betrayed by your mentor. He should have learned then. I punished him, with the spirit of a certain human, to remind him of your true nature.'

Hearing his name gave me strength. 'He doesn't seem to have learned his lesson,' I said.

'He remains in thrall to Terebell Sheratan, unable to see the true nature of the mortals he believes he can save.'

When she mentioned Terebell, her tone sent a trickle of unease through me.

'Humans have conducted their own affairs for too long. You have failed to govern yourselves,' she said. 'If we did not rule, this opportunity to save you would be lost for ever.'

'I've seen your disregard for human life,' I said. 'You expect me to believe you want to *save* us?'

'Killing you all would burden the æther beyond repair. Some will live,' she said, 'to serve the empire. But the natural order does not place human beings at the top of the hierarchy. Now is the age of the Rephaim.'

I had been naïve. I had thought of Nashira Sargas as purely evil, purely cruel – but she knew more about us than we did. We had given her the tools to bring us to our knees.

But if we also gave her our freedom, there would be no getting it back.

'This building we stand in,' I said, 'was designed by human minds and created by human hands. Through nothing but our ambition, and the freedom to create, we can turn a thought into a masterwork. We can make the intangible real.'

She was quiet. I had listened to her, and she was returning the courtesy.

'That's what humans do. We make. We remake. We build, and we rebuild. And yes, sometimes we paint with blood, and we tear down our own civilisations, and it might never stop. But if we're ever to unlearn our worst instincts, we have to be free to learn better ones. Take away the chance for us to change, and I promise you, we never will.' I looked her in the eye. 'I'm willing to fight for that chance.'

Nashira appeared to digest this. She looked out at London, a metropolis created by centuries of humanity. London, with its secret, folded layers of history and beauty, as perfectly formed as the petals of a rose. The deeper you ventured into its heart, the more there was to peel away.

'The Grand Overseer has petitioned me to stay your execution,' Nashira said. 'For a human, he is perceptive. He believes that if I do not allow your gift to continue burgeoning over the years, I risk losing its full potential. From what Suhail has told me, it is clear that your talents may not have matured. Or that you are simply weak.'

The pain had been a test, then. Perhaps she had expected me to be able to escape.

'For now, you are all I have,' she said. 'The Grand Overseer is certain that you could yet embrace our cause. If you were to serve it of your own accord, I would have no immediate need of your death. Given his conviction, I may consider sending you to France, under a new identity, to live out the rest of your natural life in Sheol II.'

'What do I have to do?'

Not even her eyes moved.

'Tell me,' she said, 'where I can find the Mime Order.'

Two words now stood between me and my execution. All I needed to say was *crisis facility*.

It was my death or theirs.

'I am Underqueen of the Scion Citadel of London,' I finally said. 'I will be Underqueen until I go to the æther, and if there's one last thing I plan to do with my life, it's protect the people who trusted me with theirs. I know you're only trying to do the same, Nashira. I just wish you'd believed there was another way than this.'

Nashira was silent. When neither of us spoke again, Alsafi came back through the doors.

'Are you finished with the prisoner, blood-sovereign?'

Her nod was hardly visible. I followed Alsafi out of the Inquisitorial Gallery.

I risked a glance as we walked down the corridors. I had no idea what the surveillance was like; better to wait for him to speak. His face was more expressive than those of other Rephs, with eyes of a bright green. This was a Reph who took his fill of aura whenever he pleased.

'We do not have long,' he said, his voice low. 'Your cell is under close surveillance. What *advice* do you have for me, Underqueen?'

'Senshield is here. The core is beneath a glass pyramid – it might be the roof – a room with pale walls,' I said. 'I think it's somewhere high up, possibly in one of the towers. There's a white light that you might be able to glimpse from outside.'

His face didn't betray whether he recognised the image.

'It can be destroyed, but not by me,' I said. 'They're keeping me sedated. I can't dreamwalk. It will have to be you.'

'It is here, then.'

His tone was musing. This must be an unwelcome surprise – the realisation that it had been right under his nose without his knowledge. It was only my gift that had allowed me to find it, and Alsafi was no dreamwalker.

'I assume you know how to deactivate it,' he said. When I didn't answer, he glanced at me. 'I cannot risk my position in the Archon for anything less than certainty. Sacrifice without gain is folly.'

'I can't be certain,' I admitted, 'but we did find evidence.'

His jaw tensed.

'The core is likely powered by one of Nashira's angels, which is bound – with her ectoplasm – to a glass sphere.' I spoke as softly as I could. 'If you destroy the casing, it should release the spirit.'

'And you believe this will stop all of the scanners.'

'Yes. So does Arcturus.'

I couldn't be certain, but to make that many scanners work, they might need to contain the spirit in one place, keeping its scores of connections stable. Warden hadn't said it, but I had my own intuition.

'There is precedent to your reasoning,' Alsafi said. 'If a spirit is released from an ethereal battery, the energy its presence generated is dispersed, and the battery ceases to function. Even if the core is a different form of ethereal technology, dislodging the spirit might impair it, if nothing else.' He slowed down, buying us a few moments. 'The executioner will be summoned soon. I cannot help you escape.'

'I know.'

His gaze slid to my face.

'Colchicum.' Pause. 'You did not intend to escape.'

I gave him no answer.

We were approaching the door to the basement now, in sight of the Vigiles who guarded it. They saluted Alsafi before they marched me back into the tomb below.

23

PERSEVERANCE

Ten days until my execution. It must be meant as a cruel delay, giving me time to wonder what kind of agony awaited me. The sword would be too good for the human who had dared to stand against the Suzerain. Perhaps she meant for me to die in one of the ways she had told me about, to prove that my faith in humanity was misplaced. They must expect me to crack under the pressure, to beg Jaxon to spare my life and take me with him to France.

I didn't. I waited quietly for death – but before I joined the æther, I wanted to know that Alsafi had destroyed Senshield.

When the drugs came, I was grateful. I submitted to the Vigiles' hands, to the needles I no longer felt – they took away the fear that my death would be in vain. With every hour that Alsafi was unwilling or unable to take action, the Mime Order remained in the Beneath.

One night, the Vigiles got me out of bed and put me on the waterboard again, seemingly for their own amusement. When they dumped me back in my cell, soaked and exhausted, there was a supper tray waiting. I inched towards it and choked down as much of the mush as I could.

That was when I found the tiny strip of paper, buried in the food. It was stained, but legible.

DOCK

I breathed easier. Dock. *Patience.* He must be biding his time, waiting for an opportunity to reach the core without compromising his position. The thought was comforting for a while.

But more days passed, and I heard nothing. And no more notes came with my food.

31 December 2059
NEW YEAR'S EVE

I was woken one morning by a Vigile aiming the beam of his torch into my eyes.

'Rise and shine, Underqueen.' I was lifted to my feet. 'Time to die.' I was too tired to fight.

The Vigiles took me to another cell, small and clean, in one of the main corridors of the Archon. I soon realised that it was a display case.

For my last few hours, I was to be exhibited as a war trophy.

The New Year Jubilee was set to be the biggest event in years. It would take place in the Grand Stadium, used for official ceremonies. There was a screen at the end of the corridor, and I could just make out the broadcast.

Murmurs echoed between the walls as dignitaries and ministers filed past my cell on their way to the show. Several of them stopped to scrutinise me. Among them were the Minister for Surveillance, the portly Minister for Arts, and the sallow-faced Minister for Transport, whose nose betrayed her illegal drinking. Luce Ménard Frère and the French emissaries spent a considerable amount of time observing what a frightening creature I was. All the while, I fixed them with a dead-eyed stare. When the French party got bored, Frère stayed behind, one hand on her rounded abdomen.

'I am pleased,' she said, 'that my children will grow up in a world without you in it.'

She walked away before I could think of a reply.

Now I understood why I was in this cell. For my last hours, I was to be displayed as a war trophy.

Jaxon came to the door for one last look. I thought I could see authentic sorrow on his features.

'So this is the end.' Somehow he sounded both angry and solemn. 'I present you with an opportunity to live, to keep your gift for yourself, and you spit at it.'

'That's my choice,' I said. 'It's called *freedom*, Jax. It's what I fought for.'

'And how hard you fought,' he said gently. 'Goodbye for now, O my lovely. I will remember you fondly, in your absence, as my unfinished masterpiece; my lost treasure. But bear this in mind: I do not like to leave things unfinished. Not masterpieces, not treasure hunts, and certainly not games. And I believe our game is only just beginning.'

I raised one eyebrow. He really was a madman. With the softest of smiles, he was gone.

Unfortunately, Jaxon was not my last visitor. The next was Bernard Hock, the Chief of Vigilance – one of the few voyants permitted in the Archon. He looked less than pleased to be in a suit as he entered my cell.

'Don't cry now, unnatural.' He grasped my arm and stabbed a needle into it. 'Just lie there nice and quiet. The executioner will be here after the Jubilee. Then you'll cry.'

I shoved him off me. 'How does it feel to hate yourself as much as you do, Hock?'

In answer, he backhanded me and left the cell. Soon, the sounds of conversation waned from the corridors.

I shivered on the floor, cold to my bones. It was a short while before the Sargas finally passed, accompanied by Frank Weaver and several other high-ranking officials, including Patricia Okonma, the Deputy Grand Commander.

Alsafi brought up the rear. The sight of him made the hairs on my nape stand on end.

None of them so much as glanced at me, but as Alsafi walked by, a tiny scroll landed within my reach. I waited until they were all out of sight before I reached between the bars, snatching the note.

EUPATORIUM ICE PLANT CLEMATIS GROUND LAUREL

Eupatorium: *delay*. Ice plant: *your looks freeze me*. Clematis: that could either mean *mental clarity* or *artifice*, if I remembered correctly. Ground laurel: *perseverance*.

I read it several times. Delay – it hadn't happened.

Frozen by a look – he was being watched.

I leaned against the wall of my cell and grasped my own arms, as if that could hold me together. I didn't know what *mental clarity* or *perseverance* were supposed to mean to me now, but one thing was clear.

He hadn't done it.

And I couldn't do it. I had already been drugged, rendering my gift useless. In a few hours, I would be dead. With a weak sound of frustration, I buried my face in my knees.

Nashira and Hildred Vance had succeeded in breaking me. I shook with silent, rib-racking sobs, loathing myself for being so stupid as to hand myself to the anchor; so arrogant as to think I could survive for long enough to carry out the mission.

Trembling, I read the note again, trying to control my breathing. Ground laurel. *Perseverance*. What the hell did that mean? How could he persevere if he was being watched?

Clematis. *Mental clarity. Artifice*. Which of the two meanings did he intend me to take from it, and why?

I crumpled the note into my hand.

Nashira will not let you go once you are in her clutches. She will chain you in the darkness, and she will drain the life and hope from you.

When music sounded in the corridor, I raised my head. The transmission screen outside my cell was now fixed on the live broadcast of the Jubilee. The walls inside the stadium were covered by black drapes, each bearing an immense white circle with a golden anchor inside it.

Hundreds of tiered seats provided the best views. The groundlings, with cheaper tickets, had gathered at the edges of the vast, ring-shaped orchestra pit, and were craning their necks to see the top of the stage.

'*Esteemed denizens of the Scion Citadel of London*,' Burnish said, and her voice resounded through the space, '*welcome, on this very special night, to the Grand Stadium.*'

The roar was deafening. I made myself listen. That was the sound of victory.

'*Tonight*,' Burnish said, '*we welcome a new year for Scion, and a new dawn for the anchor, the symbol of hope in a chaotic modern world.*' Applause answered her. '*And now, before the stroke of midnight, it is time for us to reflect upon two centuries of our rich history, brought to you by some of Scion's most talented denizens. Tonight, we celebrate our place in the world, and embrace our bright future. Let us set our bounds ever wider, and grow ever stronger – together. The Minister for Arts is proud to present the Jubilee.*'

The ovation rumbled on for almost a minute before mechanisms began to move in the stadium. A performance, then. Or a message from Vance. *Look at our imperial might. Look at what you failed to thwart.*

A platform rose, and the light ebbed to a twilight ambience. On the platform, a line of children sang the imperial anthem. When the audience gave them a standing ovation, they took a bow, and a new stage was drawn up, decked with the old symbols of the monarchy. A man performed a lively dance, dressed as Edward VII, accompanied by actors in lavish Victorian gowns. It reminded me of *The Fall of the Bloody King*, the masque Beltrame had written for the Bicentenary. Scion had never been creative.

Once the séance table was brought up, the dance became more tormented. Here, once again, was the story of Scion – heavily edited, of course, to remove the Rephs. The lighting reddened, and more performers swept on to the stage, executing acrobatic dances around the principal actor, clawing away his regalia. He was the king who had dabbled in evil, and they were the unnaturals he released into the world. Just like the play at the Bicentenary, all those months ago.

The scenery began to change. Now it was a shadow theatre, and new actors were forming the shapes of skyscrapers and towers, rising ever higher until their figures loomed over the stage, where the dancers had all fallen to their knees. This was the remaking of London, the rising from the ashes of the monarchy. The music swelled. Scion had triumphed.

The stage cleared of actors. The lights went out. When they returned, they were cool and muted.

A woman in a dark bodice and skirt, her fair hair coiled at the crown of her head, was poised on her toes in the middle of the stage. I recognised her at once: Marilena Brașoveanu, Scion Bucharest's most beloved dancer. She often performed at official ceremonies.

Brașoveanu was as still as a porcelain doll. When the camera focused on her, close enough for every viewer to see the finest details of her costume, I realised the skirt of her dress was made up of hundreds of tiny silk moths.

She was the Black Moth.

She was me.

The stadium fell silent. Brașoveanu sailed around the stage to the tune of a piano, fluid yet erratic. Then the Bloody King snatched her hand, spinning her into his arms. I watched, mesmerised, as the Black Moth danced a pas de deux with him. She was the heir of the Bloody King, the herald of unnaturalness.

The dance became faster. Brașoveanu whirled her leg out in front of her and tucked it behind her other knee, over and over, while the lights raced around her and the music became ferocious, like a storm. The Bloody King lifted her above his head, then swung her into his arms again. She was seduced by evil.

Around the pair, actors held signs reading FREEDOM and JUSTICE and THE NATURAL ORDER. Then an army stepped from the shadows – an army of unnaturals – and all of the actors fell down with their signs, murdered where they stood, while the Bloody King brought the Black Moth to a stop. She walked into the blaze of a spotlight, her arms raised high. This was the moment of my death in Edinburgh.

It was beautiful.

They had made my murder beautiful.

Slowly, Brașoveanu took centre stage. A hush had fallen. When she spoke, she raised her head high, and I was sure I saw the dark fire of hatred in her eyes.

'We need everyone,' she said, and her microphone sent it all around the stadium, into the home of every viewer in the country, 'or everyone loses.'

I froze. My own words, a call to revolution, spoken on a Scion stage.

The camera, which had just panned to the Grand Box, caught the complacent smiles of the ministers stiffening before it cut back to the stage. There was an apprehensive silence.

This had not been part of their plan for tonight.

Brașoveanu took her bow; then she drew a blade from her bun and cut her own throat.

Screams erupted from the groundlings, the only ones close enough to see the red sheeting down her neck. I stared, thunderstruck, as she dropped the blade. That blood was as real as mine.

Brașoveanu collapsed on the stage. The orchestra played on. The other dancer, who was wearing an earpiece, lifted her into his arms. He pirouetted with a plastic smile before dancing off the stage. Though the groundlings were in disorder, most of the audience was still cheering.

And something kindled, deep within me.

Marilena Brașoveanu was Romanian. She had witnessed an incursion, too – and tonight, she had used her own blood to ruin their lies.

A Vigile rattled the bars of my cell. 'Come here, 40.'

One hand beckoned me. The other held a syringe. A top-up dose of the drug.

The drug.

Goosebumps covered my arms. Seeing that needle, I realised what I hadn't before, entranced as I was by the Jubilee.

Mental clarity.

My mind was clear as ice. There was no cloud inside it. My vision was sharp, and my gift seethed inside me.

There hadn't been a first dose.

Artifice.

I stared at my hands.

Steady.

Alsafi must have swapped the syringes. Hock had shot something into my veins, but it could only have been water. And now the building was almost empty; there was only a skeleton staff in the Archon while everyone attended the Jubilee. Until the celebrations ended, only a handful of Vigiles stood between me and Senshield.

Perseverance.

The Vigile drew his gun and aimed it at my head. 'Come here,' he said. 'Now.'

'What are you going to do?' I said softly. 'Shoot me? Not without the Suzerain's permission.'

The gun stayed where it was, but I had stared death in the face once before, looked down the barrel of a gun and lived. He swore and returned his weapon to its holster. He took his keys from his belt and sifted through them. That was his mistake. Rage was pounding through my body, bubbling in my blood. It had set me on fire, and like the moth I was, I burned.

When the Vigile opened my cell door, I was ready. I sprang at him and slammed my body into his. At the same time, I lashed out with my spirit, sending us both to the floor in a heap. I clapped a hand over his mouth and nose, squeezed hard, and wrested the gun from the holster. My arms were shaking, and he was clawing at my neck and hair, breaking skin – but I hit him with the pistol, over and over, bludgeoning his skull with all my strength, until blood glinted and his head rolled to one side. I grabbed his set of keys, hauled his dead weight into the cell, and locked the door with trembling hands.

Footsteps were approaching from somewhere to my left. I ran the other way, keys in one hand, pistol in the other, my bare feet light on the marble.

I would help Marilena Braşoveanu ruin their night of glory. If I had to die tonight, I would release the Mime Order.

My head was throbbing as I rounded a corner, hoping against hope that nobody was paying attention to the cameras. I could already sense the æther again – clearly enough to avoid the Vigiles patrolling the Archon, and to know that Hildred Vance was nowhere close.

I felt for the room with the sphere and found it Following the signal, I limped across the marble floor, trying to ignore the drumbeat in my bruises. I could sense two squadrons, spread over a vast building. In one corridor, I had to duck into an office to avoid a lone Vigile, who I hadn't detected until it was almost too late. I hid behind a curtain, sweating. A wrong move could get me hauled back to my cell, and I wouldn't get out again. I might not be drugged, but I was physically weak. I couldn't fight my way to the core.

When I was sure the Vigile wasn't returning, I stumbled out of the office and back into the labyrinth, up the stairs to the next floor. Senshield was somewhere above me.

This corridor was empty, dimly lit by sconces. The darkness calmed me, just a little. The signal above me wavered, and I paused briefly to think.

If the core was high up, it was most likely in a tower. The Archon had two, one on each end of the building. Inquisitor Tower was the one that housed the bells. The other one . . .

I sifted through the keys. None of them were labelled *Victoria Tower*. But then, only Vance and the blood-sovereigns were supposed to know where the core was; no one else would have access.

With fresh resolve, I set off again. Most of the doors I had seen in this building were electronic, but if the Vigiles carried keys, they must also have mechanical locks in case of a power failure – and those locks could be picked.

An alarm began to ring, raising my pulse. Either my empty cell had been discovered, or Brașoveanu's act of defiance had activated some kind of security alert. Metal blinds were scrolling over the windows, and emergency lighting had sprung up on either side of me. Adrenalin streaked through my muscles, keeping the ache at bay. I avoided a few more Vigiles before I staggered into a corridor with a thick ebony carpet, lined by windows on one side.

At the end of this corridor was an arched door, and set into this door was a small plaque reading VICTORIA TOWER. My breath came fast as I approached it. The core was now almost directly above me.

I tried the handle, not expecting it to work. It gave way beneath my hand.

Slowly, I brought my weight to bear against the door, opening it. Vance wouldn't have left the tower vulnerable while she was at the Jubilee. Alsafi must have done this. I stepped into the darkness and closed the door behind me.

A draught blew at my hair. There were no lights in the tower.

A balustrade was wrapped around a kind of well. When I risked a glance, I saw that the opening dropped straight down into an entrance hall. A squadron of Vigiles ran through it, shining their torches. As soon as they were gone, I hit the staircase, fighting the weakness in my body, my head spinning from exhaustion and pain.

I forced myself to continue, gripping the rail for support. When I fell the first time, I thought I would never get back up. My hands reached for the next step, but it seemed as if I was at the foot of a mountain, staring up at the distant summit.

You have risen from the ashes before.

I grasped the railing again. One step. Two steps.

The only way to survive is to believe you always will.

When I reached the top of the stairs, I crumpled to my knees and folded over, trembling. There was light nearby. Almost there. I picked myself back up.

My soft footsteps broke the silence. I was at the highest level of the tower, right beneath its rooftop.

Now I could see that a glass pyramid, illuminated from beneath, made up the centre of the ceiling. And there it was, suspended underneath that glass – the memory I had seen, stolen from the mind of Hildred Vance. The core that powered every scanner, all of Senshield. And now I was this close to it, I knew that Warden had been right.

A spirit.

An immensely powerful spirit, somehow trapped inside a glass sphere. The æther there rippled with vibrations.

This was it.

'Paige Mahoney.'

The back of my neck prickled. I knew that voice.

A woman stepped from the shadows, into the pale light from above. It made her face skeletal.

'Hildred Vance,' I said.

Her dreamscape was hidden. She must have dosed herself with alysoplasm.

One last trap. The grand finale.

Vance stood with a rod-straight back and no expression. I had convinced myself that I could face the Grand Commander without fear, but sweat chilled my brow as we regarded each other. The iron hand of the anchor, the human embodiment of Rephaite ambition. The woman who was responsible, along with Abberline Mayfield and Cathal Bell, for the massacre in Dublin. The woman who had put my father to death.

She had hunted me across the country. She had used my aura – my intimate and fragile connection to the æther – to enhance her machine. She had shaped my life since I was six years old.

Thirteen years later, she was finally in front of me.

Vance looked from the core to my face. She regarded me with something I thought, at first, was contempt – but perhaps not. There was no heat in the stare. No passion. If Jaxon was right, and we were devils in the skins of men, then Vance had shed her skin already.

I was in the presence of a human being who had spent far too much time among Rephs.

She didn't care enough for my life to feel anything towards me. Not even hatred. Her expression, if it could even be called that, told me I was nothing to her – nothing but an enemy war asset that should have been destroyed.

'Even before I saw you in my dreamscape, I knew what you were searching for; what you planned to do. You wanted Senshield.' She glanced at it. 'I confess, you almost had me fooled. You responded as anticipated to the march on Edinburgh – a replication of the Dublin Incursion, calculated to make you surrender in order to avoid the same bloodshed you witnessed as a child. All went to plan. You appeared broken in mind and body. And yet, I suspected an ulterior motive.'

I watched her.

'The Trojan horse,' Vance said. 'An ancient stratagem. You presented yourself like a gift to your enemy, and your enemy took you into their house. All you had to do was deliver yourself into our custody, and you would be that much closer to the core.' Her bony hands clasped behind her back. 'I assume you had help to escape your cell.'

'None,' I said.

As I spoke, her gaze darted to the core again.

'It's brave of you to step out from behind the screen, Vance,' I went on. 'And I have something to ask you, if you'll indulge me. Do you remember the names of all the people whose lives you've stolen?'

Vance didn't answer. She must have calculated that there was no strategic advantage to speaking.

'You didn't just kill my father, Cóilín Ó Mathúna. Thirteen years ago, you killed my cousin, Finn Mac Cárthaigh, and an unarmed woman named Kayleigh Ní Dhornáin.' Saying their names to her face made my voice shake. 'You have killed thousands of innocent people – yet when I was in your dreamscape, it was *my* dream-form with blood on its hands. Do you really think I've taken more life than you have?'

Her silence continued.

She was waiting. I was trying to work out why, when I saw her gaze move – ever so slightly, back to the core. That was the fourth time.

She was nervous.

There really was a weakness.

Time seemed to slow as I looked at the core. I searched it with my eyes, then with my gift.

It took me a few moments to find the vial of ectoplasm, locked inside the sphere, emanating greenish light, holding the angel in place. I could feel the thousands of delicate connections that branched out around it, reaching towards every Senshield scanner in the country.

I didn't know its name, so I couldn't use the threnody; I doubted that would even work against a boundling of this strength. But surely if I destroyed the casing that imprisoned the spirit, it would disperse some of its energy into the æther and sever those connections.

Surely.

I raised my stolen gun. At the same time, Vance pointed a pistol at my chest.

'It will kill you,' she said, 'and achieve nothing. The spirit will continue to obey the Suzerain. It will also continue to power Senshield.'

I stayed very still.

She could be telling the truth. She could be bluffing.

'You will die in vain,' Vance said.

Perhaps I would.

But there had to be a reason she was suddenly talking, *telling* me how Senshield worked. There could be no gain in that. She would only be this free with her information if she was lying.

And Vance only lied when it was necessary.

'You know a lot about human nature, Vance,' I said, taking my time over each word, 'but you made a single, fatal error in your calculations.'

She looked at the core, then back to me.

'You assumed,' I said, 'that I had any interest in leaving here alive.'

Vance stared into my eyes. And somewhere in their depths, there was a flicker – just the softest flicker – of something I hadn't truly believed that Hildred Vance was capable of feeling.

Doubt.

It was doubt.

I pulled the trigger.

When the bullet struck it, the sphere broke apart, releasing a mass of bridled energy. The vial shattered at my feet. I hit the floor and scrambled away from Vance, slipping on spilled ectoplasm as she opened fire. Before I could get up, the fallen angel seized me by the throat.

A breacher, capable of touching the corporeal world. The Suzerain had commanded it to stay, to power the machine, and I had disturbed it. It slammed me between the wall and the floor. I choked on blood. The gun flew out of my hand.

Vance was a strategist. She knew when to retreat. As she backed towards the door, the spirit cast me aside and raced across the room to slam it shut. Vance stopped dead. She was blind to the æther, unaware of where the threat would go next. Pulling myself on to my hands and knees, I looked up at what was left of the sphere.

She had been right. Senshield was still active. Its light remained as bright as ever.

'You belong to the Suzerain.' Vance addressed the spirit, her voice full of authority. 'I am also her servant.'

I crawled across the floor, towards the gun. If my last act in this world was to rip Hildred Vance out of it, my nineteen years had been well spent.

My movements distracted the fallen angel. It whipped away from Vance and threw me over on to my back. A wall of unseen pressure descended on me like a shroud. Sparks erupted from the wreckage of the sphere and threw wild shadows on the walls as the angel began to crush me. Sweat froze on my skin. I couldn't breathe. All I could see was the light from the core.

I didn't know how to fight back. I didn't know how to stop fighting, either. Desperately, I tried to dreamwalk, but I was so weak. All around us, the corporeal world was straining at the seams.

My dreamscape was on the verge of collapse. As the air was drained from my lungs, I saw Nick smiling at me in the courtyard, surrounded by blossoms, sunlight in his hair. My father, the last day I saw him alive. Eliza laughing at the market. I saw Warden, felt his hands framing my face and his lips seeking mine behind the red drapes. The amaranth in bloom. And finally, I heard Jaxon.

I believe our game is only just beginning.

As my vision darkened, some small instinct made me hold out my left hand, as if I could push the spirit away. My arm was forced back, but I kept my palm turned outward. The scars there felt unbearably cold – the old scars from the poppy field, inflicted when I was a child.

And I felt something change.

I *was* pushing it away.

The pain began as a tiny point, a needle pushing through my palm. As it grew, a wordless scream racked my body – and just for a moment, some of the pressure released. Enough for me to gasp in one more breath.

With that breath, I whispered.

'Go.'

What happened next was unclear. I remember watching the glass pyramid shatter. It must have exploded in a split second, but in my mind, it lasted for eternity. I was flung in one direction, Vance in the other.

There came an arc of blinding white, and then oblivion.

24

THE CROSSING

I had woken like this once before, thinking I was dead.

The æther was calling me into its arms, telling me to abandon all my cares, to leave my tender bones behind. My eyelids parted, just enough to see a pale hand, clad in shards of glass. The rest of my arm sparkled, armoured in diamond and glazed with molten ruby. Even my lashes were frosted with gemstones. I was a living jewel box, a fallen star. No longer flesh, but crystalline.

Wind howled through the part of the roof where the angel had passed through. Splinters tinkled from my hair as I turned to see the ceiling.

The white light had been extinguished. All that was left of Senshield was a cavernous hole in the æther, marking a place where a spirit had dwelled for many years. Over time, it would stitch itself back together.

My hand shook. The fallen angel had carved a word into my skin, joining the old scars.

I lay back in my bed of glass. A friend had once told me that knowledge was dangerous. When I succumbed to my wounds and left my body for the final time I would have all the knowledge of the æther. This mystery would soon be solved.

And I could find the others. Even if they didn't know, I would stay with them. I would watch over them. I would not go to the last light until I knew they would be safe.

Footsteps came through the glass, drawing me back. A moment later, my head and shoulders were lifted into the crook of an arm, and yellow eyes were smouldering in the gloom.

'Dreamwalker.'

His features gradually sharpened.

'Leave me,' I murmured. 'Leave me, Alsafi.'

He took hold of my left hand and pried my fingers open, revealing the marks on my palm.

'I'm not worth it.' I was so tired. 'I'm done. Just go.'

'Some would disagree with your assessment of your worth.' He released my hand. When he scooped an arm under my knees and lifted me, I groaned. My skin bristled with broken glass. 'This is not your time.'

He carried me through the ruins, pushing the pistol into my limp hand. The fight wasn't over. As he opened the door, I caught sight of Vance in the corner, as broken as me. She bled just like the rest of us. I wanted to tell Alsafi to make sure she was dead, but I blacked out before I could.

When I came round, Alsafi was almost at the bottom of the stairs, and my cheek was pressed against his doublet. When he entered the corridor with the black carpet, I lifted a hand to his shoulder.

'Nashira,' I whispered. My gift had been weakened, but I sensed a Reph. 'Alsafi—'

He stopped in his tracks. There was no other way out of the corridor.

'Stay quiet.' He spoke quickly. 'If anything happens to me, go to the Inquisitorial Office. There, you can access a tunnel that will take you out of the Archon.'

'Alsafi—'

'And tell Arcturus—' He paused. 'Tell him I hope this redeems me.'

I had so many questions, and no time to ask them. Nashira had already swept into view. The hilt of a sword gleamed over her shoulder.

When she saw me, her eyes turned to hot coals. She looked as if she had walked straight out of hell, carrying its flames within her.

'Alsafi.'

'Blood-sovereign,' he said. 'I have come from Victoria Tower. The Grand Commander is critically injured. Senshield is destroyed.'

He must have been using English consciously, allowing me to follow the conversation.

'I am more than aware of its deactivation.' She didn't raise her voice, but something in it terrified me. 'The humans will attend to Vance. Bring 40 to the basement at once.'

Alsafi remained where he was. I was shaking. When Nashira turned back, he lifted his gaze to look her in the eye.

'Is something wrong, Alsafi?'

His whole body was tensing. Nashira took a step towards him.

'I must confess,' she said, 'I did think it extraordinary that one human, even in Inquisitorial custody, should be able to cause so much destruction in such a short period of time. 40 has done many things she should not have been able to do. She was able to escape from London as martial law was being implemented. She was able to hide the Mime Order and travel between citadels without detection. She was able to reach the core of Senshield.' Another step. 'She could not have done any of it without help.'

Alsafi did not hesitate. He gathered me close and ran.

Black carpet. Wood-panelled walls. Tiny sunbursts of pain, all over my body. He tore a tapestry aside, turned a key, and opened a hidden door in the wainscoting, thrusting me into the tunnel beyond. My left side crashed against a wall, and a shard of glass penetrated deep into my arm, drawing a scream that seared my throat. Sobbing in agony, I pressed my hands against the door.

'Alsafi, don't!'

A key card came spinning into the tunnel.

'Run,' Alsafi barked. I pulled myself back to my feet. Through a spy grate in the door, I watched him draw a sword from underneath his cloak. Nashira met it with hers. 'Go, dreamwalker!'

'Ranthen,' Nashira whispered.

Their swords clashed. Iridescent blades, like shards of opal. I leaned against the wall, unable to take my eyes from the grate. Spirits were rushing to join the war dance of the Rephs. Immobilised by the fire in my arm, I watched Alsafi Sualocin fight Nashira Sargas.

I could see at once that Nashira was faster. She moved like spindrift around Alsafi, as fluently as Brașoveanu had danced her death ballet. Alsafi used sharper swings, and stayed rooted to one spot, but he was no less elegant. The blades chimed like bells as they collided. Quick as she was, he parried her strokes, never changing his expression.

I had seen Rephs fight before, in Oxford, though never with swords. I remembered the way their steps resonated through the æther; how the proximity of two rival Rephs drank all the warmth from the air around them. As if the æther understood their hatred, intensified and nurtured it.

They circled each other like dancing partners. Nashira struck again, faster and faster, until I could hardly see her movements – just the glint of her hair, the flash of the sword. Alsafi stood his ground. When she cut his cheek, drawing ectoplasm, I flinched.

She was toying with him.

His next swipe was harder, and he broke from his position.

His blade slashed and sliced, but never touched her.

Nashira raised her open hand. The rest of her fallen angels came to her from wherever they had been wandering, drawn back to her tarnished aura.

Alsafi spat at her in Gloss. For a long time, neither of them moved.

When the poltergeist attacked him, a tear streaked down my cheek. More gashes appeared across his face, the marks of an unseen knife. He lashed out with the sword before all of her angels converged on him.

Alsafi let out an agonised sound as they tore at him like a flock of birds. As his blade finally hit the floor, Nashira lifted hers. I caught sight of his eyes for a last time, afire with hatred, before she cut straight through his neck.

I turned away, one hand over my mouth. The heavy *thud* was all I needed to hear.

Nashira stared down at the corpse for a moment – it must have been a moment, but it lasted for ever – before her head whipped around, and hellfire flooded her eyes again. And I knew, from the terrible look on her face, that she would dog my footsteps for the rest of my days, even if I could escape her tonight. A decade or a lifetime could pass, but she would not stop hunting me. She would not forget.

I snatched the key card from the floor and ran.

Dark stars erupted in the corners of my vision. Hot jolts came shooting through my feet as I hobbled across stone, breathing in bursts. I tasted salt and metal on my lips. The throbbing in my arm was making me retch. My legs gave way again, and I curled in the darkness, listening to my fitful heartbeat.

'Rise from the ashes,' I whispered to myself. 'Come on, Underqueen.'

When I rose, my hands left red prints on the walls. I couldn't take much more of this. I would die before I reached the Inquisitorial Office.

Then I saw it. Frank Weaver's Inquisitorial maxim was etched above the doors: I SHALL CAST OUR BOUNDS TO THE EDGES OF THE EARTH. THIS HOUSE FOR EVER GROWS.

There was one dreamscape inside. Dewdrops of sweat were forming on my brow. Blood soaked my shift, I was light-headed, and black gossamer was spidering across my vision. I wouldn't stay conscious for much longer. I swiped the card and shouldered the door open.

The Inquisitorial Office was an ornate room, watched over by portraits of all the previous Grand Inquisitors. An oak desk, which housed a wooden globe, sat before a floor-to-ceiling bay window. Weaver himself was nowhere to be seen. Silently, I stepped across the carpet.

Someone was standing beside the bookshelf. Red hair flowed down her back, red as the blood that plastered my skin. When she turned, I swung up the pistol. In the faint light from the citadel outside, her skin was waxen.

'Mahoney.'

I didn't move.

Scarlett Burnish stepped away from the bookshelf and raised a hand.

'Mahoney,' she said, her cool blue eyes seeking mine, 'put down the gun. We don't have much time.'

Those were the lips that told their lies.

I had threatened the Grand Inquisitor once. Now it was the Grand Raconteur who stood before me, at the mercy of my bullet. Back then it had been about leverage, but I didn't need that now. This was about self-preservation.

Burnish lifted her other hand, as if to surrender, and said: 'Winter cherry.'

At first, I didn't understand. It made no sense for her to be using the language of flowers. But then—

Winter cherry.

Deception.

Scarlett Burnish, the face and voice of ScionEye, who had read the news since I was twelve years old.

She was Alsafi's contact in the Archon. Scarlett Burnish, a Ranthen associate. A professional liar. The perfect denizen. A double agent.

Scarlett Burnish, a traitor to the anchor.

Golden light flared into the office. In a movement so fast I almost missed it, Burnish snatched a letter opener from the desk. It whistled past my head and punched through the Vigile's visor, splintering red plastic. The handle jutted from his forehead; blood wept down the bridge of his nose. He teetered before his dead weight thumped to the floor.

In the clock tower, the bells struck one. The æther heaved with the reverberations of another death.

'Quickly,' Burnish said. 'Follow me.'

More dreamscapes were already closing in. Something made me look at the surveillance cameras.

They were deactivated.

Burnish pressed the back of the bust behind her, that of Inquisitor Mayfield, opening a gap in the wall. 'Hurry,' she said, and drew me into the space beyond it.

She had barely closed the wall behind us before more Vigiles thundered into the Inquisitorial Office. Her hand clamped over my mouth.

We waited. Muffled orders could be heard through the wall for some time before their footsteps retreated.

Burnish uncovered my lips. A *crack* split the silence, and her face was illuminated by a tube of light, making her red hair shine like paint against her skin. I followed her along an unlit passage, just wide enough for us to move in single file.

She hurried me down a winding flight of steps. At the bottom, she held her light towards my face.

'Burnish,' I rasped. 'Who do you work for?'

'Good grief, Mahoney, the state of you—' She ignored my question, taking in the streams of blood, the glistening crystals lodged in my arms. 'Stay calm. Where is Alsafi?'

'Nashira, she—' I couldn't control my breathing. 'I told him to leave me.'

'Did she realise he was Ranthen?'

'Yes.'

Fuck.' Burnish started back up the stairs, then seemed to think better of it. Instead, she hit the wall, her face contorted in frustration. 'The *stupid* bastard—' Suddenly she grasped my shoulders. 'Did he mention me, Paige? Did he implicate me?'

Her grip was like iron.

'No,' I said. 'No. He didn't even tell me.'

'Did she capture him, or destroy him?'

'He's gone.'

Her eyes closed for a moment. One long breath, and she was back to business.

'We have to be quick.' She whipped off her silk scarf and used it to staunch the flow of blood from my arm, careful not to push the shard in any farther. 'You had better be worth all this, Underqueen.'

331

A few hours ago, I wouldn't have followed Scarlett Burnish anywhere, but if Alsafi had trusted her, I would have to do the same. It was this or whatever brutal death awaited me in the basement.

Burnish pulled my arm around her neck. We set off into a concrete passageway. I leaned on her as little as I could, but my strength was leaving me.

'Stay awake,' she said. 'Don't pass out on me, Paige.'

'Wait,' I managed. 'Are you . . . with Circinus?'

'No. I was already working against Scion.'

Burnish took what I thought was a handkerchief from her pocket. As she stretched it over her face, it changed her features, making her look twice her age. She tucked her famous crimson hair into a woollen hat.

I couldn't process this. She was clearly a spy, but who had planted her, and when?

After what felt like years, Burnish stopped and entered a code into a keypad, and a pair of doors opened. We stepped into an elevator that rattled as it trundled to the surface. When we reached street level, Burnish went to a wooden door and unlocked it.

We emerged into thick snow in a dead end just off Whitehall. I wouldn't have given the door a second glance.

I had made it out alive.

A lorry was parked nearby. Burnish opened its back door and helped me climb inside. I registered hands taking hold of my elbows just before I passed out.

'. . . was right. She was alive, all that time. I just can't . . .'

The floor shivered beneath me. There was pain at the top of my arm, but it was nothing compared to the sick, steady throb above my left eye.

'Nick,' the voice whispered. 'Nick, I think she's waking up.'

A hand brushed my cheek. As if he were swimming up through deep water, Nick Nygård came into focus.

My senses were still drowsy; it took me a moment to realise, to *see* him. A cut vaulted across his forehead, and his face was greased with sweat, but he was alive. I reached out to touch him, to convince myself that he was real.

'Nick.'

'Yes, sötnos. It's me.'

He pressed me gently against him, resting his chin on the top of my head. The awareness of everything that had happened hit me like a punch to the gut. I tried to speak, but a gate had given way. All I could do was weep. Hardly any sound came out; just broken, straining rasps, punctured with frail sobs. With each shock, my ribs ached and my head pounded and the water beat my lungs apart again. I could feel Nick shaking. Maria rubbed my back, shushing me, speaking to me like you would to a child: 'It's going to be okay, sweet. It's going to be okay.' I cried until I could no longer feel the pain.

My eyelids lifted again. Now I was on a threadbare blanket, and I couldn't see a thing. My ears felt stuffed with cotton wool, but I could just hear the low hum of nervous conversation.

My arms and legs were a collage of dressings. Someone must have removed the glass. I drifted off again, riding the last wave of whatever sedative I had been given, which soon broke. When my eyes flickered open, I felt more clear-headed, but at the cost of the anaesthesia. Most of the left side of my body was smarting.

Arcturus Mesarthim sat beside me, like a sentry.

'You are a fool, Paige Mahoney.' His voice was darkest velvet. 'A headstrong fool.'

'Aren't you used to it by now?'

'You exceeded my expectations.'

'I exceeded Vance's, too, I think.'

He had made questionable choices of his own. It was he who had said that war required risk, and I had chosen to risk my own life.

'Sorry for pointing a gun at you,' I rasped.

'Hm.'

He glanced down at me, his eyes burning softly. With effort, I moved my arm and laced my fingers between his knuckles. His thumb caressed my cheekbone, skirting around the cuts and bruises. In the darkness of the Archon, I had thought I would never see his face, feel his hands on me again. And I hadn't truly realised, until now, that I treasured being touched by him.

'What did they do to you?'

His voice was a low rumble. I shook my head.

'They—' I breathed in. 'I'm all right.'

But I wasn't all right. Anyone could see it. I was trembling like someone yearning for a fix of aster. He stroked my hair, his touch gentle.

'You will be pleased to know,' he said, 'that Adhara, the rightful Warden of the Sarin, has come to a decision. Seeing that our human associate had won such a significant victory against Scion, she concluded that mortals may have matured just enough to merit her allegiance to the Ranthen. Consequently, she has decided that her loyalists will be ready to fight for us. We need only call.'

I tried to still the heaving in my chest. At last, I had proven to Terebell that her investment in my leadership had been justified. It had all been worth it.

'Where are we going?'

'Dover.'

My head felt so heavy. 'The port?'

'Yes.' His hand kept moving over my curls. 'Sleep, little dreamer.'

I slipped away before I could ask anything more. When I woke again, I was opposite a sleeping Maria, lying against Nick. Pain swelled and ebbed in all my wounds with each shunt of the vehicle.

'. . . orders at some point in the next few weeks.' That was Burnish. 'In the meantime, Mahoney needs to convalesce. Alsafi chose her over himself, which leaves me as your only ally in the Westminster Archon. For all our sakes, make it count, and keep her safe.'

'Alsafi was my Ranthen-kith,' Warden replied. 'I will strive to honour his sacrifice, but I suspect that Paige will not want to be absent from the war effort for long, even to convalesce.'

I stayed still.

'If she doesn't rest, she's going to be too weak to contribute to that war effort,' Burnish said. 'She was tortured in the Archon, God alone knows what she had to do to break Senshield, and on top of that, I doubt her injuries have fully healed from the scrimmage. Honestly, I'm surprised she's able to stand up.'

'She is possessed of extraordinary resilience. It was part of why we chose her to be our associate.'

'She's human. And we all have limits,' Burnish said. 'She's a vital player in this game, Arcturus. Leaving aside her gift, she has come to . . . stand for something.' The lorry skimmed over a bump. 'My employer needs people to generate waves of revolution in different parts of the empire. If she wants to keep fighting the Sargas, joining us is her best shot.'

'The Ranthen will need to meet these employers.'

'All in good time. My orders from Domino take priority, but I'll keep helping you, if I can, for Alsafi.'

Domino.

'Did you know him well?'

'We protected each other. I hear you and Paige did the same in Oxford. It gives me hope that Rephs and humans can find common ground.'

'Yes.' Warden took his time answering. 'I will do my utmost to persuade Paige of the sense in resting for a month. But in the end, she must make her own choices, even when they hurt her. I am not her keeper.'

'But you can be her friend, if you know how. She'll need plenty of those.'

One side of my ribcage ached. I shifted my weight off it, hoping they wouldn't notice.

'What will you do next, Grand Raconteur?'

'Exactly what I always do. Lie to the loyal denizens of Scion,' Burnish said. 'I made sure I had a concrete alibi for tonight.'

'You still took a risk by leaving the citadel. Scion may come to suspect you.'

'I take risks every day. Even if someone does question my whereabouts, every human can be bought in one way or another. Everyone accepts a currency. Money, mercy, the illusion of power – there are always ways to purchase loyalty. Trust me,' she said. 'I'll be fine.'

Warden was silent after that.

When the vehicle stopped, a light switched on inside. Scarlett Burnish roused us all and handed me a bundle of clothes. With help from Nick, I eased on a dark sweater, an oilskin, and a pair of waterproof trousers, flinching at the pain when the sweater covered my left arm. The oilskin was embroidered with the anchor wrapped in rope.

'Nick,' I said, 'where's Eliza?'

'She's with the Mime Order.'

'Why isn't she with us?'

Nick breathed out through his nose.

'Paige,' he said grimly, 'we're leaving.'

I looked at him, uncomprehending.

'Burnish is a spy. In exchange for your life, her network has conscripted you, me and Maria. We had no choice but to comply.'

'I don't—' I was too exhausted to process this. 'Where?'

'We're about to find out.' He pulled on his own sweater. 'You've united the syndicate and deactivated Senshield. You've given voyants a chance to survive. You did what you set out to do as Underqueen. I don't like any of this, but it might be safest for you to leave London.'

'Scion told the world I was dead,' I said hoarsely. 'I should be fine to stay.'

'No. The rumour that you're alive will get out, and then you'll be even more of a liability to Scion. They know you're Underqueen,' Nick said. 'London will be the first place they look.' He zipped up his oilskin. 'The Ranthen agreed to send Warden with you. You won't be alone.'

'So we're being shipped off. Because it's what the Ranthen and some . . . spy network want.'

'I know.'

'Can we do anything to stop this?'

'Not that I can see,' Nick said. 'But it was worth it, in exchange for your life.'

Everything had changed so quickly. Eliza would be distraught at being separated from us. We were her only family, and I hadn't even been able to say goodbye.

'Paige,' Nick said, seeing the set of my jaw, 'it will be okay. While you're away, Eliza and Glym will rule as your interims, with Jack as mollisher supreme. They can handle things here now Senshield is gone.'

'Then I'm still Underqueen.'

'You won the scrimmage. No one else has a right to the Rose Crown.'

Eliza and Glym were two of the few people I trusted. Between them, they could keep the Mime Order together. If I had been there, they would have been the replacements I chose.

I was still losing control of my life again, just as I had when Scion arrested me, that fateful night in March. But I *was* curious about Burnish.

When she returned to the lorry, it let in a flurry of snowflakes. She stood before us and crossed her arms.

'You are now part of the Domino Programme, an espionage network working against the Republic of Scion,' she said. 'As Nick and Maria agreed with my contact, you will join our clandestine operations in mainland Europe for a maximum term of one year.'

Maria had an impressive bruise on one cheek. 'Who exactly are you working for, Burnish?'

'All I'm at liberty to say is that I'm sponsored by a free-world coalition with a vested interest in stopping Scion.' Burnish reached into a briefcase. 'Either you comply, or I shoot you. You already know too much.'

She handed Maria a thin leather dossier.

'There's your new identity, Hazurova. You're going home, to Bulgaria,' she said. 'You'll receive your orders within the next two weeks.'

Maria leafed through the documents, her face tight. The next folder Burnish handed out was mine.

'I hope your French is up to scratch, Mahoney,' she said. 'You and Arcturus are taking a merchant ship to Calais. A contact will meet you there and transport you to a safe house in the Scion Citadel of Paris.'

Paris. I didn't know what her handlers wanted from me, but if there was one place in Scion I would have chosen to go next, it was there. Sheol II would be in France, and that meant a new grey market.

I could stop both.

I opened the folder, which was embossed with the seal of the Republic of Scion England. My alias was Flora Blake. I was an English student who had taken a year out for research. My subject of interest was Scion History, specifically the establishment and development of the Scion Citadel of Paris.

Nick breathed out. 'And me?'

'Sweden, where you'll be of most use to us. You have the language, the local knowledge – and personal experience of how Tjäder runs things.'

He looked through his dossier with a knitted brow. I grasped his hand.

'I suppose I am to keep out of sight,' Warden said.

'Correct.' Burnish checked her watch. 'I don't have much time. We need to leave now.'

One by one, we emerged from the lorry. I looked out at the English Channel, not quite believing that I was heading towards it. The five of us walked to the seafront, where ships were docking. The ones from the Scion Inquisitorial Navy must have brought the soldiers here from the Isle of Wight. There were merchant vessels, too, to carry heavy cargo to other Scion countries and neutral free-world states.

'Burnish.' I walked alongside her, holding my jacket as close as I could without setting fire to my skin. 'Will you do me one favour?'

'Name it.'

'One of the Bone Season survivors, Ivy Jacob, is somewhere in the system of sewers that the River Fleet runs through. She's with a woman named Róisín. Is there any way you could get them out?'

'If one of them is a Bone Season witness, I'll make it my priority.'

'Thank you.'

It was all I could do for them now. I only hoped that Styx would let them go without a fight, and that Eliza and Glym could appease him.

After eleven years, I was leaving the Republic of Scion England. I had visualised this as a child, when I was in school or trying to sleep; wished on stars that one day, I would climb aboard a ship and sail into a future ripe with possibility. I just hadn't thought it would happen like this.

Burnish led us into the shadow of a container ship. Letters spelling FLOTTE MARCHANDE – RÉPUBLIQUE DE SCION loomed above us.

'This is yours, Mahoney,' she said. 'And yours leaves first.'

My heart pounded. It was time. Maria held out her arms first. 'It's been quite the journey, sweet.'

'Yoana,' I said, embracing her, 'thank you. For everything.'

'Don't thank me, Underqueen. Just tell me something.' She pulled away slightly and grasped my shoulder. 'Did you see Vance in there?'

I nodded. 'If she's not dead by now, she won't be getting up for a while, at least.'

'Good.' Her smile widened. 'Now, go and cause some havoc in Paris, and don't let all this have been in vain. And if you possibly can,' she added, 'try not to get killed before I can see you again.'

'Likewise.'

She kissed my cheek and went to join Burnish at the next ship. Nick looked at me, and I looked at him.

I felt as if the ground was slanting. As if my centre of gravity had changed.

'I remember when I first saw you. A little girl with blonde curls.' His voice was steady. 'I'd seen a vision of the poppies. That was how I found you.'

'You never told me that.'

'You never asked.' He gave me a tired smile. 'After that day, I didn't expect to see you again. The æther clearly had other ideas.'

I returned the smile.

'I remember wondering where you'd gone,' I said. 'Whether you ever thought about the poppy field.'

'I remember finding you at Ancroft,' he said. 'I felt so proud of you for surviving Scion, all those years, but you were almost the same age as Lina. And when I saw your aura – the only aura in the room – I knew I couldn't let you face the woods alone.'

My eyes were misting over.

'I remember when you told me you loved Zeke,' I said, my voice thick, 'and being so afraid that I would lose you. That I'd be left alone again, the way I was in Dublin. But maybe the æther ordains some friendships.'

We had never acknowledged that night out loud. Nick laid his palm against my cheek.

'I remember you being crowned in the Rose Ring,' he whispered, 'and I remember realising what a wonderful, courageous woman you'd become.' Tears spilled on to my cheeks. 'And I had never felt so privileged to have you in my life.'

He was as much a part of me as my own bones, and now he would be gone. I cried as I hadn't since I was a child. In the shadow of that merchant vessel, we clung to each other like we were ten years younger, the Pale Dreamer and the Red Vision, the last two Seals to break apart.

A French dockworker ushered me and Warden into the cargo ship. He showed us into a small freight container, warning us not to be seen. All too soon, a long blast announced our departure from Dover. I sat with Warden among the crates and boxes, trying not to think about Nick, or the ship that would carry him far away from me.

We would find each other. I would see him again.

London would always walk with me. It would live inside my blood. The place my cousin had told me never to go; the place that had been my chrysalis, my damnation, and my redemption. Its streets had won my heart. They had turned me from Paige Mahoney to the Pale Dreamer to Black Moth to the Underqueen, and then unmade me again, leaving me irrevocably changed. One day, I would return to my citadel, to see this land unchained from the anchor.

When we were some way from the port, Warden opened the door of the container, and together, we stepped on to the deck.

My hands came to rest on the railings at the stern. The merchant ship crashed through the English Channel, churning the waves to lace. The ice-cold wind tore at my cheeks, as if it wanted to expose a second face beneath my own, as I looked back at the southern coast of Britain.

I had stopped Senshield. I had weakened Hildred Vance. For now, voyants were safer than they had been. They could disappear into the shadows again; they could walk the streets invisibly. But I could do more for them. I would cast off my crown and take up my sword, and I would go to battle. Soon, an unknown woman named Flora Blake would arrive on the streets of Paris, and the theatre of war would open again.

And we would meet our new allies. Whoever they were.

'All this time, I thought we were the ones driving this revolution,' I said, 'but this is clearly bigger than we could ever have imagined.' The wind hacked at my curls. 'Someone once told me we were all puppets; that I should know who was holding my strings. Right now, I don't think I have any idea.'

'We all have our strings,' Warden said. 'A dreamwalker should know better than most that all strings can be cut.'

'Then promise me this.' I turned to face him. 'Whatever orders Domino sends us, we don't follow them without question. We find out what kind of game we're playing before we show them our own cards. And we stay together.' I sought his gaze. 'Promise me we'll stay together.'

'You have my word, Paige Mahoney.'

He stood by my side as we left England behind us. It was the first day of January. The beginning of another year, another life, another name. I looked back once more at the cliffs that loomed along the coast, at the white cliffs of Dover, limned by the promise of dawn.

And I waited for the sun to rise – as it always had, like a song from the night.

SCION: INTERNATIONAL DEFENCE EXECUTIVE
CLASSIFIED INTERNAL COMMUNICATION

SENDER: OKONMA, PATRICIA K.

SUBJECT: AUTHORITY MAXIMUM

Urgent notice to all commandants. Grand Commander VANCE, HILDRED D. has been injured in the line of duty and is unfit for command. In my capacity as Deputy Grand Commander, authority maximum rests in me until further notice.

RDT SENSHIELD has been incapacitated. All units are to return immediately to conventional munitions.

Hostile individual MAHONEY, PAIGE E. has escaped Inquisitorial custody with assistance from within the Westminster Archon. We are interrogating all personnel, up to and including those holding first-level security clearance, to uncover the identity of the collaborator.

Internal and international border authorities have been alerted that MAHONEY, PAIGE E. is at large. All measures must be taken to conceal from the public that this individual is alive. OPERATION ALBION's revised priority is to eradicate her remaining supporters, known as the MIME ORDER, in the capital.

Finally:

Due to the failure of diplomacy with the relevant foreign powers, the need for immediate action in the IBERIAN

PENINSULA is critical. OPERATION MADRIGAL will now proceed with immediate effect. All non-executive communication concerning this operation will be suspended from 6 January.

Let us look forward, as a new year dawns on our empire, to casting our bounds ever farther – and onward still, to the ends of the world. This house for ever grows.

Glory to the Suzerain.

Glory to the anchor.

Author's Note

Although the language of flowers used in *The Song Rising* is based on real nineteenth-century floriography, I have tweaked the meanings of certain flowers, such as clematis, for the purposes of the story.

Glossary

Æther: [noun] The spirit realm, which exists alongside the physical or corporeal world, Earth. Among humans, only *clairvoyants* can sense the æther.

Alysoplasm: [noun] The blood of the *Emim*. It can be used to conceal the nature of voyants' gifts, or to hide their dreamscapes in the æther, making them undetectable to a *dreamwalker*. However, it also prevents them from being able to use their clairvoyance for a time.

Amaranth: [noun] An iridescent flower that grows in the Netherworld. Its nectar can heal or calm any wound inflicted by a spirit; it can also fortify the *dreamscape*. Warden and Terebell take amaranth to ease the pain of the scars on their backs, inflicted by one of Nashira's *fallen angels*.

Amaurotic: [noun *or* adjective] A human who is not clairvoyant. This state is known as amaurosis, from an Ancient Greek word referring to a dimming or dulling, especially of the senses. Among voyants, they are known colloquially as *rotties*.

Angel: [noun] A category of *drifter*. There are several known sub-types of angels:

– A *guardian angel* is the spirit of a person who died to protect someone else, and now remains with the living person they saved

- An *archangel* protects a single bloodline for several generations
- A *fallen angel* is a spirit compelled to remain with their murderer
- All sub-types of angels can be *breachers*

Apport: [noun] The movement of physical objects by *ethereal* means, derived from Latin apportō ('I bring, I carry'). Among spirits, this ability is unique to *breachers*. Rarely, clairvoyants or Rephaim may be able to use apport.

Aster: [noun] A genus of flower. Certain kinds of aster have *ethereal* properties:

- **Blue** strengthens the link between the spirit and the dreamscape. It can sharpen recent memories and produce a feeling of wellbeing

- **Pink** strengthens the link between the spirit and the body; consequently, it is often used by voyants as an aphrodisiac

- **Purple**, highly addictive, is a deliriant that distorts the dreamscape

- **White** causes amnesia

Augurs: [noun] The second order of clairvoyance according to *On the Merits of Unnaturalness*. Like the *soothsayers*, they are reliant on *numa*. The so-called vile augurs, who use the substance of the human body to connect with the æther, were persecuted by the syndicate for many years.

Aura: [noun] A manifestation of the link between a clairvoyant and the æther, visible only with the *sight*. Since the Netherworld began to deteriorate, *Rephaim* have required human auras to sustain their own connections to the æther.

Binder: [noun] A type of clairvoyant who can compel and tether spirits. A spirit that serves a binder is called a *boundling*.

Blank: [noun] White aster.

Blood-consort: [noun] The consort of a *blood-sovereign* of the Rephaim. Following the Rephaite civil war, Nashira Sargas forced Arcturus Mesarthim to be her blood-consort for two centuries, treating him as a war trophy.

Blood-sovereign: [noun] The leader of the Rephaim. There are always two – a male and a female. Nashira and Gomeisa Sargas are the incumbent blood-sovereigns.

Bob cab: [noun] An unlicensed cab, generally used by clairvoyants.

Boglander: [noun] A hibernophobic slur in the Republic of Scion.

Boundling: [noun] A spirit controlled by a *binder*.

Breacher: [noun] A category of spirit that can affect the corporeal world, e.g. by moving objects, or injuring the living. The ability to breach is usually related to the manner of a spirit's death – a violent death is more likely to produce a breacher. The most common types of breacher are angels and poltergeists. When breachers touch either a human or a Rephaite, they can leave cold scars and a profound chill.

Brogue: [noun] A hibernophobic slur in the Republic of Scion, referring to an Irish accent.

Busking: [noun] Plying a skill for money in public. For clairvoyants, this is a type of *mime-crime*.

Buzzers: [noun] See *Emim*.

Cartomancer: [noun] A clairvoyant who uses cards to connect with the æther.

Clairvoyant: [noun] A human who can sense and interact with the spirit world, the *æther*. They are identifiable by their *aura*.

Cold spot: [noun] A portal between Earth and the Netherworld, which manifests as a perfect circle of ice. Humans cannot pass through a cold spot, but *Rephaim* and *Emim* can.

Costermonger: [noun] A street vendor.

Denizen: [noun] A resident of the Republic of Scion.

Dreamscape: [noun] The house or seat of the spirit, where memory is stored. The term is often used interchangeably with 'mind' by clairvoyants.

The dreamscape is thought to be how the brain manifests in the *æther*, and often resembles a place where an individual feels safe. Clairvoyants can access their dreamscapes at will, while amaurotics may catch glimpses in their sleep. The dreamscape is split into five zones or rings:

- **Sunlit zone**, the centre of the dreamscape, where the spirit is supposed to dwell. The *silver cord* fastens it in place
- **Twilight zone**, a darker ring that surrounds the sunlit zone. The spirit may stray here in times of mental distress. Only *dreamwalkers* can go beyond this zone without injuring themselves
- **Midnight** and **abyssal**, the next two zones
- **Hadal zone**, the outermost and darkest ring of the dreamscape. Beyond this point is the *æther*. There may be spectres – manifestations of memory – in this zone

Dreamwalker: [noun] A contraction of *dreamscape walker*, referring to an exceptionally rare and complex form of *clairvoyance*. Comparable to the esoteric concept of astral projection, dreamwalking involves the dislocation and projection of the spirit from the *dreamscape*. Dreamwalkers have an unusually flexible *silver cord*, allowing them to not only walk anywhere in their own dreamscape, but possess other people.

Drifter: [noun] Spirits that remain within reach of the living. They are broadly divided into two categories: breachers and common *drifters*. Within these categories are numerous sub-types of spirit, including angels and ghosts.

Ectoplasm: [noun] The Rephaite equivalent of blood. It is luminous and slightly gelatinous, and considered to be molten *æther*. As such, it heightens *clairvoyant* abilities.

Emim: [noun] Large and violent creatures that have infested the *Netherworld* and are now venturing to Earth. They are known colloquially as *Buzzers*, due to a distinctive sound that voyants hear when they appear. The Emim feed on human flesh to sustain their earthly forms, and are also believed to devour spirits, trapping them in their dreamscapes. Despite their immense power, they cannot enter a circle of salt.

Ethereal: [adjective] Pertaining to the *æther*.

Floxy: [noun] A brand name for scented and enriched oxygen, inhaled through a cannula. Served in most entertainment venues across the Republic of Scion, including dedicated oxygen bars. It is considered a legal alternative to alcohol and recreational drugs, both of which are forbidden under Inquisitorial law.

Flux: [noun] A colloquial name for Fluxion 14, a deliriant that has a particularly intense effect on clairvoyants. One of the key ingredients is purple *aster*. The number refers to the version of the drug.

Ghost: [noun] A spirit that prefers to dwell in one place – often their place of birth or death. Moving a ghost from its haunt will upset it.

Gloss: [noun] Glossolalia, the language of spirits and Rephaim. It is impossible to acquire Gloss; one can only be born with it. Among humans, only polyglots are capable of speaking it.

Golden cord: [noun] A connection between two spirits. It creates a seventh sense, allowing the linked individuals to track one another and share their emotions.

Grand Inquisitor: [noun] Leader of a Scion country. Each has its own Grand Inquisitor, but they all submit to the authority of the Grand Inquisitor of England, currently Frank Weaver.

Grand Raconteur: [noun] The main propagandist of a Scion country, who makes public announcements and reads the news. News reporters are known as *little raconteurs*.

Greasepaint: [noun] A slang term for makeup.

Gutterling: [noun] A young homeless person, or a child who lives with, and works for, a *kidsman*. They may go on to become hirelings for the syndicate.

Inquisitorial: [adjective] Referring to the authority of a Grand Inquisitor, e.g. Inquisitorial law.

Kern: [noun] A derogatory term for Irish defectors to the Republic of Scion, from Old Irish *ceithern*, referring to Irish or Scottish soldiers.

Kidsman: [noun] A person who employs children, who are known as *gutterlings*. Many kidsmen work for the syndicate.

Krig: [noun] A slang term for a ScionIDE soldier.

Mecks: [noun] A non-alcoholic drink. Comes in white, rose and blood (red) to imitate wine.

Mime-crime: [noun] Any act involving contact with the spirit world, especially for financial gain.

Mime-lord *or* **mime-queen**: [noun] A high-ranking member of the clairvoyant syndicate of London. Generally heads a dominant gang of five to ten followers, but maintains overall command over clairvoyants within a section of the citadel. Together, the mime-queens and mime-lords of London form the Unnatural Assembly.

Mollisher: [noun] The heir and second-in-command of a mime-lord or mime-queen. The Underqueen or Underlord's mollisher is known as the mollisher supreme.

Muse: [noun] The spirit of a person who specialised in any sort of art or music.

Netherworld: [noun] The home world of the *Rephaim*, which once functioned as an intermediary realm between the æther and Earth. At some point, the Netherworld was overrun by the *Emim* and began to fall into decay, forcing the Rephaim to relocate to Earth.

Numa: [noun] [singular: numen] Objects used by soothsayers and augurs to connect with the æther, e.g. mirrors, tarot cards and bones. The term originates from the seventeenth century and refers to a divine presence or will.

Off the cot: [adjective] A slang term for mad.

Oracle: [noun] One of the two categories of jumper, i.e. members of the seventh order of clairvoyance. Oracles receive sporadic visions of the future from the æther, often experiencing intense migraines at the same time. They can also learn to make and project their own visions. Like dreamwalkers, they have red auras.

Poppy anemone: [noun] A red flower, also known as the wind-flower. In Greek myth, it grew from the blood of the hunter Adonis, a lover of Aphrodite. Though named for its short-lived fragility, its pollen can inflict serious damage on *Rephaim*.

Querent: [noun] A person who seeks knowledge of the æther. They may ask questions or offer part of themselves, e.g. their palm, for a reading. The *Querent* is also the name of an illegal penny paper in Manchester.

Ranthen: [noun] A group of Rephaim who supported the doomed Mothallath family during the Rephaite civil war. The surviving Ranthen see the Sargas family as usurpers and do not wish to subjugate humans. They are currently in a tenuous alliance with Paige Mahoney.

Red-jacket: [noun] The highest rank for humans in Oxford. Red-jackets were primarily responsible for patrolling Gallows Wood to protect the city from the *Emim*.

Regal: [noun] Purple aster.

Rephaim: [noun] [singular: Rephaite] Humanoid beings of the Netherworld. Among humans, they are known colloquially as Rephs. Since their world fell into decay, the Rephaim have been forced to use human *aura* to sustain themselves.

Rookery: [noun] A Victorian slang term for a slum. In Oxford, it referred to a shantytown on the Broad, where the performers lived.

Rottie: See *amaurotic*.

Saloop: [noun] A hot, starchy drink made from orchid root, seasoned with rosewater and orange blossom.

Sarx: [noun] A name given to the skin and substance of Netherworld beings. Rephaite sarx is slightly metallic and more durable than human skin, showing no signs of age. While Earth-made weapons may pierce it, it will heal quickly, while *breachers* and Netherworld metals cause significantly more damage.

Scion East: [noun] The collective name for the Scion Republics of Bulgaria, Cyprus, Greece, Romania and Serbia. Scion North is used to refer to Sweden, while Scion West refers to England, France and Ireland.

ScionIDE: [noun] Short for Scion: International Defence Executive, the armed forces of the Republic of Scion. The First Inquisitorial Division is responsible for home security; the Second Inquisitorial Division is used for invasions; the Third Inquisitorial Division – the largest – is used to defend and keep control of Scion's conquered territories.

SciORE: [noun] Short for Scion: Organisation for Robotics and Engineering. Danica Panić works for this sector of Scion.

Scrying: [noun] The art of seeing into and gaining insight from the æther, especially through *numa*.

Séance: [noun] An event where voyants seek to invoke and communicate with a spirit. Most séances are performed in groups, but they may also be conducted alone. The *Ranthen* most often use séances to converse with their messengers, the psychopomps.

Sensors: [noun] The fourth order of clairvoyance according to *On the Merits of Unnaturalness*. Most sensors can perceive and interact with the æther through smell (sniffers), sound (whisperers) or taste (gustants), while the polyglots can speak and understand *Gloss*.

Seven Orders of Clairvoyance: [noun] A system for categorising clairvoyants, first proposed by Jaxon Hall in his pamphlet *On the Merits of Unnaturalness*. Despite its controversial implication of higher and lower sorts of clairvoyance, the system was adopted as the official method of categorisation in the London underworld, resulting in a spate of gang wars and the persecution of the so-called vile augurs.

Shade: [noun] A type of *drifter*, older than a *wisp*.

Shew stone: [noun] A type of *numen* used by seers. Like a crystal ball, a shew stone can offer glimpses of the future.

Silver cord: [noun] The link between the body and the spirit. The silver cord wears down over the years and eventually snaps, resulting in death.

Soothsayers: [noun] The first order of clairvoyance according to *On the Merits of Unnaturalness*. Broadly agreed to be the most populous order, soothsayers are reliant on *numa* to connect with the æther.

Sovereign-elect: [noun] The leader of the *Ranthen*, currently Terebellum 'Terebell' Sheratan.

Spirit sight: [noun] Sometimes referred to as the *third eye* or simply as the *sight*. The ability to perceive the æther visually, indicated by one or both pupils being shaped like a keyhole. Most voyants are sighted, but some are not. Half-sighted voyants can choose when to see the æther, while full-sighted voyants must see it all the time.

Spool: [1] [noun] A group of spirits; [2] [verb] to draw spirits together. All *clairvoyants* are capable of spooling.

Strides: [noun] A slang term for trousers.

Summoner: [noun] A clairvoyant who can call spirits across great distances. Jaxon classifies summoners as part of his own order, the guardians.

Syndicate rent: [noun] A monthly sum of money paid by London clairvoyants to their local mime-lord or mime-queen, to buy a place on their turf.

Syndicate tax: [noun] A monthly sum of money paid by clairvoyant business owners to their local mime-lord or mime-queen, on top of *syndicate rent*. After receiving both rent and tax, the mime-lords and mime-queens give a sum of their money to the Underlord or Underqueen, known as the rose tax.

Syndies: [noun] Members of the clairvoyant syndicate of London.

Threnody: [noun] A series of words used to banish spirits to the outer darkness, the end of the æther. There are many threnodies, developed by clairvoyant communities across the world. The threnody is not always effective, and will often fail to banish a *boundling*.

Underlord *or* **Underqueen**: [noun] The head of the Unnatural Assembly and mob boss of the clairvoyant syndicate of London. The incumbent Underqueen is Paige Mahoney, known as Black Moth.

Unnatural: [adjective *or* noun] The formal name for clairvoyants under Inquisitorial law.

Veil: [noun] A word used to describe the boundaries between the three known planes of being – the corporeal world, the æther, and the Netherworld.

Vigile: [noun] A member of the police forces of Scion. Day Vigiles are amaurotic and work for the Sunlight Vigilance Division (SVD), while night Vigiles are clairvoyant and work for the Night Vigilance Division (NVD). Night Vigiles agree to be euthanised after thirty years of service.

Voyant: [noun] A common shorthand for *clairvoyant*.

Waitron: [noun] A gender-neutral term for anyone in the service industry of the Republic of Scion.

Wisp: [noun] The weakest type of drifter. Wisps are often used in *spools* to bolster their strength.

Yellow-jacket: [noun] A rank given to humans in Oxford if they showed defiance or cowardice. Earning a yellow tunic three times was called the yellow streak and usually resulted in permanent eviction to the *Rookery*.

A Note on the Author

SAMANTHA SHANNON is the *New York Times* bestselling author of the Bone Season series and the Roots of Chaos series. Her work has been translated into twenty-eight languages. She lives in London.

samanthashannon.co.uk

@say_shannon

A Note on the Type

The text of this book is set Adobe Garamond. It is one of several versions of Garamond based on the designs of Claude Garamond. It is thought that Garamond based his font on Bembo, cut in 1495 by Francesco Griffo in collaboration with the Italian printer Aldus Manutius. Garamond types were first used in books printed in Paris around 1532. Many of the present-day versions of this type are based on the *Typi Academiae* of Jean Jannon cut in Sedan in 1615.

Claude Garamond was born in Paris in 1480. He learned how to cut type from his father and by the age of fifteen he was able to fashion steel punches the size of a pica with great precision. At the age of sixty he was commissioned by King Francis I to design a Greek alphabet, and for this he was given the honourable title of royal type founder. He died in 1561.